THE GATES OF MEMORY

RYAN KIRK

Created with Vellum

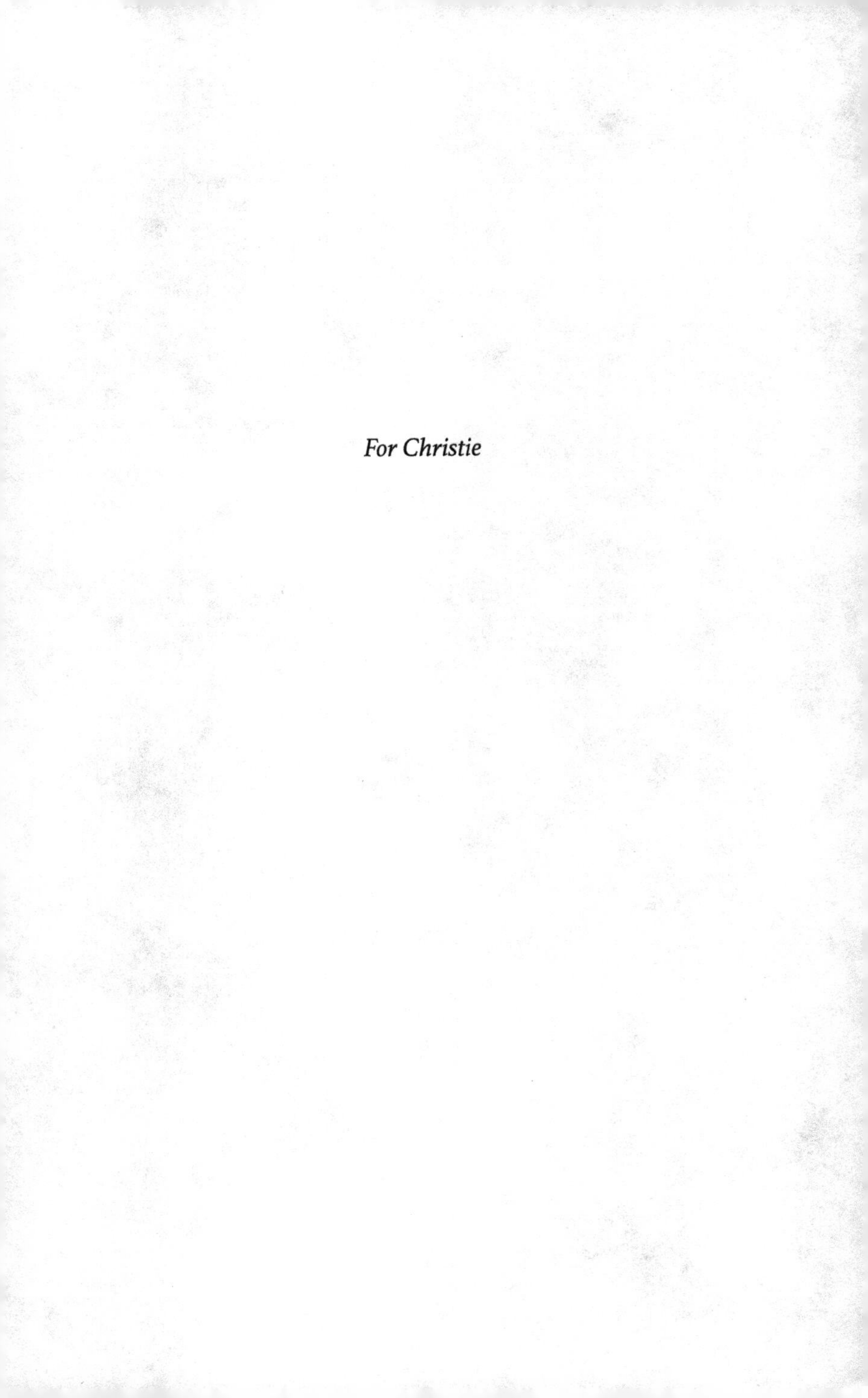

For Christie

PROLOGUE

She observed her creation from afar even as it spun away, churning and growing into an attack she hoped would cripple an empire. It was so nearly perfect. It just needed a little something more.

So much was instinct. No manual had ever been written on these techniques. No master could teach this power. As far as she knew, no one else in the long history of this planet had developed these skills.

And she had hundreds of years of memory to draw on.

There.

She pulled some heat from far away and added it. Then she pushed with wind, a force not much stronger than blowing the seeds off a dandelion.

Every action she took was echoed by the priests chanting below her. They possessed no true skill of their own. Their greatest talent was to follow her lead without question, to duplicate her efforts in exact amounts. They were mirrors of different sizes. No more.

Perfect.

She leaned back and tracked her creation. It moved

slowly now, but it gathered speed. By the time it hit the empire, there would be little warning. Hopefully her aim was true, but she could never be sure. Her talents had improved, but to even strike close required skill beyond the imagining of most mortals.

It didn't matter.

His death would cause certain, predictable consequences she had planned for.

His survival would lead to predictable outcomes as well.

Both paths had been prepared for, and both led to her goal.

She spared a thought for him. He'd been in her thoughts frequently, a trend she sometimes worried about.

He had called her a queen.

Long ago that might have been true.

Her memories of ages long past were broken, shattered by the unyielding weight of countless years.

Once she had tried to hold onto those memories. She'd crystallized them in her mind, forced herself to remember.

But even diamond cracked, and her mind had come close. It seemed, perhaps, that a person was only allotted so many memories. When a new one was made, an old one must die.

She didn't know. Again, there was no one to compare experiences with. She walked paths no mortal dared approach. That first emperor, he had come close. But then he had passed through the gates, his foolishness costing him his life.

It didn't matter.

Humans sought to order their universe, to categorize all things.

The dream of a whole species of fools.

The universe was more vast than their limited comprehension. They couldn't explain what was seen, much less unseen. She had acquired lifetimes of knowledge, but all she knew was that her knowledge only scratched the surface of the deep mysteries.

If she were to pass through the gates, all would be lost. She hadn't yet found one worthy of her instruction.

She focused on her attack once again. These first few moments were critical. A small error here doomed the entire attempt.

It was as perfect as she could make it. Nothing more remained for her.

She allowed herself to lean back in her throne. Physically, her body was young, continually healed by powers she used but didn't comprehend. But her body still ached. Her soul was heavy, carrying the weight of all those years.

No one understood.

She glanced one last time at the swirling mass of moisture, wind, and heat.

Perhaps if he survived, he would someday understand. In all her years, she'd never met someone with his potential. Even as he'd shattered her gate and delayed her carefully laid plans, he'd proven his worth.

He could be turned. He coveted her strength, and that would be his downfall.

She'd failed in her attempt before, a fact remarkable by itself. But that didn't mean he wouldn't come to her side.

Even if he traveled to the gate, she would meet him there and make him beg for her welcome.

Brute force wasn't the answer. His spirit was too strong to be cowed, even by one such as her.

But there were other ways.

Subtle, yet more effective.

Like the storm she had just launched across the sea, a person could be manipulated by small degrees.

Humans always thought themselves so rational. After the fact, they could justify any action.

She understood truth, though.

Humans were emotional and chaotic, manipulated by forces they didn't even consciously recognize.

A glance at a lover that lasted too long.

A quiet whisper between friends.

A disappointed parental glare burrowing into the heart of a child.

Small events, quickly burned from memory, but not from behavior.

She'd planted seeds when they first met. In the intervening years, those seeds had grown and would continue to grow.

Safer if he died.

But if he survived, even this attack would nudge him in the direction she wished him to travel.

He had called her a queen.

But she was no queen.

Not anymore.

She was a god.

1

Brandt gave Kurl a small nod as he walked across the courtyard. The other monk was on gate duty this afternoon. Passing the alert guardian, Brandt remembered his own entrance into the monastery so many years ago. Kurl had been on duty that day as well. He'd recognized Brandt's compulsion and let him inside, literally opening the gates to the next stage of Brandt's life.

Without Kurl, then, there was no Brandt. Had that gate remained closed all those years ago, Brandt imagined his life would have been darker and much shorter.

That fateful decision had been a small one, at least from Kurl's perspective. He'd admitted a visitor to the monastery whom he had every right and reason to turn away. The choice meant little to him, but it meant everything to Brandt.

Brandt found it easy to find countless such points in his life. When one started searching, dozens of moments burned like stars, choices and decisions that seemed meaningless at the time, but eventually changed the course of a life.

Cause and effect.

He'd been thinking too often about the concept lately. Everywhere he looked, he saw a vast web of interdependence.

He blamed Alena.

They might be separated by distance, but she had figured out a way to connect with him. They met in her mental world every week, comparing their learnings. They met in a construct of her mother's kitchen, the place she felt most comfortable.

Together they advanced faster than Brandt believed possible.

But it wasn't enough.

Even Highkeep served as evidence of Brandt's concern. When Brandt had first come here the monastery had been a hive of activity. It always appeared quiet from outside the walls, but inside, dozens of monks threw themselves into daily training.

Today a bare handful remained. Brandt and Ana lived here, as did Kyla, the abbot. Kurl and six others rounded out the monastery's current inhabitants. The rest were scattered throughout the empire, teaching their skills to the army and to city watches. Though the citizens of the empire weren't aware of it, they were preparing for a war they had little chance of winning.

In another two weeks a group of monks were scheduled to return. Then Brandt and Ana would leave and continue the instruction while the others continued developing their own skills.

Train yourself. Then train others.

That had been the emperor's last command to the monasteries after Landow.

So Brandt trained. More than most monks, he was given

the time and space to learn more about the powers that infused their world. Though Kyla would never order him to do so, Brandt still volunteered to train nearby city watches. He didn't believe it was right for the other monks to bear the burden of preparing the people without him.

Besides, sometimes teaching led him to new discoveries.

Brandt finished crossing the empty courtyard, coming to the abbot's study. He knocked and was welcomed in.

Kyla had served as the abbot of Highkeep since before Brandt's arrival. She kept her hair cut short, betraying her own distant past in the military. Brandt gave her a short bow as he entered.

She wasted no time in pleasantries. "Ready?"

"I am."

Kyla put her hand on her desk. Brandt heard the sounds of stone shifting within, unlocking a hidden compartment.

She pulled an uncut diamond out of the desk, clutching it tightly in her hand. "Which element shall we begin with?"

"Water."

Without a word, she pulled some water from a nearby cup, letting it gather in the air between them. Then she pushed it at him.

Brandt heard the song of Kyla's power and felt the water rushing toward his face. Pushing directly against the water would only cause it to disperse, soaking him.

Like a grappler, Brandt elected to use Kyla's strength against her. Instead of fighting against her, he let his own strength redirect the water. The small sphere of water distorted as it whipped around his head and back at Kyla.

They could redirect the water back and forth for days with no winner. The task wasn't particularly difficult for either of them. As Kyla mimicked Brandt's redirection, sending the water back his way, she split it, not into two parts, but four.

A hint of a grin broke out on Brandt's face. He redirected all four smaller spheres, splitting one into two. He sent three straight at her while allowing two to orbit around his head one more time.

It was training, but it was also playful, at least with water. Failure cost no more than a wet face most days. Other elements were less forgiving.

The water danced between them. Pushed, pulled, and redirected, at least one attack was always headed his way.

Stone followed water, and fire after that. In each element the pattern repeated. By the time the last flickering ball of flame was extinguished, both Brandt and Kyla were short of breath, sweat beading down their foreheads.

Kyla placed the stone back in her desk, straining against the effort of locking the hidden compartment after her exertions. She held Brandt's gaze.

"I don't know what more you hope to accomplish here," she admitted.

Brandt wiped the sweat from his eyes. "I don't know what else to do."

"You're as strong as any unaided warrior the empire has ever seen. Only the emperor is stronger, but without his gates, I suspect even you could challenge him."

Brandt stood, pacing Kyla's small room. He wanted to argue with the abbot, but to what end? They'd explored the problem from every direction. They had no answers, and his frustration had no outlet.

He rested his forehead against a cool stone wall, imagining the solid peace of the stone seeping into his bones. "It's not enough."

"I still think you should leave to study with the other

abbots. Even a change of scenery may lead to the breakthrough you seek."

Brandt thought of his last encounter with the queen of the Lolani. Two years had passed since that moment, and every day he felt her strength, imprinted somewhere deep in his heart. He might be one of the strongest in the empire, but whatever light he displayed was a dying candle against the roaring bonfire of the Lolani queen's ability.

He could wander the empire for an age, meeting new teachers in every corner. It still wouldn't be enough.

Now that he knew what was possible, nothing less was acceptable.

Given the futility of his efforts, why not stay where he was comfortable and welcome? In Highkeep he could put away daily concerns and focus on developing his skill.

"I'll consider your wisdom." They both knew it was a lie, but neither would point it out. "Thank you for your time, as always."

Kyla nodded and Brandt took his leave. Kyla, aided by Highkeep's gatestone, could barely keep up with him. As he continued to get stronger, that would become untrue. Then he would have no one to train with, no one to push him.

Perhaps Alena could construct some sort of mental training ground where he could further hone his skills. She claimed she had done something similar for herself.

He ran into Ana in the courtyard and his worries dissipated. If anything, the years had only increased her beauty in his eyes. She stood straight, her long dark hair undone today. He stepped close and grabbed her hands.

"How did it go today?" she asked.

Brandt sighed. "Well. Even when she is aided, I suspect that I will soon surpass her."

"That is something to be proud of. But?"

"But it still doesn't matter. This new strength still equates to nothing against the Lolani. I might win against their warriors, but against their queen I am nothing."

Ana stepped closer to him. "I don't like to hear you say that."

"What?"

"That you are nothing. A person is more than just their strength. Once you begin to forget that, I'm not sure there's a return."

She was right, of course. Ana always was.

They'd all come back changed from the caves outside Landow. Alena discovered powers not yet developed by anyone in the empire. Brandt lived with the knowledge of his own limits and the power they faced. And Ana had become something of a philosopher. Each of them had brushed death. By Alena's accounts she had even been to the gate. But Ana had perhaps been changed the most by the experience.

She held onto serenity now, a quality he admired more with every passing day. She would say it was because she had discovered what mattered to her, but Brandt wondered if the change went even deeper than that.

"I'll try. I promise."

Then he frowned. Ana's presence had distracted him, but the hair on the back of his neck was standing on end. Why?

Ana sensed the disturbance at the same time he did.

"What is that?"

It felt familiar, yet his memory refused to dig up the appropriate event. Where had he felt this?

Then it hit him. The heavy air, filled with moisture and unseasonable heat. The atmosphere held a menace to it, an intent.

This was what it was like before the queen had tried to assassinate the emperor years ago.

Brandt shouted. "Everyone run! Down the road! And ring the bell!"

The few monks in earshot hesitated, then leaped to action. The bell began to clang. Monks came out into the courtyard, ready for danger and confused when none appeared. They looked to him for answers.

"Get away from the monastery," he said. "Leave, down the path." They didn't understand the queen's ability to manipulate the weather, but they knew the attack couldn't be aimed at a person, not exactly. Instead she aimed for a place where she knew a person would be. In this case, the monastery was the only reasonable target. If they put distance between them and the walls, no lives would be lost.

Orders were passed among the monks. Kurl opened up the gate as the first handful rushed to safety. Storm clouds appeared over the mountaintops, darker and taller than any storm had a right to be, racing across the sky with unnatural speed. Brandt wouldn't have much time to effect his own escape.

He made himself light, running through the hallways and corridors of his home. Off in the distance he heard the first rumbles of thunder, deeper than normal. He felt the reverberations in his stomach. He woke one monk sleeping undisturbed through the bells and shooed him out, still groggy. Other than that, the monastery was empty.

The rain started, a sudden downpour that drenched every stone in sight. Brandt ran, sprinting toward the gate as fast as his legs and lightness could carry him. He passed the gate just as the first bolt of lightning struck behind him, a blinding flash and deafening roar washing over him.

For several agonizing moments he ran on instinct alone.

Off to the edge, the path ended precipitously, but he needed every bit of distance he could get between him and the monastery.

Fortunately, his instincts guided him well. He remained on the path and his vision cleared after just a couple of heartbeats.

A second flash hit, far more powerful than the first. His world became light and sound. The blast threw him into the air and tossed him to the ground face first. Brandt knew he needed to move. He was too close.

But he couldn't convince his body. He cowered, burying his face into the stonework of the road and covering his head with his hands.

In time, the echoes of the blast faded, the mountains echoing the final reverberations.

Brandt blinked and slowly raised his head.

He lived.

He lifted his gaze higher, to the threatening sky. The impossibly tall clouds had already diminished as they passed beyond the monastery. So many forces of nature had been manipulated to bring one powerful event into being. As unnatural as it was, it couldn't last.

The order of the world reasserted itself in time.

Perhaps that was some consolation.

It was all that he had. Brandt sat up and for the first time saw his home.

Or what remained of it.

The queen's attack had struck true. Perhaps it had looked and sounded like lightning, but it had been something more. The blast had destroyed three of the monastery's buildings and damaged the rest.

Brandt couldn't conceive of the energies required for such an attack.

He knew he was weak compared to the queen, but the ability to work this technique seemed impossible. For every step he took toward her skill, she ran a league.

Brandt didn't know how he would catch her, but looking at the remains of his home, he swore a vow that he would never stop trying.

2

Rolle was an enormous man, making the front room of the smithy look small when he stood within it. Most days two or three customers could browse through the space comfortably, but Rolle alone looked like he barely had room to turn. His arms were as thick as Alena's waist, but it was hard not to laugh at his infectious smile and quick wit.

Rolle's kindness was even more expansive than he was. He worked as one of the town's butchers, and his generosity was legendary. He provided liberal portions, a business practice that worked well for him, guaranteeing customer loyalty. Alena's own mother bypassed the nearest butcher in favor of Rolle because she knew it helped their family's money stretch further.

Rolle chose one cleaver from the table between them and held it close to his eye. He examined the edge of the blade and took some practice swings, as though cutting through the air was the same as cutting through flesh and bone. Then he picked up a second cleaver and repeated the process.

The two tools were the same except for the steel used. An apprentice had made the first out of a lesser steel. It served as practice for the apprentice and a cheaper option for those who couldn't afford nicer. The other had been made by her father.

Alena's eyes tracked Rolle's movements closely. She saw the years of experience ingrained in his cuts. Rolle was no warrior, but she suspected he could butcher a cow faster than anyone in town.

"The grip feels a bit small," Rolle said, "and I prefer my cleavers to be a bit longer and heavier."

"If you're interested," Alena replied, "we could forge something custom for you, but it would require some time. We've been busy."

Rolle laughed at that. "So I hear. Drok's smithy is worried they'll be run out of town."

Alena shook her head. "We can't handle all the work this town requires. And Drok does fine work."

"True," Rolle admitted. "But everyone knows where to go when they need a blade they can count on." He picked up each cleaver in turn again. "These feel nearly identical. Different steel?"

"Yes."

"I think I like this one more," he said, handing her the cheaper cleaver.

Alena saw how Rolle's eyes lingered on the more expensive cleaver. He knew it was better, but couldn't convince himself to spend the extra money. He was a man careful with his money.

She'd seen such expressions on many faces in the last two years.

Part of the challenge was her father. He insisted that his shop be known for quality of all its products, not just his own. The whole town knew of her father's gift with steel, but he rarely marked his personal creations in any way. Perhaps an expert would notice the difference between a blade crafted by her father and one crafted by an apprentice, but most wouldn't, and her father preferred it that way. If the shop sold it, the product had earned his approval.

Alena was also prohibited from speaking about who made what. Custom work was an exception, but for items up front she had strict orders. She knew who made which cleaver, and could have easily sold Rolle on the more expensive one if he knew her father had crafted it himself.

She admitted that it allowed the smithy to charge more for all its work, and the practice fueled avid speculation about who made what, but she did sometimes find the restriction annoying.

"If you don't mind me saying," she began, and Rolle nodded for her to continue. "More than many professions, the quality of steel will matter for you. The less expensive cleaver will serve you well, but it has its own cost. It will require more time to maintain, won't hold its edge as long, and will need replacing sooner."

She paused. "You're a man who lives by the quality of his blade. Although this blade costs more," she pointed to her father's cleaver, "you'll be more satisfied with the purchase, and it will save you time in the long run."

Rolle wavered, but Alena didn't push. Sometimes the art of the sale was in knowing when not to say more.

Rolle let out an explosive sigh, a grin lighting his face. He had wanted the more expensive one all along; he just hadn't been able to justify it to himself.

Alena had given him just the reason he'd been looking for.

Not long later he left, the proud new owner of her father's cleaver.

Her father came out from behind the corner. Alena hadn't seen him from her position, but she'd thought she heard the rustle of cloth and shifting of weight that signified his presence. He didn't come forward very often. It distracted the customers too much.

Father looked at the pile of silver on the counter. His look was mildly disapproving. "You didn't—"

Alena smiled at her father's discomfort. "You know I promised not to. And I didn't need to. He just needed a reason to get what he wanted all along."

Father nodded, not quite convinced, but trusting anyway. "It's a good sale. I suppose I'll have to get to work on another one. If he does come in for custom work, offer him a bargain. He's been good to our family over the years."

"Yes, Father."

Before Father could reply, the door to the shop opened again. The young man who stepped in stood tall. Though he wasn't half the size of Rolle, his presence still filled the room.

"I came by to escort Alena home, Father, if she's done making all your sales for the day."

"Hello to you, too, Jace," Father said. He nodded his permission. "I can have the apprentices finish closing up."

Alena glanced suspiciously at her younger brother. "I don't need an escort."

"The streets are filled with pickpockets and thieves, my dear sister. I couldn't bear the blemish on my honor if any harm were to befall you."

Alena raised an eyebrow. "You're that bored?"

He laughed. "I am, indeed. And we haven't had any time to ourselves lately. I want to know how my sister is doing."

Alena gathered what few belongings she had brought to the shop, then remembered to call after Father. "Don't be late tonight!"

"I won't!"

The siblings left the shop, turning in the direction of their house. They shared the events of their day, though nothing momentous had happened to either of them. Alena noticed her brother containing his excitement about something, but he didn't want to spill the story yet. Perhaps he'd finally met a young woman? Their mother would swoon at that news. She feared Jace spent too much time working and not enough time looking to start a family.

Pleasantries exhausted, Jace dug into weightier subjects. "How are you?"

She noticed the shift in tone. A glance confirmed it wasn't simply a polite question. "Is it that obvious?"

His smile was wide. "Only to anyone who knows you at all. I think you were better at pretending when you were younger."

"I had more practice." She paused. "Did they put you up to this?"

"Yes, but I would have asked on my own soon enough."

"I'm not sure what to do," she admitted. "When I returned home, all I could think about was how I wanted to stay here forever. And I've loved the past two years."

"But you want more?" Jace completed the sentence for her.

She nodded. "I need to find a teacher. Someone in the empire has to know more about soulwalking. And I want to visit Etar and see my family there."

Jace's shoulders tensed for a moment at that, but he relaxed them quickly. If she hadn't been looking for it she wasn't sure she would have noticed. Unlike her, Jace had gotten better at disguising his emotions.

They walked in silence for a block, each lost in their own thoughts.

"What will you do?" Jace asked.

"I'm not sure yet. It will break their heart if I leave, but I don't think I'll be happy to remain in Landow for much longer."

Their house came into view. "Whatever you decide, you know I'll support you, right?"

"I know."

Their conversation came to an end as they entered their family house together. Their mother welcomed them, then immediately put them to work. Jace, being better in the kitchen than Alena, helped finish the meal. Alena put out the bowls they would eat from. She had a little time to read before Father's heavy footsteps could be heard in the hallway.

Family meals were still boisterous. Jace served as a commander in the city watch, and he had no shortage of stories to share. From celebrants who had gotten a little too deep in their cups to thieves that knocked themselves out while trying to evade pursuit, he had a new story every time they gathered.

Father still groused about his apprentices, but less than he had many years ago. He had trained them well over the years, and several were becoming masters in their own right. Father paid well and cared for his smiths. If not for that, Alena suspected several of them would have moved on. Many were skilled enough to start their own smithies.

Alena didn't have stories to share. She enjoyed working for Father, but stories from the front of the shop didn't entertain the way Jace's did. And she didn't speak about the far more interesting aspects of her life. Her abilities made her family nervous whenever she mentioned them.

Eventually Jace called for silence. "I have news!"

The family obediently quieted, plates long since finished.

"The governor came to see me today," Jace said, and Alena's heart dropped for a moment. She'd been hoping the news was about a young woman, too. Jace worked too hard. "He wants to create a new position, a lieutenant governor for the region. And he wants me to fill it."

Mother beamed and Father clapped his son on the shoulder. They were proud, and why shouldn't they be? Jace had become not just an admirable soldier, but a competent leader as well.

Alena smiled, but doing so required an effort. She was proud of her brother, but it hurt to see him succeeding while she felt stuck.

It wasn't fair to him, but it was true.

Their father went into the cellar and pulled out a bottle of wine. Their family rarely drank, but Jace's promotion merited the occasion.

They laughed and drank until the sun kissed the horizon.

Then they were interrupted by a knock on the door. Jace, in high spirits, went to answer it.

Alena's heart skipped a beat when her brother let in a figure cloaked in red, a familiar shade to any trader in the empire. Those cloaks denoted Etari traders.

The Etari threw back his hood once he had crossed the threshold into their house. His eyes met Alena's. "Sooni has summoned you," he said. "Your aid is required."

3

Brandt stood with his fellow monks on the path, staring slack-jawed at the monastery that had been his home for over a decade. He saw the ruins before him, but he still struggled to believe. The monastery had been something solid, a place where the ravages of time raged ineffectively against the sturdy construction. But now?

It would take years to rebuild what *she* destroyed in moments.

He didn't understand.

The destruction wrought by that last blast was orders of magnitude greater than her previous attacks.

He'd run.

Retreat had been the only way to survive.

Questions plagued his lethargic mind. The how bothered him, but he already knew the Lolani queen was stronger than him. This was simply more evidence of a fact he already understood. The questions that demanded answers were the whys. Why now? Why here? Brandt took pride in his abilities, but he was no threat to the Lolani queen.

Had this been simple revenge, attacking him because he'd prevented her invasion years ago?

Ana's hand clutching his stopped his questions cold. He'd been so obsessed with the attack and its meaning he'd forgotten to check on her. Thanks to their efforts, and the mostly empty monastery, every monk still lived. Ana appeared unharmed and remarkably calm. A look passed between them, and her slight nod let him know that she was fine.

Kyla stepped in front of the assembled monks. "The danger has passed. Let's return and search for what can be salvaged. We need to know if we can sleep here tonight, or if we have to make our way down the road."

Brandt hoped they would find enough bunks to remain at the monastery tonight. The nearest village with space for them to sleep was a full day's walk away. At the moment, he didn't find the idea of such a walk inviting.

The monks followed Kyla into the ruins of Highkeep. The gate had shattered and the short journey was slow. They stepped carefully, cognizant of the fact that a twisted ankle now would only increase the already weighty burden on friends.

They paused inside the gate. A blackened crater silently smoked inside the destroyed courtyard. Nearly two hundred years of history, wiped away in a flash of power. Brandt clenched his fist and looked over the rest of the monastery.

The blast had destroyed the abbot's quarters and study. Brandt stepped toward the last standing structure. The guesthouse, which had been the target of the queen's previous attack on the monastery, remained unbroken. Brandt put his hand to the stone and closed his eyes, listening to the song the element sang to him.

He had always heard stone as a steady hum, and today

was no different. The building stood and would give them shelter, at least for tonight.

Kyla issued the monks' orders. Several began searching the rubble. The monastery housed no small number of valuable items. Any that could be easily recovered would be moved to the guesthouse and protected by the remaining monks. Brandt, Ana, and two others cleared a path to the guesthouse and ensured it was ready to host an influx of unexpected residents.

Brandt threw himself into the work, grateful for the opportunity to bend his body to a difficult task. He left himself no time for questions. All that mattered was moving stone out of the way, clearing the way to the guesthouse.

Brandt used his affinity at times, but for the most part relied on his hands and muscles to perform the labor. Thanks to the cost, using his affinity expended as much energy as picking the rocks up by hand would, but sometimes the affinity made the task easier.

By the time the sun descended to the tops of the peaks, casting long shadows, Kyla declared the work done for the day. Others had found food and the well was undamaged. For tonight, survival wouldn't be a problem.

The meal was quiet, the only sound that of utensils scraping against the bottoms of bowls. No one said as much, but no one knew when their next meal would be. Brandt imagined the other monks were also lost in their thoughts, memories of their home mixed with fears for their future.

Brandt and Ana retired early, seeking solace in one another. Brandt held onto her tightly that night. Despite the loss of the monastery, she remained. Her presence shielded him from the worst of the attack's effects.

He woke up first the next morning, staring at the ceiling as Ana breathed softly on his neck. Over the course of the night she had rolled over and curled up next to him, her arm draped over his chest and her nose next to his ear.

He matched his breath to hers, slow and steady.

Ana's transition from sleep to wakefulness was instant, the same as his had been. Some habits from their days as soldiers refused to die. He only noticed because their breaths suddenly didn't match. She spoke before he could greet her. "What's on your mind?"

"What comes next."

Her hand reached up and played with his hair. She waited for him to elaborate.

"I need to see the emperor."

Her hand paused for a moment, then resumed. Two years ago the emperor had offered to make Brandt one of his personal honor guard. Brandt had declined, insisting he could study better at Highkeep. Anders VI, or Hanns, depending on the formality of the situation, had conceded the point and stopped short of ordering Brandt to remain by his side.

At the time, Brandt's feelings had been complicated. He had inherited some of Alena's anger over the lies the empire told to sustain itself. But unlike Alena, he understood that truth didn't always govern best. He had genuinely believed that Highkeep was the best place for him to study. Hanns freely admitted that even with the knowledge only known to the line of emperors, he didn't possess any greater understanding of the queen's power than they did. The monastery offered him more time to practice and monks who would help push him. As part of the emperor's honor guard, Brandt would have had to travel, stand guard over meetings, and complete dozens of other tasks that weren't a part of monastic life.

But, if he forced himself to confront his own shortcomings, a large part of his decision was the woman lying next to him. Ana would have traveled with him to the capital. She was a strong warrior in her own right, but the emperor's offer hadn't extended to her. Accepting the offer would have meant more time apart from her.

They'd enjoyed the past two years together, but more than once Brandt had questioned his decision. All the time to study hadn't resulted in the gains he needed. In his moodier moments he worried his decision to return to Highkeep had struck a blow against the empire he served.

"You're sure?"

"I am. Perhaps the emperor doesn't understand the Lolani queen, but he still has the most powerful affinities in the empire. There has to be something he can teach me."

Ana didn't reply immediately. Her hand kept running through his hair, though, slowing his thoughts and his breath. "You're probably right. I don't like it, though."

"Why not?"

She didn't answer at first, seeking the right words. "It's nothing I can point to, nothing rational. But this feels like the beginning of the end to me. When we leave Highkeep, I doubt we'll ever return."

Brandt hadn't considered beyond their trip to the capital, but Ana's words rang true. This did feel like a door closing.

But it opened upon another part of their journey.

Outside, Brandt listened to the sounds of the monastery coming to life. Mostly, he heard the sounds of rock being moved by some of the early-rising monks. But he didn't want to get out of bed, not quite yet.

"There's something else," Ana said.

Brandt turned his head so he was looking at her.

"You won't expect this," she warned.

He reached up and brushed the hair out of her face. She'd grown it even longer these past two years.

Ana took a deep breath. "I'd like to start a family."

Brandt's hand tangled in her hair. He tugged at the tangle hopelessly for a moment, then simply removed his hand. "What?"

Her eyes twinkled with mirth. "I'm sure you heard me the first time."

Brandt pushed himself gently away from her so they weren't entangled. "Now?"

Now that she had expressed herself, she had no problem defending her decision. "Yes."

"I'm sure there are worse times to start a family, but I can't think of one."

She kicked him in the shin under the covers, then turned serious. "I understand. But there is no perfect time to have a child, especially for us. There will always be another danger. In the past it was Falari incursions. Now it's the Lolani. Who knows what we'll discover five years from now?"

She paused, her gaze steady on his. "But that's no reason not to try. Children are another reason for us to keep fighting for a better tomorrow."

Brandt sat up in bed, and Ana's hand met his. She held it tightly. He returned her grip. "What about your training?"

She smiled at that. "I'll continue as best I can, but my skill won't matter. We both know that."

"You're one of the stronger affinities in the monastery."

"And I haven't made any progress in months. I'm near the limits of my ability."

It was the first time either of them had said as much out loud, even though Brandt had suspected it for a while. The admission still hit him like a punch to the stomach, though.

He wanted her to grow stronger. They'd been on this journey together, and he didn't want to leave her behind.

But there were limits, and Ana had found hers.

He considered her proposal. They had talked about having children before, but it had never felt quite right. Brandt enjoyed the idea of raising children, but he found himself with cold feet now that the actual opportunity presented itself.

He snuck a look at Ana. She was gorgeous, kind, and strong. And he suspected she would make a wonderful mother.

In the end, his decision was simpler than he expected. This was what she wanted, and he couldn't refuse her.

"Very well," he said.

A smile grew on her face, and a mischievous look flashed on it immediately after. "You want to start now?" She threw the covers off, revealing nearly her entire body.

He should probably tell Kyla they were leaving, and there was no shortage of work around the monastery to complete. The rebuilding had just barely begun.

But it was important to have priorities.

4

Despite their initial confusion, her family's good manners prevailed. They welcomed the trader into their home and offered what little remained of their meal. The Etari, who introduced himself as Ligt, accepted the hospitality and dug into the remains of the meal with the enthusiasm of a man close to dying from starvation.

Alena laughed to herself as Mother and Father attempted the polite conversation that dominated imperial meals. They asked about his travels and the weather on the road. He answered them kindly enough, no doubt used to imperial customs, but his patience for such questions was clearly limited.

Her mirth died when she caught sight of Jace out of the corner of her vision. He stood near the door of the dining room, stiff as steel. He crossed his arms and fixed Ligt with a glare meant to kill.

Alena didn't need to soulwalk to understand her brother's reaction. He understood why Alena had run to the Etari years ago, but his heart still wrestled with her decision and the dark consequences it had spawned. Most days it felt like they had put their past behind them. But Ligt's presence threatened to destroy in a night what they had spent two years trying to rebuild.

Still, he probably wouldn't draw his sword within their family house. Her brother could be rash, but he matured day by day. His new promotion was evidence enough of that.

Thought of his promotion saddened her. Tonight should have been his night to celebrate.

Alena interrupted her mother's question about Etari food. Ligt didn't bring welcome news, so it was best to deal with it now. Alena raised a hand and her mother went silent. "You said Sooni summoned me. Why?"

Ligt scraped the last of his food from the plate, then turned to face her, hand signing a gesture of appreciation for her intervention. He switched to the Etari language. "Do you still speak and understand Etari?"

"With ease," she replied, in the same language.

A sign of gratitude. "I do not know the words for some concepts in imperial." He signed an apology.

"There's nothing to apologize for."

She sensed the tension growing among her family members. They all knew she'd spent years among the Etari, but Jace wasn't alone in his discomfort in being reminded. She turned to them. "He doesn't know enough imperial to explain Sooni's summons. It's not because he desires to keep anything a secret."

"She speaks true," Ligt added.

"If it makes you uncomfortable," Alena said, "I can speak with him in another room. You will know everything before we're done."

Father shook his head. "Anything that affects you affects us. We'll stay."

Ligt spoke to Alena in Etari. "Your family loves you."

She turned back to him. "They both do."

A sign of affirmation, respect indicated in the gesture.

Ligt, in Etari fashion, spoke directly to the problem. "The great scourge threatens us again."

Alena started. "The Lolani have returned?"

Ligt signed for her to remain calm. "Not in person, but in other ways."

"Explain."

"It is our gatestones. Have you noticed anything strange with yours?"

She signed a negative. She missed Etari communication, so rich in its combination of gestures and words. It felt so much more free than imperial.

"Some of our more recent family members have experienced challenges with the gatestones. The problem seems to be worse the closer one gets to the remains of the shattered gate. But at times, our gatestones fail us completely."

"How so?"

"Some who use them vomit. Others complain of strong headaches. A few have come close to death's gate. For others, the connection briefly vanishes. The problems are increasing in frequency, severity, and duration."

Alena frowned, then signed her confusion. She hadn't noticed any such problems, but she very rarely connected to her gatestone.

"Many believe the Lolani queen has infected our gate."

Alena leaned forward. Through all her years with the Etari, she'd never learned much about their gate. Hanns, her emperor, had told her the Etari possessed the remains of a gate that had been shattered. It was the source of the small gatestones every adult Etari embedded somewhere in their skin, usually near the navel. It allowed them to connect to a power greater than their own, bypassing the cost that plagued imperial warriors gifted with affinities.

But Alena didn't know where the Etari gate was, or anything else about it. Sooni, the leader of her family, had never spoken with her about it, despite Alena's inquiries.

"I'm sorry," Alena said. "Why does Sooni want me?"

"She says that you can soulwalk."

Then Alena understood. Among the Etari, soulwalking was taboo, for reasons they had never explained to her. Alena only discovered her own ability to soulwalk after leaving the Etari, so the subject hadn't come up.

After their last battle with the Lolani queen, Alena had written a long letter to Sooni explaining everything. She was obligated to inform them of Azaleth's death, the outcome of the battle, and her own role in it. That had also been the letter where she told Sooni she wouldn't be returning to Etar anytime soon. Explaining it had been difficult, and Alena still didn't believe she'd expressed herself well.

Sooni deserved better from her.

Sooni had done more than just save Alena's life. She'd given Alena a second family. And Alena was responsible for Azaleth's death. Several reasons complicated any return to Etar, but it was her fear of facing Sooni again that prevented her from venturing near the border again.

But thanks to the letter, Sooni knew she could soulwalk and somehow thought Alena's gift might be exactly what the Etari needed. Alena swore, in Etari. She didn't need her mother yelling at her for her language.

"Will you come?" Ligt asked. "There is concern that if something is not done soon, the infection will worsen." He paused, giving her a meaningful look. "We might lose all the power of the gatestones."

Alena had mixed feelings about that threat. She didn't

treasure her gatestone quite the same way the Etari did. For them, the gatestone represented their passage into adulthood. It remained with them until the moment of their passing, when it would be given to another, often within the same family.

Her stone wasn't without sentimental value. It hadn't marked her adulthood, but instead her formal acceptance into Sooni's family.

Her more pressing concern was that her gatestone fueled her soulwalking abilities. It had been a large part of the reason they'd defeated the Lolani queen and her minions. Losing the gatestone wouldn't be difficult. Losing its power would be.

"I'll need to discuss it with my family," Alena replied.

Ligt signed his acknowledgement. "Perhaps it would be best if I waited somewhere else?"

Alena glanced at the looks on her family's faces. "That might be wise."

After Alena got Ligt settled in their family room, she returned to the dining room. Jace had taken a seat. She completed the circle. Then she took a deep breath and recounted the conversation that had just taken place.

"But you don't have to go," Mother said.

Alena signed the negative, then remembered she was with her family. She shook her head. "No. There are no immediate consequences to refusing the summons. If I choose not to go, Ligt will leave without complaint."

Ligt might leave, but if disaster befell the Etari, they would hold her at least partially responsible. Then she would feel the consequences. But she didn't want to make this decision about what the Etari might do or not do to her. She wanted to do the right thing.

And as soon as she understood that, she realized she had already made her decision.

It tore her in two.

Father, always more attuned to her thoughts than she guessed, realized the same. "You want to go."

She nodded, feeling the pain in her heart mirrored in the faces of her family. "If the attack has anything to do with soulwalking, then I'm the only one who can help. And I don't want to see the Etari suffer."

Jace's fists clenched at that, but he said nothing. At best, most citizens of the empire viewed the Etari with ambivalence. But no small number saw their existence as an affront to the empire. Jace might not have felt so strongly as a child, but Alena's time among them soured any generous views he might have had. He couldn't view them as anything more than the people that had taken his sister away from him.

"I don't want you to go," Mother said. "What if it's dangerous?"

Alena had no good answer to her mother's concerns. She felt little threat from the Etari, but she had no way to evaluate the danger from the gate. "I'll be as safe as I can."

Mother looked to Father, worry in her eyes. Father, in turn, watched Alena closely.

She remembered that gaze from when she was younger. It wasn't a soulwalk, but the sensations weren't dissimilar. Father didn't have an affinity, but his careful observations and slow wisdom served him nearly as well. "Why do you really want to go?"

Alena swallowed. "The Etari saved my life, and I owe them a debt for that. If I can serve them in this, I would like to." She paused, knowing the answer wouldn't satisfy her father's insight into his daughter. "And perhaps there are answers. For all my training, I still don't understand my powers well, and this might be a path in the right direction."

"And you've been eager to leave for weeks now, anyway."

"Yes." She wanted to tell them more, to tell them that she loved them but she had to go. But this was her family. They all understood her, and she hoped they trusted her, too.

Father leaned back in his chair, a sigh escaping his lips. "Then I suppose you should go. But you will keep in touch, and you will return when you are able."

Mother protested, but Father calmed her with a hand on her shoulder. He waited for Alena to answer.

"I will," she said. "If you wish, I can form a connection with you the same way I did with Brandt before he left. I should be able to reach you that way."

Alena looked to Jace. Mother would eventually follow Father's lead, but Jace was another matter entirely. He stared at the table, fists still clenched. When he did look up, his jaw was set. "I will go with you," he declared.

"What?" Alena asked, her question joining the chorus of inquiries coming from their parents.

Jace shrugged. Once he made a decision, he rarely retreated from it. "I lost you once to the Etari. I don't mean for it to happen again."

A dozen challenges presented themselves to Alena, but one above all else. "But what about your promotion?"

His only answer was to meet her gaze. She saw then that nothing she could say would change his mind. He would follow at a distance if she didn't let him join them. She gave him a small nod and he relaxed. He'd been preparing for a fight.

There was little else to discuss. Alena hated seeing Mother distraught, but there was little she could do to ease a mother's worries. She would form a connection with both of them. It was the only comfort she could offer. She would reach out to them when she had the time.

"I'll let Ligt know," she said. "I imagine we'll leave in the next day or two."

"And I'll let the governor know that I'll be gone for a while," Jace said.

And just like that, the decision was made.

She was going back to Etar.

And this time, she was bringing her brother.

5

Estern came into view long before they reached its walls. When he first saw it clearly, Brandt stopped to take it all in. He shook his head at the changes visible even from afar. The city had grown since he'd been here last.

He shouldn't be surprised. It had been, what, a dozen years since he'd last visited? His travels with the wolfblades occasionally brought him through, but not for a while before his fateful visit to Landow. And since then the vast majority of his days had been spent in Highkeep.

Beside him, Ana seemed less impressed. "Looks dirty."

Brandt smiled. "Still not interested in moving to the city?"

"Give me open air and clean water any day."

Brandt and Ana shared a dislike of cities, although for different reasons. Brandt had grown up within one, the youngest son of a family of wage-earners. He admired his family, but growing up in a city where so much of the empire's coin had been on display left him with little but bitter memories. He despised ostentatious displays of wealth, and there were plenty to go around in the larger imperial cities.

They spent the rest of the day reaching the walls of the city. Farms gave way to homes built beyond the walls. Brandt wondered if the city had run out of space or if those who elected to live outside the walls found life to be cheaper and the space more welcoming.

The wolfblade within him frowned at the new construction. He understood why people built in such places. Whether due to cost or space, they could build their homes outside the walls but still retreat inside in case danger threatened the area.

But there was little to worry about here. Estern, while not quite in the center of the empire, was hundreds of leagues away from any border that threatened it. There hadn't been a meaningful threat in this region since Anders I established the empire two hundred years ago.

He still disliked it. Should the worst come to pass, the houses were a liability. They could shelter invaders or be burned, obscuring enemy movements. Though he didn't feel the need to circumnavigate the city to prove his suspicion, it appeared as though the construction encircled it.

The houses ended about five hundred paces from the wall. From that point, nothing protected would-be invaders from the sight of the wall. Brandt supposed the short open field was better than nothing.

The gates to Estern stood open, and Brandt and Ana entered without problem. Brandt stopped before he made it a dozen paces into the city. How could such a city even be possible?

Every building in sight was more than a story tall. Several were more than three, and they all seemed crammed together. The noise, especially after the weeks on the road, deafened him. How did anyone get used to such a cacophony?

Ana gave him a small push. "You're making us look like country folk who've never seen a city before."

"It's so much bigger than I remember it."

"It's still a city."

"Let's find someplace to sleep tonight. We can try for an audience with the emperor tomorrow."

Brandt didn't have any particular worries on that count. By now, Kyla would have sent a message ahead making the emperor aware of their impending visit. Hopefully accessing the palace wouldn't prove too difficult.

They faced an overwhelming number of choices for food and shelter. Eventually, Brandt chose one more or less at random. The space seemed clean and the room and food affordable. They weren't anywhere near the heart of the city, but Brandt suspected they didn't have the coin for such places.

This suited them better, anyhow.

They enjoyed a quiet meal together, eating before most of the crowd arrived for the evening. That night they retired early. As had often been the case, even after long days on the road, they worked to make Ana's dream of a family a reality.

That night Brandt fell asleep completely exhausted.

They greeted the rising of the sun with another attempt. Then they called for bathwater, scrubbing the last remains of the road off. Hanns hadn't stood on ceremony when Brandt had met him in the past, but they'd never met at court before.

After a filling breakfast, they made their way toward the palace.

The buildings grew larger the closer they came to the

heart of the city. To Brandt's relief, the streets also quieted. The buildings had space between them, and while the roads were still full of people, it wasn't nearly as crowded as the outer reaches had been. Here, the wheels of commerce dressed citizens in fine clothes and provided luxuries unknown to most.

Brandt felt tension growing within him. Memories of mistreatment at the hands of such people still echoed faintly in his mind. He cursed Kye for stealing the memories of his friends, but Brandt would have thanked him for stealing those of his childhood.

Their first full view of the palace reassured him. It, at least, hadn't changed. Built during the reign of Anders I, the palace was a fortress. Perhaps some found it beautiful, but its intent was to protect. Now that Brandt understood that it guarded a gate, the design choice made even more sense.

The guards surrounding the palace paid close attention to all guests entering and leaving. Brandt's critical eye found few flaws in the emperor's defenses. He and Ana were interrogated multiple times, and while they made it through with little difficulty, Brandt easily saw how the precautions would have stopped any intruders.

Eventually they found themselves in a small nondescript room in the palace. A few paintings representing the reign of the Anders served as the only decoration. Brandt gave them little attention. They were depictions of stories any school child could recite.

The door behind them opened again and a group of four guards entered. Brandt recognized two of them as guards who had served Hanns back when he'd first visited the monastery all those years ago. The recognition was mutual, and short bows of acknowledgment were exchanged. The guards performed a quick check of the room to ensure its safety.

Then they left and Hanns entered.

He looked older than his years. Only two had passed since Brandt had seen him last, but it looked more like a dozen had. Both Brandt and Ana bowed deeply, a gesture barely returned by the emperor.

A younger man with more than a passing resemblance to Hanns followed. The emperor introduced him, though Brandt had already guessed. "Brandt, Ana, this is my younger son, Regar. He wished to meet you, as the ones who discovered the gate outside Landow."

Brandt knew little about the young man besides what was common knowledge. Rumor had it that Regar had been a troublesome child, but like any prince, he had gone into military service as soon as he'd come of age. He'd served on the Falari border, dealing with the never-ending incursions. Brandt had never served under the prince. His own tenure as a wolfblade had ended before Regar reached the border.

Brandt had heard stories of Regar's time, but details differed. All that Brandt knew as fact was that the prince had been captured by the Falari in some skirmish. Some said he escaped and fought his way back to imperial territory. Others claimed a rescue mission had been launched. Still others believed Hanns had bought his youngest son back with promises of gold and alliances.

Whatever had happened, the young man didn't seem scarred in any noticeable way, and the conflict with the Falari hadn't changed, either. They still constantly harassed the imperial borders. Brandt saw a proud young man, attentive and strong by his father's side.

The emperor's eldest son, Olen, Brandt knew even less about. He was considered more of an academic than a warrior and wasn't well-regarded among military units. Though Hanns had never made an official announcement, Olen was widely expected to be next in line to the throne.

They all sat. "Tea?" the emperor asked.

For a time they spoke of meaningless topics. The emperor asked them about their journey, and in return Ana inquired as to the emperor's health. All the while they sipped at tea poured by Regar, a potent green liquid that started with just the slightest hint of bitterness but ended with a pleasant sweetness. It was some of the best tea Brandt had ever tasted.

The formalities surprised him, though he didn't let the surprise reach his face. In their previous interactions Hanns had never been anything but direct and informal. Brandt wondered how much of this was show for Regar's sake.

Hanns, as the host of the gathering, was the first to broach the subject that had brought them all together. "I was saddened to hear of the loss of Highkeep."

Brandt and Ana bowed their heads. "Thank you for your condolences," Ana replied.

"Kyla's messenger described the power of the attack," the emperor said. "It sounded much stronger than the one we endured while I visited."

"I've never felt its like," Brandt confirmed.

"What aid do you seek?"

"Knowledge," Brandt answered.

A ghost of a smile played across the emperor's lips. "I seem to recall that we discussed this two years ago. I know little more now than I did then."

Brandt noted Regar's sudden attention, a light in his eyes that hadn't been there before. He looked close to speaking, but Hanns answered Brandt first. "You are welcome to any knowledge I possess, save only that known to the Anders about the gates. But I fear I will be less help than you hope."

"You've made no progress in understanding her power?"

"None."

"Father," Regar interrupted, "perhaps I—"

"No." Hanns' reply was that of a parent who has already had a familiar argument with their child too many times.

Regar glowered for a moment, then regained his composure.

Hanns explained. "Prince Regar believes that some of the techniques the line of Anders use to control the gate might be the key to unlocking the queen's power. I don't agree, but Anders also decreed the techniques never be passed beyond the emperor and those who might succeed him."

Brandt wondered how applicable a two-hundred-year-old decree should be, considering the weight of the consequences. But he didn't question Hanns. It clearly hadn't done Regar any good.

The emperor stood up suddenly, surprising everyone. "Follow me. Prince Regar, you may leave now."

Regar left, leaving an angry wake behind him.

"I apologize," Hanns said. "He means well, but he doesn't understand how important it is we obey the laws Anders set for his line."

Brandt quickly finished the last of his tea, unwilling to waste a single precious drop. Then he hurried after Hanns. They returned to the palace hallway where they were surrounded by guards. Brandt noted their movement and training. The guards remained far enough away so as not to be bothersome, but effectively blocked both directions of the hall as they moved. No one would get close to the emperor and his retinue without permission.

Hanns walked with a determined stride, taking the myriad turns of the palace with confidence inspired by a lifetime within its walls. Though Brandt considered himself an expert navigator, he soon found himself lost among the twists and turns. Another defensive feature designed to confuse invaders.

They came to a room with a single door. They waited for Hanns' guards to sweep the room for threats before entering, then they stepped into an orderly study.

Hanns went to a shelf of scrolls and books. Reaching into a crack between books he pulled on a lever and a concealed door swung open on silent hinges. An eerie but familiar blue glow emanated from a stone hallway. Hanns looked back at them. "Ready to see one of the greatest secrets of the empire?"

Brandt and Ana nodded, and Hanns led the way below.

The narrow stone corridor led them steadily down. The steps were wide and gentle, but the path snaked as it descended. The blue light reflected in an unnatural manner off the walls, nearly glowing, though they seemed no closer to the source of the light.

At first, Brandt's attention was focused on the blue light, memories flooding through him. The last time he'd seen that light he had been certain he was going to die. He found the memories alone were enough to twist his stomach into knots.

But as they descended and Brandt mastered his reaction, he began to notice the walls of the corridor. They were unnaturally smooth. No matter how hard he looked, he couldn't see a mark of a chisel anywhere. The connection snapped together in his thoughts.

"This tunnel was built by the same people who built the tunnels under the mountain outside of Landow."

"Astute observation," the emperor confirmed.

They passed entrances to other tunnels. Brandt noted one had smooth walls but another's were rougher, similar to more that he'd been in.

"You've dug your own access, haven't you?"

"Not me, but Anders III," Hanns said. "He worried that in an emergency he wouldn't be able to reach the chamber in time."

"Did those that come before build the palace, too?"

Hanns shook his head. "No. As near as I can tell, most of the foundation was left by them, but the palace was built by Anders. The actual Anders."

Brandt nodded. More and more, it seemed that history seemed to revolve around the emperor who had founded their empire over two hundred years ago.

Eventually they reached the chamber Brandt had known they would.

Hanns stopped in the center of the room and gestured. "The gate that founded our empire. The gate that Anders discovered."

Like the gate near Landow, this one was a stone arch, carved by diamonds lit by a mysterious blue glow. This close to it, Brandt could feel its power thrumming through his bones. He hadn't visited Landow's gate since he'd left the area years ago, but he would swear this gate had a different feel to it.

The light from the gate flickered then, almost as though it had been snuffed for a moment. The light recovered quickly enough, but Brandt didn't remember the other gate doing that in the short time it had been active. "What was that?"

The emperor looked as though the weight of the answer

would crush him. "Better you feel it for yourself. Touch it and funnel a bit of air affinity into it."

Brandt looked at the emperor skeptically, who gave a halfhearted smile. "It will be a very different experience from before. It's under my control. There's nothing to fear."

Brandt wasn't sure he agreed. Touching the first gate he had encountered had filled him with a power that had nearly torn him limb from limb. But he trusted Hanns.

So he did as he was asked.

Sensations blasted him the moment he opened his affinity to the gate. He remembered to ride the power, the way Alena had once shown him. The torrent of power became manageable and Brandt sensed a pattern underneath it all.

Almost as soon as he found his bearings, they were torn away. A force of massive power tore into the pattern, seeking to rip it and tear it apart. The pattern of power bent and folded, but snapped back when the assault vanished.

Brandt broke contact with the gate, gasping for air. He had felt that dark power before.

"She's attacking the gate."

Hanns nodded. "It's actually worse than that."

"How?"

Hanns exhaled deeply, the weight of the confession seeming to hang about his neck.

"I believe she's attacking all the gates at once."

6

"Show me again," Jace asked.

Alena smiled and made one of the affirmative gestures the Etari used. Jace's eyes missed little, but his attempt looked stiff. Beside her, Ligt watched on with amusement.

Jace noticed. "It's wrong, isn't it?"

"A little."

"He looks like a fish trying to swim on land," Ligt said in Etari.

"He's trying," Alena replied in the same language.

Jace frowned. "What?"

"Ligt is applauding your efforts," Alena said sweetly.

"That's not what it sounded like."

Alena smiled. They were nearing the Etari border, and Jace had spent the entirety of the trip learning as much about Etari language and customs as he could.

She found her brother remarkable.

Back in Landow, he, more than her parents, had struggled with the years she'd spent away and her sudden and unexpected return. He found the Etari an easy target for his accusations, blaming them for problems that weren't of their making.

Alena didn't fault him, as much as she sometimes wished to. The Etari weren't popular around Landow, and years of insults and distrust weren't easily undone. Jace wasn't the type to bully the occasional Etari trader who came through town, but he wouldn't speak to them unless necessary, and he did his best to act as though they didn't exist.

Now, though, he needed to learn that which he had disdained for years. His ignorance probably wasn't a matter of life and death, in Alena's estimation, but Jace attacked the problem as though he might die if his Etari wasn't perfect.

From sunrise to sundown they worked on teaching Jace Etari customs. Most of the burden fell on Alena's shoulders. Ligt's imperial was surprisingly limited, and his desire even more so. More than once he'd indicated his displeasure at bringing two imperials back into his land.

Jace's efforts impressed her. Though it pained her to admit it, he learned faster than she had on her own journey into Etar. It had taken her a few weeks to fully accept Etar as her new home, so she'd lacked motivation. If not for Azaleth—

She had to cut that thought off as quickly as it appeared.

If it was possible, years after his death, his memory stung worse than it did immediately after he'd died. Perhaps it was because she was returning to Etar, forced to face their family once again. But that wasn't all.

The young Etari warrior had loved her, and she hadn't realized her own feelings until it was too late. Though a fair number of suitors had approached her in Landow, she denied them all, telling herself they would tie her to a city that grew smaller by the day.

True, perhaps. But he'd been part of the reason, too.

The easiest solution was not to think about him. For two years she'd tried daily not to, and she'd gotten better, until the day Ligt appeared at her door.

Her brother's uncoordinated attempts provided welcome relief from her memories. She smiled. "Your motions are correct, but you're not relaxing into it. It comes across almost like sarcasm, the way you perform the motion."

Jace shook his head. "It doesn't feel like it should be this hard. Why can't one motion mean one thing? Why does their language have to be so backwards?"

"Our own language does the same," Alena pointed out. "If I say, 'Oh, stop!' like this," she laughed and pretended to pull away from him, "it's far different from saying, 'Stop!'" She yelled the final word. "It's the same word, but context and delivery matters. Does that make sense?"

Jace nodded. "Sure, but those are words, not gestures."

"It's all language. Your stance, tone, and words are all parts of the whole."

Jace rolled his eyes, but Alena saw that he at least understood what she meant. A hint of a smile played across her lips. Without knowing, he proved her point. "Comfort will come with practice. I think most Etari will understand your attempts. They were generous with my own mistakes. Just try not to appear threatening."

That, she thought, might be the more difficult problem. On the road, she saw her brother in a new light, one she hadn't paid much attention to in Landow. In her absence, Jace had achieved his goal of becoming a warrior, and a strong one at that. She remembered him as a child, diligently practicing every form he learned, the calluses on his palms thick even at a young age. Those years of dedication hadn't been wasted. He didn't puff out his chest like a tavern brawler, but danger rolled off him in waves. The Etari, sensitive to such posturing, might perceive him as more of a threat than he intended.

But that was a problem to be faced another day.

The sun was near its midpoint when they reached the Etari border, delineated by the Alna River. Here the river ran wide and slow, and Ligt went to find a ferryman to bring them across. The crossing was one of several that the Etari permitted.

While they waited for Ligt to return, Alena studied the river and the land beyond. Something about it felt different to her, a sensation she couldn't quite identify. Curious, she closed her eyes and dropped into a soulwalk.

She'd first experienced the state when fighting a soulwalker outside Landow. And while Jace trained with a sword, she sharpened her own abilities, pushing them at night among the rooftops of the city.

A vast web of life revealed itself to her, ghostly strands that ran through the whole world. Soulwalking opened the mind to other planes of existence and revealed the connections that bound them together. Alena tended to see them as threads, though she suspected that was only her mind's interpretation of a more complex experience.

She knew she'd grown stronger, but she didn't know how much. At times, she almost wished to meet another Lolani soulwalker. Then she could once again test her ability. But the Etari thought her affinity shameful, few imperials even knew of mental affinities, and the Falari didn't train affinities at all.

The exploration of her affinity was a lonely one.

In the immediate vicinity, a few threads glowed brighter than others. One was a thread she had tied between her and

Jace. Jace knew of it, and it allowed her a small connection to him at all times. Two others led to her parents back in Landow. And a final led to Brandt, brighter and stronger than the others.

Her perception didn't stretch to the Etari border, so she tapped into the gatestone embedded near her navel. The web expanded, and then she saw it.

Alena gasped softly.

It was beautiful, a working of a scale and intricacy beyond her wildest imagining.

On the other side of the Alna, a translucent wall rose before her. Gossamer threads of infinite complexity intertwined in a pattern Alena could almost understand.

Jace's voice brought her back to her body. She could have gotten lost in that wall for ages. How was such a working possible? It made the impossible stonework hidden in the mountains outside Landow look like child's play in comparison.

She tightened her grip on the reins of her horse. The sight before her was wondrous. But it was another mystery to which she foresaw no easy answers. That wall was a soulworking, but the Etari despised any mental affinity.

Yet they relied on it to guard their border.

Alena remembered the first time she had crossed into Etar. Something about it had felt different, she remembered. But she hadn't thought much of it at the time.

That wall explained the feeling, and it explained how the Etari always knew when someone crossed their border without permission.

And now she understood the importance of an Etari welcome. Alena remembered her own, remembered feeling like it was more than it seemed. Sooni, at least, had given her that impression.

She filed all her questions away as Ligt returned, signing that he had found a ferryman.

They rode their horses down to the bank, following Ligt's lead.

The river crossing was uneventful, and Alena didn't even bother trying to soulwalk. The wall had clearly been on the other side of the Alna, and when they dismounted on the opposite bank she didn't feel any different.

She stopped the party before they had taken more than a few steps on the other shore. She wanted to see with her own senses how this wall worked. Ligt and Jace obliged her as she settled herself and extended her senses. The invisible wall flared to life not more than fifteen paces away. This close, the tapestry was even more mesmerizing. The threads which built the thin barrier shone with prismatic brilliance, ever shifting.

"Ligt, would you go first? Thirty paces."

The Etari trader walked through the wall, which parted before him like a spiderweb cut by a knife. But in less than a heartbeat the wall had reformed, the gentle movement of the threads closing the wound. Alena frowned. There had been interactions between Ligt and the wall, but they were too subtle for her to track.

She considered asking him to walk back and forth a few times but didn't want to press her luck. He already indulged her.

"Jace."

When her brother walked through the wall, she couldn't miss the change. Ligt's passage made the threads flow like liquid, parting and reforming around him. To her senses, her brother's passage ripped the threads apart like an angry child tearing a blanket by hand. Alena flinched away from the sight. To destroy such a beautiful weaving seemed a crime.

As she watched, the wound healed. Not as smoothly as when Ligt passed, but Alena guessed the wall repaired itself within thirty heartbeats.

The threads Jace walked through clung to him. Alena felt their echoes clearly.

Now she knew how the Etari could keep their borders so safe. Not only could they detect intrusions, they could always find an intruder once in their land.

Did they even know this was a soulworking? Alena guessed not. Their dislike of mental affinities was well-established. But at the very least, someone in each family knew how to track the broken threads.

Only one test remained.

Alena walked toward the wall, hand outstretched. When her hand touched, she felt nothing at all.

The threads parted for her like water.

Her welcome still held.

She was still Etari, at least in the eyes of this soulworking. She let out a breath she didn't even know she'd been holding onto. Though not a complete answer to the worries that plagued her, it indicated a hopeful outcome.

"Did you feel anything?" she asked Jace.

Her brother shook his head. "The air seems different somehow, but that's about it."

Her own experience long before hadn't been much different. Still, she'd hoped for more. With one last look at the barrier, Alena dropped from her soulwalk. Remaining in that space for too long exhausted her.

They resumed their journey. They traveled southwest, to an ultimate destination Ligt refused to share.

Late in the afternoon, a group of riders approached them. They rode at speed.

Their posture, even from a distance, worried Alena. In the back of her mind she remembered that Jace had broken the barrier and he had no welcome to these lands. More than once she had soulwalked and seen the threads clinging to him as vigorously as they had when he first tore the barrier.

Her fears were confirmed as the horses surrounded them. Four riders circled about fifteen paces away, and two riders had a stone spinning in the air next to them. They came prepared to fight.

Alena let Ligt handle the discussion.

Ligt made the hand sign for peace, but it only settled the riders a bit. Their leader stopped her horse while the others continued circling. "Why do you bring an outsider, trader?" she asked in Etari.

Alena didn't like the sound of that. Etari culture was separated along several lines, but those who chose to become warriors and defend the land often looked upon the traders with some amount of disdain. Alena heard the attitude in the tone of the question.

Ligt took no offense. "The woman has been summoned by Sooni."

The commander of the group barely reacted, but Alena noticed the riders falter for a moment. They were expecting her arrival?

"She's the one?" the commander asked.

Yes, Ligt hand signed.

"And the other?"

"Her brother. He insisted on protecting her," Ligt explained. Alena almost smiled at the condescending attitude in their guide's voice. Ligt really didn't like Jace.

"He has no welcome," the commander pointed out.

"It was not mine to give," Ligt answered.

"Alena, what are they saying?" Jace asked. "I don't like their tone."

Alena grimaced. Jace might not speak their language, but the Etari knew enough imperial to understand him.

"We're deciding whether or not to kill you," the commander answered, in imperial.

Jace drew his sword.

In response, the riders circled a bit further away. Alena now saw three riders had stones spinning.

Alena wasn't worried for her own life. She had welcome and the riders knew who she was. But Jace wasn't making it easy for himself.

She stepped forward, speaking fluent Etari. "Forgive my brother. He is ignorant of Etari ways, but he means well. He only wishes to protect me. Is there any way he may earn your welcome?"

As a trader, Ligt had good reasons to withhold his welcome into the land. For all Alena knew, he didn't even have the ability. But anyone who could sense the threads, as at least one among the riders must, should.

The commander considered the question. "A test. Single combat, unarmed. I wish to see an imperial fighting style for myself. If he can last sixty heartbeats, I will permit his escort."

Thank you. Alena used the most formal and polite form of the sign. She turned to her brother. "They want to fight. One on one, unarmed. If you can last sixty heartbeats, you'll gain formal entry into their land."

Jace glanced at the commander of the riders, who stared at him impassively.

He smiled and sheathed his sword. Alena wondered if

the commander had already measured and understood her brother. Such a test was perfect for him. If the commander had guessed as much, Alena wouldn't be surprised. She'd often found the Etari, with their focus on physicality, to be deeply intuitive.

It didn't take long for the riders to dismount and select their champion. They chose the largest of them, a man who stood at least a head taller than Jace.

Jace grinned at the challenge. He offered the rider a short bow, which was returned awkwardly by the Etari.

The commander gave the signal to begin, clapping her hands once.

Jace wasted no time. Alena knew her brother wouldn't fight to survive the count of sixty, but to win. His aggression could easily become his greatest enemy. But it also might be just what was needed to impress the Etari.

Alena watched the duel with undisguised interest. Not just because it determined her brother's fate, but because she'd never seen her brother actually fight in the past few years.

The Etari rider was fast and strong, a warrior shaped by a life of strenuous living.

But Jace was faster and just as strong, a fact the Etari warrior quickly learned.

Jace threw a quick series of punches, none of them particularly damaging, but enough to get in the rider's head. The Etari responded, but his strikes never quite connected. Jace dipped and ducked. His movements didn't appear any faster than the rider's, but the rider couldn't land a single significant hit.

In return, Jace drove fists and knees into the rider's torso.

The rider, frustrated, attempted to tackle Jace and bring the fight to the ground.

Alena missed Jace's manipulation, but he threw the warrior away from him with a casual toss.

Even the other Etari appeared impressed.

He might be her younger brother, but he was also as much a warrior as any rider here.

The Etari warrior came smoothly to his feet, but the commander clapped her hands again. She looked satisfied with the display. "Welcome to Etar, imperial."

Alena quickly soulwalked, just in time to see the threads drift off Jace. She watched them flutter into the sky and vanish.

Her brother had earned his welcome.

7

Brandt stood and stretched, then rolled his head in a large, slow circle. He blinked quickly, trying to clear the dryness from his eyes. How much time had passed? He emerged from between two shelves of books to look at the window outside. The sun already dipped below the horizon.

Far too much, then.

He contained his sigh of frustration and returned to the table where Ana combed through books that had been old when her grandparents were born. She glanced up at him. "Done for the day?"

"Not quite. I'll look through one more set of books, then report to the emperor."

She raised an eyebrow. "We could retire to our chambers for a bit."

He smiled and shook his head. "Tempting, though."

The emperor filled their days with studies of different flavors. Sometimes Regar trained them. The prince presented an enigma to Brandt. Regar's affinities surpassed even Brandt's, making him one of the strongest warriors in the empire. Yet Brandt had never heard so much as a whisper about the prince's skill.

Their sparring revealed hidden depths to the prince's character. In the halls and chambers of power, Regar was polite, if distant. Had Brandt never fought the prince, he would have called him cold and calculating, studying people like pieces on a board.

In the training hall he revealed his true nature. Regar fought with passion, wrestling against positions a wiser warrior would have disengaged from. He never surrendered.

Unarmed, or with a blade, Brandt was the stronger warrior. But if affinities came into play, Brandt couldn't win. Their differing skills made for the only excitement in Brandt's day, and it was where he began to respect Regar.

Regar was skilled and strong, but he would probably never be emperor. That title would pass to his older brother, rarely seen in the palace. When Brandt asked after Olen, all he was told was that the prince was on a mission for the empire.

Other times, Brandt trained with Hanns. Unfortunately, their time together rarely taught Brandt anything useful. Hanns knew a handful of techniques Brandt didn't, but none of them were the key to greater power. Most of Hanns' skill came from his connection to the gate underneath the palace. The only other techniques he knew that Brandt didn't were mental, and he refused to teach Brandt those, claiming they were too dangerous.

When he wasn't with royalty, Brandt practically lived in the library, which housed the greatest collection of books in the empire. None of which taught him that which he most desired to learn.

Secretly, Brandt became more convinced every day that his questions could only be answered by Anders I. The first emperor had been pivotal in more ways than anyone seemed to understand, but little was known about the man outside of the legends that had grown after his death. And almost nothing at all was known of the time before Anders. The emperor had destroyed everything, a process he'd been surprisingly thorough about. Nothing in the library dated back more than two hundred years.

Ana prevented him from surrendering to frustration. She helped him, guided him, and pushed him when he needed it. And in the evenings her desire to start a family had become infectious. Her enthusiasm rubbed off on him, and he looked forward to returning to their shared room after a full day of study and training.

The last set of books Brandt examined gave him no further clues than any others. When only torches lit the hallways, they bid each other farewell so Brandt could meet with the emperor.

The guards welcomed him, giving him the slightest of bows as he passed. When he reached the emperor's private training hall he knocked on the door and was invited to enter.

Brandt did, relaxing the moment he stepped through the door. Libraries didn't often suit his disposition. The stacks of books intimidated him with the weight of their knowledge. But a training hall he understood. The smell of sweat and blood clung to the walls, a silent testament to the generations of emperors who had trained within. It smelled like home to Brandt.

The emperor was already seated cross-legged at one end of the hall. He was in meditation, so Brandt took up a position across from him and did the same. His breathing slowed and his heart beat steady. As he slipped deeper into meditation he heard the songs of the elements more clearly. The fire from the torches still sang loudest, but the low hum of stone wasn't far behind. Even the whisper of the wind offered promises of secret knowledge.

Though they weren't physically close to the gate, Brandt noticed its influence. The songs were louder, the notes clearer. Here he was stronger.

The sound of the emperor shifting his weight brought Brandt out of his meditation. Their gazes met, and as usual, the emperor began. "What did you learn today?"

"Nothing useful. One monk in the time of Anders II developed a wind technique similar to the stone technique the Etari use. By manipulating a mass of air one bit at a time, continually adding to the movement of the element, he was able to create small tornadoes. But the scale was hundreds of times smaller than the Lolani queen's efforts."

"Has it occurred to you that perhaps the queen's strength is the result of nothing more than her connection with her gate? Perhaps she has no secret knowledge."

"Then why does her strength so far surpass your own?"

Hanns took no offense at the question that would have cost Brandt his command had he said it when he served as a wolfblade. "Her connection is stronger."

Brandt narrowed his eyes. "Do you believe that?"

Hanns offered a slight smile, as though he'd been trapped by his own argument. "I do not."

"Why not?"

"Because Anders I mastered the gates, and although he didn't pass down everything, I believe he passed down all we needed to know about them. If there was a way to make a stronger bond, he would have found it."

Brandt stopped himself from arguing. The two of them had speculated plenty on the source of the Lolani queen's strength. But no amount of speculation changed the truth: they had no idea why the queen was so strong.

Hanns' defense of Anders did lead Brandt to another question, though. "Do you know why he destroyed so much? I feel like the answers are in our past, but we have no past to look back on."

Hanns didn't answer immediately. "I think I understand, but this is only my guess. I do not know."

Brandt indicated that he understood.

"I think, in a way, you answered your own question. Anders was driven by a single purpose. He wanted to create an empire that would protect and serve as many people as possible. I agree with you. I think the answers to some of our most pressing questions are locked in the past, before Anders rose to power. But I suspect there is a danger there, too. Knowledge can cut the knowledgeable just as easily as it can control the ignorant. By destroying our past, I believe Anders sought to protect us."

"That decision might be what dooms us in this war."

Hanns acknowledged the point. "And it might be the decision that allowed this empire to flourish for two hundred years. How does one weigh such a choice?"

Brandt didn't like the direction of that argument. "Why do you defend him?"

Again, Brandt was grateful the emperor didn't take offense. In public, any word spoken against the emperor could cost the speaker their tongue, or even their head. But in person, nothing could be further from the truth. "Because, like you, I have met him. My power is descended from his. I do not know his memories and I cannot always speak to his reasons, but I trust him."

The answer didn't suffice, but Brandt felt that Hanns was telling the truth. "Then what do we do?" he asked. "How do we get strong enough to fight the queen?"

"I wish I knew the answer to that question, Brandt. But for now, all I can do is offer you what I can. I know it doesn't feel like much, but I know nothing better."

Brandt sighed. If there was nothing else to do, there was nothing else to do. "Let's get to it, then."

Today they began with fire. Small orbs of flame danced between the two men, faster and faster, the pattern growing ever more intricate.

Hanns faltered first, two of the balls flickering out of existence as the energy feeding them died.

Brandt frowned. Hanns never made the first mistake.

He studied the emperor. Beads of sweat dripped down his forehead. "Hanns?"

The emperor waved away Brandt's attention. "I'll be fine. I just need a moment."

Brandt didn't argue. Hanns looked pale, but he was also the emperor. Brandt followed his requests as though they were commands. Eventually his ruler composed himself. "Again."

Brandt created more orbs, pulling one each from several torches along the wall. They began their dance again, but Hanns never found the rhythm. One of the orbs almost exploded in Brandt's face. He caught the wild fire and directed it harmlessly around him.

Hanns had collapsed.

Brandt stood and rushed to the emperor. Hanns still breathed, but he came back to consciousness slowly. When his eyes met Brandt's, they were alert and aware.

"Her attacks grow in strength."

Brandt helped Hanns back to sitting, then gave the emperor some distance. "What can we do?"

"I need to fight her, push her back from trying to influence our gate."

"Can you?"

"There is no choice. She attacks my connection to the gate. If it fails, the empire will fall as well." Hanns took a deep breath. "Will you aid me? You have fought her once before. Your presence might make a difference."

Brandt's jaw clenched as he thought of his last battle with the queen. "In that same space?"

The emperor heard the concern in Brandt's voice. "I'm afraid so, yes."

"I'm not sure how much use I can be to you. If not for Alena, I would have given myself to the queen."

"You're still tied to her, are you not?"

"You can tell?" Brandt hadn't mentioned it to Hanns.

"I can. If you wish, I think your connection would allow her to take part in our endeavor as well."

Brandt didn't want to return. The dreamscape he'd last fought the queen in still haunted his memories. That fight took place in a world he didn't understand. "Is there anyone else who could do it? Wouldn't Regar be a better choice?"

The emperor shook his head. "Regar might be stronger, but I can't risk him becoming entangled with the gate. It needs to be you or no one at all."

Brandt closed his eyes and tried to master his fear. "I'll do it. I'll talk to Alena as well."

"Good." Hanns stood, his feet unsteady. "Tomorrow, then, or the day after. I'll let you know. I'll need my rest tonight, and we should put affairs in order in case the worst should befall us."

Brandt's eyes widened at that. He knew the danger he

faced, but for some reason it hadn't occurred to him the emperor would be putting his own life at risk.

Knowing he would fight next to Hanns gave him strength.

He hoped it would be enough. Because if they failed, the empire might lose Emperor Anders VI.

8

Jace's sparring match against the rider earned him the goodwill of the border patrol. The riders accompanied them, and Jace amused them all with his rough attempts at communicating in Etari. Most of the riders spoke at least some imperial, though, so the language barrier wasn't insurmountable.

If anything, Jace's entrance into the world of the Etari was smoother than Alena's. He was a warrior, a profession given more respect in Etari culture than thief, the only profession Alena claimed when she first crossed the border. Every night, while Alena and Ligt prepared the meal, Jace and the riders would spar, both open-handed and with wooden sticks. Jace's skill earned him respect overnight that Alena had fought for years to obtain.

He'd worked hard for his skills and she couldn't begrudge him using those skills to his advantage, even if she occasionally felt a pang of jealousy at the ease with which he inserted himself into the other half of her life.

When she wasn't jealous, though, it warmed her heart to see Jace with the Etari. He no longer held them in contempt, and she guessed he'd be disappointed when their path parted from that of the border riders. For most of the last ten years of her life, she'd thought of herself as being torn between two worlds. Watching Jace form new friendships changed her mind. He was a bridge between Landow and Etar, and he reminded her they were all part of one much larger world.

That night they sat together around a fire, the group watching Jace with bemused expressions as they tested some of his Etari hand signs. As she laughed, Alena felt a tug near the base of her skull.

She closed her eyes and fell into a soulwalk, the process almost as natural as breathing to her now.

Brandt.

Alena took a deep breath and focused her attention. Distance wasn't completely irrelevant while soulwalking, but it didn't separate souls the same way it did bodies. She visualized herself running along the thread that connected them. The soulwork at the Etari border slowed her for a moment, but then she was through. She found Brandt and created a space for them to meet.

As she usually did, she chose her family's kitchen. It was a room she knew well, one she could summon with little effort. And it brought her comfort. Brandt appeared within the kitchen, standing. He looked around, gaining his bearings.

"It always smells like bread here."

Alena smiled at the comment. "It's not intentional, but my mother grew up in a family of bakers. She bakes fresh bread several times a week, and I guess the smell must be ingrained in my memories."

Brandt's eyes became unfocused and Alena felt a ripple pass through her illusion. Brandt remembered something, the memory threatening the safe space she'd created. Fortunately, a small effort on her part dispelled Brandt's interference. In a fight, he could beat her a dozen ways before she could blink. But here, the power was hers.

"Sorry," Brandt said. "I was thinking of our fight with the queen. Was there a smell then?"

"Not one that I remember."

"Me neither." He paused, lost in thought. Then he sat down and explained why he had called for her. Alena listened, then sat in silence as she considered Brandt's request for aid.

"When?" she asked.

"Soon. Tomorrow or the day after."

The timing worked out well enough. Ligt said it would take them another four days of travel to reach Sooni. Alena realized she hadn't spoken to Brandt about her own movement and the problems with the Etari gate, and did so then.

"It can't be a coincidence," Brandt said.

Alena nodded.

"I'm glad your brother is with you. He's a good man."

"Thanks. How's Ana?"

"We're trying to start a family."

It took a heartbeat for the words to register, then the fire in the kitchen suddenly bloomed brighter. Alena blushed. If she didn't keep her emotions controlled they were reflected in the space in small ways. "Congratulations! That's great news."

"Is it?"

"Of course it is. You two are wonderful together, and think of how strong your child will be."

"Thanks. I wish I shared your confidence." Brandt gestured around the room, taking everything in. "I ask myself all the time—with everything happening now, is bringing a child into this world wise? Look at me. I'm terrified of facing the queen again, even with you and Hanns supporting me. I know I might not return. How can I ask a child to endure that? How can I ask Ana to bear that burden?"

Alena reached across the table and grabbed his hand. "Don't you think Ana knows all this?"

Brandt admitted she did.

"Then trust her. If she's willing, and you're willing, you two will find the path. I'm certain of it."

Brandt breathed out slowly. "Thank you." Then he changed the subject. "Will you help us?"

"There isn't much choice, is there? You believe Hanns needs the connection to the gate?"

Brandt nodded.

"Then we need to protect it."

Brandt looked around the room, as though worried someone might be eavesdropping on them. "I don't want to go back. Not after last time."

Alena tried to ignore her own memories of their last encounter. "Neither do I."

They sat in silence together for a few moments. Then Brandt squeezed her hand. "I'll be in touch soon."

"I'll be ready."

When Alena was certain that Brandt had said all he needed, she banished the illusion and returned to her own body.

The scene around the campfire had become very quiet. Alena opened her eyes to see everyone staring at her. The Etari, in particular, looked as though they were close to drawing their weapons.

In the intervening years Alena had forgotten how much

the Etari despised soulwalkers. It hadn't occurred to her to hide her actions from them out of respect for their beliefs.

At the same time, her ability to soulwalk was the very reason they had summoned her.

I'm fine, she gestured.

The Etari didn't look convinced, but they let her be. Jace offered to spar all comers again, even though he looked exhausted from his long day on the road. The riders eagerly took him up on his offer.

The tension around the fire dissipated. After a few rounds, Jace called the sparring to a halt and everyone gathered closer to the fire. Jace sat down next to Alena.

"You look horrible," she said. He had new bruises on his face and welts on his arm where he'd been hit with a stick.

"They're tough fighters," he admitted. "Where were you?"

"With Brandt." Alena told Jace everything, including her decision to fight again against the Lolani queen. As she spoke, the Etari quieted their conversation to pay closer attention to hers. She addressed them all. "We may need to stop for a bit to allow me to fight, either tomorrow or the day after."

Ligt signed an affirmative gesture, which was about all Alena expected. The riders spoke quietly among themselves and then announced they would be leaving the party in the morning. They gave no reason, but Alena guessed easily enough.

Jace had been a fun distraction, but they didn't want to be anywhere near a soulwalker as she fought. Alena wished them well. Their presence meant little this far into Etar. At the moment, there were probably few places safer in the world.

She would miss the company, though. And the look on Jace's face was almost enough to ask them to stay.

Early the next morning she took Jace away from the camp. The riders were packing up and Jace was eager to see them off, but Alena wanted to ensure one last task was taken care of before she was summoned by Brandt.

When they were well away from the camp, she sat down. Jace followed suit. Hidden in the tall grasses of the prairie, they might as well have been alone in the world. Which was exactly the feeling she was searching for.

Jace followed her without question, though she saw the curiosity in his eyes, and the worry he would miss the riders' departure. Once they were settled, she spoke. "I'm nervous about what Brandt has asked of me. The queen frightens me, and I don't fully understand her powers. The place that I'm going—" She hesitated, not quite sure how to say what she meant. "Where I'm going, I want an anchor. Something that I'm tied tightly to."

"I'll do it," Jace said, preempting her question.

"It means wrapping threads tightly around both of us. In some ways, it might feel like compulsion. Do you understand?"

Somehow her brother's eyes managed to be both hard and welcoming at the same time. "I do."

"And you'll still do it?"

His stare was answer enough.

She exhaled deeply. "Thank you."

Alena hadn't been certain how he would respond. She'd compelled him once before, and that deed hung over their relationship like a dark cloud. To willingly submit to it again spoke volumes about his trust in her.

Trust she wasn't sure she deserved.

She closed her eyes. The web of life appeared around

her, the thread connecting her to Jace brighter than the rest. As she had with Brandt the night before, she followed the thread until they were together.

In her studies, Alena had discovered that most people possessed some deep-seated and natural defense against soulwalking. It wasn't enough to deter a trained soulwalker, but some part of the human spirit rejected the interference of others. Souls wanted to be free.

She knew Jace possessed the same innate defense, but she didn't encounter it today. He left himself completely vulnerable.

She swore to herself she would never abuse that trust. Never again.

Jace appeared before her, but it wasn't him in the same way it had been Brandt earlier. This was her representation of him, her own mental model. As she willed it, strings appeared in her hand.

Like most of her training, Alena didn't quite understand how her techniques worked. This was no different. She wanted to strengthen the bond between them, to have something to hold onto when they faced the queen. But she didn't know exactly how to achieve that.

So she followed her instincts. She took the string in her hand and tied one piece to his right wrist. Then she tied that string to her own wrist. Another string appeared in her hand and she repeated the process with the other wrist, then again with each ankle.

With every connection, she felt her brother more clearly. Some of his emotions bled into her. He was calm. She couldn't understand how he could remain clearheaded in such difficult times.

How many connections should she create? Her instinct told her that more connections would secure the two of them more tightly together, but there was a danger. With every string that connected them she could see his thoughts more clearly. If she bound them too tightly she feared they might not remain as individuals.

Not for the first time, she wished she had a guide to this affinity.

When she thought she had found a safe balance, she stepped back and viewed her work. The strings lengthened as needed.

Alena stepped out of the soulwalk. Even with her eyes open she felt her brother, calm and rooted like a tree beside her. "How do you feel?"

He held up his hand and stared at it. "Fine. But nervous." He bit his lower lip. "That's you, isn't it?"

"Probably."

Jace grunted. "That's strange. Do you always feel so uncertain?"

"Not always. Sometimes I'm terrified, too."

He laughed.

"It's not every day I tie myself to someone like this. But thank you. I can't believe how calm you are."

He gave a small shrug. "It's nothing. Are we done? I don't want to miss the others' departure."

They stood and rejoined the Etari and wished the riders well. As Jace said his farewells, Alena paid attention to the emotions running through her. She could feel Jace's, more subtle than her own. He was sorry to see the riders go.

Jace's emotions reminded her of a lesson she'd learned two years ago. She understood the temptation to use soulwalking to fix so many common problems. How strong could a relationship be if each partner were tied together in this way? There would be no guesswork, no lies.

She couldn't see it working, though. People needed

separation. As soon as she returned from her defense of the gate, she intended to sever these connections.

The riders broke away, riding hard toward the north. Jace waved farewell, the imperial gesture out of place in the plains of Etar. Then it was just the three of them. Ligt looked to her, seeking guidance.

She hadn't heard from Brandt. "We can travel. When the time comes, I will let you know."

They packed up their own camp and resumed their journey. Alena steeled herself for the fight to come. The last time, her fight had brought her to the gates of death, a myth made suddenly real.

She kept sneaking glances at Jace, knowing that he could feel her turbulent emotions. But his face was impassive.

She would return to her family. She wouldn't abandon Jace, never again.

But one thought troubled her.

If the queen defeated her and sent her to the gates, would her connection with Jace kill him, too?

9

Brandt broke away from Ana's embrace. As they separated he ran his hand down her arm, stopping to clasp her hand one last time before turning his back on her.

They both understood danger. Before their marriage, they had fought side by side as wolfblades, among the first warriors the emperor sent into battle. But this felt different. This moment held a finality he didn't usually experience. He couldn't imagine not seeing her again.

Brandt shook his head and forced his eyes forward. Behind him, Ana closed the door to their chambers, leaving Brandt alone in the long hallway.

Two days had passed since the decision to attack was made. The days had crawled by since, Brandt's normal routine disrupted by the emperor's various preparations. He'd done little but dread this moment.

Now he wished he had squeezed more out of that time.

He passed through the rows of guards and into the study beyond, where the emperor waited alone.

The emperor stood up from the chair he'd been reclining in, not wasting a moment. "Ready?"

"Not at all."

Hanns' smile was grim. "Me neither. Shall we?"

Brandt nodded.

He followed the emperor down the secret passage. At times he ran his hands along the walls of the tunnel, still amazed by the craftsmanship.

So many mysteries.

And not an answer to be found.

They reached the gate, glowing with unworldly energies. The two men stood in silence, pausing before the task. The emperor broke the silence. "Alena?"

"She will join us."

"Summon her."

Brandt closed his eyes. He didn't understand mental affinities, and a part of him remained surprised every time they worked for him. He imagined standing on a cliff overlooking an expansive valley. In his imagination he cupped his hands to his mouth. "Alena!"

His voice echoed in his imagination, so loud he almost clapped his hands over his ears.

The power of the gate, he supposed. This close, everything was stronger.

In return he felt an assurance she would arrive. In his experiences in this space, Brandt had learned to trust his emotions, to read more into them than he usually did. The mental affinity intertwined with emotions in ways that defied easy explanation. But he was confident that the assurance he felt was most likely from Alena.

Brandt opened his eyes. "She will be with us soon."

The emperor nodded, studying the gate as though for the first time. "It makes you wonder, doesn't it?"

"What?"

"I forget sometimes, lost in the details, how miraculous these gates are. Why do they even exist? What was their original purpose?"

"You really don't know?"

"No. Anders I learned how to use them, and was the first in the empire to have some inkling of what they were capable of, but all he passed on was his knowledge of the use of them. I know no more about their origins than you do."

Brandt stood by his emperor, studying the enigma before him. He wished for answers, but none would come today.

A while later he felt Alena more clearly. "She's here."

Hanns took a deep breath and stepped toward the gate. He put his hand on one arch, a slight tensing of his body the only indication of the tremendous powers flowing through him. When Brandt had touched the gate near Landow, it almost tore his body into pieces. Hanns turned to him, still able to focus on events in the physical world. That in itself told Brandt how impressive the emperor's control was.

"Be careful not to touch the gate itself. Once you are certain you and Alena are connected, touch my shoulder. Allow me to be your conduit."

"I will."

Hanns closed his eyes, trusting Brandt to follow his guidance.

Brandt closed his own eyes, dropping once again into Alena's kitchen. He'd visited the actual room a few times when he had recuperated in Landow. and Alena's eye for detail was evident in every corner of the room. She stood next to the fire, playing idly with her hair, the same as she always did when she was scared. "It's time?"

Brandt's reply caught in his throat. He could feel his heart pulsing in his chest. He nodded.

Alena came up to him and wrapped a cord around her wrist and his. Then she met his eyes.

In the real world, Brandt took a step forward and put his hand on Hanns' shoulder.

The power of the gate crashed over him, overwhelming his control in an instant. But Alena was there, guiding him through the transition. The forces tearing through him faded, and he thought of being wrapped in blankets inside a sturdy house as a storm raged beyond the walls.

He found himself in darkness, standing next to Hanns. In this soulscape Hanns appeared younger, muscles still taut under tanned skin. This was his emperor decades ago.

Alena, less impressed by authority, spoke first, her voice behind Brandt making him jump. "This place suits you."

Hanns' grin was mirthless. "A lesson for you, Alena. In this place, your self-image is part of your strength. This form isn't just vanity, although I'll admit it feels good to erase the aches and pains of an aging body."

Alena nodded, her eyes searching for clues Brandt couldn't guess at. She studied Hanns carefully. Then her eyes widened. "You connected to the second gate."

Hanns kept his face neutral, but Brandt knew Alena's statement was true and had caught him off guard. Something in the shift of Hanns' weight gave him away.

"You're perceptive," was all he said.

Brandt glanced between the two. Then he settled on the emperor. "You connected with the gate outside Landow?"

"I did."

"I thought you were going to use it to defeat the queen for good."

Hanns gave a bitter laugh. "I said no such thing. I did

hope it would allow me to fight her on more even terms. But that might have been optimistic. I haven't revealed my connection yet, and have taken great pains to hide it." He glared at Alena.

"This close to a gate, I don't think hiding it is possible," Alena said.

"Apparently." The emperor paused. "Are we ready?"

"What should we expect?" Brandt asked.

"I wish I knew."

Before they could respond, Brandt felt the space around them change. They traveled from darkness to darkness, but this darkness felt different. The air was cool and clammy against his skin. Off in the distance he thought he heard the drip of water into a puddle.

Alena fell to her knees, holding her head in her hands.

Brandt turned to her, but before he could even ask a question, a voice echoed in his head. For a moment it was all he could hear. His whole world became *her* voice.

He had missed her.

Why had he ever feared? Under her, he was safe. He would fall on his own sword, if only for her smile.

Beside him, Alena screamed, but the sound was muffled. It still grated against his ears, though. If he killed her, the sound would stop.

Hanns stepped toward Alena. He reached down and hauled her up by the arm. The emperor grimaced at the effort required. But as soon as he touched her arm the screaming stopped.

A moment later, Brandt's trance was broken. He blinked, and the realization of what had just happened made his knees shake. With a sword in hand he had once believed he could fight any enemy. But how could he fight a queen whose weapons were unlike any he understood?

Alena nodded her thanks to Hanns. "I wasn't ready for that. I'm sorry."

"Nothing to apologize for," the emperor grunted. "I suspect she expected us."

Laughter cackled in the background. "I certainly did."

Brandt turned toward her voice, though he couldn't see her.

Hanns gritted his teeth and groaned. The area around them brightened, even though there was no light source. They stood in a large cave, tunnels to other caves found in all directions. Across the cave from them, the queen lounged on her throne, two priests standing to attention on either side.

The queen waved her hand and the light faded. "You're ruining the atmosphere," she said.

"Where is this?" The emperor sounded as though an enormous weight rested on his chest.

"I grew up in these," the queen replied. "We all seek places of comfort, and this is mine."

"It doesn't seem terribly comfortable," Alena replied flippantly.

Brandt couldn't see, but he could *feel* the queen's attention focus on their young ally. "Ahh. Alena. You are not welcome here."

The air around them pulsed with life. Brandt inhaled and found he couldn't breathe. A thousand needles burned into his skin.

And then the pain vanished.

Alena's breath now came in ragged gasps.

"My." Brandt thought the queen sounded impressed. "You've grown, haven't you? And with no one to train you, either."

The queen's voice circled the chamber. Brandt didn't

know if she walked around them or if it was a trick of this place. "Comfort means something different to us each. To you, Alena, it means your mother's kitchen, or maybe even your father's smithy. To Brandt it's Ana. And for poor Hanns we must go far back, before he was identified as a candidate for Anders VI, before his affinity manifested. Back when he longed for his mother's embrace."

Light flared within the cave. Fire flickered in Hanns' eyes, and a bow appeared in his hands. With a shout, Hanns released an arrow at the queen's heart.

She batted the shaft away as though it were a fly.

Brandt's veins ran cold. The queen knew them, far better than they had guessed. Was Ana safe? The queen's touch spanned whole continents. Had he made a mistake in agreeing to come?

"Stop doubting," Alena whispered.

Brandt looked over at her. She appeared worn. "This is a realm of belief, Brandt. You're not making this easier."

Ashamed his weakness was so public, he focused on the task at hand. Both the emperor and Alena fought against the queen in their own ways. He needed to find a way to contribute.

The queen's cold eyes glittered. "This is my home. Those who sought my life never found this place. Here I could sleep and dream of the power I would one day wield. Perhaps the beds aren't soft, but this is still my sanctum."

Brandt heard the queen's words, but his mind was elsewhere. He remembered their last fight, the way he'd manipulated his sword to destroy the gate.

The queen had threatened Ana by naming her in this place.

It lit a fire inside him, a small coal burning as bright as

the sun. He held onto that, knowing how volatile his emotions could be in this place.

Brandt stepped in front of the others.

The queen glanced at him, then returned her attention to Alena, who she perceived as a greater threat.

He would make that her final mistake.

Brandt shifted his position, the technique ingrained in every bone and muscle in his body, a move practiced thousands of times.

His sword slid out of its sheath, the steel of the blade glowing. Brandt cut horizontally, the draw and the cut blending into one movement.

As he cut, he willed the blade to grow.

Here, the idea became reality. Brandt's sword lengthened, quickly extending the entire width of the cave.

It cut into the stone on the other side. Brandt flexed his muscles, willing the cut to be easy. His sword didn't even slow as it sliced through rock like thin parchment.

The first priest didn't have enough time to respond. The sword passed through her cleanly. The second priest resisted, but only slowed Brandt for a moment. Then she, too, died. Brandt's blade passed through an empty throne and met the knife of the third priest.

This one fought, nearly bringing Brandt's whole swing to a stop. Caught in the moment, Brandt could think of nothing but to press harder.

Then the queen reappeared, standing tall in front of them. Her eyes blazed, glowing with an inhuman red light. She extended her arms and pure power blasted from the center of her being.

Hanns yelled, the sound of a soul crushed with despair. The emperor fell to his knees and the cave dimmed even more.

All Brandt saw was the queen's glowing eyes.

He heard a whisper, not in his ears but in his mind. "I saved your life once. I own you."

Something punched him in the stomach. He looked down, unable to see what had happened. He looked up and found himself face to face with the queen. She towered over him.

Brandt felt himself lifted bodily off the floor. His legs dangled helplessly, kicking at the air.

For a moment, the light returned to the cave and Brandt saw it was the queen's fist that had punched him. It had pierced his stomach, and now she lifted him with one arm by his intestines.

The agony was excruciating, and cold. Ice spread through his veins, slowing his heart.

And then silence.

10

Emotions flooded this world, and Alena felt them all. Hanns didn't reveal his torment on his face, but desperation leeched off him like a stink. She'd known the import of this task, but it wasn't until she noticed Hanns controlling two gates that she understood how much they had staked on this attempt. If they failed here, the empire would eventually fall with them.

And they were failing. The cave reeked of death, the stone silent witness to the end of countless lives. Alena saw the barrier the emperor held between them and the queen, the only reason any of them were capable of logical thought. The queen's power crashed against the barrier, one relentless wave after another.

So far, Hanns had only drawn on the power of a single gate. He would only surprise the queen once, so the moment had to matter.

But Alena wasn't sure how many moments they had left.

Then the queen attacked Brandt in retaliation for his assault on her priests. The emperor's boundary crumbled as the queen revealed a taste of her true power.

Alena froze when she saw the queen's fist impale Brandt. Her friend roared in agony, but Alena wasn't sure what she could do to save him. The queen could kill her with ease.

Then she noticed the threads tying the priests to the queen. Hanns needed to fight the queen, but Alena could weaken her.

Alena's own defenses shattered as the emperor's protection finally failed.

Somewhere far away, her brother waited for her to return. She felt him, his emotions calm, reassuring her.

Alena willed herself to appear next to the priest who had just defended himself against Brandt's attack, not sure if such a feat was possible.

It worked.

The priest's eyes opened wide as Alena appeared directly in front of him. Alena found the threads of his soul, wrapped herself around them, then plunged a dagger into his eye.

The priest's soul pulled her into a familiar place.

No longer did Alena feel the fear of the cave. This was a flat plain decorated only by a single gate, somehow more real than the imitation Alena had seen outside Landow.

Alena kept a grip on the threads as the priest walked to the gate. It flared briefly as the priest stepped through, and a rush of fresh energy filled her.

A presence appeared, not quite solid.

They'd met before, but this time she recognized him.

Anders I.

The man who had founded the empire. The man whose lies and secrets threatened to destroy that same empire.

She turned away from him, but a gesture from his hand froze her in place.

"Coming here again was foolish," he said. "Blood has limits."

Her body was frozen, but her mouth still moved. "I need the strength to kill the queen."

Anders shook his head. "Do you know how many you would need to face her on even footing?" He sighed. "Literal rivers of blood have been shed for that woman. Is that a burden you're willing to place upon your own soul?"

"I'm open to other suggestions," Alena said bitterly. "But there's too much we don't know." Her gaze focused on him.

Her stare didn't intimidate the emperor, although she thought she caught a flash of sadness cross his face. He didn't rise to her disrespect. "You need to return. I understand Hanns' choice, but it was a poor one. Her control of that realm is unmatched. When he reveals his possession of the second gate, you'll need to take advantage of the moment."

"What do I do?"

"Cut off her connections."

With that, Anders disappeared, nothing but empty space where he had stood.

Alena swore the next time she saw him she would begin their discussion by punching him in the face. She hated cryptic answers.

She took one last look at the gate, feeling the new power flowing through her.

The feeling didn't seem as strong as she remembered it the first time.

She returned to the cave, slammed into an assault on all her senses. Vomit rose in her throat but she forced it down. She threw a barrier over herself. It wouldn't last long, but it gave her a moment to catch her bearings.

Brandt was dying. He was impaled on the queen's fist and his eyes were glassy. Death here was every bit as permanent as it was in the physical world.

But his death gave Hanns time to recover from the queen's assault. Alena saw him gathering his strength. With the queen distracted by Brandt's last breaths, there would never be a better time to attack.

Alena twitched, eager to throw herself into Brandt's rescue. Anders I's words stuck with her, though. She needed to break the connection between Hanns and the queen.

But what connection?

Her vision swam with the attacks and defenses the two rulers launched at each other. Even with one distracted and the other recovering, their assaults never halted. They lacked intensity, but an undefended attack could still change the course of this battle.

Alena didn't sense a connection between them.

Alena's own barrier faltered. She didn't have Hanns' gate-assisted strength, and she suspected that if she didn't act soon, Hanns would unveil his second gate to no effect.

The gate connection.

Was that it?

The queen wasn't attacking Hanns directly. She was attacking him through his gate.

Alena sensed Hanns' connection to the gate easily enough. It burned brightly here.

And there, a wispy thread from the queen that led to the same place, a thread that seemed insignificant.

That was what she needed to cut.

But Brandt needed her help, too.

She couldn't save him and the empire.

So she chose the empire.

Alena allowed her barrier to break under the queen's

constant assault. She appeared behind the final priest, now approaching Hanns. A dagger appeared in her hand. Part of her desperately hungered to entwine their souls as she sent the priest to the gate. Only Anders I's warning stopped her. She drove the dagger into the back of the priest's skull. It resisted for a time, the priest's defenses almost as strong as Alena's skill.

Then the blade slipped in and the priest collapsed.

The death of the priest earned her the queen's attention once again. A dozen spears appeared in the air, all pointing at her heart. Alena swore. She'd experienced this attack before.

The spears leaped at her.

Alena vanished and reappeared at the other end of the cave. The spears passed through empty space, embedding deeply in the stone.

The queen raised an eyebrow, giving Alena even more of her attention.

Hanns chose that moment to unveil his second gate. The world exploded with light.

No longer were they in the caves.

Alena looked around. Tall trees surrounded her. Sunlight filtered through a dense canopy of deciduous trees. The air held a stillness, a peace Alena felt in every breath. Off in the distance, birds chirped a morning song.

The queen dropped Brandt to the ground, crossing her arms in front of her as though warding off a physical assault.

Hanns stood tall, waves of light emanating off him.

Alena blinked and Hanns was gone.

He reappeared directly in front of the queen. His fist glowed as he drove a powerful uppercut into her chin.

The world warped, shattered, and reassembled itself as the energies collided.

The force of the blow knocked Alena off her feet. She landed and rolled, coming up awkwardly against a tree trunk.

She found the two combatants again.

Through all that, the queen had only been knocked back a single step. Surprise was painted on her face.

Alena understood the queen's strength then. Or perhaps more accurately, she understood she couldn't comprehend the depths of that strength. The emperor's punch would have killed a dozen Alenas working together.

Hanns wasn't deterred, but Alena felt the desperation in his actions. Both fists glowing, he laid into the queen, a combination of blows any wolfblade would have been proud of.

Alena hadn't realized Hanns possessed such a deep knowledge of martial arts.

The world rumbled.

Trees tore from their stumps and cracked in half with earsplitting claps. A moment later the trees would return, only to suffer the same fate again, trapped in a loop of destruction and rebirth.

Against the chaos, Alena focused on the thread between the queen and the empire's gate.

It took her several moments to find it again.

Her father's knife appeared in her hand. She leaped toward the string and cut at it. Her knife bounced off the wispy thread like it was made of steel.

Alena tried again, this time pressing her entire weight into it. She connected to her gatestone and pulled on the strength there.

The knife bit into the thread, slowly.

Off in the distance, the queen screamed in rage. Alena

risked a glance. The queen's eyes were on her, filled with fire, but the emperor held her in an unbreakable embrace.

That wouldn't last long.

Alena focused on the blade. She thought of Azaleth dying in the dark passages under the mountains. She thought of her family, waiting for her to return.

And the knife cut deeper.

Bit by bit, it cut.

A roar of pain. The emperor.

Alena didn't dare look.

Another yell, all too familiar.

Somehow Brandt had found his feet. She couldn't help but look.

The former wolfblade blasted fire from his hands, flames billowing over the queen. She stepped through them, unscathed, and backhanded Brandt through a tree.

With a final heave of desperation, Alena cut through the string.

The queen stopped in her tracks.

Alena had never seen such hate. It was cold, freezing her where she stood.

"Enough," the queen growled.

The world shattered around them. Hanns fought the change, but could only hold on for a moment.

The trees disappeared, replaced by a freezing void of perfect blackness. Alena felt the air freeze in her nostrils. She imagined being outside on a warm sunny day, but her efforts counted for nothing. "Brandt?" She meant to shout, but her voice came out a whisper.

"Here." She could barely hear him. Words didn't seem to carry in this new place.

She visualized appearing next to him, but she didn't

know if it worked. The darkness was too absolute. But when she reached out she felt his skin, cold against hers.

She brought him close.

Next to her, Hanns spoke. "I'm here, too."

She jumped at the proximity of his voice.

"Where are we?" she asked.

Her question was greeted with silence.

They floated in nothingness. The cold creeped ever closer. Alena lost feeling in her fingers first, then her arms. Her teeth chattered. But somehow she knew the cold would never kill her. It would only torment her.

"Any ideas?" she asked.

Again, silence. For a few moments she wondered if the others were dead.

She closed her eyes. In the perfect darkness, it made no difference to what she saw, but the action helped her focus. She went inside and focused on her breath.

There had to be something.

Alena lost the feeling in her legs. She felt drowsy and had trouble focusing on her thoughts. There was only the pain of the cold and the darkness of their surroundings.

Then she heard it.

A whisper, barely heard, even in the silence of the eternal void.

It sounded like her brother.

She reached out to him, her consciousness stretching along the bond she'd built with him.

Then she found him.

She pulled the others toward her, then Alena dove toward Jace, pulling at the threads connecting them with all her strength.

The void dissolved, light and sound slamming against her battered senses.

The sun beat down on her and she raised her head. She was lying in the grass and Jace stood over her, a concerned look on his face.

She tried to speak, but the words wouldn't come.

Alena's head collapsed back into the grass and she surrendered to the encroaching darkness.

11

Brandt awoke, sitting bolt upright in bed as he suppressed the urge to scream.

His nightmare vanished as soon as his eyes opened. Had it been the endless darkness, or the cave this time?

Over the past two nights his nightmares had blended together with haunting memories, a repeating kaleidoscope of dark terror. Sleep no longer rejuvenated his body or his soul, and he dreaded the falling of the sun each evening. If not for Ana, Brandt wasn't sure he'd even seek rest willingly.

Ana woke a moment later, her arm reaching out to him.

Her grip was solid and steady. Without a word, she said all he needed to hear.

Guilt flooded him. She deserved better than this, night after night. Like him, she woke in the morning with bags under her eyes.

The fight in the cave against the queen gave him nightmares, but those, at least, felt familiar. He always relived the battles he fought, but they faded in time. The cave would fade, too, buried by time with all the rest.

But something about the void afterward haunted him. It buried itself in his thoughts and lurked in every shadow. Describing it to Ana had been simple. It was perfect emptiness. But the words didn't capture the heart of the horror of that experience.

He shook just thinking about it.

Ana held him, silent support against the void, the warmth of her body and the brush of her breath against his arm a reminder that he was here. He existed.

His shivering subsided, but all thoughts of sleep fled. He stood and walked to the window. Their room in the palace was high enough he could look over the wall and into Estern. The night beyond was quiet, but flickers of firelight could be seen in places.

He wasn't alone.

His thoughts wandered, but they always returned to that endless expanse of emptiness.

"Come back to bed." Ana's voice held a hint of request and a hint of an order.

Brandt looked out on the city one last time, then returned to her. She snuggled next to him. "It will pass," she said.

He grunted, wishing he shared her confidence.

"What's on your mind?"

"Someday, I'll have to soulwalk again. And that terrifies me."

Even confessing that helped. Ana's ears would be the only ones that heard his fears. He wouldn't be called a coward, and if the emperor requested his presence in another soulwalk, Brandt would step forward without complaint.

But soulwalking was a reality he feared, wrapped in mysteries he couldn't penetrate. He understood the basic principles well enough, but his entire lifetime of training counted for next to nothing there. The queen had destroyed him with a thought. The memory of her hand gripped around his organs sent another chill down his spine. "If not for Alena, I think I would still be in the void."

That was another thought he hated. When one died, one went to the gate. Brandt didn't have to believe. He'd been there, long before. He'd seen the gate awaiting his arrival, had felt its welcoming embrace. But that void knew no death. Time had no meaning. Every heartbeat passed in a moment, yet lasted an eternity. Had they been trapped there, it would have lasted forever.

He owed Alena more than he could repay in a lifetime of service. Ana was sympathetic, but she couldn't understand. No one who hadn't been there could.

"From the sound of it," Ana replied, "If not for Alena the whole expedition would have been a failure."

She was right about that, too. When they had returned, Hanns was horrified. He hadn't said anything, but Brandt saw enough to guess. Hanns, with the power of two gates behind him, hadn't won the small victory they'd achieved. Alena had.

Brandt was proud of Alena, but Hanns' weakness wounded his confidence. Hanns was supposed to be their best defense against the queen.

Brandt pressed the palms of his hands to his eyes, trying to push the thoughts out of his mind. His nightmares would fade. They would find a way to protect the empire.

He had to believe that.

THE NEXT MORNING, a knock interrupted Brandt's sleep. Ana, already awake, answered the door and accepted a message.

She frowned as she looked at it. It bore the emperor's seal and Brandt's name. Ana broke the seal and read it.

"The emperor requests our presence for lunch."

Brandt let out a slow exhale. He'd been expecting a summons, but his stomach still clenched at the thought of facing Hanns again. They hadn't spoken since the gate.

When the appointed time arrived, they found themselves in a small dining area, a table set for three. Hanns entered last. Brandt studied him. He appeared unharmed, but he refused to meet their gazes. He sat heavily on the final open chair, rubbing his chin before beginning. "I'm sorry." He held up a hand to forestall objections. "I knew the task would be difficult. I didn't expect to be overwhelmed so easily."

Hanns finally looked up. "Have you spoken with Alena?"

Brandt shook his head. When he focused, he could feel the thread between them. But he hadn't called for her, nor her him. He couldn't. The idea of being transported into that realm again, even if only to her kitchen, made bile rise in his throat. "She lives. That is all I know."

"We owe her everything," the emperor said.

Brandt heard the edge in his ruler's voice. Apparently he wasn't the only one unsettled by their encounter.

"Why have you asked us here?" Ana asked.

The question snapped Hanns out of his reverie. "My failure has been instructive. We've seen what the queen is capable of. And we know I'm not strong enough. I need another gate."

"Another gate?" Brandt frowned, trying to remember what the emperor had told them about the gates. He thought only two existed in the empire, and Hanns controlled them both.

Ana's mind was quicker. "You want us to go to Falar."

"Yes. In an official capacity."

Brandt scooted his chair back. "I'm no diplomat."

The emperor arched an eyebrow. "And you think a diplomat would have any chance with the Falari? I'm sending you because you're *not* a diplomat. You're a warrior, and you know what's at stake."

Brandt's mouth opened and closed, but nothing came out. "There must be someone better."

"Name them and I'll send them."

Brandt couldn't answer.

The emperor ticked points off on his fingers. "One, you're familiar with the Falari. Two, you know more about the gates than almost anyone alive in the empire. Three, you've proven your loyalty to the empire several times over."

"None of that makes this a good idea."

"And you'll be escorting Regar."

Brandt blinked. "What?"

The emperor smiled and clapped his hands. Lunch was brought in. The meal was surprisingly simple for palace fare. A hearty chicken stew. Fresh bread and butter, all completed with some wine. An expensive meal, but not ostentatious. Brandt's stomach rumbled as his eyes wandered over the dishes.

"Eat up," the emperor commanded. "I'll explain what I can."

Brandt dug in without needing further encouragement.

Hanns began. "Several years ago, Regar served along the Falari border. Although Olen will most likely become Anders VII, Regar needed to be prepared, and I needed to see how troops would respond to his command."

The emperor popped a grape into his mouth. "Initial reports were promising. Regar had always been an," Hanns searched for the best word, "intense child. That intensity found a welcome home in the armies. Commanders praised his decisions. He earned the loyalty of those he served with and those he commanded. There were some small incidents of disobedience, but compared to his younger exploits, they were nothing.

"Then he got captured in a skirmish. He pushed too far into a Falari advance and lost the support of his squad. He was captured."

Hanns' eyes stared off into the distance, the only hint of how those days had affected him. After a moment, he continued.

"He was held for one month. The commanders at the border wanted blood, but I refused to give the order."

"Why?" Ana interrupted.

"Because one man, even if that man is my son, is not worth the lives it would cost to retrieve him. The line of Anders doesn't require sons, and I believe Olen the better leader. Don't misunderstand: Regar's loss pained me, and I sent diplomats to secure his release, but I refused to send warriors to their death."

The decision was a cold one, but rational. Brandt remembered his own time at the border. Falar was a mountainous region of the continent. Those who lived there were hard, and they knew the mountains in ways the imperials never could.

As a young soldier, Brandt had gone into those mountains frequently, pursuing Falari raids. Many of his companions had been killed without ever seeing their enemies. The Falari warriors trained extensively in archery, masters of delivering death from a distance.

Those days had led to his first nightmares as a soldier. Going to sleep anywhere near those mountains was almost impossible. More than once Brandt had woken in the middle of the night, the watch vanished as though it had never existed. But the Falar would leave the sleeping untouched, their threat silent but explicit.

Expeditions into Falar never lasted long.

To retrieve the prince, Hanns could have sent the entire army and still failed to save his son.

"I had given him up for dead," the emperor confessed. "And then a month later he reappeared. He was lean and hard, but he had escaped."

"How?"

"A story better told by him. Suffice it to say, the journey was not easy, and he came back a far different man."

"Are you certain it's a good idea to send him? His feelings are sure to be strained among them again."

"I expect they will," Hanns said.

"It's another test," Ana intuited.

Hanns grimaced. "Of a sort. I do need to ensure that he is capable of calm and rationality while dealing with the Falari. You two are a large part of that. No matter what role he assumes in the empire, emotion can't control his decisions."

"And if emotion does get the best of him?" Ana asked.

"Prevent it from becoming a problem," Hanns said. "His presence will give the negotiation another advantage. His escape earned him the respect of the Falari."

Brandt hadn't thought of that. They didn't know many details about the Falari, but they seemed to be far more militant than the empire. They respected martial skills, even in their enemies. An imperial soldier caught off guard might have their body mutilated as a warning to others. But a warrior who died after besting several Falari was left untouched where they fell.

If Regar had earned the Falari's respect, he might be the best person to bargain with them.

"What are our objectives?" Brandt asked.

"I need the gate. I'm willing to consider almost any option so long as they give us that."

"Do you know what they might request in return?" Brandt asked.

Hanns shook his head. "No. I know they are ruled by a council of elders, but my impression is that they rarely act as a unified whole."

And that, Brandt thought, was why the empire would eventually win. The line of Anders had unified much of the continent, and Hanns had a whole people supporting him.

Hanns reiterated his points. "I need that gate. It's the only one left on the continent, and if we're going to fight the queen, it's our only option."

Brandt glanced over at Ana. There was no question they'd accept. Familiar as he preferred to be around them, Hanns was still their emperor. She gave a small nod, though.

Hanns noticed. "Good. Preparations have already begun. I spoke to Regar this morning."

Brandt and Ana stood to leave. Hanns held up a hand. "One last thing. Should you succeed and come close to the Falari gate, keep a close eye on Regar. I trust him, but the power of the gate is a temptation not to be underestimated. He knows enough about them to feel that temptation acutely. Help him not give in to it."

"We'll do our best," Brandt said.

"It's all any of us can do," Hanns replied. "Now let's hope it's good enough."

12

Despite her years in Etar, navigation over the endless plains challenged Alena. Beyond the occasional grouping of trees or a small pond, few landmarks existed to guide her way. Thanks to the motion of the sun she could tell their direction, but little else.

Today they would meet Sooni. Ligt was giving them advice for the meeting, and Alena signed an affirmation, but her mind was in other places. It was stuck in the past, as it too often was these days.

Ligt didn't push her, though Alena sensed that he wanted to. He gave her space, just as Jace had, ever since her last soulwalk.

She'd returned to the physical world in pain. Then she'd slept for almost a full day. Her sleep was restless, troubled by nameless horrors.

She shuddered every time she closed her eyes, the darkness behind her eyelids a pale imitation of that perfect emptiness.

Only her connection to Jace had saved them.

Jace's own emotions cut even deeper. She felt his love

and concern, his fear that he might lose her again. It was too much to bear, and as soon as she felt up to the task, she cut most of their ties. It had taken her longer than usual to enter the soulwalk, but once started the work had gone quickly. Only the original thread between the siblings remained.

She thought constantly of the Lolani queen. Returning from her first battle with the queen had been difficult, but they'd won that fight. She had no such comfort after this second meeting. Alena might have broken the queen's connection to the imperial gate, but it had been dependent on Hanns surprising the queen with his control of a second gate.

Alena couldn't shake the "what if" questions.

What if she hadn't tied herself so tightly to Jace?

What if she hadn't used the strength from the priest to break the final thread to the gate?

What if she hadn't been able to return? That had clearly been the queen's intent, to strand them there.

Jace would have been left with her body, its heart still beating but its soul gone, a living death.

And her soul would have been trapped, forever.

As the leagues passed, Alena retreated into herself. She didn't want to. All she wanted was to keep Jace close, to hear his voice telling her his exaggerated tales of heroism. She thought she needed that now.

But she couldn't. Whenever she tried, all she thought of was the void, or of Anders I's warnings.

She'd learned something valuable in that warning, though. The Lolani queen tied her soul to others, then killed them to gain her strength. That was how she paid the cost.

With the lives of others.

Alena should tell Brandt, but couldn't bear to reach out

to him. She wasn't sure she could face him after their failure.

Was telling Brandt wise? She trusted him, but plenty of monks had been looking for ways to negate the cost. It required little stretching of the imagination to understand the terrible consequences of her knowledge falling into the wrong hands.

If anything good had come from this, it was Jace and Ligt learning to tolerate one another. Ligt was Etari, so he knew how to fight, but he lived as a trader. As Alena remained lost in her own thoughts, the other two were forced to interact more. They'd developed something of a master-student relationship. When they stopped for the evenings, Ligt and Jace trained together. Jace showed the trader combative techniques the Etari didn't use. In exchange, Ligt took over Jace's instruction in Etari language and customs.

Jace hadn't been a great student in academy, but Alena now realized it was because he hadn't found the proper motivation. With no one to speak to but an Etari trader, he picked the language up quickly. Growing up, she'd always prided herself on strong academics, but now she realized that Jace might be just as quick to learn as she was.

We're here, Jace signed. His movements looked much more relaxed than they had seven days ago.

The motion snapped her to attention. She looked around and saw nothing. Then they crested a small hill. In a shallow valley on the other side, a collection of tents stood. Even from a distance, Alena recognized familiar faces.

Their arrival was noticed, of course. Alena suspected scouts around the camp had actually spotted them a while ago, also explaining why Jace knew they were getting close. She looked higher. Lost in her thoughts, she had little sense of time. It appeared to be late afternoon.

They rode slowly into camp, dismounting their horses and taking care of them. Ligt glanced over at Alena. "She'll want to see you, soon."

Alena forced her nerves down. The fact Sooni hadn't come out to greet her was a message, and one that didn't necessarily bode well. Alena might be welcome in Etar, but maybe not among her own family. When Alena had last left, she'd been accompanied by Azaleth, one of the few healthy young warriors left after the battle with the Lolani. She returned without him.

Alena finished taking the saddle off her horse.

Ligt reached out and grabbed her wrist, gently.

"I'll take care of your belongings."

Alena stepped back. Jace looked to her, concern etched in his expression. "Don't worry," she said. "This is something I need to do alone. You'll meet Sooni before long."

She turned her horse over to Ligt's care. Then she made her way to the center of the camp, where Sooni's tent would be. She passed several of her family on the way. Their gazes assessed her, but they withheld judgment, at least for now.

Were they still her family?

She thought of them that way.

But she hadn't seen them for years.

Two families in two different lands. One through blood, one through ties that went even deeper.

How did she honor both?

She knew, as those familiar faces watched her, that she had failed again. She had failed her birth family when she'd run away all those years ago. And she'd failed this family, perhaps even worse. She'd led one of their treasured sons to his death. And she hadn't even returned to them after.

Back in Landow, surrounded by her parents and Jace, her decision had made sense.

Now it seemed wrong.

Alena remembered Sooni's tent well, for she'd spent no small amount of time within it over the years. She didn't enter, but instead kneeled in front of the tent. "Sooni."

She kept her voice soft, just loud enough to be heard over the sounds of camp. Alena heard the matriarch of the family move within the tent. A flap lifted, revealing the woman who had saved Alena's life on one of her darkest days.

Alena's emotions were almost as strong as when she'd met her own family back in Landow. Sooni had aged, but if anything, the years had made her stronger. Her sharp eyes took Alena in, and she made the hand sign for entrance.

There were two signs for *enter.*

One was formal, used when meeting a new family or clan, or used when the status between the two people was unknown. The second was informal, an invitation between friends and family.

Sooni's was the first.

Alena entered the tent and sat. Sooni sat across from her.

Despite the addition of years, Sooni seemed much the same as when Alena last saw her. The first hints of gray had begun to show in her hair, but her sharp gaze missed nothing.

Alena looked around the tent. Sooni hadn't carried much back when they'd first met, and little appeared to have changed. But Alena did see a sword resting in the corner, a Lolani design. A piece of the battle that had wreaked havoc on her clan, and a reminder of the last day Alena had spent among her family.

"I'm sorry," Alena said. The words weren't sufficient, but they were all she had.

She forced herself to meet Sooni's stare. At first, it seemed cold, and Alena wondered if she had stepped into a trap.

Then the ice broke and Alena saw the woman's sorrow.

Alena came up to her knees and shuffled forward quickly, wrapping Sooni in an embrace. It was returned, Sooni's strength making breathing difficult.

They held each other for several long heartbeats, then broke apart. Alena remained close. The Etari were generally more physical than imperials, with less emphasis on personal space. Alena fell into the rhythms of the life with ease.

"I'm sorry," Alena repeated. She couldn't think of anything else to say.

"As am I," Sooni said. "Tell me everything."

And Alena did. She spoke of Azaleth's final days, of how he had died in a mysterious chamber far below the mountains outside Landow. She spoke of the gates and the power that resided within. And she spoke of her own affinity and the ways in which it grew.

Alena left nothing out. Much of it Sooni already knew. Alena's long letter after Azaleth's death had covered most of this, but it needed to be spoken.

"Your other family, they are well?"

"They are. My brother insisted on escorting me."

A thin smile grew from the corner of Sooni's lips. "We've heard. He's a skilled warrior, by all accounts."

"So he is. I hadn't realized how skilled until we crossed the border."

Sooni stiffened slightly at the mention of the border. Alena didn't miss it. "I saw the weaves. More complex and beautiful than anything I've seen before. It's a soulworking."

Yes, Sooni signed. "But I can't answer your questions. Those secrets are not mine to tell."

Alena had hoped for more, but she wasn't surprised she'd have to go all the way to a clan elder to find them. Maybe even higher.

"We missed you," Sooni said.

"And I you."

"There are questions about whether or not you are Etari enough for what is to come."

Alena shrugged, then signed indifference, remembering where she was. "There always have been. It's not for me to worry about anymore."

Sooni's gaze ran up and down her. "You've grown these last two years."

"But I still have much to learn."

"There is little I can tell you directly. I was ordered by the clan elders to summon you. I insisted on meeting you first, but now that you are here, we will continue our journey."

"To do what?"

Sooni looked uncertain, an appearance she didn't wear well. As head of the family, Alena had always found Sooni's decisiveness to be a matter of course. "I don't know. The elders won't give me even a hint."

Alena frowned. The Etari, in her experience, didn't keep many secrets from one another. For them to hide information from Sooni was concerning.

Sooni must have sensed her concern. "Let us not worry. Today is a reunion. Go, bring your brother. It's time for your two families to know each other better."

13

Brandt enjoyed traveling. He always had. Ana, riding next to him, didn't. She longed for a way to reach their destination moments after departing their origin.

So Brandt's delight at leaving Estern was Ana's torment.

She foresaw endless leagues of riding and days filled with little to do.

Brandt basked in the simplicity of a day on the road. Whenever one remained stationary, particularly in a city, a plethora of options demanded consideration. What should he eat? How should he spend his time?

On the road, all those decisions were made. They ate what food they had brought, simple fare designed for the rigors of the road. Their only choice every day was how far to travel.

With nothing to do except ride, Brandt felt an incredible sense of freedom. This, he felt, was how people were supposed to live. Perhaps the Etari had it right, never allowing themselves to settle into cities.

Unfortunately, with little to do, and with Ana's mood

sour due to the long days on the road, it was too easy to fall into disagreements.

Like the one they currently were engaged in.

Ana shrugged again. "I don't care."

"Then why come?"

"The emperor gave you an order. And I'd rather remain by your side, so long as I can."

Brandt believed Ana, but still found her lack of interest difficult to understand. "You don't have the slightest curiosity about the gate?"

"No. I've seen the gate underneath Landow. You say the one under the palace looks the same. I don't personally care about the power they provide. So why should I be interested?"

"They could change the world!"

"Sure, but that doesn't matter much to me."

"You don't mean that."

She sighed. "It's not that I want the world to burn. But I believe in letting the world do as it will. I just want to focus on what matters to me."

"Which is?"

"You, for one. Starting a family. Building a home."

The last statement made him pause. "You want to build a home?"

She raised her right eyebrow. "I wasn't planning on raising our child in the monastery."

Brandt hadn't considered that problem. They rode silently for several heartbeats before she laughed. "You really didn't think this through, did you?"

Another few moments passed. "No, I did not."

He liked the idea of starting a family. He thought that he would make a good father, and Ana would be a wonderful mother. Obviously it would come with changes, but he realized now those changes would be more substantial than he had thought.

Would being a father mean giving up all of this?

He looked at the endless expanse of prairie surrounding them. They had countless leagues to go before they reached the mountains of Falar, but their journey mattered. It could shape the future of the empire.

How did he choose between that and a family?

"You don't need to worry yet," Ana said. "But you should probably figure it out soon."

"Figure what out soon?" The voice was the prince's.

"Life," answered Ana, saving Brandt from having to explain their conversation to Regar.

"No small feat," Regar remarked dryly.

"He's got that gleam in his eye again," Ana noted.

Brandt studied the prince for a moment. Ana was right. Regar had a question that he was dying to ask. Brandt knew the signs by now.

Ana shook her head. "I'll leave you two to that. Enjoy." She nudged her horse forward to join a group of female guards that rode off to the side. Ana had grown fond of them over the long days of riding.

"A remarkable woman," Regar commented.

"She is."

"You are loyal to the empire, correct?"

Brandt looked over. From anyone else, he might have considered the question offensive. But they'd come to understand Regar better in the course of their travels. The prince possessed an undying curiosity that peeled away assumptions to strike at the heart of problems. He questioned everything, though he meant no offense by any of it.

Ana found the constant questioning annoying, and that was the term she used if she felt charitable. Ana was content. She understood herself, she knew her skills, and she knew what role she had in the world. It wasn't that she wasn't curious, but her curiosity had a different flavor than Regar's, and it didn't extend nearly so far.

In Regar, Brandt found something of a kindred spirit. Brandt's curiosity, at least for the past decade, had focused on how to become stronger. Specifically, he looked for a way to surpass the cost which limited the elemental affinities.

The gatestones were one way, but the Etari controlled those.

Regar shared Brandt's curiosity, but his extended further in all directions. As near as Brandt could tell, no question was too small for prolonged consideration. "How" and "Why" were the words that began most of his sentences, and Brandt had learned much from Regar's relentless questioning. Though he had several years on the prince, the prince forced him to question ideas he never had before.

So he wasn't offended by the question. Regar meant only to explore. "I am."

"Why?"

Brandt smiled. He had wondered if that would be the next question. "Because the empire has given me everything. Why shouldn't I repay it with my service?"

"Did you join the military only because you wanted to serve?"

Brandt shook his head. "My parents were wage-earners. Service was an opportunity to leave town and earn money."

"So it wasn't loyalty to the empire that motivated your service, but money?"

That question stung. Brandt figured it was a bit of both.

Regar kept digging. "If I offered you half my gold to kill my father, would you?"

"Never."

"If I offered you all my gold to do nothing while the Falari attacked, would you?"

"Never." Despite his familiarity with Regar's questions, Brandt found his anger rising.

"So, while you might have joined the military for gold, gold is no longer the reason you serve."

Brandt's anger dissipated. Speaking with Regar was like that. He twisted and pulled at your beliefs, then let go just before he took a step too far. Brandt considered Regar's statement. He liked how it sounded. "I don't think it's that simple."

"Why not?"

Brandt thought of Alena and their conversations after Landow. "It's tempting to make people simple, but I don't think they are. There's some truth to your idea. I did join the army for money. But that wasn't my only reason. I wanted to see more of the world. I wanted to get out of the town where I had spent my entire life. And I did want to serve. My parents survived as wage-earners, and I think even when I was young I recognized how helpful that was."

Regar looked like he wanted to interrupt, but Brandt held up a hand. "And I wouldn't turn down your offers simply because I want to serve the empire. I don't want to betray your father because he has earned my respect. I wouldn't allow the Falari to attack because I've served in those units and I know how dangerous the Falari are. Decisions might have a single reason, but even that decision is shaped by countless influences."

Regar absorbed that for a while. "I think your answer is wise, but incomplete."

"How so?"

"Sometimes the reasons are simple. People fight because

they are hungry, or because if they don't, they will surely die."

Brandt acknowledged the point. "Why do you ask?"

"I seek to understand why people serve one another, or an idea."

"Not always an easy question."

"It is not."

"What of the Falari?" Brandt didn't often ask anything that might be related to Regar's captivity, but it seemed foolish to avoid the subject. He trusted Regar not to take offense at a question.

Regar stared in the direction they traveled, his sight crossing the untold leagues still ahead of them. "The Falari fight because they believe they must."

Brandt frowned. He'd never heard that explanation before. Most said the Falari fought because they were poor and desperate for the riches of the empire. "But we never attack them, at least not without provocation."

Regar scratched at the back of his neck. "No, we don't. Their belief isn't predicated on our existence."

"What do you mean?"

Regar didn't answer for several heartbeats. "What do you think is the greatest flaw of the empire?"

The question brought Brandt up short. He'd not really considered such thoughts before. The empire took good care of its citizens. So long as people were willing to work, their basic necessities were always taken care of. Of course, there were small things he would change, but were there major flaws?

Alena's voice came to him again. She had a complaint, and although it didn't bother him quite the same, it would serve well enough for this discussion. "It relies too much on secrecy."

Regar looked surprised. "You believe the emperor should tell more of his secrets?"

"I do. People should know about Palagia and the queen."

"And what would they do with that knowledge?"

Brandt didn't have an easy answer to that. "Prepare?"

"How?"

Brandt didn't have any answer to that either. All reasonable preparations for an invasion were already being made. The army didn't know the true reasons, but they drilled harder than they ever had before. Then he had an idea. "The more people who know, the more who can work on the problem."

"Conceded," Regar replied. "I'm not certain the benefit outweighs the cost, though. How well would people react if they knew an invasion was coming? It's not hard to imagine chaos in the streets, costing innocent lives."

Brandt saw the point. "If not secrecy, what is the empire's greatest weakness?"

"Stagnancy."

"What?"

"In what meaningful ways has our empire changed since Anders I?"

Brandt found he couldn't think of a way.

"That is why it's so hard for us to think like the Falari. Anders I imposed an order on the empire that has lasted for two hundred years. How often has my father invoked the first Anders as the reason something must be?"

Brandt could think of a few times, off the top of his head.

"The Falari believe the only constant is change. They fight because they seek to test new weapons and new strategies against us. When I was a captive, they tried questioning me in several ways. Some were violent, some were kind, but all were tested. I was tested."

Brandt noticed a hint of something surprising in Regar's voice.

Respect.

"You sound thankful."

"I am." Regar turned to him. "I've learned something of your own history. Do you think you would be as strong as you are today if not for the conflict you've faced?"

"That doesn't mean I would seek conflict out."

"Perhaps you should. My captivity taught me what I am capable of. The Falari seek that challenge, but throughout their entire society. Whereas we allow only a small number of individuals to protect us all. Only one or two of every ten in the empire knows how to wield a weapon. But every Falari is armed and eager to defend their land."

Brandt joined Regar in looking out into the distance. "And all we have to do is convince them to let us control one of their most powerful weapons."

Regar's smile was grim. "If it was easy, my father would have sent someone else."

14

The next day, Alena, Jace, and Sooni's family packed their camp and made their way toward Cardon, the final destination of Alena's journey. The trip took a little less than three days. When the tent city first came into view, Alena pulled her horse to a halt.

This visit marked her fifth to Cardon, but she'd never seen it so small. Jace stopped beside her. "I thought you said it was a city."

"It was."

Her last visit had been in response to the Lolani invasion. Clans from throughout the land had gathered. Now only a few dozen tents clustered around the main tent, a structure Alena had never before entered. None but elders and the guardian clan of Cardon were allowed entrance.

She'd never even seen the tent before today. It wasn't taller than any other, but its length and width far surpassed the others. Sooni joined them. "Most of the clans have left. Only the guardian clan and a few of our own clan are here."

"Why so few?" Alena asked.

"You'll soon know for yourself," Sooni answered. "But the elders asked me not to say more."

This tight secrecy seemed more like the empire than the Etari. "Why not?"

"It's a problem at the heart of Etar," Sooni said. "The elders fear the reaction the news will bring, though it will inevitably spread. It is not a secret we keep lightly."

Sooni urged her horse forward and Jace and Alena followed. Jace kept his horse beside hers. "Worried?"

Alena nodded. "Secrecy is unlike them. And I've never seen Cardon half so empty."

They pitched their tents near the current outskirts of the city. On previous visits, such a location would have been considered an inner ring, a place of honor. Now nothing but trampled grassland stood beyond their camp.

The ground showed plenty of evidence of habitation. No grass grew around Cardon, every green plant trampled into dust by years of people walking and living in the same places.

Alena had just finished raising her shelter when a messenger entered their camp. She approached Sooni and spoke quickly. Sooni glanced their way, indication enough of a summons. Alena threw her gear haphazardly in the tent and walked to Sooni.

Jace followed, but Sooni held out a hand. "Where we go, I'm not even sure Alena will be welcome. For now, you must remain here."

Jace gave Alena a questioning glance.

"I'll be fine," she said. Some part of her had worried Azaleth's death would carry repercussions, that something would be required of her. But her actions had harmed only her relationships. If Sooni or the Etari had planned anything more, it already would have happened.

Jace acquiesced, although he didn't seem pleased. Ligt approached, and the two young men went off to train. Alena silently thanked their grouchy guide. At least Jace would be distracted.

Alena followed Sooni deeper into Cardon. They entered a tent halfway between their camp and the center of the city. Inside sat an old woman, with long gray hair braided down her back. She welcomed them formally with a gesture and invited the two to sit.

She didn't speak at first, instead studying Alena.

Alena didn't shy away from the examination, instead returning the look. Etari didn't have any compunctions about staring, and over time Alena had grown past her discomfort. The woman was clearly an elder, but she possessed a vitality many would be jealous of.

After about fifteen heartbeats, Sooni made introductions. "Alena, this is Dunne. She is the head elder of our clan. She is the one who summoned you."

Alena bowed deeply, offering her respect.

No imperial pleasantries were exchanged here. Dunne's voice was lower than Alena expected, and it held a tone of confident command. "Sooni tells us that you are a soulwalker. Is this true?"

Yes, she signed.

A hint of a smile played across Dunne's lips. "How strong are you?"

"I have little to compare to," Alena answered. She thought of the power of the two Lolani that now coursed through her blood. "But I believe I am strong. Twice now I have confronted the Lolani queen, and twice I've survived."

"You are as strong as their queen?" Dunne couldn't hide the surprise from her voice.

Or her hope.

Alena's stomach sank. She'd expected her summons to have something to do with the queen, but knowing it to be true still frightened her. "No," she said. "I have survived, which is all the achievement I can claim."

"Their queen is strong?"

"Beyond imagination."

Alena thought she saw fear lurking behind Dunne's eyes. "That is troubling." She looked around the tent, considering her next question. "What do you know about gates?"

"There are four known on this continent. Two imperial. One in Falar. One in Etar, I imagine within the tent at the center of Cardon. The Etari gate is shattered and is the source of all gatestones. I know little else about the shattered gate."

That same hint of a smile played across Dunne's lips. "Gates might be almost unknown to the imperials, thanks to Anders, but they are hardly a mystery to us."

Alena realized her mouth was hanging open, and she felt a fool. She had puzzled over the mysteries of the gates for years, but she learned little useful. But she'd forgotten the Etari didn't have the same break in their history the empire did. Of course they would know more about the gates. She should have returned years ago, if only to visit.

"What do you know?" Alena asked, unable to keep the curiosity or eagerness out of her voice.

"There is much knowledge that could be traded," Dunne said.

Alena held up a hand, sensing the direction of the conversation. *No*, she signed. "There is no trade. Not for this. If I may aid you, I will. I ask for nothing in return."

Dunne shared a glance with Sooni. Though Sooni's

posture had barely changed, Alena thought she detected a hint of pride there.

Agreed, Dunne signed. "Sooni raised you well."

"The credit is hers," Alena replied. She felt her own flush of pride. Something about this family of hers made her want to impress them. She wanted them to know she was worth the risk they had taken with her so many years ago.

"Our gate is failing," Dunne announced.

Alena took several heartbeats to work that statement out, but she couldn't unravel Dunne's meaning. "Isn't the gate shattered?"

"Shattered and broken aren't necessarily the same thing," Dunne replied. "Perhaps it would be easier to show than to tell." She came to her feet smoothly, moving like a woman half her age.

Dunne led Sooni and Alena deeper into Cardon, toward the tent at the center of the city.

Alena's heart raced. She'd seen one gate in person and it had changed her life. The objects were the most powerful in the land, and few even knew they existed, at least in the empire.

Another bit of pride made her grin. Not bad for a child from Landow. All she had ever wanted was to escape, and now her emperor knew her by name and she was summoned by the elders of the Etari. She had done well for herself, and if she learned more about the gates, there was no telling what she might accomplish.

She squashed the thoughts before long. Her brother was near, and her actions had torn his life into shreds for years. Accomplishment meant nothing if it required such sacrifices.

Dunne passed the layers of guards around the tent

without slowing, Alena and Sooni having to step faster just to keep up.

Alena whispered to Sooni, "Have you ever seen it?"

No, she signed. Alena wasn't surprised. Sooni would be an elder one day, but hadn't earned that honor yet.

The three women entered the tent together. Two men sat within, but Alena barely noticed them. The broken gate at the heart of the tent claimed her entire attention.

That the gate was here had been nothing but a guess on Alena's part. In her years with the clans, no one had mentioned it. But Cardon made sense. It had been Alena's guess from the moment she learned the Etari possessed a gate. Cardon was the only permanent settlement in Etar. One clan was always responsible for guarding Cardon, though the responsibility shifted between clans. When she'd lived among the Etari, she'd assumed Cardon had some cultural or religious significance.

But it was always the gate.

The shattered gate.

At first glance, it had much in common with the one outside Landow. It was made of diamond, lit by a dim blue glow.

The glow surprised her.

The gate was active.

Even though it had been shattered.

The gate outside Landow had been an arch, a shape shared by this one. But only a fragment remained here, jutting from the ground at a slight angle. Where the other foundation of the arch should have been there was nothing but a hole.

A hole that glowed with pale blue light.

Alena glanced over at Dunne for permission. The elder gave her an affirmative hand sign.

Alena stepped closer, looking down into the hole.

It was deeper than she imagined. If she climbed in, it would have swallowed her and then some. At the bottom of the hole she saw the now-familiar glowing blue diamond.

Alena took a step back and kneeled down. She closed her eyes and brushed the world of souls. She sensed the gate, bright against her senses.

Alena opened her eyes and looked over at Dunne. "It's not an arch. It's an oval."

Dunne grunted and turned to Sooni. "Is she always this observant?" The jest was made without malice.

Sooni chuckled.

Alena defended herself. "The one I encountered before was embedded in stone. I never imagined it was anything more than an arch."

"A closed loop is more powerful than a broken one," Dunne replied. Her words sounded like something she'd memorized long ago.

The light in the tent suddenly dimmed. Again, it took Alena a heartbeat to understand. Then she saw the glow had faded from the gate.

Dunne spoke before Alena could ask a question. "Try to use your gatestone."

Alena frowned but obeyed. She focused on the stone embedded near her navel, focusing her affinity through it.

Nothing happened.

The light in the gate returned.

Alena felt the power in her gatestone return with the light.

She turned to Dunne. "Your gate is failing."

The elder arched an eyebrow. "That is what I said."

Alena had a dozen questions, but she started with the easiest. "How?"

"If I knew the answer to that I wouldn't have had Sooni summon you. Soulwalking has been outlawed from our land for generations. This is a problem far beyond our skill."

Alena forgot herself and nodded. Her mind was already working on the problem. As much as she wished otherwise, it had to be the queen. Somehow she attacked the Etari as well as the empire.

"Can you repair it?"

"I don't know," Alena admitted. "But I'll try."

15

The mountains of Falar reached for the sky before them. During their breaks, Brandt stared at the pristine peaks, considering it a pity that such a beautiful sight only pulled terrible memories from his past.

He'd been sent to the Falari border as one of his first assignments, long before his acceptance as a candidate for wolfblade training. He'd been young, filled with both excitement and fear, like nearly everyone in his unit.

The empire rotated almost all its troops through service at the border. The army believed it important for all active warriors to possess battle experience, and on a largely peaceful continent, the Falari border was the only real option.

Brandt remembered chasing after a Falari unit that had ambushed a farm close to the border.

He had thought himself the hunter that day, not realizing until too late that his unit was acting exactly as the Falari expected. The Falari sent a small raid, then attacked in force when imperial soldiers pursued the raid back over the border. The Falari ambushed his unit and Brandt nearly died alongside his warriors.

He'd returned to the border several times since. Once he became a wolfblade, several of his missions took place deep in Falari territory. Most of those assignments ended successfully.

But the fear from that first experience still remained, a slight twisting of his insides whenever he thought of Falar.

In his mind, the mountains ahead of them were more intimidating than majestic. Brandt's heart beat a little faster as he looked at them. Others no doubt felt the same. The friendly conversations that had broken the silence on the journey thus far faded away the closer they came to the border.

Their first stop was an outpost hugging the border. The structure was small, built from stone from the nearby mountains. It housed nearly a hundred soldiers, though. Brandt had never visited this particular location, though he'd slept in similar outposts in other parts of the border.

They passed through checkpoints quickly and left their horses in care of the soldiers stationed at the post. The prince, Brandt, and Ana met with the commander in his quarters.

The commander was a type Brandt was well familiar with, one of dozens Brandt had crossed paths with over the years. Clean and orderly, Brandt suspected the officer bathed twice a day. He ran his outpost well and was determined to prove it to the prince.

Brandt smiled to himself. When he'd been a wolfblade he'd received no such welcome. Wolfblades were a part of the army and yet separate. Other soldiers and officers were polite enough, but a wolfblade didn't often make friends on their assignments.

Their briefing with the officer was short and to the point. The Falari had increased their activity over the past few months, but that same increase had been seen across the border. The officer insisted he'd been zealous in his duties, punishing any incursion.

Brandt saw Ana's fist clench at the pride in the officer's voice.

He understood her gesture.

Most imperial units now understood that pursuing the Falari into the mountains was a fool's errand. Smart commanders kept to the border and developed cavalry units that could respond immediately to incursions. Foolish commanders who believed themselves tactical geniuses threw their troops into Falar, often to disastrous results. This commander was one of the latter. Brandt suspected that if he asked the troops for their thoughts he'd receive a very different report.

If Regar understood any of this, he said nothing. He accepted the commander's information without question. Then he announced his intent to leave the next morning.

The commander offered more troops, but the prince declined.

That decision Brandt approved of. The number of troops brought across the border wouldn't matter. In his own experience, it was easier to travel in Falar with smaller numbers. As it was, Regar's guard was large enough that stealth wasn't an option.

The next morning, they mounted up and pushed forward. Brandt silently wished the soldiers well. They deserved a better commander, but there was nothing he could do for them at the moment.

The tension in Brandt's shoulders grew as they passed the border and began climbing the foothills.

Though they seemed alone, Brandt suspected there were already Falari eyes upon them. The Falari guarded their border every bit as zealously as the empire guarded its own. They made no overt attempt at stealth, by Regar's command. Brandt only hoped the prince knew the risk of his actions.

A day later they climbed through a mountain pass, following a well-established trail. Every sense Brandt possessed searched the world for evidence of ambush.

He didn't notice anything specific, but the hairs on the back of his neck stood up. He trusted the instinct and ordered a halt.

Dozens of heartbeats passed. Brandt searched the mountain, both up and down the slope, for signs of hidden warriors. He sniffed the air as the cool mountain wind blew through his short hair.

There.

A hint of movement, far up the mountain. Brandt looked, watching a single arrow arc into the sky. At first glance, the angle and distance seemed impossible, but the Falari trained such shots. As the arrow plummeted straight at him Brandt lost sight of it.

He called on the air. Though it was the weakest of his elemental affinities, he was strong enough to deflect a single shaft. He forced the wind to blow faster over his head, a small gale that threw the arrow off course. To ensure his safety, he backed his horse up two steps.

The arrow clattered to the path in front of him.

Regar took command. "On me!"

Brandt almost countermanded the order. Bunching up on the trail provided easy pickings for the Falari. Then he turned around and saw Regar's confidence. Against his better judgment, he followed Regar's orders.

Brandt kicked his horse forward, joining the rest of the entourage.

Up the mountain, Brandt caught sight of more movement. Dozens of arrows launched into the air.

Brandt cursed and almost ordered them to break apart, but Regar sat tall on his horse. "Stay calm," he said.

Then he closed his eyes and the wind picked up around them.

On his own, Brandt had managed to create a small gust, just strong enough to deflect the arrow a few paces.

Regar's technique was something else entirely. Brandt heard the high notes of the wind, his own affinity informing him that the air surrounding them had become a maelstrom. The air picked up stone and dust, obscuring his vision.

The incoming arrows got caught, joining the stones as they spun around the group. With a breath, Regar released his technique, sending stone and shaft harmlessly to the ground.

Brandt looked up, curious how the Falari would respond. The Falari disliked affinities and refused to make use of them. Would they push and try to tire Regar? Or would they attempt a different attack? The Falari were no less dangerous for their lack of affinities, even if they'd never come across one as strong.

And how had Regar done that? Brandt knew the man was strong, but such power was beyond human. Moving that much air that quickly was beyond the cost a mortal could bear. Regar barely looked perturbed.

That question would wait. For now, they needed safety. He addressed Regar. "We should separate into groups of two or three and leave the path. It will make us harder to ambush."

Regar shook his head. "The threat has passed. We will continue."

"It's too risky."

Regar smiled, as though addressing a child. "To the contrary, now that we have shown them our strength, it is the safest decision we can make."

Trust and reason warred within Brandt.

Ultimately, his obedience won out. The emperor had given this task to Regar for a reason. Any answers he desired were ahead of them. "Very well."

"Keep a sharp eye, Brandt. I do not believe they will attack again, but caution is well warranted."

Brandt nodded and retook his place at the head of the column.

They continued up the path, but two bends later, they came upon a clearing filled with Falari.

Brandt almost drew his sword, but held off. The Falari stood in two lines. Archers had arrows nocked but their bowstrings were loose. Behind them stood another line of warriors carrying all manner of bladed implements. Behind them all stood a single man wearing robes Brandt recognized as belonging to a warleader.

The other guards pulled up in a line. Then Regar rode around the bend and saw the formation blocking their path. He nodded to himself, as though he'd expected nothing different. He dismounted and pushed his way through his line of guards.

Regar paused next to Brandt, the pair of them slightly ahead of the rest of the line.

The Falari ranks broke for their warleader to step through. "You are recognized, prince. Many years have passed since you last visited our lands."

The warrior's imperial was difficult for Brandt to understand. But Regar had no such problems. He offered a bow to the warleader. "We seek audience with the council."

The line of Falari warriors chuckled among themselves. The warleader's grin was wide. "You know what you ask?"

"I do."

"You are not worthy."

"In my captivity I defeated Lozen at the board. I defeated Makun in the ring. And I defeated Isha with the blade. I am worthy enough."

Brandt didn't understand what Regar spoke of, but the gathered Falari seemed suitably impressed. Even the warleader's grin had vanished. Now he studied Regar. A long moment passed. "Pass one trial and be welcomed. Pass three and I shall escort you to the council to make your plea. But even then, I will not promise a return journey."

"It is understood," Regar said, a hint of solemnity in his voice.

"The ring, then."

Regar nodded and turned to Brandt. "It's a grappling match."

Brandt dismounted. "I'll make short work of any opponent, sir."

Regar laughed. "I was the one who asked to speak to the council. It is I who will be tested."

Brandt made to protest, but Regar held up a hand. "This is the way of it. Order the guards to form half a ring. The Falari will complete the other half. And no matter what happens, no one must interfere."

With that, Regar stepped forward. Apparently the warleader was not under a personal obligation to meet Regar's challenge, as he selected a larger man as Regar's challenger. Brandt tore his eyes away from the scene and ordered the guards to form their circle.

It took some time, but eventually the ring was set. While the perimeter formed, Regar moved through a complex warm-up, loosening the muscles from long days of riding.

Brandt worried. In their own sparring, Regar had been less skilled than Brandt. He was still superior to most fighters, but the challenge he faced wasn't small. Literally and figuratively.

He saw no other option but to play along. Not only was their small expedition outnumbered, but they had the care of the prince. The only successful fight was one they won and kept the prince alive through.

No small feat when a group of archers waited for the slightest provocation to leash a deadly volley of arrows.

The match began without preamble. The two fighters circled one another, the distance between them slowly closing.

The Falari warrior seized the initiative, stepping in and attempting to throw Regar. Regar slipped the man's grip. He tried to throw the warrior, but the Falari seemed rooted to the stone underfoot.

Brandt observed with a critical eye. From the initial exchange Regar appeared to be the superior grappler. But his opponent's size and strength would prove a challenge.

The next exchange went poorly for Regar. The prince attempted to take the offensive, but the Falari was quick enough to muscle through a counter. He seized Regar before the prince could escape. The hold wasn't secure, but it lasted long enough for the Falari to throw Regar bodily to the ground.

The prince took the impact and rose to his feet, a smile playing across his lips.

Ana's hand on Brandt's arm stopped him. He looked

down and saw he'd taken a step into the ring. She pulled him back.

The next moments became Brandt's personal nightmare. He was forced to watch, unable to take any action that would influence the outcome.

It felt like he was trapped in the dreamscape again.

He clenched his fist and forced himself to remain still.

When the Falari warrior made a mistake, Regar didn't let him recover. The fight had gone to the ground, and the Falari relied on strength instead of positioning to hold Regar down.

Like an eel, Regar slid around, managing to wrap his legs around the Falari's arm. With both hands on the Falari's captured wrist he pulled, extending the elbow further than it was meant to travel.

The Falari bellowed something and Regar released the hold.

The two combatants broke apart.

And just like that, it was over.

The commander of the Falari smiled. "Well fought, prince. Come, we shall escort you to our town. There you can meet the other two challenges."

Regar grinned from ear to ear. He looked to be the happiest that Brandt had ever seen. His joy contrasted strongly with Brandt's misery.

"Lead us on, then," the prince said.

16

The next morning Alena prepared to return to the gate. Overnight the gate's power faded twice more. Though she hadn't been using her gatestone during either attempt, she felt the loss in her bones. Now she understood why so few remained in Cardon. Closer to the gate, the effect was more pronounced. Though each incident only lasted a few heartbeats, it felt like an absence long afterward.

She and Jace broke their fast in silence. Alena's thoughts focused on the gate and approaches she might try to restore it. Jace's, she suspected, were focused on protecting his older sister from a threat he couldn't fight.

Visitors arrived just as they finished their meal. Sooni and Dunne brought a young man with them. He appeared to be about Alena's age. He possessed the wiry build so common among the nomadic clans, forged by a lifetime of endless travel.

But Alena found herself drawn to his eyes.

They were dark brown, but his gaze seemed to take in

everything at once. He projected a presence Alena felt across the tent.

Sooni provided the introductions. "This is Toren. He's not a member of our clan, but he will assist you in your task."

"Assist me?" Alena couldn't imagine how. This was soul-work, and there were no soulwalkers among the Etari. Or at least, so she had thought.

"Toren has shown some skill in soulwork, or at least he claims as much."

Alena understood. "You want me to train him."

Yes, Sooni signed.

The whole situation grated on her. Had her powers been discovered in her time here, she suspected her welcome would have been rescinded. But now that the Etari needed soulwalkers, they wanted her to train one.

She understood. Necessity often forced change.

But she didn't like it, and Dunne didn't either. She looked as though someone had made her sit on a needle.

Alena knew the answer, but the question escaped her lips anyway. "Why train him, if his skills will be considered a curse among his family?"

Dunne answered. "The ability to influence another's spirit is a crime against nature. And it was soulwalkers that destroyed our gate many generations ago. But—"

"But now you need us."

"We do," Dunne acknowledged. "And maybe Toren can prove us wrong. But don't confuse our necessity with our acceptance."

"What?" Alena wasn't sure she'd heard correctly.

Dunne didn't back down from her statement. "Our people need your skill, and you have already earned our gratitude. But that does not mean soulwalking belongs among our people. Toren knows what he risks by undertaking this task."

With that, Dunne turned and left, leaving a cold silence in her wake.

Sooni, for once, seemed at a loss for words. After a few moments, she tried. "Alena—"

No, Alena gestured. She took a deep breath and looked over at Jace. Two years ago, in desperation, she learned how easy it would be to destroy her brother's spirit. Brandt had suffered some of the same. Dunne's outburst sharpened those memories, making them fresh in her thoughts. "She's right. Soulwalking isn't natural." She took a long breath. "But the affinity exists, so it must be mastered."

Alena studied Toren. "And what about you? Why go through with this?"

Toren's face was almost impassive, but she thought she caught a hint of respect in his voice. "Because soulwalking exists, and it must be mastered."

Alena looked at the Etari, wondering if he was respecting her or mocking her. She truly couldn't decide.

Jace chuckled. "I like him."

"The grounds around the gate have been cleared today," Sooni announced. "Is there anything you require?"

Alena thought for a moment, then signed the negative. She didn't know what to expect.

"If there is anything, I'll be close all day," Sooni said. Then she left.

Curious, Alena dropped into a soulwalk. The lines leading to and from Toren did seem to glow with a more vivid brightness. He hadn't lied about his affinity, then.

Together the three of them made their way to the center tent. Their passage was uncontested, although no small number of guards surrounded the area. As Sooni promised, the tent itself was unoccupied.

Alena pointed her question at Toren. "What do you sense?"

"The gate is alive. I feel its presence."

An interesting observation. Alena wasn't sure she agreed on the gate being alive, but she wouldn't discount the possibility. She didn't know what to expect on this soulwalk.

Precautions came first. She turned to Jace, who nodded. They'd discussed this the night before. Alena didn't like relying on the technique, but she wasn't aware of any other methods of staying safe in strange waters.

With the gate's proximity strengthening her abilities, it didn't take her long to bind her spirit to her brother's. Once again he served as her anchor.

Then it was back to Toren. "I've never trained anyone. I'm still learning much of this for myself."

"I understand."

"Close your eyes. Remain calm."

Alena dropped into her soulwalk, forcing herself not to look at the gate yet. That moment would come soon enough, but for now she felt it as a pulsing beacon behind her. Instead she approached Toren, creating a shared world for them. They both appeared in her mother's kitchen back in Landow. "Open your eyes."

He obeyed and stared in wonder. "Where are we?"

"A memory, perhaps? A world that I've shaped, a place that I'm comfortable with."

Toren held out his hands and looked at them. He pinched himself.

"It's real," explained Alena, "but also not. Your physical body is still in the tent. Here, imagination and will shape reality. You try it. Imagine a place for us."

She felt his power, tiny compared to her own, but she allowed it to overwhelm hers. She blinked and found herself on a hill overlooking an endless expanse of water. The view took her breath away. She'd never been to the sea before. Never would she have guessed how vast it was.

"This was the first time I saw it," Toren said. "All my life I'd known nothing but endless stretches of grassland. When I saw this, I knew just how small my world was." He looked over at her. "A little like now."

"Thank you for showing me this. I've never been."

She asserted her will, returning them to her mother's kitchen.

A string appeared in her hands. "This will help the two of us stay connected. I wish I knew a better way to train you, but hopefully this will allow you to sense what I do. But the connection runs both ways. I will feel your emotions as well. Are you comfortable with that?"

Toren looked uncertain, but he nodded. Alena wondered what motivated him. Orders from his elders? Curiosity? Whatever pushed him, she envied his courage. In a similar situation, she wasn't sure she could summon such trust of a stranger.

She tied the string to his wrist and to her own. As soon as the knots were formed she felt the connection between them grow stronger. "Do you feel it?"

Yes, he signed.

She pushed them out of their soulwalk, back into the world of flesh and bone. Toren blinked, regaining his bearings.

"You connected yourself to him," Jace observed.

"I didn't think you'd be able to feel that."

"It's slight, but he's there."

Toren looked up at the two of them. He frowned,

puzzling something out. When he spoke, he was hesitant. "I feel both of your spirits."

Alena hadn't considered that, but a glance at Jace revealed he didn't mind.

Toren continued. "I can feel your love for your sister."

Alena's eyes widened. That was a problem she hadn't considered. But it made sense. Toren picked up on Jace's emotion through her. She wondered if Brandt, hundreds of leagues away, now suddenly felt a deep unintended affection for her.

She hoped not.

Dunne's angry words came back to her. For all she'd learned, Alena still knew nothing about this power. Her continued meddling, even with the best of intentions, didn't come without risk.

There was nothing for it, now. She needed to examine the gate and she didn't dare do anything that dealt with the Lolani queen without Jace's connection. So that was that.

They turned to the gate and Alena stepped forward. Her curiosity pulled her ever closer to the exposed fragment, but fear slowed her steps and made her heart beat like a drum. The forces balanced when she was two paces away. She couldn't bring herself to step any closer.

Toren stood several paces away. This close to the gate Alena could almost see the connection between them with her eyes open.

Jace followed her, step for step. When she hesitated, he leaned closer. "I'm here. I'll always be here."

Alena nodded, took a deep breath, and took the final two steps toward the gate. She reached out her hand and touched it before she could convince herself it was unwise.

Nothing happened. Alena channeled no affinity at the

moment, so it felt much the same as touching any other stone.

Except it wasn't any other stone. Though thousands of cuts had formed the gate, it felt strangely smooth under her fingertips. She ran her finger gently over the surface, awed by the craftsmanship. No skill like this existed today. Even if Hanns ordered something similar built, it would never compare.

And it thrummed with energy. At times she could feel the vibration strong in her fingertips. Then it would fade until it was barely discernible, no stronger than a weak pulse. Perhaps Toren wasn't so wrong. Perhaps it was alive.

Alena closed her eyes and dropped into the soulwalk, ready to explore what damage the queen had done.

She rode the wave of power, this connection with the gate made easier through her previous experiences. Her imagination shaped the dreamscape, resolving into the plains of Etar. Behind her, in another world, she felt Jace, and to a lesser extent, Toren.

And nothing else.

Alena scanned the horizon and searched the sky, searching for any sign of the queen. Where the Lolani ruler struck she left blackness and despair, sometimes obvious, sometimes less so.

Alena searched and found nothing. She searched harder, remembering the thin tendrils of power the queen had relied on in their last encounter. But even those couldn't be found.

Frowning, Alena changed the landscape to the rooftops of Landow, then to the tent she and Jace had slept in last night. Each change flowed without resistance, and in no place did she sense the queen's presence.

If the queen was responsible, her working on the gate was more subtle than any Alena had so far encountered.

Suddenly, her world bulged and erupted, a bubble of pure energy popping directly in front of her. The energy threw her into the air, reality warping like a blanket being shook free of dust.

She was helpless against the forces. Her own image was a part of this reality and it bent and warped the same as the rest. She felt molded and squeezed by inexplicable powers.

Alena screamed, the sound rising and falling in pitch as her world collapsed and expanded.

Smells assaulted her nose, some sweet and fragrant, others rancid.

Time lost meaning. One heartbeat passed quickly, then froze in the next.

Overwhelmed, something in her mind finally snapped. This was beyond understanding, beyond explanation. It simply was.

And then the disturbance passed. Alena crashed face-first into the ground. Her entire body quivered. Somehow she felt both cold and hot.

She broke her connection to the gate.

Beside her, Jace vomited on hands and knees, a small pool of bile created between his hands.

She wobbled, only to lose her balance a moment later.

Toren was there and she fell into his arms.

17

The Falari warleader introduced himself as Weylen. He appeared to find Prince Regar's entourage an endless source of amusement, but for what reason, Brandt couldn't tell. The man had an easy smile, but Brandt suspected that smile hid a dangerous mind.

Any worries about Regar's composure in the face of the Falari soon vanished. Brandt had found the prince's company on the ride to Falar pleasant. Now, as Regar navigated their initial negotiations with the war party, he understood the wisdom of the emperor's choice. Though once their prisoner, Regar treated the warriors as he would his own soldiers. The Falari returned the respect in equal measure.

The initial meeting went almost entirely against Brandt's expectations. Regar's escape from Falar was a tale Weylen knew, and one Brandt now desperately wanted to hear. The Falari warleader almost seemed pleased to meet the imperial prince, and it didn't take long for Regar to sort out the details of their onward journey.

Weylen led the combined parties into Falar. Brandt

remained wary, though no one gave him the slightest cause for worry. By the end of the day they were deeper into Falar than Brandt had ever been. Imperial forces never reached this far.

If anyone had made it so far from friendly borders, they had never returned.

The terrain awed him with every vista. Snow-capped peaks loomed overhead as they made their way through evergreen forests. They walked past small glacial lakes and crystal-clear streams. They saw few people, and Brandt wondered just how populated Falar was. He hadn't seen a single house or farm yet, though he supposed the terrain made farming difficult.

Two days later they reached an idyllic town nestled deep in a valley. When Brandt first saw it, he paused to study it more carefully. Never before had he seen a town that appeared so vertical. Everything from the homes to the streets were built from stone, and from a distance, buildings appeared to be stacked on top of one another. Ladders and the occasional rope bridge connected homes and shops, creating a confusing maze of options.

Beyond the construction, though, the town seemed much the same as any imperial village. Children ran in the streets while adults went about daily chores. The familiarity of it unsettled him. In his mind the Falari were different on some fundamental level. But the scene before him made him question that belief.

Weylen paused soon after and addressed the group. "Your prince has earned your welcome, at least for a time. But if any one of you so much as draw a sword within the village, all will be executed."

Weylen ran his eyes over the group, making sure they understood. Then he turned and continued down the path.

Ana stepped close to Brandt and spoke softly, her voice barely carrying to his ears. "Does this seem too easy to you?"

Brandt nodded. He didn't suspect duplicity, though. He believed the Falari would have just killed them if that had been their plan.

Brandt gestured toward Regar. "I suspect there is more happening here than we understand."

Weylen stopped the group again at the boundary of the village. Faces poked out of windows, curious about the strangers. A lone man stepped from the assembling crowds, his expression eager. The man spoke with Weylen in Falari, a quick exchange that ended with both men smiling.

Weylen turned to the group. "This is Ren. He is the best sword in the village. He meets your prince's challenge."

Regar nodded, as though he'd expected this. The prince turned to his entourage. "No interference." He didn't even wait for acknowledgment, and just turned and faced this new enemy.

Brandt tensed when Regar drew his sword. Ren did the same, and the two men faced each other, six paces apart. The Falari noncombatants backed away, an action mirrored by the imperial contingent.

Brandt was the only one who stepped forward. He couldn't let his prince duel with live steel. Not if he could help it.

"Brandt." Ana's voice froze him.

He hesitated, torn between Regar's command and his desire to protect his prince, to do *something* helpful.

Ana tipped the scale. He respected her calm in these situations. Gritting his teeth, he stepped back and joined the others.

The Falari favored swords that were slightly shorter than the imperial standard, and had a slight curve. Traditionally, imperial sword schools taught fighters to use the greater length of the imperial sword to its full advantage against a Falari warrior. Unfortunately, the Falari expertise with and reliance on bows made the advice largely useless. Few imperial warriors ever got close enough to cross swords with the mountain warriors.

As before, the duel started without a formal announcement. Regar struck first, leading with the point of his sword. Ren swiped the blade away, and for a moment Brandt expected to endure a prolonged duel.

The next heartbeat proved him wrong.

Regar moved with a speed and strength Brandt hadn't seen before. Instead of a technical match, Regar simply overpowered his opponent.

Regar attacked again, and Brandt's practiced eye saw Ren unbalanced by the strength of the blow.

The shift was slight, but it meant Ren couldn't get in position to defend against Regar's next strike, which flashed out, fast and precise.

The two combatants froze. Regar's sword hovered a hair away from Ren's chest. They stood like that for a moment, then Ren stepped away and put his right fist to his chest. Regar mirrored the movement and sheathed his blade. Brandt let out a long breath.

"You've improved," Ren said.

"Thank you," Regar replied.

Brandt and Ana's eyes met. The two had met before?

When Brandt had the opportunity, he expected Regar to tell him a very long and detailed story.

Weylen welcomed them all to the village, reminding them once again never to draw a sword. He announced that beds would be made available. The town had no inn, so the imperial contingent would be welcomed into homes as guests.

Brandt stepped up to Regar. "Is this wise? Separated, we are far easier to ambush."

Regar shook his head. "There is no need to worry. So long as no sword is drawn, you are safe in the village until tomorrow."

"You sound certain."

"I am."

"You also said until tomorrow. What happens then?"

"The contest of the boards. The most serious of the three, I suspect."

"What is it?"

"You'll see."

"That's not particularly helpful."

Regar smiled. "There's nothing you can do to change the outcome, Brandt, so why bother yourself? If I win, I'll answer your questions."

"And if you lose?"

"Then I can answer your questions on the other side of the gate."

Brandt growled at that.

Regar laughed. "Sorry, Brandt. But it's easier this way. Trust me that you have nothing to fear tonight. Sleep well, and enjoy your wife's company."

Regar turned away, leaving Brandt standing alone and uncertain. He shook his head, then found Ana.

In time, Weylen introduced him and Ana to their host family, and as the sun set Brandt found himself a guest of the very people he once fought against, being treated to a savory meal. Fish from a nearby stream made up the heart of the meal, but they also enjoyed fresh bread and carrots. After so many days traveling, the meal was a feast.

Their hosts were kind, but their kindness didn't make the meal feel any less awkward. Neither Brandt nor Ana spoke Falari, and their host family didn't speak imperial. There were smiles all around, but the meal was eaten in silence.

After the meal, the family ushered them into a room filled with cushions. They poured drinks into tiny cups. Brandt accepted, then sniffed at the clear beverage. The aroma stung his nostrils. He must have made a face, because his hosts laughed at him. The father threw the entire drink down his throat at once and smiled, gesturing for them to do the same.

Brandt and Ana glanced at one another. Ana shrugged, smiled, and threw her drink back.

She coughed, and his hosts laughed harder. The laughter wasn't unkind. The father poured Ana another drink.

Brandt frowned, then followed suit.

The drink burned all the way down his throat. He coughed hard, not nearly prepared for the strength of the drink.

Ana joined in the laughter, and Brandt soon lost track of the night.

After a few of the drinks he couldn't find it in him to worry. Their hosts played music on stringed instruments and the moon rose overhead.

That night Ana guided him to bed. Their lips met, and between the drink and the abstinence of the road, Brandt's inhibitions disappeared. She pushed him down onto the bed, and the rest of his memories dissolved into a pleasurable blur.

Nightmares woke him, and a splitting headache prevented him from returning to sleep. He watched the sun rise over the mountains, the sight almost making his suffering worth it.

Ana woke up much later. She grimaced as she did. She sat up and held her head in her hands, the covers slipping from her, reminding Brandt of the previous night. A groan escaped her lips. "Who hit me?"

Brandt grinned and sat down next to her on the edge of the bed. "I don't think you would have noticed if someone did last night."

She punched him lightly in the leg. "You've been up for a while?"

"Yeah."

"Nightmares?"

"Yeah."

"Sorry."

He massaged her scalp, hoping it would do some good. As he did, he brought up the subject that had troubled him throughout the morning. "Do you ever feel useless?"

"Not often. Do you?"

Brandt nodded. "First it was with the emperor with the gates and the queen. Now it's Regar. He planned all of this, but he's not saying anything. Which means there's nothing I can do to help him."

"This was always his task, Brandt. The emperor made that clear. We're here to keep him as safe as we can. And now it's clear we had no reason to worry about him meeting with the Falari again."

"We should be doing more."

"No, we shouldn't. We should be supporting Regar, in whatever way we can. You don't always have to be the hero."

"I—" Brandt stopped. He was no hero. He just believed in doing all he could.

Just then, a wave of nausea passed over him. His whole

world twisted for a moment, bending and expanding. He held his head in his hands, waiting for the spell to pass. This was no hangover, but something far worse.

"Brandt?" He could hear the worry in Ana's voice.

"Something's happening to Alena."

After a few long moments, the sensation passed. Brandt took a deep breath, then cursed. If he wanted to know what happened, he'd have to soulwalk again.

He could tell that she was still alive, though, so he pushed the matter to the back of his mind. They had more important problems right in front of them. Regar had only promised them safety until today.

They met with their host family to break their fast, enduring the knowing smiles of the family, then joined a growing crowd near the center of the village. A table had been set there. Three wooden boards rested upon it, as well as two containers of stones, one painted black, the other white.

"The boards," he whispered to himself.

Before long, Regar came into the square and seated himself at the table. Weylen came and sat across from him. Each man raised a fist to their heart and the game began.

The rules of the game were beyond Brandt. Each player, with Regar starting, took turns playing a single stone on the board. There did seem to be exceptions where one player could place two stones, but Brandt didn't understand. Stones could also be moved and captured. The game was played simultaneously on all three boards, and it seemed as though each board played by slightly different rules.

The crowd around the table grew closer as the game went on. Parents whispered to their children, pointing to moves each player made.

After some time, Brandt stopped trying to understand

the game. The rules didn't seem too complex, but there were just enough exceptions he couldn't piece everything together. Instead, he watched the crowd.

The Falari were some of the greatest warriors he'd ever seen. Though he understood little, he did know that much of their society was bent toward warfare.

But it was easy to forget that even a society devoted to warfare would be a complex affair. Brandt didn't think of families, food, and entertainment when he thought of the Falari. But they possessed all this and more.

Brandt hoped he made it back to the empire so he could share some of what he learned. He'd never expected to see a group of Falari townspeople gather around a board game.

A collective intake of breath brought Brandt's attention back to the board. Weylen was nodding and looked impressed. Both players once again raised their fist to their heart and stood up.

Regar found them in the crowd. "You didn't seem so eager to leap to my rescue this time, Brandt."

"There's nothing I could have done to help you with whatever that was," Brandt admitted.

"I know the past few days have been difficult, but thank you for your patience. We've earned our audience with the elders."

"*You've* earned our audience," Brandt said.

Regar frowned. "Not at all. You've been tested just as much as I."

"What do you mean?"

"Last night in town, the rings surrounding the combat, they've all been tests. Can my warriors follow orders? If even one person had drawn a blade last night or tried to sneak from a house, none of us would have woken this morning.

And we wouldn't have even made it into town if anyone had interfered with the duels."

Brandt didn't understand.

Regar saw as much. "In a way, you could consider it a fourth test, but one of my leadership. Would I be worthy of meeting the elders if I couldn't even control my own soldiers?"

Brandt just shook his head.

Regar gave him a reassuring smile. "On the road I'll explain more. I promise."

Regar left them, and Brandt reached out for Ana's hand. If not for her, he might have interfered, a decision with more dangerous consequences than he realized. "Thank you."

She laughed and squeezed his hand. "Someone has to keep you from getting yourself killed."

18

Alena sipped at her tea, hoping that in time her nerves would fade and she wouldn't have to worry about spilling all over her lap. The tea served as an anchor, the warmth of the cup in her hands reminding her that she was real and whole.

Jace and Toren sat next to her, nursing their own cups. They both looked shaken, but not like her. Of the two, Jace was worse. Thanks to the bonds between them he had felt much of those agonizing moments. Even Toren, with his single thread, had felt some unease.

Sooni and Dunne sat across from them. Both women stared at her like she was a mystery to be solved.

Dunne, in particular, had little patience for Alena's recovery. "Can you stop her?"

No, Alena signed. When she saw the expression of dismay on Dunne's face, she hurried to explain. "It's not the queen."

"Then what's happening?"

"I don't know. There's something wrong with the gate itself."

Dunne made a dismissive gesture. "That gate has stood for longer than our legends. There is nothing wrong with it."

Alena saw no point in arguing, especially with Dunne. So she sought knowledge, instead. "What do your legends tell of the gate?"

Sooni made a questioning gesture, indicating her uncertainty. "Those are stories only told among the elders." She looked meaningfully toward Dunne.

"True," Dunne said. "And so they shall stay."

Alena pressed. "You summoned me here to help. Perhaps I can, but I know little about the gates. They are secreted away within the empire."

Dunne waved a dismissive hand. "This was a foolish idea from the beginning." She made to leave.

"I believe her," Toren said, stopping Dunne in her tracks. He didn't elaborate, but his corroboration seemed to surprise the elder.

Sooni chimed in. "She's come this far. You wouldn't send a warrior into battle without their stones. Why do you ask her to solve this problem without your knowledge?"

Dunne glared at them all, but she didn't move. She looked at Alena for a long moment before speaking. "Ask your questions."

Alena took a deep breath to restrain herself. She had dozens. "What are the gates? When were they made, and by whom?" She stopped before she asked more.

"No one knows exactly what the gates are," Dunne answered. "They were built in a time before legend by those who came before."

Alena hid her disappointment. Too often her questions were met with more questions. "Who were those that came before?"

Dunne glanced at Sooni, as though questioning Alena's competence. "The empire erased its history prior to Anders I," Sooni said. "She knows nothing."

Dunne sighed, clearly disappointed to be forced into the role of a teacher of basic information. "We do not know who they were, but they predate the empire, the Etari, and the Falari. For all we know, they existed long before the Lolani as well. From what survives, we know they were masters of the world, more powerful than we can imagine. They built the gates, and long ago, they disappeared."

"How?"

"No one knows."

Alena thought of the path into the mountains outside Landow and the tunnels underneath those mountains. They too must have been built by those that came before.

"Do you know when they lived?"

"We're not sure. At least five hundred years ago. Perhaps as many as a thousand. The stories are unclear."

"Do you know why the gates were built?"

"We have one story that tells of a threat from the skies. We do not know if it is a true story, but it is one that comes from our earliest days."

Jace shook his head. "Like giant birds?" His skepticism was clear.

"Perhaps. Our story simply said that the greatest threat of all is from the skies. Some wondered if there is a link between the gates and that threat, although we know nothing for certain."

Alena understood her brother's skepticism, but who was she to say? Many years ago she might have been more critical of Dunne's answers, but if she'd learned one lesson, it was that the world was far stranger than she'd imagined.

The gates had a purpose, even if she couldn't guess

at it. They must have been difficult to build. And the power they summoned was immense. It took almost all her skill to simply skim across the top of that power. To harness it and direct it remained well beyond her ability.

Dunne still knew more. Alena was sure of it. "How did the gate shatter?"

"That is a story we do know." Dunne fixed her with a piercing stare. "A soulwalker shattered it."

Alena's breath caught in her throat. "Who?"

"A woman named Zolene. An Etari."

"You had Etari soulwalkers?"

"Her generation was the last, but yes."

"That's why you detest us."

Yes. "Among other reasons."

"What happened?"

"Zolene was the greatest soulwalker the Etari ever produced. Stories of her abilities are still passed among the elders as a warning. But she was disciplined and Etari to her very heart. She served the people."

Dunne paused to sip at her own tea. "This was over two hundred years ago, but rumor reached us of a man growing in power, a man to the east bringing one fiefdom after another to their knees."

"Anders I," Alena whispered.

"Yes. The other elders thought little of the trouble, for it didn't concern us. But Zolene alone argued against the prevailing wisdom. She claimed Anders I had awakened a power long dormant. A power that would change everything."

Some of the mystery began to clear. "He discovered how to use the gates."

Yes. "At the time, Cardon didn't exist. This land was

considered sacred. We had our stories of the gate, but none attempted to harness its power."

Alena had some idea where this was going. "And Zolene wished to do so."

"She did. Through the gate she was the one who placed the working on the border, the one who taught us how to sense disturbances within it. Then one day, without explanation, she ran to the gate and embraced it. The stories say she stood there for three full days. The gate glowed brighter than the sun and burned any who came close. But she remained.

"And on the third day observers reported that the earth and sky tore open. What was left was a shattered gate. Some of Zolene's pupils realized some small power of the gate could be channeled through the debris. It was their last gift to the people. The elders determined that from that day the practice of soulwalking was too dangerous to practice."

Alena considered the story. In her own history lessons, teachers said that Anders had never found the Etari land valuable enough to conquer. But Dunne's stories implied a different truth. Perhaps Zolene had beaten him in a battle between their gates.

"What about Zolene?"

"She was never seen again. Her body wasn't found, but no one close to that disaster could have survived."

Every answer unveiled another mystery.

But her course was clear. The Etari relied on their gatestones. If the gate failed, the Etari would struggle to defend themselves against an attack. If the Lolani came again, the Etari would be overrun. "I'd like to continue working with the gate."

Sooni looked pleased to hear it, but Dunne less so. "Are

you certain that's wise? The gate, even shattered, is not an object to take lightly."

"I don't. But if I give up, I fear your gatestones will fail. If I can prevent that, I will."

Dunne stared at her for several long moments. "Then continue. Speak with me after every attempt, even if little happens. I want to know everything."

"I will."

Sooni and Dunne stood up and left together. They weren't more than a few steps out the door when Jace turned angrily on her. "Why would you do that?"

She held up a hand to stall him. "I'm the only one who can help."

"But you're risking your life for the Etari!"

Alena answered his outbursts with quiet certitude. "I know."

They glared at each other, but Jace broke first. "We should leave. This isn't our problem."

Alena stepped closer to him and grabbed his hand. "They are my family, too. Do you understand what that means to me?"

He took a deep, shuddering breath. "I do."

"Then I need your support. This is hard enough as it is."

Jace looked up, determination in his gaze. "You want me to anchor you again?"

She could tell how much he feared the idea, but she also knew he would volunteer without a second thought.

She shook her head. "I don't think so."

Alena saw relief and wounded pride war on his face.

"Whatever is happening inside that gate is powerful. You got a taste of what I felt today. In time, I think I can defend against it. But you can't. And if I make a mistake, I will not let our parents lose both their children."

"Don't talk like that."

"I'm being pragmatic."

Beside them, Toren spoke up. "I'll do it."

They stopped in mid-argument, glancing over at the Etari soulwalker. Alena was ashamed to realize she'd forgotten he was there.

Alena weighed her options. Though they hadn't known each other long, she trusted Toren. He didn't speak much, but his words were earnest. Having another soulwalker might be a great help. It wasn't like she knew what she was doing.

Alena stopped Jace from protesting again. "Jace, I know. I do. But your skills and ability are in this world. Will you protect my body when we visit the gate again?"

She'd been expecting him to struggle, but she was surprised how hard he wrestled with the problem. Finally, he acquiesced.

With that settled, Alena turned to Toren. "Get your rest. Tomorrow morning we're going to attempt the gate again."

19

After the board game, the Falari provided a meal to the visiting warriors. As Brandt and Ana finished their final scraps, the swordsman who had dueled Regar the day before came to join them. "Regar claims you two are the strongest warriors who joined him on this journey."

"He is kind to say so," Ana replied.

"Would you do me the honor of training with me this afternoon?"

Brandt, suspecting a trap, shook his head. "We are honored by your invitation, but no steel is to be drawn in this town."

Ren didn't relent. "The prohibition doesn't apply to practice weapons. If it eases your mind, we can speak to Weylen before."

On another day Brandt might have resisted longer, but this, at least, was something he could do. They did speak with Regar and Weylen, seated together near the head of the table. Both rulers gave their permission.

Ren led them through town, and Brandt seized the

opportunity to ask the questions he hadn't had anyone to ask. Ren was the first Falari who spoke imperial they'd had any time with. Ren told them the town was larger than most, and that not all Falari lived in towns. Many, it seemed, preferred a more nomadic life in the mountains, far closer to what Brandt had originally envisioned.

Children played in the street. Some games seemed familiar. In one, children chased and tried to tackle one child holding a ball. Whenever the ball was dropped or forced out, another child would pick it up and become the target of all. Then they turned a corner and saw two youths, a boy and a girl, squaring off against one another, short wooden practice swords in hand. Brandt stopped to watch them.

The boy had the edge in size, but after the first pass it was clear the girl's speed surpassed her opponent's. Three passes later the boy had three new bruises to show for his efforts. Ren excused himself and approached the pair, offering advice to both. The children listened attentively and nodded as he spoke.

Ana spoke softly. "Physicality and combat appear to be at the heart of most of their games."

Brandt nodded. His own thoughts ran in the same direction.

Ren returned and led them to the ground floor of a larger building. They stepped into the largest space Brandt had seen in town. Its polished floors and weapons-laden walls made its purpose perfectly clear.

Behind them, Brandt heard the sound of dozens of young voices. He turned to see a small army of children running toward the training hall. Ren smiled. "I hope you don't mind that I invited guests."

Brandt stood speechless as the children piled in. Each

put a fist to their heart as they entered the space. They took spaces along a wall without a whisper. For all the rambunctious behavior Brandt had observed on the way here, he couldn't imagine a more disciplined group inside the training hall. They made the imperial military seem lax in comparison.

"Shall we begin?" Ren asked.

Ana stepped forward. "I'll be your first opponent."

Brandt appreciated the gesture. Though he no longer suspected a trap, having Ana go first allowed him to observe Ren's style. It gave him the space to decide how much of his own skill to display to the swordsman.

Ana selected a practice sword from the wall, testing its weight. When she was satisfied, she met Ren in the center of the room. Brandt stood alone against a wall opposite the children. They looked as interested in the outcome of this fight as he was, if not more so.

From the fight against Regar, Brandt assumed this match would be close. Ren raised his fist to heart and Ana returned the gesture.

Then the match began, and Brandt's assumption proved correct. Ren was skilled, and fast.

He'd also been holding back against Regar. Brandt realized that fact after two passes.

If Ana was surprised, she didn't show it. Practice swords met and broke apart, each combatant seeking an opening.

Brandt should have watched Ren, but he found his gaze drawn to Ana. Her martial arts had improved considerably over the past few years. When they were wolfblades, Ana had been plenty skilled, but a certain timidity had held her back. With her water affinity she often found herself in supporting roles on their missions.

Landow had changed her.

Her lithe body evaded Ren's cuts, her own sword darting at him like an angry snake, forcing him back.

Now she fought with confidence.

Not the false confidence of a guaranteed victory, but the confidence that came from knowing exactly what she was capable of.

The swords clacked together. Brandt saw how Ana manipulated her internal energies. When she needed speed, she became light. But when she needed strength her lightness vanished and she rooted her feet to the ground.

The technique was risky, and almost impossible to perform consistently. One mistake, one lapse in focus, and she was just as likely to hurt herself as Ren.

The duel continued. Brandt saw the openings he'd exploit when he and Ren met.

If Ana let the Falari warrior stand.

Eventually the two fighters broke apart. Brandt hadn't kept track of touches, but he'd seen both warriors make contact with the other. They repeated the fists-to-heart gesture and the wall of children erupted in cheers.

Ren spoke to the children in Falari. Though Brandt couldn't understand the words, he recognized a lesson when he saw one. Ren spoke with the cadence of a practiced teacher.

Beside him, Ana was beaming from ear to ear. Sweat poured off her, but she hadn't looked so happy in days. "He was still holding back. He's good."

Brandt nodded. He'd wondered as much. "You fought well."

Brandt watched his wife as she brushed the sweat from her eyes. At that moment he wanted nothing more than a private space and time alone with her. Sober, this time.

But that wasn't to be, at least not for a while.

Ren welcomed him to the floor. Like Ana, Brandt searched for a wooden sword he felt most familiar with.

Brandt considered how best to approach the duel. Knowing the Falari respect for warriors, he decided not to hold back.

Their first pass ended in a heartbeat. Ren came in with a quick but light cut. Brandt knocked it off line and stabbed at Ren's heart, scoring the first touch.

Ren was surprised, but not offended. His own smile grew as he understood Brandt didn't intend to restrain himself.

They met again. As Ana had predicted, Ren had been holding back. He was faster and stronger than he'd shown against Ana.

It made no difference.

Brandt scored again and again. Ren couldn't match his strength, speed, and accuracy, and years of daily practice allowed Brandt to know exactly when to move and where to strike. The duel ended quickly, but this time there were no cheers. The students sat openmouthed along the wall.

Ren chuckled as he brought his fist to his heart. "If the empire was filled with warriors as skilled as you, no Falari would dare cross the border."

Brandt appreciated the compliment. It eased, a little, the helplessness he'd felt over the past few weeks.

Ren took no offense at being bested. Instead, he worked with Brandt to teach the children. Brandt only understood parts of the lesson, but Ren explained why he had been beaten.

The students were nearly ideal. They listened intently, asking questions and practicing on their own as Ren instructed. Brandt and Ana ended up teaching for most of the afternoon.

Two thoughts dominated Brandt's mind as he taught. The first was that combat knew no language barriers. Without words, he could correct a student's form, and many of Ren's students were quick studies. The second was that the Falari continued to surprise him. That they were dedicated to the pursuit of war came as no surprise. The empire had known that since it had been founded. What surprised him was how welcoming they could be.

Part of him worried that he might someday be training those who would fight against the empire. But the emperor had sent them here to make peace and find an agreement. This, at least, felt like a step in the right direction.

They left the training hall in time for the evening meal. Again Brandt found himself seated in front of a plate of wonderful food. Ren hadn't left his side since their training, and he seemed as fascinated by Brandt's life and world as Brandt was with his.

As they spoke, Brandt realized Ren had never crossed the border. "You've never been to the empire, have you?"

Ren hesitated for a moment, but Brandt didn't think his uncertainty had to do with Brandt's impolite manners. Brandt had stumbled upon something, a truth he hadn't understood yet. Finally, Ren shook his head. "Warriors from this town patrol the border, but we never cross. We never raid."

"Never?"

"Not even Weylen."

Brandt frowned. This village wasn't more than a week from the border, and he was certain the imperial outpost they'd left from had experienced nearby raids in the past few years. At least some of them had to have come from here.

Ren must have seen the unspoken question on his face,

because he continued, his voice lower now. "Regar hasn't informed you?"

Brandt shook his head.

Ren let out a long breath. "I suppose you'll learn soon enough. You come at a time when much is in doubt. Our elders argue constantly, and the Falari are nearly split evenly into two groups."

Beside him, Ana leaned in closer to hear what Ren said.

Ren continued. "There are many who believe we must wage endless war against your land. Others, like those who live in this village, have chosen a different path. We do not attack the empire. Our goal is to improve through training and the development of our martial arts."

Some part of a larger plan unfolded in Brandt's imagination. "That's why you allowed Regar to win."

Ren nodded. "Our trials were mostly for show. They are required for one who isn't a warleader to speak to an elder, but we only sought to challenge, not to defeat."

"You hope for peace, don't you?" Ana asked.

"Not an imperial peace, no."

Brandt frowned, confused again. "Why not?"

Ren gestured around the table. "Everyone here is willing and able to take up a sword when needed. Most would defeat the average imperial soldier."

Brandt conceded the point.

"Peace is only possible when one is prepared for war. Your empire is not prepared. It rots at the core. We do not want your ways polluting ours."

"So why let us in?"

"Being prepared for war doesn't mean that war must be waged. We hope that Regar will help the other warleaders and elders see that. A larger threat looms on the horizon, and it's there we must focus our attention."

"You know about the Lolani?" Brandt asked.

"We do. Some among us hope the Lolani will cleanse the land of the empire. But in this town, we recognize the danger for what it is. The will of the people rests on the edge of a knife, though. That is why I'll be among your escort tomorrow."

"You expect trouble?"

Ren nodded. "Once those who oppose us realize Regar is here and journeying toward the elders, I believe they will attack."

Brandt ate in silence for some time. He'd never thought the Falari would be so divided. Though he knew they acted as war parties, it had never occurred to him some of those war parties might wish for peace.

That night, they returned to the same home they'd had the night before. The family welcomed them in, although this night there was no music. That suited Brandt just fine. His head still spun with new thoughts.

He fell asleep as soon as his head hit the pillow. Between the higher altitude and the afternoon full of training, he was exhausted.

That night, he woke to the sound of a single bell pealing in the darkness. He came to his feet in a heartbeat, and his sword was in hand a moment later. Was this the trap part of him had always expected?

He went to the door as he heard footsteps approaching. Brandt swung it open, sword ready.

The whole family stood in the hallway. The father and mother were armed with the short, curved swords common among the Falari. The children all held knives, and they looked ready to use them.

Brandt took in the family in a moment. They were uncertain.

They thought Brandt meant to attack.

And he didn't speak their language.

A memory of the training hall returned to him.

Warriors didn't need words.

The safe approach was to keep the family at bay.

But they'd welcomed him into their home.

In a single smooth motion he sheathed his sword and stepped away from them.

He remained ready to draw again if it was necessary, but his action confused the parents. They had expected him to attack.

Behind him, Ana called for him. He turned to look at her. She was pointing out their window at something he couldn't see. She seemed worried.

"It's fire. The town is under attack."

20

Alena woke well before the dawn the next morning. Her night had been long and largely restless. Whenever she fell into sleep, a fresh nightmare ambushed her. First it was the cold emptiness of the void she didn't understand. Then it was visions of Jace, dead on a battlefield littered as far as the eye could see with corpses. Finally it became a variation of her last attempt to explore the gate, twisting and bending her soul in ways it would never recover from.

When she woke from that last nightmare she felt the twisting deep in her stomach. She saw little point in trying to sleep again. Her mind roiled with images she'd rather forget.

She slipped from the tent without disturbing Jace's slumber. He slept with the same enthusiasm he lived his days with. Jace's snoring threatened to collapse their tent while they slept inside. Already Sooni was half-joking about moving the siblings' tent nearer to some mortal enemy for the evenings.

Alena walked until her brother's snoring faded into the

background, until all she heard were the crickets and the sound of the wind through the tall grass. She made herself a comfortable place to lie and watched the constellations lazily spin overhead.

They didn't make her drowsy, but they did bring her a sense of peace. No matter what happened to her, the stars would shine on. Her life, for all that had happened, meant little when one considered the whole of history, and she always found that thought peaceful.

When the sun rose on the new day, she heard footsteps behind her. She sat up and saw Toren approach. He sat down beside her and offered her a cup of tea. She gratefully accepted it.

"How did you find me?"

"I could feel you." His tone was matter-of-fact.

Alena frowned a bit at that. She didn't understand the full extent of his abilities yet, but he seemed quite sensitive to soulwalking. One question troubled her, though. No one would have judged him for putting all this behind him. "Why join me today?"

"Curiosity."

She smiled a little at that. Curiosity had nearly destroyed her life once. More than most, she understood its irresistible pull.

Toren wasn't particularly verbose, even by Etari standards. But she trusted him. He'd caught her when she fell, supported her with Dunne, and brought her tea.

Thank you.

You're welcome.

Alena sipped at the last bit of her tea. "Well, shall we?"

Yes.

They stood and returned to the tents. They found Jace,

who had mercifully woken up, and together they approached the center of Cardon.

Alena's stomach rumbled, both out of fear and hunger. But after her experience yesterday she didn't think working with the gate on a full stomach was a wise choice. Toren, it seemed, agreed. The tea would suffice until they were done for the day.

Jace reached the center tent first, holding the flap aside for her to enter. The sight of the broken gate almost stopped her in her tracks.

The gates represented opportunity. Hanns believed as much, and one would be a fool not to realize the possibilities inherent in such power. But they presented a danger as well. Power without control, without understanding, was as dangerous to the wielder as to the wielder's enemies.

Her legs carried her into the tent. The gate glowed, and she felt the power in the room.

The small group took time to prepare. They had nothing to gain by haste. Alena checked her connections with Toren and with Jace. Then she reached out and connected with the gate.

As always, the power was indescribable. Her imagination painted it as a river, impossibly wide, deep, and fast. She rode on top of the power, dragging Toren with her. When she felt enough control, she shaped the landscape with her imagination. She brought them to the plains of Etar, a place they both felt comfortable.

Toren gained his bearings with surprising speed. He stood and looked around. "Are we *in* the gate?"

Alena shook her head. "I don't think so. Connected, but not in."

Toren looked into the sky. He flexed his muscles and jumped. His leap took him forty or fifty paces high, but he landed softly. He saw her staring. "Imagination and will, right?"

She shook her head. His actions had never occurred to her.

She let him explore for a bit. He ran like the wind and created balls of flame in his hand. While he was otherwise distracted, Alena studied their surroundings. Her mindscape existed on top of the power of the gate, like a boat carried down by a swift current. She was connected, but that connection was weak, almost superficial.

Alena allowed her memories to pull her back to when they'd first encountered the Lolani queen. That environment had felt different. That wasn't this. That was control over a gate. Command.

She suspected that any problems with the gate required a deeper connection to uncover. Which meant diving into that terrifying current instead of riding on top. She'd pulled Brandt out of that current before. It had almost killed him.

But she didn't see a choice. She kept the Etari in the front of her mind. Without answers, they would fall.

She caught Toren's attention. "I want you to imagine a place you feel very comfortable in."

She felt him trying and let him overwhelm her. Once again they were by the sea. Alena nodded. This place would do. It felt solid underneath her feet. Toren had control over it, which might be needed. "I want you to anchor me."

"From here?"

Yes. "I'm going to try to connect more deeply with the gate. I'm not sure how I'll manage once I'm within. If you feel like I'm in danger of losing my life, I want you to pull me out."

He signed his acceptance. In his hand a thin but strong line appeared. She held out her wrist and waited for him to tie it tight. He did, and she felt his emotion through the bond. His feelings were as calm as a mountain lake. "You don't seem terribly concerned."

He signed indifference. "I will do what I can. The results are beyond my control."

She wished she felt some of that same calm. It would do her good now, when her focus was needed.

There was no point in delaying. Every moment she waited was one more where second thoughts threatened her confidence. Taking a deep breath, she dropped through the surface of Toren's world and into the powerful energy underneath.

It slammed into her, pulling her like a fish caught on a line. Power filled every muscle and bone in her body. Her skin burned as it threatened to explode.

Her first instinct was to control it, to try to hold it within herself. But her body was weak, a vessel poked full of holes ready to burst.

Let it flow through you.

The voice was that of a woman, one Alena had never heard before.

She couldn't, though. The idea of letting that amount of power flow through her was tantamount to suicide. No living being could endure the onslaught of energy.

Stop fighting!

She wouldn't. Fighting meant survival, and she wouldn't surrender.

But she was losing the battle.

Moment by moment, the strength of the gate filled her closer to bursting. For this task, she wasn't enough.

She searched for the way back but couldn't find one. Forces beyond comprehension filled her mind. She couldn't find her ties to Jace or Toren, blinded by the energies surrounding her.

There was nothing she could do.

Except surrender.

Lacking all other options, Alena gave up. She closed her eyes, stopped fighting, and let the current wash over her. Her heart felt as though it would go first, pumping faster than any heart ever had. Every hair on her skin sizzled, thousands of pinpricks of agony stabbing into her.

And then it passed.

She figured she was dead. It was the only explanation for such peace. She opened her eyes, fully expecting to see death's gate, as she had before.

But she didn't. She perceived only a milky whiteness. She imagined it like flying through a very thick cloud. Her whole body felt as though it were in motion, although she couldn't see as much with her eyes.

She wasn't controlling the flow of power, but had become part of it.

The longer she spent in the space, the further her vision resolved. She reminded herself that none of this was real. It was her mind trying to make sense of a vast power. She floated along the currents, completely at peace. There was a sense of correctness here, of things being exactly the way they should be.

She closed her eyes and relaxed more deeply. Time lost meaning, and she wondered if it even passed in this place.

Eventually, she opened her eyes again. Instead of the fog she'd encountered before, she was greeted with a vast web of connections. She recognized it immediately. This was a soulwalk on a completely different scale. The web stretched forever. The immensity of it defied comprehension. Thousands and thousands of connections. Perhaps all of them.

But some were brighter than others. She counted five.

The gates.

Turning her attention to them was a slow process. Her mind didn't react with its customary swiftness. Even shifting her attention felt like an effort from a legendary story.

As she studied the gates, two facts became apparent. The first was that they stood outside the web of interconnectedness that bound all living creatures.

But they shared another connection. All five were linked to something else, the heart of the whole web.

What was it?

Even connected to the power of the gate, she perceived the heart as something immense. If the strength of the gates strained her imagination, this broke it completely. It was the source of the gates' power.

When she understood that connection, Alena also saw the problem, the reason why the Etari gate was failing. Three of the five gates drew immense power from the source. Two of those three shared another bond, providing Alena another clue. Those were the gates Hanns was connected to. She assumed the third was the Lolani queen's.

They were pulling too much from the source, choking the life from the other two.

But perhaps Alena could fix that.

She looked to the two gates that were more closely connected, then sought the thread which bound them. Like everything in this place, the process seemed to take forever. But her patience was rewarded. She found a single point of light that connected the two gates.

Hanns.

She reached out to him.

In a flash, the scene changed. She was sitting once again in her mother's kitchen, the smell of freshly baked bread filling her nose. Hanns sat across from her, slack-jawed and open-eyed. He took in the scene in an instant, then fixed his gaze on her. "This should be impossible."

Alena shrugged. She didn't fully understand herself. But she had wanted to talk to Hanns, and once she had found him, her mind had shaped the power.

His stare was hard, reminding her that though he didn't demand formality from her, he was still her emperor. He wasn't a man others summoned.

Unsure how long this audience would last, Alena skipped the polite formalities. "The Etari gate is dying, and I think I know why."

It took Hanns a few heartbeats to put everything together. "You're at their gate, aren't you? That's how you did this."

A hunger came into his eyes, one she hadn't seen there before.

It frightened her.

But she wouldn't lie, not unless she saw no other option. She'd learned that lesson the hard way. "I am. And it's dying. Do you know that all the gates draw from the same source?"

Hanns didn't react at first, but his gaze never left her face. "Anders I left information which implied as much."

The confession rocked Alena. She realized that she might understand as much, or more, about the gates as the emperor himself. "Do you know what the source is?"

Again, Hanns didn't answer immediately. She knew his mind was churning, but to what end she couldn't guess. "I am not sure. Anders I believed that it might be the planet itself."

"The planet?" Alena couldn't figure out how she felt about the idea. "How could the planet generate so much power?"

This question Hanns answered quickly, as though he'd already decided something. "I don't know, but I don't find it hard to believe. This planet has the power to raise mountains, or to cause volcanoes to erupt. Is it so hard to imagine the gates tap that vast power?"

Alena wasn't sure what to think, but she felt her anger rising.

Secrets dominated the empire.

How could Hanns know so much and not share it? How much better could she have helped the Etari if she knew half of what Hanns did? "That would have been nice to know."

He grunted at that. "Knowledge is the most dangerous of weapons, and it can wound its wielder with surprising ease. These are secrets for a reason."

Alena didn't miss the hint of threat in the statement. But she refused to bow to his pressure. This was about the Etari, not about his own precious secrets.

"You and the Lolani queen are pulling too much power. It's preventing this gate from working the way it should. Can you draw less?"

A long silence settled over the table. They had come to the crux of the matter.

"No."

His answer had a ring of finality to it, little different than if he had given an official command.

But Alena wouldn't let it go. "It's causing the Etari gatestones to fail. And if they fail, the Etari won't be able to protect themselves. This gate is their lifeblood."

Hanns' tone was surprisingly harsh. "And why should I care about the Etari? My concern is the empire." He swept his hand over the kitchen they were in. "Would you rather I worry about protecting your parents, or sacrificing the empire's safety for the Etari? Because you can't have both!"

His verbal assault rocked her back, leaving her speechless. Her mouth opened and closed, but nothing came from it.

Hanns stood up. His anger, brief as it was, had vanished. "I'm sorry, Alena. I have nothing but respect for the Etari. But I have my own people to protect, and they must take priority."

With that he was gone, leaving her with nothing but the certain knowledge that the Etari gate would continue to fade until it died, bringing her second family with it.

21

Brandt ran to the window, poking his head around the corner to see what he could. Down the block one of the houses had started on fire, the flames crawling up from level to level, hungry for more fuel. He watched as a family scrambled across a rope bridge to safety before one end caught fire, burned, and fell.

Below, the shadows appeared alive.

For all the destruction, the town was surprisingly quiet. Brandt only heard the fading sound of the bell and an occasional clash of steel. But he heard no screams.

He glanced across the window to Ana, looking down on the same scene. "Should we fight?"

"We won't know who is who."

Brandt grimaced. She was right, but they needed to do something. The attack couldn't be anything but an assassination attempt on Regar.

"We need to get to the prince," he decided.

Ana agreed.

Their first obstacle was their host family. The family might not see them as an immediate threat, but they weren't about to let foreign warriors loose in the village during an attack. Brandt pleaded with the father, not wanting to fight their way past the family that had been so kind. The lack of shared language made it difficult. "Prince," Brandt tried.

The father stared at him blankly.

"Regar," Ana said.

The father understood that. He glanced between the two former wolfblades, then nodded. He gestured for them to follow.

Brandt hesitated. Another person complicated matters if they had to fight. But he supposed a guide couldn't hurt. In the night, confused with small clashes, it would be easy to get turned around.

They ran down the stairs to the front door. After studying the street, the father grabbed a bow and led them out. He began down the street, then turned left and then right in short order.

The group hit trouble after turning the second corner. Three figures, silhouetted by the light of a torch, were prying a door open. As Brandt watched, one threw the lit torch into the house.

Fire had been a poor choice on their part.

The three invaders turned at the sound of their approach, weapons already drawn. Brandt pulled the flame from the fire and funneled more heat into it from the surrounding air. The flame erupted into a fireball, lighting the invaders' clothes on fire. They swiped at their burning garments, as though that would somehow put them out.

Brandt charged as their host fired his bow, killing one of the invaders. Brandt made one pass through the other two, felling them both.

For a heartbeat their host stared at Brandt, then found

his senses and continued on. But he stopped at the next corner. Brandt came close and glanced around the corner.

He didn't notice anything until their host pointed. Three stories above them, two archers watched the street below. They wore the same dark clothing as the previous invaders.

Their host readied himself for a difficult shot, but Brandt grabbed his shoulder and stopped him. Brandt flashed a series of gestures toward Ana. She signed that she understood, then used her lightness to scamper up the side of the building they currently hid behind.

In a few moments she was behind the watchers. Caught by surprise, they stood no chance against her. She signaled from the roof and indicated she would stay high.

Brandt gestured for their host to continue. If not for the man's sharp eye, Brandt would have been caught. He knew enough to look up high, but he hadn't seen the archers. He'd forgotten how much he hated fighting against Falari tactics.

They made it another block before the sounds of a fight above them brought them to another halt. Brandt looked up, searching for Ana. He couldn't find her and assumed the worst. Using what gestures he could, he told their host he was going up to the roofs, and that their host should stay in place.

Brandt didn't wait for the argument. He made himself light and ran into a small alley between tall buildings. He zigzagged between the walls, kicking higher off of each until he landed on the rooftops.

He didn't believe what he first saw. High above the streets the moon's illumination was stronger, but Ana was covered in shadows. At least three warriors attacked her, but Brandt couldn't be sure of the number.

He charged in, heedless of the danger. His sword cut

down one thanks to surprise, then another after a single pass.

An arrow zipped past his head as he ducked under one shadow's cut. Brandt closed with his assailant just as another arrow sliced through the robes over his shoulder.

If their attackers were Falari, which Brandt suspected, they would only rarely close with their opponents. Instead, they would hide in the shadows, firing whenever the opportunity presented itself.

Brandt cursed. He wasn't skilled fighting on such terms.

It also meant killing their immediate opponents posed a problem. Right now, the archers restrained themselves out of fear for hitting their fellow warriors. If their friends fell, far more arrows would fly.

Leaving them alive wasn't much wiser, though.

So he fought through the shadows, and when the last one dropped he shoved Ana off the ledge and followed her down.

Ana landed lightly on the street below and rolled, easily distributing the impact. Brandt tried the same, but his lightness wasn't as well-developed. He crashed to the ground, cursing whatever names he could come up with. Fortunately, if he had twisted an ankle, the blood in his veins was too hot to notice.

Darting from cover to cover they made their way back to where their host waited. They rested there for a moment, catching their breath before pushing on. Brandt tested his ankle, finding it strong.

They reached Regar's quarters not long after. Their host again stopped them as the building loomed overhead.

This section of the town was quiet.

Far too quiet.

Brandt and the others hid deep in the shadows, examining their surroundings for the traps that surely existed.

Two members of Regar's bodyguard were dead, face down on the street, several arrows in each. Brandt pushed his feelings aside for the moment. He'd gotten to know those guards on the journey here and had liked them. They deserved better than arrows in the back.

Judging from the angles of the arrows, the attacks had come from up high. Brandt allowed his gaze to travel up and search the buildings. Shadows crawled over the rooftops and Brandt saw at least one archer perched on a corner, watching Regar's quarters with unbroken concentration.

Brandt whispered softly in Ana's ears. "Any ideas?"

She shook her head.

Brandt figured he had even odds of reaching the building. If he moved fast and shifted directions frequently they might not hit him. It wasn't much of a plan, but it was all he had. If they climbed the roofs they would just find themselves in the same situation as they had before. The archers would bide their time and pick them off.

Still, he had to act. Regar couldn't last in there forever, if he still lived. The silence surrounding the quarters portended an ominous future.

Brandt collected a few stones and started twirling them around his body. He still hadn't found his way past the cost, so he couldn't launch them with lethal force like the Etari, but they still served as a useful tool. He whispered his plan to Ana. If he could distract the archers for long enough, she could help the prince escape to someplace safer.

He sprinted from cover, drawing the attention of at least two archers. His quick direction changes kept them from hitting him, but both arrows passed too close for comfort. Again he kicked from one wall to the next, reaching the rooftops with record speed.

He saw four archers as soon as he crested the roof. He sent stones their way at the same time that he dove. Two shafts sailed overhead as he split his focus between the stones and his own movement.

The stones weren't large enough or fast enough to do anything more than stun the archers, but it was the distraction he was going for. One stone hit an archer square between the eyes, knocking him onto his back. Another caught an enemy in the chest. The others missed, but they'd forced the archers to evade, which was all Brandt could have asked for.

Brandt didn't know how long he fought for. He didn't pause, his body in constant motion. Between his own movement and the circling stones, Brandt managed not to get shot.

He gained ground against the invaders. Whenever one of his stones hit a nearby archer hard enough to keep them off-balance for several moments, he was there, his sword nearly invisible in the darkness.

His defense wasn't perfect. One arrow caught him high in the left shoulder, embedded at an awkward angle. The arrowhead didn't penetrate all the way through the light armor Brandt wore. Another arrow grazed his left leg, causing a burning line of pain to erupt whenever his weight settled on the limb.

Then the pressure against him eased.

He saw her moving on another rooftop, liquid death.

Ana had joined the fight.

Something below had gone wrong. They should be escorting Regar away. But the archers gave Brandt no time to ask Ana what had happened. He simply had to trust. If she was fighting, so would he.

He kept pushing. His weariness grew, his body growing

heavier with every beat of his heart. He held his focus, using the stones against any archer he noticed, but the effort cost him.

Brandt stumbled, then pushed himself back to his feet.

He couldn't keep this up for much longer.

An arrow glanced off his torso, the shallow angle causing the shaft to skip off his armor.

He was failing.

And then the attacks stopped.

Brandt kept moving, kept spinning, but there were no more arrows and he couldn't make out any archers. On some silent signal they had all vanished into the darkness they'd come from.

Brant slowed and came to a stop, nervous that this was all some feint. Unable to keep his focus any longer, the stones dropped, clattering to the roofs.

He stood on his rooftop, expecting the assault to resume. Now that he had come to a stop he wasn't sure he could start moving again.

But he saw no more enemies and no arrows came his way. Ana became light and leaped from her rooftop to his.

That alone impressed him. His exhaustion was complete. He would need a ladder to come down off the roof.

Ana answered his question before he could even ask it. "He refused to leave."

"Of course he did. But why?"

"He said the town would help defend him. To leave would be an insult to their honor."

Shapes moved in the darkness at the edges of Brandt's vision. They were townspeople. No one wore the dark clothing of the invaders, and Brandt caught sight of a few faces he recognized.

He gave in to his exhaustion, collapsing back and sitting on the angled roof.

The fight had taken place near the limits of his abilities. The constant movement combined with the use of affinities had drained him of everything.

But with the exhaustion came a certain satisfaction. A pride.

He'd given everything, and he'd helped keep the archers away from Regar. His talents had always been on the battlefield.

But his satisfaction wasn't complete. He'd pushed to the very limits of his ability, and if the attack hadn't broken when it had, he wasn't sure how much longer he could have lasted.

The cost still plagued him. He knew the Etari used gatestones to bypass the cost, opening up the technique Brandt had seen the young Etari, Azaleth, use to such great effect outside Landow. But he didn't think the Etari would give him a gatestone anytime soon.

The empire had a few, but they were in the care of the emperor and the monasteries. They weren't given to individuals under any circumstances.

Which left him in the same place. He felt like he was nearing the edges of his ability, and if this ambush was any indication, it wouldn't be enough. He needed more strength, but he didn't know how to obtain it.

Ana sat down, putting an end to that string of thoughts. They sat in silence as the sky above the mountain peaks turned pink with the dawning of a new day. He grabbed her hand and held it in his, and together they watched their allies begin to heal one another.

22

Although she felt the temptation to remain connected to the gate and explore its abilities further, Alena decided her efforts were enough for the day. She made her way back to Toren, who was calmly sitting upon the imaginary plains of Etar. Then she severed their connection completely.

Back in the tent, she found that not much time had passed at all. Jace, vigilantly guarding the two of them, looked surprised to see them so soon. She'd noticed that aspect to soulwalking before, but within the gate the effect seemed stronger.

Toren had questions about their experience and what he had felt through their bond, but Alena begged for some space. Hanns' refusal to cooperate irritated her, and she found it impossible to focus. Jace, thankfully, sensed Alena's state of mind. He promised Toren they would meet for a midday meal, then escorted Alena to their tent.

Once alone, Jace settled near the entrance, protecting her from interruption and giving Alena all the space she needed. She paced the short length of the tent, sorting her thoughts. It didn't take her long to realize these weren't problems she could sort on her own.

She recruited Jace, explaining everything that happened. He asked insightful clarifying questions, then sat in silence when she finished.

When he did answer, it was carefully. "Alena, I think I agree with Anders VI." Jace hadn't had the same interactions with Hanns and refused to use the emperor's given name.

Before Alena could object, Jace held up his hands. "I understand. I really do. But hear me out."

Through a force of will, Alena shut her jaw and listened.

"There's no doubt that if the Etari lose their gate it will be difficult for them. But it doesn't necessarily mean disaster. Even without their gatestones they all possess affinities and the ability to use them. They're still skilled hunters and warriors. Losing the gate would change their culture, but it doesn't endanger their lives."

Alena took a deep breath. Her brother had a point. She nodded, sensing that he still had more to his argument.

"So the question, then, is this: Is the loss of the Etari way of life worth the potential gain for the empire?" Jace paused. "I believe it is. I know you're angry at the emperor, but remember that he's using this power to protect the whole continent, including the Etari and the Falari. He's a capable commander. He knows the only way to remain safe against the Lolani is to keep them on their own land. He can't sacrifice either Etar or Falar—if the Lolani gain a foothold it's only a matter of time before they bring the fight to the heart of the empire. So even if the Etari lose the gatestones, they'll still have the emperor's protection."

At that moment, Alena appreciated Jace more than anyone else in the world. Not because he had convinced her, but because his calm argument helped focus her own. Blades only became sharpened against a whetstone. Arguments only became clear when one could see both sides.

"You're right, but I don't think it's only Etari culture at stake." Alena moved her hands through the air randomly, searching for the right words. "Soulwalking has taught me that everything is connected, and that's true of the gates, too. They weren't built to be used the way Hanns or the queen is using them." She searched for an explanation. "I think the balance is important."

"And what happens if that balance is disrupted?"

Alena shook her head. "I don't know, but I doubt Hanns does, either. The power we're talking about is beyond incredible, Jace. The risk of making a mistake is too high."

"But you said the queen is drawing too much power through her gate, too."

"And?"

"So you've still got a problem. Even if you convinced Anders VI, you haven't fixed anything. Maybe you even make it easier for the queen."

Alena grimaced. She hadn't considered that possibility, but Jace had a point, again.

She returned to pacing their tent. What could she do?

She could tie herself to the Etari gate the same way Hanns tied himself to the other gates. She'd seen the emperor's connection a couple of times now and thought she could duplicate it. That idea was intoxicating. She imagined the good she could do with such power. Perhaps control of the gate would give her enough strength to challenge the Lolani queen.

Thankfully, reason reasserted itself before she followed her imagination too far. She doubted the Etari would give her permission to control their gate, and to attempt it without permission was a betrayal of the trust Sooni had shown her.

It was also the same trap Hanns found himself in. If he couldn't defeat the queen with two gates, what luck would she have with one?

She dismissed the idea, as tempting as it was.

She turned to Jace. "What would you do?"

Jace stared at the ground. "I'm not the person to ask. I don't understand nearly enough of this. So I'd listen to my superior. In this case, that's the emperor."

Alena felt a pang of sympathy for her brother. Ever since he'd been little he'd admired his sister's rebelliousness, but it had never been his. He craved a life of adventure, but he lived his life within the rules created by others.

Alena needed guidance. Any other opinion would help. She didn't want to turn to Sooni, who was closest. Sooni's interests, with good cause, lay with her own people. She wouldn't be able to examine the whole problem.

Brandt was the only person who came to mind.

They hadn't been in touch since their battle with the queen, but she knew he was alive and well. It would be good to see him, regardless. She dropped into a soulwalk and pulled on the thread that connected them.

When she told Jace what she intended, he nodded and left the tent. She suspected he meant to get in some training while she waited for Brandt to reply.

Alena sat down cross-legged in the tent and dropped into the soulwalk again. Eventually she felt the return tug. She traveled the connection between them, defaulting once again to her mother's kitchen.

They appeared together, both seated at her mother's table.

Brandt looked frightened.

He hid it well, but Alena now understood the wolfblade. His eyes darted left and right and his hand was never far from his sword. But why was he nervous?

Then she knew.

This was his first visit to this realm since the battle with the queen.

"I'm sorry to bring you back here," she said.

"I'll be fine." He gave her a smile that she didn't believe at all. "I don't like this realm much, though."

"I still have nightmares about the void," she confessed.

Brandt said nothing, but the look in his eyes was enough for Alena. He'd been haunted by the same dreams.

"Thank you for meeting me here. I need your help."

Brandt did his best to relax, but his efforts only appeared partially successful.

Alena launched into her story. She started at the beginning, when Ligt came to her door in Landow, running through the pertinent events. She finished with her last dive into the gate and her realizations. When she finished, Brandt's discomfort had vanished. He sat, enraptured by her story.

"How certain are you of what you experienced?"

"Fairly. And Hanns didn't dispute anything I said."

He nodded and looked off in the distance. "What would you ask of me?" The question seemed to make him nervous.

"Your advice. I believe that Hanns is making a gamble that could have consequences far beyond what he expects. I'm hoping you have some way to make him see that."

Brandt looked uncertain. "That's a difficult ask. I don't doubt what you felt, but all you're dealing with is your feelings. No rational emperor would stop without more evidence."

"Isn't the Etari gate dying enough?"

"Not even close. Again, you tell me that you have a feeling. You don't actually know what will happen if Hanns continues to pull more from the gates. Maybe the problem with the Etari gate is something completely different. Maybe it can't pull from the source because it was shattered."

Alena clenched her fist. She *knew* she was right. It was a certainty, right up there with the knowledge that her family loved her. But like her family's love, how did she prove it? First Jace and now Brandt. Both seemed to understand the opposing argument better than they understood hers.

"Could you at least speak with him? Perhaps he'll reveal something to you that will at least put my mind at ease."

Brandt shook his head. "I'm not in the palace anymore."

Of course. She'd felt him moving and forgotten that fact. In her rush to tell him everything, she hadn't even asked how he was or what he was doing. So she did.

"I'm in Falar, actually. On a diplomatic mission guarding Prince Regar."

"Sounds important."

"I think it will be. We fought off an assassination attempt last night."

"Really?"

"Apparently the Falari have strong disagreements among themselves. A warleader who objected to Regar's visit decided to put an early end to it."

"But you saved the day?"

Brandt's laugh was grim. "Hardly. Ana and I helped hold them off, but it was the Falari hosting us that drove the attack off. I was near my limit. The cost still holds me back."

Alena chewed on her lower lip. She hadn't told Brandt her other discovery. But was it wise?

She trusted Brandt, though. If he couldn't do the right thing, no one could. "I know how to avoid the cost," she said.

His eyes shot to hers with a startling intensity. "Not the gatestones?"

She shook her head. "No. I know how the queen gained such strength, even without her gate."

"How?"

"It's horrible."

His eyes didn't waver. She'd only seen him this intense in the middle of battle, and now she regretted saying anything. Perhaps this was a secret she should take to her grave.

But it was Brandt.

"It's a soulwalking technique. If you create a connection with a living being and it dies, you gain its energy when it passes through the gate. That's how I've gotten stronger."

"Can you teach it to me?"

"Brandt—"

"Can you teach it to me?" It wasn't a question, but a demand.

"Maybe? It requires at least a basic knowledge of soul-walking."

"Figure out how to teach it, Alena."

She found her spine then. She liked Brandt and trusted him, but no one ordered her around. If he forgot, she would remind him that in this place she was far stronger than him. "So you can do what? Go on a killing spree?" She let the venom in her voice reflect her anger.

It caught him by surprise. He held up his hands, as if to surrender. His eyes fell. "Not like that, no." Then his eyes came back up. "But I'm a wolfblade, and a soldier of the empire. Just last night I must have killed nearly a dozen warriors. If I can gain something from those deaths, don't you think I should?"

"But we don't know what the technique does to those who die. What if it prevents them from passing through the gate? What if it strands them in the same void we experienced?" Alena blurted out her worries.

The words of the original Anders echoed in her thoughts. Perhaps the technique allowed one to bypass the cost in using affinities, but it still came with a steep price.

She didn't know what to tell Brandt, but delaying was easy enough. "I'll see if I can learn how," she said, the words feeling dirty even as she said them. "I have a pupil now who I can attempt to teach."

"Thank you. It might make the difference as we travel deeper into Falar."

Alena frowned. "You got attacked and you're going deeper in. Why?"

Brandt's eyes fell back down to the table, and he looked as though he'd been caught saying something he hadn't intended to.

"Brandt, why are you going deeper into Falar? Why, exactly, are you there?"

He looked up, chagrined, "You're not going to like the answer, especially now."

She hoped her stare burned him.

"Hanns has asked us to treat with the Falari. He wants to control their gate as well."

23

Brandt admired the townspeople's resilience. Not only did they all rise to defend their homes, they went about the rebuilding of their town with a quiet determination that left him speechless.

The morning after the attack, the residents of the village gathered bodies for a large fire, set to consume neighbors and invaders alike. While the Etari and imperials tended to bury their dead, the Falari preferred the quick end of fire.

Brandt heard no wailing as the town cleared its streets and rooftops. He didn't doubt their grief for a moment. Tears ran freely on many faces, but they contained their grief and kept it within.

In a way, that made the morning harder.

This had been Regar's fault, shared by all who accompanied him. The enemy Falari had attacked Regar and the town had been in their way. Brandt would have welcomed an angry spouse or sibling. He would have endured a torrent of hate, if only it would wash away a part of what he felt.

But no one spoke a word against them. Brandt didn't even catch an angry glare.

It made Falar feel more foreign than before.

When his host family offered them generous amounts of food for the road, Brandt almost lost his composure. He tried to refuse, but they wouldn't take no for an answer.

They left the village not long after the sun rose above the peaks, the work in town still unfinished. Brandt wished the village well as it disappeared behind them. It was the least he could do.

His worries faded as they hiked into the mountains. The paths through the heart of Falar were often demanding, and they began their morning with a stretch that climbed relentlessly uphill. The effort finally succeeded in pushing away his guilt.

Alena's message came later that morning. Brandt spoke to her while they rested near the high point of a pass.

When she severed their connection, he couldn't hide his new distress from Ana, who asked, "How is she?"

"Well, as far as I can tell. She's currently at the Etari gate."

"What?" She looked as confused as Brandt had felt when he spoke with Alena.

"I know."

"Isn't their gate shattered? Isn't that what Hanns told us?"

"It is, but Alena says part of it still exists and it's active."

"Huh." Ana accepted the fact easier than he had. "And she's fine?"

"I think so."

When Brandt didn't volunteer further information, Ana pushed. "So what's bothering you?"

"She found a way to surpass the cost."

That piqued Ana's curiosity. "How?"

Brandt explained. Ana's face fell. By the time he finished his explanation, Ana looked horrified. "Would you consider it?"

"I asked her to figure out how to teach me."

Word came that their journey would soon be resuming. They walked down the path, near the rear of the column. Regar, Ren, and Weylen were close to the front, leading a mixed column of imperial guards and Falari warriors. After last night, the distinction meant less than ever. Both sides had lost friends. Brandt and Ana remained in their own bubble, undisturbed by the others.

"You shouldn't pursue that," Ana said.

Brandt glanced at her. "I don't like it either, but what if there's no other choice?"

Ana's reply was harsh. "There's always a choice."

"If not for Regar, the first Falari ambush would have killed most of us. And against the queen, I'm nothing. This is the only way I know of to protect you and to protect the empire."

"Which is why we have an emperor. Hanns is the one connected to the gates. It's his duty to fight the queen."

"It's everyone's."

Ana stopped walking, forcing Brandt to stop as well. She gestured to some warriors behind them to continue on. Soon the couple was alone behind the column. Brandt looked around for places where enemy Falari might ambush them, but no one had been seen all day.

Ana didn't care. Her eyes were focused entirely on him. "Do you really believe that the fate of the empire rests on your shoulders?"

Brandt hesitated.

She nodded, as though his silence answered her question well enough. "You're a student of war, Brandt. How often does a single warrior change the outcome of a battle?"

"All the time." The answer sounded weak, even to him.

"Nonsense. We may pick out stories of individuals, but a battle never relies on just one person. You know this. The empire won't rise or fall based on your own strength."

"But if I'm stronger I can better protect the people I love—"

"No." She stepped closer to him. "Don't use me as justification for something you want. I've fought for myself my entire life."

Brandt flinched back, surprised by Ana's vehemence. They'd spent the better part of a decade training together, seeking more strength together. She'd always sought to improve, just like him. He thought she'd be excited to learn of Alena's breakthrough.

Ana took one step closer, bringing them together. She held his hands. "Will you promise me you won't learn that technique?"

Brandt wanted to promise. He saw the depth of Ana's conviction. And he hated to hurt her. But he didn't agree, and he refused to lie. "I will think on what you've said."

It was the best he could offer.

Ana held his gaze for another moment. He wasn't sure exactly what she was searching for, but she didn't find it. She stepped away from him, and together they drifted back toward the rest of the column.

Brandt searched for something he could say that would make her feel better. But every option was a lie. So he gave her space.

When they returned to the column, he excused himself. Ana's emotions rolled off her, making Brandt uncomfortable. He wandered toward the front of the line, seeking Regar and Ren. It wasn't just a technique for surpassing the cost that Alena had discussed. Her concerns about the gates needed to be raised to Regar.

When he reached the pair of leaders they were discussing various paths through the mountains. Brandt listened with interest. From the sound of it, paths crisscrossed Falar in every direction. What the land lacked in paved roads it more than made up for with options. Ren listed three or four different paths. Some were longer, others involved more altitude changes, and two ran through territory of unfriendly warleaders. No path came without challenges.

Regar glanced over at Brandt. "Do you have an opinion?"

Brandt shook his head. "This isn't my land. I trust Ren to guide us by the path he seems best."

Regar agreed. "Then it's settled. We place the choosing of our path in your hands, Ren."

The swordsman didn't seem disappointed in the result. He excused himself to walk ahead, to pass new instructions onto the scouts.

Once they were relatively alone, Brandt told Regar about his conversation. Regar listened intently.

"You say this woman has the ability to work with the gates?"

"She does. Outside Landow she saved my life. And she was instrumental in our last fight against the queen."

Regar looked discomfited by the knowledge. When he saw that Brandt noticed, he explained. "The gates are incredibly powerful. My father's training has drilled that into me. It makes me uncomfortable to know someone is playing with one."

"She's not playing, and she, more than most, understands how dangerous they are."

"Does she? If she truly did she wouldn't be anywhere near a gate. Even my father only approaches his when absolutely necessary."

Brandt conceded that point. "Is she right to worry?"

Regar shrugged. "I don't know. For all my training, your friend apparently has more direct experience than me."

Brandt thought he caught a hint of jealousy in the prince's voice. "Is there a way to make your father aware?"

"It sounds like she's already tried."

"It might have more weight, coming from you."

Regar shook his head. "Perhaps, but I have no way of reaching out to my father. We do not share this bond you and Alena do. It sounds as though we should explore it. The use of communication over distance would revolutionize warfare."

Brandt had thought the same. But it required soulwalkers, an affinity most imperial citizens didn't even know existed. No doubt, they could be found and trained, but it would take precious time.

They rode together for a while, Regar lost in his own thoughts. One seemed to worry him most of all, though. Eventually he turned to Brandt to ask his question. "Your friend, Alena, is she trustworthy? She dabbles with forces even my father fears."

Brandt considered the question. Alena had been thrust onto this path as a thief. She was clever and skilled. But her past still troubled him at times.

"I do. She's young, but I would put my life in her hands."

Regar nodded. "I'm glad to hear that."

But his voice lacked conviction.

Brandt put it aside. He was surprised Hanns hadn't mentioned Alena at some point to Regar, but he couldn't presume to know the emperor's mind.

Not long after, Ren came running up to them in a hurry. He looked concerned.

"I apologize, Regar, but it appears your journey to the elders will be more eventful than I'd expected."

"How so?"

"Our scouts report a war party in our path."

"Hostile?" the prince asked.

"I don't know. Their warleader doesn't proclaim his beliefs as loudly as most do."

"They're on the path?"

"They are. Our scouts haven't seen any enemies waiting in ambush, but that doesn't mean it isn't a trap. We can either ride toward them or we can take another path."

"How large is their party?"

"Visible? About the size of ours."

Regar nodded. Behind them, the entire column had come to a halt. Regar stood in silence, considering his options. "Lead me to them."

Ren kept his facial expressions neutral, but he seemed pleased. It seemed the prince was winning over their Falari allies.

Brandt respected Regar's decisions. The prince asked for help when he needed it, then gave orders when they were called for. He was a leader worth following.

Attempting to avoid conflict for the two weeks it would take them to reach the elders was foolish. This party waited in the open. From what little Brandt knew about the Falari, that boded well for them.

He walked back to Ana, who was watching the nearby

rocks for movement. Word had traveled down the line. “Another war party?”

“Yes. Regar’s leading us right to them.”

“Do we know if they’re allies?”

Brandt’s smile was grim. “I think we’re going to find out soon enough.”

24

Alena faced off against Ligt. His smile, so uncommon on the journey here, was more menacing than any glare. It was a smile of supreme confidence. Alena supposed the confidence was well-earned. This was their fourth round, and Ligt won all three previous rounds with ease.

Alena didn't mind. She wasn't a warrior. Every Etari youth trained extensively in the martial arts. Alena had focused her own education on different subjects, barely paying any attention at all to the martial skills taught at academy. She'd learned enough to protect herself while living with the Etari, but martial arts had never been her strength.

She did want to wipe that smile off Ligt's face, though.

He beckoned her forward, offering her the opportunity for the first move. Alena knew it was a trap. Ligt excelled at countering attacks. What appeared generous was nothing more than the warrior fighting to his strengths.

But she couldn't defeat him standing five paces away, either.

Well, she could. She could have him on his knees screaming in horror in a few moments.

But she wasn't looking to test her soulwalking.

She advanced, every sense tuned to Ligt's movement. He remained still, a predator waiting for his prey.

Alena snapped a kick at his shin. He switched his stance, pulling his leading leg back to avoid her low kick. As he did, Alena darted forward, grabbing his shoulders and pulling him down.

Ligt wasn't surprised. He allowed himself to be pulled, grabbing onto her as he fell, bringing the two of them down together. They rolled until Ligt was on top of her. He fought for a mount position.

Alena positioned her legs between them and pushed him off, then scrambled to take control of the new position.

She swore as he got a grip on her wrist and pulled. Although they were of similar size, Ligt was stronger, and she felt him pulling her into a lock.

In her moment of panic, though, there was nothing she could do. Once the lock was applied, the fight was over. Alena tapped and Ligt immediately released the hold.

That irritating smile remained plastered on his face.

"You almost beat him," a voice remarked from behind her.

She turned to see Toren standing there. She was surprised to see him, but she didn't need his sympathy. "No, not this time."

"Let me show you."

Not sympathy, then, but an observation.

She glanced at the sky. Soon she would meet with the elders, but she had a little time. She signed an affirmative. Toren approached and grabbed her arm with the same lock that Ligt had used. They duplicated the position just before the end of the match.

"Here," Toren said. "If you keep your weight moving like this—" he manipulated her leg with his free hand, "you end here and win."

His hand on her leg was strong. For some reason, Alena thought of when she'd been torn apart by the gate and he had caught her.

Ligt scoffed. "She can't beat me."

Toren didn't reply. But he stood up, the lesson over.

Without another word he walked away. Ligt watched him go. "He's a strange one, isn't he? Rarely speaks, rarely spars, and he studies soulwalking."

Alena watched Toren walk away. Ligt didn't like Toren, but it seemed few Etari did. She wouldn't call him strange.

She'd say interesting.

Brushing herself off, she thanked Ligt for the match. After her last two days she had needed something physical, something that grounded her in her real body. She'd lost track of the number of times she argued with Sooni and Dunne. But she had convinced them. They agreed to present her findings to all the elders of Cardon.

Ligt had been the most obvious sparring partner. Jace would have if she asked, but any fight against her brother, no matter how controlled, reminded her of their duel in the caves outside Landow. That was a memory better sealed in a vault than relived.

Ligt's willingness to spar probably reflected his own frustration. All Etari were nomadic, but to varying degrees. Sooni's family, as one of the trading families, spent more time moving than most. Waiting in Cardon for Alena to finish her task no doubt irritated many in her family who itched for open spaces and constant movement.

Hopefully their time of waiting would end soon, though.

After cleaning up, Alena met Sooni. Jace had wanted to accompany them, but he possessed no gatestone, the mark of an Etari adult and necessary to speak before the elders.

Alena kept expecting Jace to tire of all this and leave. He still had his new post waiting for him in Landow. But he made no complaint, no matter what he felt. She wouldn't have held leaving against him, but his continual presence grounded her. She was glad he was here.

The tent the elders held council in was quite small. In the past, Alena had visited a larger tent, when more of a crowd was present. Today only the elders, Sooni, and Alena sat under the tent.

Sooni knelt next to Alena in front of the line of five elders. Dunne was one of the five, but Alena didn't recognize the others. Sooni began. As head of Alena's family, she was responsible for Alena's conduct throughout the interview. "Honored elders. Thank you for this audience. My daughter, Alena, is known to you. She was welcomed into my family over a decade ago. She has worn her gatestone proudly for years, and her gifts helped defeat the Lolani invaders."

Alena winced at that. She had helped quell the Lolani invasion, but her own contribution felt insignificant. She'd simply done what she could when she could.

"She's the soulwalker." The statement was half a question and uttered by the man who sat on Alena's far right. His defining feature was the baldness of his scalp, a rare trait even among the elders.

Alena bit back a response. She still hadn't been invited to speak. Sooni replied on her behalf. "She is."

Alena worried she might collapse under the weight of the elders' glares. But she kept her back straight and met their gazes. She would serve, but she would not let them intimidate her.

The elder who sat in the center, a woman as thin as a stick, spoke, her voice ringing with command. "You may speak, Alena. Dunne tells us you fought hard for this audience, so say what you came to say."

Alena spoke of her discoveries about the gate. No doubt Dunne had already informed the elders, but Alena recounted all the pertinent details.

A heavy silence hung over the gathering as she finished describing her conversation with the emperor.

She wasn't sure how they would react. In all her years with the Etari, she'd never quite figured out exactly how they viewed the empire. The forces skirmished on occasion. Once every few years, an imperial trader believed they could use a shortcut through Etari lands. The Etari would end the practice whenever they discovered it, raising tensions along the border for a year or so. Then the worry would fade and another trader would begin to think they would be the one who snuck through undetected.

The elders' reactions, such as they were, were muted. She'd expected outrage or questions, but none came.

Eventually, Dunne asked a single question. "What would you have us do with this knowledge?"

This had been the source of their arguments the past few days. Alena insisted that the Etari link someone to command their gate in the same way that Hanns commanded his. To say that Dunne didn't view that possibility favorably was an understatement.

The first time Alena had mentioned the idea, Dunne spat at her feet.

The elder still hadn't apologized.

But Alena insisted the possibility be presented. "It is for the elders to decide. This is your gate. If nothing is done, I believe that eventually your gate will fail and the gatestones will become useless. Either an Etari must command the gate or efforts must be made to prevent more power being pulled to the other gates."

The backs of the elders stiffened at her first suggestion. The thin woman sitting in the center of the elders responded. "We will not consider 'commanding' the gate, as you call it. But how might less power be pulled from the other gates? You've already said the emperor has no desire to cooperate."

Alena had been chewing on that exact problem since she'd realized it was the most likely possibility. The Etari reticence to command their own gate complicated matters. "The most straightforward option is to command your gate and attempt to pull more of the source toward it." She saw their reactions and charged forward. "But if that is truly out of the question, there are only two options. Either we break Hanns' connection with one of his two gates, or we find some way to use the Falari gate."

"Breaking Hanns' connection to the gate might be considered an act of war," Dunne mentioned casually, as though such an event wouldn't cost thousands of lives and break the treaty that had largely held for two hundred years.

"And it would harm his ability to keep the Lolani queen at bay," Alena added. She'd come to the same conclusion. She hated admitting it, but allowing Hanns only one gate didn't solve their problems. The Lolani queen was part of the problem, too. It only took the poor management of one gate to throw the balance of the system off.

She knew she treaded the edges of proper address, but

the simplest answer remained in front of them. "Why won't you allow someone to command your gate?"

Alena had asked Dunne the same question and never received an answer. The Etari detested soulwalking, but they rarely turned away from a pragmatic option.

The elder in the center answered. "The gates are not to be commanded. This is an edict passed down among the elders. What the emperor and the Lolani queen do is against the very purpose of the gates, and their punishment will not be long in coming."

The elder spoke with certainty, but Alena intuited a hole in the heart of the elder's words. The Etari elders didn't know the actual reasons why they avoided the gate. They had nothing but a command passed down through the years.

That lack of knowledge encouraged her. Perhaps they could be persuaded.

Then she thought again. The Etari had more history to call on than the empire did. Anders I had destroyed too much of what was known before. Even if the elders didn't understand why their edict stood, the command had the weight of history behind it. The elders wouldn't bend so easily.

"In that case, we must ensure that Anders VI doesn't gain control of the Falari gate."

It was the conclusion Alena had hoped to avoid, but one that had appeared inevitable for days.

Dunne didn't approve. Any attempt to stop Hanns carried innumerable risks, and its odds of success were slim. Why waste precious Etari lives on a mission so likely to fail?

The head elder spoke. "Elder Dunne has spoken of your ideas. But we are of her mind. Besides the possibility of sparking a war upon the land, it seems foolish to risk Etari lives on such a scheme."

And so they came to the crux, just as Alena had dreaded they would. She'd hoped for a different outcome, but none of the elders would bend. It left her no choice. "Then send me. Give me permission to act on your behalf."

She understood the weight of her request. Despite her adopted status, she was an outsider. If they said yes, they put some of their destiny in the hands of one who hadn't even been born in their lands.

If they were surprised by her offer, they didn't show it. The elders weren't fools. They likely predicted the course of this interview, just as she had. A part of Alena hated having to jump over the obstacles they put before her, but this was the Etari way. The elders wouldn't make this decision without seeing her face and hearing her voice.

Dunne dismissed her. "Wait outside the tent, Alena. We must talk."

Jace waited for her outside. His gaze was questioning. She shook her head. "They won't allow anyone control of their gate."

He didn't look surprised. "So it's Falar, then."

"Hopefully."

Jace gave a grim laugh. "No one hopes to travel to Falar, sister."

"You don't have to go."

"You know that I do."

Alena let the argument go. It was one they had already had, and she had lost. Jace refused to leave her, no matter what opportunities awaited him at home.

She was glad, even if she didn't understand.

They waited together. The ring of guards around the

tent of the elders ensured the two of them were out of hearing range. They had nothing to do but wait.

Eventually, Sooni came out of the tent. She looked distraught, but Alena wasn't sure what that implied.

Sooni didn't leave them in suspense long.

"You've been granted permission to travel to Falar on behalf of the Etari people. You leave soon."

25

Though they knew a war party waited in the open, Weylen observed every caution as they approached. The loose column broke further apart, the Falari warriors leaving the path and scrambling up and down the rocky terrain like gazelles.

Archers nocked arrows as the group advanced. Their progress slowed to a crawl, each warrior alert for traps, ambushes, and other unforeseen unpleasantness.

Brandt, Ana, and the imperial guards closed tighter upon Regar. The maneuver was half noble, half self-preservation. They might take an arrow for him, but close to him, most hoped his powerful affinities would prevent them from having to.

Brandt rarely regretted not practicing more archery. He possessed a basic competence, as all imperial soldiers did. As he watched Weylen's war party advance, though, he was reminded of how little a blade meant in these mountains. Even if he made himself light, in the time it took him to scramble from one enemy to the next, he'd be riddled with arrows.

Even at their cautious pace, they came face to face with the other war party before long. Brandt took the scene in with a glance. If this was an ambush, it was either far more clever than he could comprehend, or it had been set by an overeager child.

The location was terrible. The opposing war party stood in a clearing. Brandt couldn't spot useful cover for almost two hundred paces. If he'd been in charge, he saw a half dozen better locations.

The other war party held their bows loosely. Arrows remained in quivers. They gave no sign of hostility, but at the same time, Brandt didn't see a relaxed face in the group.

Regar approached to within a hundred paces. Brandt followed a pace behind, eyes searching for any clue as to the war party's intentions.

Ren, Weylen, and a handful of their Falari escorts joined them. Weylen spoke softly to Regar. "Their warleader is named Merek. They are a mountain clan, and I am not sure of their intentions."

Regar nodded. Brandt saw the plans forming in his eyes. "Remain in place."

Without further warning he stepped forward, alone. After ten paces he stopped again. Brandt forced his hand to relax its grip on his sword. Regar was skilled enough to protect himself from attack for the two heartbeats it would take Brandt to close the distance, but Brandt's heart still raced as he saw the prince standing alone before a Falari war party.

Merek stepped forward. He surpassed Regar's ten paces, stopping halfway between the forces.

A gust of wind coming down the mountains kicked up a cloud of dust. Brandt tensed. The momentary distraction was all an astute enemy required. He searched the air for arrows but saw none.

When Merek spoke, his voice wasn't loud, but it reached every ear. "Word has spread through the mountains that Weylen's village hosts a strong warrior. Where is he?"

Regar stepped forward, but Merek shook his head. "Not you, prince. The man who fought on the rooftops when Shulin attacked."

Brandt glanced at Ren, who gestured him forward. "Don't kill anyone if you can help it." A hint of a smile played across his face.

Brandt stepped forward. Merek nodded once. "You match the description given. Are you the warrior who defended the prince's rooftops the night of the raid?"

"I am."

"Then we have come to test our skill against you."

Merek waved, and a single warrior emerged from his ranks. A woman, smaller than average, but she carried herself with a deadly grace. Too often warriors confused size with danger.

Brandt didn't.

This woman would slice him open in a heartbeat if he gave her the chance.

He cursed under his breath as the woman drew not one, but two short blades. They danced a quick, intricate pattern he barely followed.

With no other explanation, and no chance for him to understand what was proper, the woman charged, her footsteps light over the ground.

She was fast.

Brandt reacted, years of training forcing his muscles into motion. The woman's blades were shorter and lighter than his own sword. She would expect him to retreat, to use his longer reach to his advantage. In response, her own strategy would be relentless advance.

So Brandt did the unexpected. He charged forward the moment she was within ten paces.

If the move caught her off guard, she didn't show it. One of her blades caught his attack while the other aimed for his throat.

Brandt pressed harder on his blade. He couldn't slide past her defense, but the extra pressure pushed her off her line, and the stab at his throat missed wide.

She twisted her blade and sliced at his neck.

Brandt expected the move. He lowered himself, and her blade passed over his head.

Then he stood up quickly and smashed his forehead into her nose.

The blow caught her by surprise and she staggered back two paces.

To her credit, she recovered quickly, but Brandt was too fast. The point of his sword rested at her throat. She froze. Brandt remembered Ren's advice and moved the tip of his sword away.

Brandt looked over to Merek, who grinned from ear to ear. He clapped once and the woman disengaged. She stepped back into line, doing nothing to staunch the flow of blood from her nose.

"Impressive." Merek looked at his assembled warriors, noting the various affirmations he received. "We will join you on your journey to the elders and add our voices to your own."

Behind Brandt, Weylen spoke. "We would be honored."

With that, Merek turned and walked back to his people.

The tension between the two groups vanished as though they had always been allies. Merek's warriors slung their bows over their shoulders and Weylen's war party returned from their vantage points to the trail. Not a single Falari seemed concerned that just a few moments ago the forces had been ready to fight.

Brandt frowned.

What had he just done?

MEREK'S WAR party joined their own as easily as if the whole episode had been planned. Brandt held onto his questions. The path was now crowded and he figured his wondering could continue until they made camp that night. Then he could take Ren or Weylen aside.

They hiked through the mountains for the rest of the day without incident. They moved quickly and quietly, and by the end of the day Brandt's legs and lungs demanded rest.

They came to a clearing as the sun dipped below the mountain peaks and began making camp. Ren found Brandt before Brandt could seek the warrior out. "Come," he said.

They left camp, climbing higher up a short cliff that overlooked the clearing. Brandt's body protested the additional effort, but he refused to complain.

They reached the top, where Brandt was surprised to find the woman he'd dueled with earlier. She had started a small fire and roasted a fresh killed hare over it.

If not for Ren's presence, Brandt's suspicions would have had him reaching for his sword. But Ren appeared at ease.

"Brandt, this is Leana," Ren said.

"You fought well today," Leana said. "If the rumors of your skill hadn't already spread, I might no longer be Senki."

"Senki?" Brandt asked, looking to Ren for guidance.

"A title. It has no direct translation into imperial.

Perhaps the closest would be 'last arrow.' It is the title given to the most skilled warrior in a clan. I am Weylen's Senki, and Leana is Merek's. You've now bested both of us."

Brandt let that information sink in.

"You look confused," Ren said.

Brandt shook his head. "I guess I assumed the warleader was the most skilled warrior."

"What sense does that make?" Ren asked. "A warleader must possess a deep understanding of strategy and navigate his war party's own interests. They must keep their mind focused on goals too distant for most to worry about. A Senki must only be the best with bow and sword."

"In our land," Brandt answered, "it is often tradition for those who fight well to be given command."

"But command of a war party and command of a bow are very different skills."

Brandt thought of the commanders he'd served under in his time, of the commander they'd met in the fort at the border. He thought of his own doomed command. Even after all these years, the deaths of his wolfblades remained a wound that refused to heal. "Perhaps there is wisdom in your way," he admitted.

The three warriors sat around the small fire while watching over the campground. Up here, there was no formality. Ren and Leana seemed acquainted, but they spoke imperial for Brandt.

Ren pulled out a flask, took a long pull, and handed it to Brandt.

Brandt didn't drink often anymore. But a flask had rarely looked more inviting. He took a long sip.

And almost spit it out.

The blend was stronger than anything he'd put down his

throat before. It burned, and he coughed as he passed it over to Leana, who drank without reaction.

Ren laughed. "Good, yes?"

Brandt just coughed again and nodded. But when Ren offered him another pull, he didn't refuse.

It wasn't just the taste that was strong, either. Granted, he'd been walking all day and hadn't had much to eat, but before long he felt a lightness in his soul that hadn't been there in some time.

Before long they were swapping stories. Through the tales of his new friends, Brandt learned more about life in Falar. Both Ren and Leana had been shaped by lives of continual fighting. If they weren't on the border with the empire they were out patrolling their own lands, a practice that sounded far less safe than an imperial guard patrolling the walls of a town. Attacks from neighboring clans were as common as summer storms.

In time, the flask was empty and the rabbit eaten. Their conversation turned to more serious matters.

Brandt directed his question at Ren. "What happened this morning?"

"You were being judged."

"Why me?"

"Because you are Regar's Senki."

"Shouldn't Regar have been tested?"

Leana answered that question. "Regar's purpose is known. His true test will come before the elders. Merek wanted to know what kind of warrior Regar had in his service."

"Why?" Brandt asked.

"Because a warleader is judged by the skill and actions of his warriors, and a Senki most of all," Leana answered.

"So if I lost, Merek would have fought?"

Ren shook his head. "You don't understand. Winning or losing was only part of it. Merek wanted to see *how* you fight. You could have killed Leana without consequence, just as she could have killed you. You could have raged, either in victory or defeat. It was your character he most sought to learn, not your skill. Even if you'd won, but not impressed him, he might have left or blocked our way."

"Because my character is a reflection of Regar's?"

Both his friends nodded.

The idea didn't sit well with him. "He could have just asked."

"There are times when speaking isn't nearly enough," Leana said. "The only way to truly know a person is to fight them."

Brandt nodded. That, at least, was a philosophy he'd espoused for many years.

Strangely, at that moment he felt more at home here than he did in the empire. He was fond of his fellow monks and admired their dedication to their development, but they were a small part of the larger empire. Most citizens never fought for anything. They never risked their lives or livelihood for anything.

Brandt heard the echoes of Regar's arguments in his own thoughts. For the first time, he understood. Perhaps Falar had something to teach them.

"So Merek and his clan have joined us? It's that simple?" Brandt was still confused on that point.

Ren laughed. "It's never simple, Brandt. Merek leads a mountain tribe. They are more nomadic and keep closer to the old ways than we do. Regar's arrival couldn't have come at a more challenging time for our people. We are split between the old ways and the desire for change. Merek has kept his own thoughts and intentions well-hidden over the years."

Leana jumped in. "He hasn't been willing to commit to either cause. He sees strengths and faults in both approaches. But the matter must be decided."

"What matter?" Brandt asked.

The two warriors glanced at each other, as though wondering if the other would speak first. Eventually, Ren answered. "Whether we should seek peace with the empire or invade it."

26

Although Alena understood the importance of haste, she couldn't leave Etar without exploring the gate one last time. Answers hid within the object, knowledge that had been buried for generations.

When Alena asked for permission, Dunne's uncertainty was evident. Certainly the elders worried Alena might not obey their commands regarding control of the gate.

And Alena *was* tempted.

Command of a gate opened up possibilities of tremendous power. Hanns' desire was one she understood. She could help in the fight against the queen and she could pull enough power to ensure the Etari gatestones never failed in her lifetime. Controlling the gate solved several of her problems.

On her own, the temptation might have been too great. But she wouldn't disobey the Etari elders. She owed them too much.

Dunne, at least, trusted her enough to connect again with the gate. The elder reluctantly gave Alena permission to explore the gate one more time. Alena swore she wouldn't disappoint Dunne.

She and Toren woke early the next morning. Accompanied by Jace, they made their way to the center tent. A now-familiar twisting sensation in Alena's stomach told her the gate had just failed. This close, she didn't even have to use her gatestone to know.

After perhaps a dozen heartbeats, the sensation faded. Alena connected with her gatestone to confirm. The gate had resumed working.

That, at least, was one worry off her shoulders. In her time here, the gate didn't fail often. At most, maybe once or twice a day. She and Toren would be safe to explore for a while.

The process of connecting with the gate was almost familiar to her now. She didn't hurry, despite her eagerness.

She escorted Toren to a safe place, as usual, taking the form of the plains beyond the sea. His growing comfort with the gate helped. Soon, maybe, she would take him deeper, if more opportunities came. But for now he anchored her. His curiosity and desire to go deeper were apparent, but he accepted his role without complaint.

After he wished her luck, Alena dropped deeper into the limitless power of the gate. Again, energy threatened to rip her limb from limb. She still fought the instinct to control. Muscle by muscle she relaxed her body, and in time, the feeling of being filled beyond bursting passed.

The vast web of interdependency formed around her. She floated within it, giving her mind time to come to terms with the flood of information pouring into her. Her reactions seemed a bit faster than before. Perhaps it was illusion, or perhaps her mind was learning to navigate this space. She hoped for the latter.

The representation of the gate stood before her, bright yet insubstantial. She drifted closer, studying it.

The temptation to dive deeper still nearly overpowered her. But she waited and observed.

The gate shifted in front of her as her mind wrestled with concepts beyond her understanding. At times she saw the diamond structure of the gate. At other times she thought she noticed something underneath, a latticework of indescribable complexity.

Alena drifted closer, careful not to interact directly with it. The latticework resolved as she focused, countless tiny threads woven and knotted in a pattern that remained just outside her understanding.

Ever so slowly, she ran her eyes up and down the lattice. It was a soulwork, but more. It seemed to include threads of the other elements as well. The barrier at the border looked like a child's craft in comparison. If this was the work of those who came before, what else had they been capable of, and why had they disappeared?

Abruptly, the pattern changed. She squinted, unsure of what had shifted. Carefully she ran her eyes back and the pattern returned to familiarity.

Alena focused on the change. The pattern of the gate remained, but threads had been woven on top.

She frowned. The new threads were intricate, but not of the same quality of the gate itself. With a start, she realized they'd been added later.

"I'm impressed."

The voice came from behind her, and Alena lost all focus. The latticework disappeared, replaced by the diamond exterior of the gate. Alena spun around, but in this space it turned into more of a slow twirl. She saw nothing.

"Relax. Focus on me here."

This time, it sounded like the voice came from in front of her. Alena focused on where she believed the voice had come from.

Just as the latticework resolved itself before her attention, a figure slowly began to appear, a ghostly apparition. Before long she looked into the face of a middle-aged woman. Her features were Etari. Alena guessed who she was looking at. "Zolene."

The woman smiled. She still didn't appear solid. Webs of life glowed behind her, almost making it look as though the web surrounded her. "You know me."

Alena nodded, then realized she didn't know if her actions translated here. "Your people still tell stories of you."

"And you have heard them."

"I have."

"Then why are you here?"

"The gate is failing. My family summoned me to see if there was anything I could do."

Zolene made a hand sign, but it wasn't substantial enough in Alena's vision for her to catch. "I have seen glimpses of your life. You are not Etari."

"I am not. I come from the empire."

"You are a servant of Anders?" The voice sounded disembodied, but Alena felt the emotion behind it. Zolene hated Anders.

Alena wasn't sure how to answer. She knew Zolene considered her response important. "No. I am of two worlds. I serve my blood family and my Etari family."

Alena sensed confusion, but faintly. Zolene stood in front of her, but she wasn't whole. Every emotion Alena noticed felt mild, nearly lethargic. She tried a different approach. "I want to stop your gate from failing. Can you help me?"

The apparition didn't answer. "Are there no soulwalkers among the Etari?"

"No. You were among the last."

A surge of pride rushed over Alena, the satisfaction of a task completed well.

Alena's curiosity burned hot. "What happened? Why did you demand the Etari give up soulwalking?"

"Because soulwalking calls *them*."

Frustrated at the nonsensical answer, Alena reached out to grab the apparition. It was the act of a moment. She didn't know if she meant to shake Zolene or support her, but when her hand touched the ghost, something passed between them.

Visions flashed through her, fragmented. She glimpsed the battle that Zolene had waged against Anders, watched as Zolene wove her own spirit with that of the Etari gate, granting her control over the object.

And she saw more. Shadows crossing over the land, enormous and filled with power.

Danger from the skies.

The moment passed. When her eyes refocused, Zolene stood in front of her, more solid than before. Alena understood that Zolene now drew on the connection between them. Alena felt Zolene's emotions like a blanket over her own.

When Zolene spoke again, her voice was clear. "Anders only understood near the end. His aims were noble enough, I suppose. He wanted peace and yet enemies gathered on all sides. And he was clever. Too much so for his own good. He was the one who first commanded the gate, and it was the mistake that led to all others."

Alena shook her head. "I don't understand."

Zolene's smile was sad. "You will. Thank you for

assisting my people. Perhaps you can right what Anders, myself, and Sofra wronged."

"Sofra?"

Zolene focused for a moment. "The one you call the Lolani queen."

"You knew her?"

"In a way."

"Can you help me repair your gate?"

No. Now that Zolene was more solid Alena had no problem deciphering the gesture. "Not directly. But we can take the first step today."

"What do you mean?"

She fixed Alena with a stare that froze Alena in place. Back home, eyes were considered windows to the soul, but here, Zolene could actually see Alena's thoughts. And Alena could see the weight Zolene carried. She was proud of her people, but barely contained a sadness that knew no limits.

"The gates *cannot* be controlled, Alena. I think you will learn that soon enough, but for now you must trust, the way the Etari elders do. We were fools to try. I tied myself to the gate to control it, and today you must cut me free."

"What?"

"My soul is tied to the gate. I should have died long ago, but I cannot pass death's gate. And I must."

"You want me to kill you?"

"I want you to free me. I died a long time ago."

"But I need your help. I need your guidance!"

The sad smile reappeared on Zolene's face. "That, you certainly don't. If you trust my words and don't attempt to control the gate, you will be fine. The gates can be guided, and they can be learned from, but control is an illusion. A dangerous one."

Alena was frozen. Zolene had the answers she desired. She couldn't release Zolene, not when she was this close.

Zolene, in this space, understood her conflict. "Your answers shouldn't come from me." She stepped toward the gate. "The gate already possesses my memories, as it does so many others. It is power, but it is also history. Everything you need to know is in this gate. In all the gates."

"But we're leaving tomorrow," Alena protested, and the words sounded weak even to her.

"And you can speak to friends nearly on the other side of the continent. What does distance matter? Being close to the gate simply makes it easier."

"Why won't you just answer my questions?"

"Because I don't want you trapped in my patterns of thinking. The only answers that will serve you are those that you find yourself. If we had taken the time to study these gates more closely, we would have learned, too. But we were driven by more immediate, petty needs."

Alena didn't know what to say to that. She didn't know what to say to any of this. But she sensed no deception from Zolene. The Etari legend desired her release. Alena alone could make that happen, and after the woman had spent two hundred years trapped here, who was she to deny the wish?

"Will you free me?"

"I will. But is there nothing you can tell me to guide me?"

She felt Zolene's sympathy. "Do not make the same mistakes we did. Explore. Understand. Trust your instincts. We're all connected to a web that knows and understands far more than we can comprehend. Listen to it. And trust in yourself. I do."

Alena frowned. "That's less useful than I'd hoped."

Zolene didn't take offense. "If there is one direction that I hope is useful, it is this: control is always an illusion. Never fall for the same fallacy we did. Events can be guided, but no more."

Alena realized she wouldn't get anything more from Zolene's spirit. It would have to be enough. "Thank you."

Together they stared at the gate. "You're the weaving on top of the gate, aren't you?"

Yes. "It was my attempt at control."

"Removing you won't harm the gate further?"

No. "If anything, it will allow the source to flow more reliably to it."

Alena remembered how intricate the weaving had been. "What if I cut part of the gate?"

Zolene smiled. "The weaving of the gate is capable of fixing itself, to an extent. So long as you don't intentionally seek to destroy the gate, I do not think there is anything you could do that would injure it permanently."

"You think I could destroy the gate?"

To that, Zolene gave no answer, and Alena caught no hint of emotion in their bond.

Their bond. "I won't accompany you to death's gate, will I?" The idea of stealing Zolene's power in that way struck Alena as wrong.

"No."

Alena nodded. "Is there nothing else?"

The other woman thought for a moment. "Trust yourself, Alena. And thank you."

Zolene's words had a feeling of finality about them. Alena didn't like it, but she accepted Zolene's wishes.

Alena called to mind her father's knife. It had carried her through more difficult situations than she could count. It formed slowly in her hand. With another effort, she visualized the connection between Zolene and herself. It appeared as a glowing thread.

Alena watched Zolene for any reaction. She'd never taken any academy classes that prepared her for this. She was guessing. But Zolene looked serene. Happy, even.

Alena cut the cord and Zolene faded again to an apparition. As Alena turned her attention to the gate, the apparition faded away into nothingness.

Finding Zolene's handiwork required a sustained focus. It was more difficult than before. Alena wondered if she was finding the limits of her own ability here.

Moving carefully, Alena began working at the threads. In this space, her knife was always sharp and it only required the smallest motions to slice through the threads. One at a time, Alena worked her way around the edges of the weaving.

It was slow, painstaking work. As she neared the end, her concentration frequently lapsed. She cut the gate more than once, and hoped Zolene's comments about the gate's ability to heal were true. She had to pause more frequently the longer she worked.

And then it was done. Alena only hesitated for a moment on the last thread. Then she sliced through it.

The pressure around her changed, as though a soft breeze had just blown through.

Though she couldn't say why, a sense of peace overwhelmed her for a moment.

She was exhausted, but satisfied with her work.

She'd sent the Etari legend to the gates of death.

Now it was time for her own journey to a very different gate.

27

Regar and his growing entourage continued deeper into Falar. Brandt was no stranger to mountains, but Falar held scenic surprises with every league. They passed waterfalls and hiked along majestic vistas, then plunged into woods so thick the sunlight never truly broke through.

Though their pace never slowed, Brandt did find himself less exhausted at the end of every day. In many ways, the Falari reminded Brandt of the Etari. While one people controlled the plains and the other the mountains, both were conditioned to long days on foot. He'd heard rumors that some Etari warriors could run down a horse if given enough time.

In the mountains of Falar, a war horse was a liability. The trails they took were barely wide enough for humans, at times barely the width of a foot. Brandt suspected that a fear of high places was quickly eliminated from a child's world-view here. Though he didn't mind heights, at least once a day his heart pounded in his chest as they walked a sharp ridge or were journeyed near the edge of a cliff.

He, Ana, Leana, and Ren formed something resembling a small group of friends. They ate together in the evening and often walked close by during the day. Ana, of course, dueled Leana after their second day together. Most nights around a Falari cookfire featured at least one good-natured sparring session.

Ren informed Brandt that as Prince Regar's Senki he did not have to accept most challenges, and Brandt took advantage of his unofficial role. Which was for the best, because every young warrior among the Falari wanted to test Regar's Senki. He *wanted* to duel all challengers, but he couldn't risk injury, not with the task that awaited them. Protecting Regar took precedence over his own desire to test his skills.

As they continued south, other war parties joined their own. Brandt wasn't sure by what means the Falari communicated so quickly, but it seemed that everyone knew of Regar and his audience with the elders. In time, Brandt began to believe the Falari saw in the imperial prince some turning point in history. Whether he was correct about their attitude or not, Regar attracted far more attention than Brandt was comfortable with. They couldn't go three days without meeting another warleader.

Sometimes there was a test, although that was uncommon. Merek's indecisiveness was an exception rather than a rule. Most warleaders who joined their journey were predisposed to Regar's cause.

Brandt found it fascinating that the empire had kept the gates such a closely guarded secret from its people. From conversations with Alena, Brandt knew all adult Etari knew of their broken gate, and the gate here was viewed by the Falari with some mixture of fear and respect Brandt hadn't yet deciphered. Only in the empire did most people know nothing.

Similar observations had fascinated him when he was younger and leaving home for the first time. Thanks to his service with the military, he traveled frequently throughout the empire. For a young man who had never once left the town of his birth, the endless marches leading to obscure corners of the land had been a treat. He saw the world and got paid for doing it.

At first it had been the unusual that seized his attention. From the food, to the architecture, to the people, his first impressions were all differences. He'd thought about those differences and what they meant on the long marches between new places. In class, his instructors had explained how the empire was one land. Like a child, Brandt thought that meant all places would be like the home he grew up in.

So at first he was bothered by the lack of uniformity throughout the empire. Different places both sparked his curiosity and offended his sensibility. The empire was enormous, and Anders I had conquered a wide variety of people to create his dream. The intervening two hundred years and more had knitted the land more tightly together, but differences still abounded.

In time, though, Brandt's understanding expanded. It wasn't the food one ate or the style of house one lived in that made one an imperial. It was a shared dream, an obedience to laws that were greater than them all. Anders I had a vision of an orderly, peaceful society, the society that Brandt grew up in. Once he understood what bound them together, he could much better appreciate the differences.

All of which made traveling in Falar a trying experience. In his mind, the Falari had been his enemies for most of his adult life. And now he traveled among them, respecting their ways a great deal. What did it say about him as an imperial that he got along so well with them?

Despite their similarities, there was no law here, no fundamental truth they agreed on. Falar was ruled by custom and agreements between war parties. One of the reasons they'd never win an invasion against the empire was because they resisted the coordination that defined the empire's forces.

He also thought constantly about where the Falari stood. Regar never spoke about this, but the prince's visit possibly meant more to the Falari than it did to the emperor. Ren and Leana both confirmed that the Falari were split on their ultimate direction as a people. Generally, it seemed that those who still wandered the mountains wished for war and for the maintenance of their most cherished traditions. Those like Weylen, who ruled over small towns, saw the path of peace as being the way forward.

Regar, it seemed, would be the weight that tipped the scale to one side or the other.

Ana, of course, derived no small amount of pleasure from Brandt's discomfort and endless speculation. It wasn't that she didn't observe the same differences, but those observations barely bothered her.

His thoughts tended to wander far and wide, especially with the ample travel time in which to indulge the practice. Small events and details often served as metaphors for something much larger. The turning of the autumn leaves was for him a reminder of the circle of life, death, and rebirth. For Ana, they were gorgeous colors that came once a year.

Likewise, the differences in food, language, and culture were little more than useful details to her. They added zest to her world, but she saw no greater meaning in their existence. Brandt wondered endlessly about the Falari emphasis on combat, whether with a bow, sword, or on the boards they so treasured. Ana settled for finally having an answer to their historic enemy's skill.

But even her attitude shifted when they came in sight of the Falari capital.

Faldun didn't reveal itself until they were nearly upon it. It was nestled deep in a valley, but in a manner that Brandt had never seen.

In his experience, towns and villages that grew in valleys were typically located in the land between the peaks. Houses and shops might be built from the stone of the nearby mountains, but they stood on the fertile and level land between heights.

Faldun turned that concept on its head. Here the city was carved into the walls of the mountain. The buildings and the mountain blended as one vertical structure of impossible proportions. Brandt had thought Weylen's village the most vertical he had ever seen, but this dwarfed Weylen's village in every way. Buildings rose to absurd heights. Brandt couldn't imagine living with such a view. Even from a distance, Brandt observed the narrow stairs that climbed in all directions.

Not a city, then, for those who struggled to move.

But again, Falar itself wasn't very welcoming to such.

Still, as impressive and awe-inspiring as the city looked, Faldun was still smaller than Brandt expected. It raised a question Ren had refused to answer. Just how many Falari were there? From what they had seen, the numbers seemed lower than Brandt had expected.

Ren stood beside Brandt and gestured at the sight. "It is impressive, is it not?"

Brandt agreed. There was nothing like it in the empire. The effort needed to construct such a city boggled his mind.

It was, he was certain, impossible.

Yet the city rose before him, the lively ghost of an age long past.

They entered Faldun properly later that afternoon. Messengers had spent several days traveling between the approaching war parties and the capital, so their arrival was anything but a secret.

Regar received a royal welcome. They entered through the main gate and followed a narrow path to a large square overlooking the valley. As they walked, Brandt felt sorry for any who considered entering the city by force. Its construction made it one of the most deadly approaches Brandt had ever seen.

Several elders came to greet Regar in the square. Regar met with them, and Brandt's attention wandered while formalities were exchanged. This was, after all, the first official royal visit in a generation.

Part of Brandt's distraction was the lack of threats against Regar's life. He'd worried on the road for a time, but now Regar travelled with hundreds of Falari warriors who pinned their hopes on him. It didn't make Regar invincible, but attacking him had become much harder in the past few weeks.

The larger part of Brandt's distraction was Faldun itself. Brandt's initial suspicions, upon closer inspection, were true.

The masonry and the construction were simply too perfect. Rocks were fitted perfectly with barely any mortar, and the stone was smooth, far smoother than any imperial chisel work Brandt had ever seen. Even more noticeable to Brandt's eye, the perfection in construction was ubiquitous. Every house and building exhibited the same craftsmanship. Even the stones in the square exhibited an exacting level of care and attention. This town had been wrought with affinities. A strength of affinity that no longer existed in the world save for a select few.

Though he couldn't be sure, he had a suspicion. There were no coincidences in life. The Falari capital had been built by the same people who built the caves outside Landow, a people that had disappeared a long, long time ago.

The gate was here, and this whole city had been built to protect it.

28

Say one thing about the Etari: once they reached a decision, it was as good as done. She'd seen some examples when she lived among them, but never experienced that truth as directly as in the days leading up to their departure. At times, it seemed every Etari in sight was aiding them.

They were outfitted with new clothes, lightweight and durable. Alena received lighter clothes for the plains of Etar and heavier ones for the mountains.

Other supplies soon followed. They received food for the road and horses of incredible quality, prized among the clans, given by the elders themselves. Unfortunately, the horses wouldn't actually travel into Falar. The steep and narrow mountain paths allowed travel only on foot. But until then, the horses would speed the journey to the border.

All of this happened within a day, and on the next they were sent on their way. Alena offered Sooni a proper farewell, and a promise to return when she could. They rode to the Alna river, where a trade boat awaited them and their horses. Before Alena had even had time to properly reflect on her past few days, she was beyond any land she had traveled before.

Her party was small, a decision the Etari elders had reached quickly. This expedition required stealth, not force. The terms of the treaty that bound the three nations of the continent together in relative peace contained strict stipulations on what size groups were allowed over the borders.

Alena would have felt safer with her whole Etari clan beside her, but a party of such size would have amounted to a declaration of war.

In the end, only three traveled toward the border.

She was accompanied by Jace and Toren. By now, Alena knew Jace wouldn't be turned aside, no matter how poorly she understood his reasoning. Toren had surprised her, though. He was a promising soulwalker with the opportunity to develop his skills near a gate. Even the elders had implied he should remain. But he wanted to join them, and no other Etari was eager to do so. Being as the elders insisted on having a full-blooded Etari on the expedition, they'd been trapped into accepting Toren's offer. Even after all she'd done for them, Alena still felt the sting of the elders' distrust.

Alena led the group, though she felt nothing like a leader. A leader possessed a vision and a map to get from where they stood to the desired future. Alena had neither of those things. Doubts constantly worried at her but she kept them hidden.

A leader was also supposed to be confident.

The first days of travel passed by in a blur. They traveled, they talked, and at times they trained. Alena admired Toren's determination to learn soulwalking, but she wasn't sure her lessons were very helpful. So much of what she knew had developed as an intuition. She didn't have a certain set of steps she followed, nor did she have the equivalent of a martial arts form that she could give him to improve his skills. Her method was trial and error and reflection. She fell down, got up, then repeated the process until the technique felt right. It worked for her, but it made her feel like a poor teacher.

Toren never complained, but she sensed the frustration lurking in his attempts.

Of the three of them, Jace seemed the most content. He possessed an ability to flow with changes in life in a way that boggled Alena's mind. He spent his days learning about rivers and currents from the crew of the boat, and he regularly sparred with all takers.

Nothing quenched his energy, and Alena grew to depend on her brother as a source of stability.

They followed the river for as long as it made sense, then disembarked to cross the empire on horseback. A small group of Etari rode with them. Here they made good time, and long days of travel ended with them exhausted as the sun went down. As Alena had guessed, the horses possessed the strength and stamina to carry them faster and farther than even lesser horses.

Then one day they found themselves at the Falari border. Though many days had passed, the first part of their journey passed far quicker than Alena expected. When they reached the border, marked by a small stream, she dropped into a soulwalk, curious if the Falari had put in place any defenses similar to those of the Etari. She sensed nothing. The border was nothing more than an imaginary line dividing the two lands. Alena and her group left the horses in the care of the Etari who had accompanied them this far. From here on, they traveled alone.

They shouldered their packs and crossed the border.

The experience was something of a disappointment. Alena had hoped for some difference she could point to, something that separated Falar from the empire where they had crossed. But there was nothing. Less than a league away from the stream rose foothills that would very soon become the mountains that grew larger with every step.

After two days on foot Alena finally broke and asked the question that had tormented her endlessly the past weeks. She approached her brother and walked by his side. Toren took the hint well enough and left them alone, falling back to allow them their privacy.

Alena didn't know how to broach the subject politely, so she jumped in instead. "Why are you here, Jace?"

A flicker of annoyance passed over his face. She had asked this question before. "Because of you."

She persisted. His rote answer didn't satisfy her curiosity. "But really, why? I can understand escorting me to the Etari border, and maybe even all the way to Cardon, but I don't understand why you persist even into Falar. You're leaving so much behind. Don't you worry that nothing will be there for you when you return? That your reputation will have diminished and you won't have the opportunities that you worked so hard for?"

He smiled. "Do you worry about these things?"

"Of course I do! I love you, and I'm grateful for your escort, but you have so much to lose. I don't want you to lose even more on my account."

Jace shrugged again, and for a moment Alena felt her own annoyance. How could her younger brother be so flippant about these things? He may act a fool, but he had to realize what was at stake. He was an intelligent young man, despite all the evidence he created to contradict that fact.

That thought led to another. Her brother *was* indifferent, but her mistake was in thinking that his indifference was born from a lack of consideration.

She should know him better than that. Her brother was intelligent, and he *did* think through his decisions. If there was a lack of understanding, it was on her part.

"Will you tell me what you're thinking?" When he still appeared hesitant, she went further. "I don't understand your choice, and I want to understand."

He considered, nodded, then took a moment to gather his thoughts. "Your concerns about the future are not mine. Opportunities will come and go. Reputation grows and fades. But some relationships matter more. Keeping you safe matters more to me than my own rise in the ranks or the lieutenant governorship."

"I can protect myself," Alena pointed out. She didn't need her younger brother to keep her safe.

Jace smiled at that. "Yes, you can. I don't dispute that. But," he gestured to the small mountain trail they were following, rising higher and higher into a foreign land, "you do have a tendency to put yourself in situations in which some extra company could be helpful."

She conceded the point and he continued.

"Protecting you is the reason I'm here, but there's more." He paused. "I believe that all of this is far more serious than anything happening in Landow. These gates of yours are tied to everything, and I believe that if I truly wish to serve the empire, the place where I can do the best is by your side. Remember, I have some glimpse of what the Lolani want. Kye showed me."

Truthfully, Alena had forgotten. Her brother had been carefully misled by Kye while she had been in Etar. Kye's misdirection hadn't been compulsion, at least not through the use of a mental affinity, but Jace had willingly served in the first attempt to bring the Lolani armies into the empire.

It raised another, more uncomfortable question. She also believed that her brother was a good man and yet had almost done unspeakable evil. In all their years reunited she had never asked the question. Perhaps she'd been too scared of the answer. "Why did you help him?"

"I was angry," he began. "I had learned that you were a criminal, and because of that I believed that criminals and the weak were a rot destroying the empire. Kye convinced me. He believed in strength and the power it bestows. It is, as near as I can tell, the Lolani way. The weak are winnowed out and the strong survive to create a society that is far superior to what the empire offers. Kye believed, and I believed him."

Alena heard the shame in his voice, but also acceptance. He knew that he had made a mistake.

"Are you doing this because you feel guilty?"

Jace pursed his lips. "I cannot say that guilt isn't a part of it, but I do not think it is what compels me."

Alena stepped closer to her brother until their arms were practically bumping. She reached out and grabbed his hand. "For what it's worth, thank you."

He gripped her hand more tightly, then let it go. They walked on in silence for a time. Then, he suddenly stopped, reaching out to hold her back.

"What?" Alena asked.

"The Falari," Jace said. "I think they found us."

29

After a full day of introductions, tours, and welcomes, Brandt decided that if Hanns ever again invited him to become an imperial guard, he would run the other way. Guarding Regar mixed mind-numbing tedium with bursts of sheer panic.

The tedium grew because even in Falar, official greetings took too long, involved too many conversations, and meant absolutely nothing. But because those greetings involved too many people in spaces with too many dark corners, Brandt feared constantly for Regar's safety. He couldn't imagine a life filled with days like today. Guarding royalty might be an honor, but it also seemed like a shortcut to madness.

Beside him, Ana's demeanor reflected similar thoughts. Only when they stuffed Regar safe into quarters that would require an army to breach did either of them relax. They went to their own quarters, not far from Regar's, and collapsed into the bed, staring up at the ceiling, exhausted but unable to sleep.

Shortly thereafter, a knock on their door brought them again to their feet. They relaxed when they saw who it was.

Leana stood at their door and invited them for a drink with her and Ren. Brandt accepted. Ana begged off, claiming that the only company she wanted tonight was that of a soft bed. Brandt kissed Ana goodnight and closed the door softly behind him.

Their route took them up stairway after stairway, climbing higher until they reached an elevation where Brandt could see most of the valley. He wasn't sure he'd ever worked harder in his life for a drink. He arrived at the tavern out of breath, but the view gave meaning to his exhaustion.

Ren waited for them. He had saved them a table, though the act appeared unnecessary. Only a few patrons graced the establishment, but they all looked dangerous. They weren't ruffians, by any means. They sipped at drinks as they spoke quietly to one another. But Brandt noticed their studious glances, the gazes that never rested long in one place. Each of the warriors radiated a dangerous calm.

The effect was enhanced by the tavern itself. Weapons served as the wall decor, several of them notched from frequent use. Brandt's entrance, accompanied by Leana, drew a handful of respectful nods.

A sense of belonging settled over Brandt. He never felt more comfortable than when he was in the presence of competent warriors. And this tavern held nothing but.

Ren's smile grew as he watched Brandt's reactions. "I thought you might appreciate it here."

"What is this?"

"It's run by a former Senki for one of the elder warleaders. When he fell to age, he started his third life as the owner here. He caters to warriors who seek companionship and no quarrel. It attracts many strong fighters who are passing through Faldun."

"Thank you for introducing me."

Before long, Brandt had lost count of the number of mugs he'd finished. It couldn't have been more than five or six, but he couldn't remember, despite his best efforts.

On the road, they had imbibed whenever Leana could get her hands on alcohol, a skill in which she showed remarkable competence. The companionship of the other Senkis led Brandt to drinking more than he had in the past. That wasn't saying much—since joining the monasteries, he'd barely consumed any. He didn't care much one way or the other about the drink, but he enjoyed the nightly conversations with the other warriors. They reminded him of his evenings with his wolfblades long ago.

"You said the owner was on his 'third life' when I came in," Brandt said. "What does that mean?"

"We live three lives before we go to the gate," Leana answered, her words slurred just a little. She'd had more to drink than either of the others, finishing two mugs for every one of Brandt's. "Not everyone gets all three, of course. But there is the life of training to become a warrior, the life of the warrior, and the life that comes after."

"What marks the transitions?"

Ren answered. "The transition from the first life to the second is clear enough. Sometime between the ages of twelve and sixteen the trials are offered to children. Passage of those trials marks the beginning of the second life and the right to start a family. The move from the second life to the third varies more widely. Sometimes it is due to injury. For others it is age, and yet for others it is usefulness. In his case," Ren gestured to the massive owner of the tavern, "his role in his party was to draw an enormous bow. When he could no longer reliably draw and aim the bow, he passed his duty on to another and began his third life."

Leana chimed in. "Some are eager to begin a third life and do so when they are younger, perhaps in their thirties. But such choices are frowned upon and uncommon."

As often happened during such explanations, Brandt found himself leaning forward as he listened.

Another round found its way to their table, but Brandt insisted it be the last. His head was already pleasantly fuzzy, and he didn't dare go further while in Faldun. It was easy, among Ren and Leana, to forget where he was and why he was here.

"When will Regar speak to the elders?" Brandt asked.

"Soon," Ren answered. "Most likely in the next day or two. As much as the elders might want to delay, I do not think they will risk it."

"Why do you say that?"

"Tensions in the city, and throughout the land, are high. Though they might not wish to make a decision, I believe they recognize the time has come. Delay only invites disaster."

"Disaster?"

Ren nodded, his look serious. "Conflicts between war parties have increased the last few years." He made a gesture to reassure Brandt. "There's always some in-fighting. But recently, it's become more violent, and more frequent." Ren's face went dark with memory.

Leana continued. "Most fighting between war parties happens when scouts run across one another. Warrior against warrior. But this spring, one war party killed three whole families of another war party on a raid. Years ago, such an act would have brought retribution down on the offending war party. This spring it brought none. The warleaders were too worried it would lead to outright civil war."

"All because some war parties seek peace with the empire?"

Ren nodded. "It's a simplification, but yes. Those of us who seek peace often believe some of our traditions and ways are outdated. Those who disagree believe it is our traditions that made us who we are, and that abandoning them means disaster. It's dozens of small disagreements that have found their focus in this single issue."

"And Regar's visit is the center of this now."

"It is," Ren said. "It's surprising the warleaders opposed to us haven't done more to stop our progress. They plan something, but I haven't heard even a whisper of what it might be, which concerns me."

Brandt sat up straighter, though the effort didn't come easy. "Is Regar safe?"

Leana laughed. "Regar has never been safe. But the expected attacks haven't come."

"I don't understand. The road here seemed peaceful."

Ren grimaced. "Too peaceful. We should have been attacked at least twice passing through land controlled by hostile war parties."

"Even with all those who accompanied us?"

Ren chuckled, the sound grim. "Have you ever known a Falari war party to turn around because they were outnumbered?"

Brandt acknowledged the point.

Ren put the subject to rest. "We don't know why our approach was as easy as it was. It may be they lie in wait here, where it is more difficult to protect Regar. Assassination isn't common, but they might resort to such means if they feel desperate. But I fear their plan is even more devious."

The end of that conversation left a bitter taste in Brandt's mouth.

Eventually, though, the talk turned to other, lighter matters. They finished their final round and remained for a while longer, allowing the effects of the drink to fade before beginning their return journey. Leana pointed out that traveling up and down hundreds of stairs while unsteady might not be the wisest course of action.

When they felt confident in their abilities, they left together. Ren and Leana insisted on escorting Brandt back to his quarters, even though he was reasonably certain he could find them without help.

As they neared Brandt's quarters they ran into imperial guards. Both Ren and Leana appeared uncomfortable with the guards' presence, so Brandt informed them he could make it the rest of the way on his own. After their farewells, Brandt continued on, uncontested by the guards.

He found the reason for their expanded presence soon enough. Regar stood on a balcony overlooking the valley. Brandt approached and looked out with him.

"You've been drinking," Regar observed, no judgment in his voice.

"Ren and Leana introduced me to a new tavern, one where warriors gather."

"Sounds nice."

Completely sober, Brandt wasn't sure he would have had the courage to ask, but at the moment, the question seemed pertinent. "You and your father knew what this visit would mean to the Falari, didn't you?"

Regar's smile was grim. "My father is an exceedingly clever man."

"You sound bitter."

Regar sighed. "Perhaps." He paused and turned to Brandt. "Tell me, what do you think of the Falari?"

Again, had Brandt been sober his answer might have been more reserved. "I admire their focus. Now, more than ever, I understand why the empire never conquered Falar."

Regar nodded. "I feel the same."

"Even after your capture?"

"Especially then. I'd been taken by surprise, and didn't fight well against their ambush. So when I was taken, those first few days were hard."

Brandt thought of the victims the Falari had left behind. His imagination easily filled in the sufferings Regar had endured.

"One day," Regar continued, "they threw me in a circle with another captured warrior. An empire soldier. I fought and I killed the man with my bare hands."

Regar didn't need to say any more about that either. Killing with a bow was easier than killing with a sword, and even that was easier than killing with bare hands. Even veterans shied away from such killing. To have it be one of your own allies, Brandt didn't even want to contemplate the horror.

"I threw up afterward," Regar said, his eyes staring off at a memory long in his past. "But when the time came to do it again, I did. And it was easier. And they treated me better. I learned from the Falari, and eventually challenged them to the trials to leave. Grappling, sword, and board. I won all three."

"And that's how you escaped?"

"I didn't escape," Regar answered. "After I won the trials, a war party escorted me to the border."

"That why your father knew you'd have the best chance with the Falari."

Regar's laugh was sharp and bitter, almost a cough. "I'm the only one who has *any* chance with them. My father and Olen are obsessed with knowledge and philosophy. Neither of them understands the value of struggling for what matters, or the strength that results from overcoming adversity."

Brandt frowned. "Governor Kye said something similar outside Landow. He believed he acted in the empire's interest. He wanted it to suffer so it would become strong."

"Kye was a fool, but I sympathize with some of his thoughts. The empire is weaker than it once was. I've tried to suggest changes to my father and to Olen, but both are so rooted in what Anders I commanded there's little opportunity to make changes." Regar let out a long, slow breath. "I believe we can learn from the Falari, and the Etari, and even the Lolani. But we need to abandon the ways that have locked us in place."

"Just like Ren believes the Falari must do."

Regar smiled at that, but Brandt didn't understand why. "We all reflect one another, don't we?"

Brandt didn't know what to say to that, but Regar turned aside and walked back to his quarters.

Brandt knew he shouldn't ask the question, but he felt closer to Regar than before, and he'd never have a better opportunity. "How did you surpass the cost, back when we were first ambushed?"

Regar stopped and turned back to Brandt. "I didn't." He patted his stomach. "After I was captured, my father insisted that both Olen and I have gatestones like the Etari." He turned and kept walking, calling over his shoulder, "It's like I said. Learning from others will make us stronger."

Brandt remained on the balcony a while longer. Something about Regar's tone, or the words he spoke, bothered him. But he couldn't put his finger on why. After a few moments, he pushed the thoughts aside. He had to believe that if they had a chance at succeeding, it lay with Regar.

30

"How do you know?" Alena asked. They kept walking, not wanting to give away their knowledge of the ambush.

"Just a feeling," Jace answered. "Someone is watching us."

Jace stopped, reaching for his waterskin. Toren joined them. His eyes studied the landscape carefully. "I believe we are being watched," the Etari whispered.

Jace gave Alena a knowing look.

Alena glanced between the two men, then tried to see what they saw as she took a sip from the offered waterskin. She saw nothing that made her wary. As far as she was concerned, they were alone.

But she didn't doubt her brother or Toren.

"Where?" Alena asked.

Jace shook his head. "Not sure. Could a soulwalk reveal them?"

Alena bit her lower lip. She'd never considered that use of her ability. "Perhaps. It'll take a few moments."

"Fine. We'll pretend to take a longer break." He pointed

to a stone with a flat top about ten paces in front of them. "There's a good place to rest."

When Alena reached the rock she sat on it, the stone hard but the seat itself welcome. They'd been walking throughout the day, and although Alena was in good condition, she could feel the effects of the elevation. If it came to a fight, she wouldn't be as fast as she'd like.

Jace and Toren took up position on either side of her. They sipped from waterskins and spoke about the view. Alena lay back against the rock and closed her eyes, pretending she was resting.

She dropped into the soulwalk, unveiling the web of life around her. Picking out Toren and Jace was simple enough, but finding the ambush proved difficult.

There was only so much information a mind could understand, which limited the distance she could travel the web of interconnectedness. Typically she couldn't sense a person's spirit more than thirty paces away. But she'd been practicing, learning how to filter out the information to allow her understanding to expand. Every blade of grass connected to the web of life, but she hardly cared about them.

Alena breathed deeply and evenly. Picking out a human from the web wasn't as simple as looking at two different paintings of vastly separate creatures. The differences between a blade of grass and a human, so far as soulwalking revealed, were subtle.

In time she found a human, and then another. The distance was difficult to judge. Soulwalking distance was different than physical distance. But the ambushers were a ways away, and at a higher elevation.

She sat up and opened her eyes, looking for places her sense of the humans might have come from. Up ahead she saw several outcroppings of rock that would serve as excellent cover. She described the one she thought hid the ambush, careful not to stare.

"How certain are you?" Jace asked.

"A little."

Jace looked to Toren. "Thoughts?"

"The ambush we expect is better than the one we don't. If we go around, they'll likely try again, and with more caution."

Jace nodded.

She could almost see him planning their next moves. In times like these, his leadership came to the fore. Alena smiled as he effortlessly assumed command of the trio. "I'll stay close to Alena. They'll attack with bow first, and with any luck I can deflect or dodge any that get close. Toren, we'll rely on your stones to counter them."

Toren signed his agreement, and Jace had now learned enough of the sign language to understand.

"Our destination is the outcropping below the path. Alena can take cover there while we attempt to fend off the ambush. Alena, did you get any sense of how many there were?"

She shook her head. "At least two, but there could be more. I barely sensed them."

"Excellent." The sarcasm dripped from his voice.

They stoppered their waterskins and continued. Toren reached into the pouch at his hip and withdrew a few stones. He clutched them in his hand, not setting them spinning yet. Once he did, those stones would be their best defense against a Falari attack.

The closer they came to the outcroppings, the more certain she was of her guess. Not because of her soulwalking, but because the boulders were an ideal place for an ambush. The rocks above them provided ample cover, and the path they walked had none for almost fifty paces.

Though she expected the attack, her heart still skipped a beat when a line of Falari archers rose like ghosts from their hiding spots, arrows trained on them.

Alena possessed no defense against archers, so she dove to the ground as arrows sliced the air overhead. Jace side-stepped two. He took a step forward, then froze when another set of archers appeared from the outcropping of rocks Jace had identified as their destination.

Like Jace, Toren stood his ground. Alena didn't see him launch the stone, but she heard a cry from above. He'd at least injured one of the Falari attackers.

Alena swore. There were too many opponents for their small group to survive.

Her reaction was instinctive. She dropped from the physical world into a soulwalk.

Alena had no plan. But she couldn't defend herself against the nearly dozen archers in any other way.

Soulwalking was where her true power lay.

Time altered, the space between her heartbeats extended.

She darted along the threads that connected her to one of the archers above.

In a moment she understood the archer. The third son of a well-respected family, she saw the ways in which he tried to prove himself. He wanted to become as well-regarded as his oldest sister.

Alena almost smiled. The parallels to Jace's life were impossible not to see.

But no obvious path of compulsion appeared. The technique only worked if there was something to latch onto, some unspoken desire that she could form into an obsession. This young Falari was filled with nothing but righteous vengeance and patriotic duty to defend his home from invaders. He possessed no secret that aided her.

Alena didn't allow the panic creeping into her mind a foothold. In this world, she still had time.

The next Falari she examined had a much richer backstory. She was a young woman, and she possessed a tight bond with one of the Falari in the outcropping in front of Alena's party.

And it wasn't a bond of friendship.

The Falari woman had been wronged by a woman in the other group. Alena saw flashes of a young man and a long friendship broken.

Alena couldn't have asked for better material to work with.

Alena found the necessary memories and brought them to the front of the Falari archer's mind, intertwined with other thoughts.

She betrayed me.

Is my friendship worth so little?

No one will know. It was in battle.

Alena pushed energy into the traitorous thoughts, making them all-consuming, then rode the woman's soul as she turned her bow onto the Falari in the lower outcropping. The shot was open, the Falari unconcerned about betrayal from their own war party.

Alena knew the thoughts she'd inserted didn't make sense, but they didn't have to. Emotions alone mattered, and the justifications came later. Such was always the way of humans, though they didn't realize it.

She only held onto the soulwalk long enough to make sure the shot was released.

Then she returned to the physical world, connecting to

the gatestone near her navel. Her strongest affinity, by far, was mental. But second was air. She summoned a gust as a second volley of arrows was launched at them.

Alena put everything into her affinity, but the effect was pitifully weak. One arrow embedded itself in the dirt next to her, its flight barely affected.

But then confusion fell upon the Falari.

The woman Alena soulwalked into might have believed no one would notice, but that couldn't be further from the truth. The Falari realized what had happened in a moment, though they knew not the reason why.

From the outcropping in front of them came a strangled cry of grief, and Alena saw a young man fall to his knees.

In the next heartbeat the same young man stood tall, an arrow nocked and aimed at the outcropping above Alena.

He released, and Alena knew their moment had come. "Follow me!" she yelled.

She made herself light and dashed toward the outcropping ahead of them. A single arrow passed behind her, but the attention of the attackers had been torn.

Alena launched herself at an archer, both feet aimed at his unprotected chest.

She wasn't nearly the martial artist her brother was, but she wasn't completely useless, either. Her kick landed solidly, knocking the archer back into a sharp boulder behind him.

Alena landed on her side, groaning as sharp rocks cut her hip. She looked up to see another archer bringing his drawn bow down so the arrowhead was aimed at her chest. At this distance she had no hope of evasion.

Then Jace was there, his sword cutting through the drawn arrow.

Alena couldn't convince her body to move. Jace drew

every bit of her attention, his strength finally brought to bear against an enemy he could fight.

His sword was an extension of his hand, and when it moved it brought death with it.

Alena almost felt sorry for the archers. At a distance, they'd had Jace at a disadvantage. But up close, he finished them in two heartbeats, done before the first body had even hit the ground.

She adored her younger brother.

But she felt a fear of him, too. A fear she hadn't felt for years.

An arrow skipping off a boulder beside her focused her attention on their current predicament.

Where was Toren?

Alena forced herself to hands and knees, keeping her body behind a boulder. Her eyes found Toren.

He had not followed the siblings, but instead stood his ground. Focused on him, Alena saw the spinning stones before he launched them into the outcropping above.

Toren's assault was methodical. He launched whenever he saw any exposed Falari. By himself, he had pinned down the rest of the ambushers.

Jace realized the same, and a moment later he was sprinting up the hill. Alena felt a small sense of satisfaction that she was still faster than her brother, but that satisfaction vanished when his sword went to work.

Alena turned her eyes away from the scene that followed. As soon as her brother safely reached the last of the Falari, the outcome was never in doubt, and she struggled to reconcile the warrior her brother was with the boy he had been. Jace had always loved to fight, but there had been something endearing about it when he'd been a boy.

His skill held no such attraction for her anymore.

Her eyes traveled to the Falari who had fallen among this outcropping. There were four men and two women, but only one of the dead had an arrow through her chest.

Alena recognized her.

Soulwalking unveiled memories, and those memories carried an emotional weight.

Alena's first reaction when she saw the body was a cold satisfaction. The woman had betrayed her and earned her just reward.

She grimaced.

No. This woman had never wronged her. Those thoughts weren't Alena's, but a nameless Falari warrior now falling to her brother's blade, or to Toren's stones.

A chill settled over her bones, causing her to shiver. Who was she to judge Jace for his ability? He'd met bow with sword, and on this occasion had emerged triumphant. But there was an honor, at least, to that. Alena might not have released the arrow, but she'd killed this woman all the same.

And she'd done it through the hands of a former friend.

Jace wasn't the monster here.

She was.

31

Three long days passed without incident. Regar met with a constant stream of guests, but rarely left his quarters to do so. It left Brandt and Ana with little to do.

They didn't leave their own rooms much. Food was provided for them and neither felt particularly comfortable wandering Faldun on their own. They spent most of their time in bed, making up for the time lost on the road.

As pleasant as the time was, Brandt welcomed the eventual knock against their door. He rose and answered, his hand at his sword. Ren stood framed in their doorway, the early afternoon sun bright in the valley beyond. He appeared solemn. "It's time."

"The elders?"

"They request your presence as well."

Brandt looked down at his clothes. They were those he had traveled in, and although they'd been washed, they were still tattered and well-worn. "Am I presentable?"

A hint of a smile played across Ren's face. "The elders

will not judge you based on your clothing. Of that, you can rest easy."

"May I carry my sword?"

Ren frowned. "Of course. Why would you not?"

Brandt smiled. "If there is ever true peace between our lands, Ren, I'll have to introduce you to imperial customs."

"I am not certain such an education would be enjoyable."

Brandt and Ana followed Ren through the city. Brandt kept his eyes moving, searching rooftops, stairs, and corners for potential assassins. Faldun was an architectural wonder, but its design also made it nearly impossible to spot an ambush.

Ren shared the same concern. Brandt saw it in the careful step of his friend.

They eventually turned into a narrow hallway carved deep into the mountain. Guards stood outside. Torches, placed at long intervals, lit the way. Ren relaxed once they were in the hall.

They followed the hallway into the mountain, eventually coming to a branching path. Ren walked the tunnels with easy familiarity, and Brandt found some of the warrior's relaxation creeping into his own posture. The tunnel itself drew his attention, and in time, he asked Ren to pause for a moment so he could examine the walls more carefully.

He and Ana ran their hands along the walls. Script decorated the stone, carved with a precision no chisel could achieve. It almost looked as though the stone had been melted away by a calligrapher's brush. "Does this look like the same script?" he asked.

Ana knew he referred to the caves outside Landow. She

squinted. "It does, but that's no surprise. Who else could have built these?"

Brandt turned to Ren. "Can you read these?"

Ren shook his head. "It is the language of those who came before. The study of such script is forbidden."

The warrior looked more uncomfortable than Brandt had ever seen him.

Out of sympathy, Brandt motioned for them to continue. "Why?"

"Some knowledge is better left buried. It is why none but elders and their guests are allowed in these tunnels."

Ren took them through several more turns, straining Brandt's memory. He remained certain he could leave this place on his own, but the task became more challenging with every turn.

The air here was cold and damp, the torches doing little to disguise how deep under the mountain they traveled. In places, holes brought in fresh air, though Brandt could see no light through them.

Their journey ended in a large antechamber, perhaps two dozen paces wide. Torches ringed the circular room, and Brandt was surprised to find Regar already there.

If Regar was nervous, it didn't show on his face. He greeted Brandt and Ana warmly. "Were you summoned, as well?"

"I was," Brandt replied. "To what end, I'm not certain."

"You are my Senki. Your word will carry nearly as much weight as my own in there."

Brandt looked to Ren, who confirmed the prince's statement.

"What do I say?" Brandt asked.

"The truth," Regar replied. "The burden is still mine, Brandt. You are just a tool they will use to judge me by."

Brandt wasn't sure he appreciated the label, but before he could complain, a woman summoned the prince.

"Fight well," Brandt said.

"Always," said Regar.

With that, Regar stepped into the next room, leaving Brandt and Ana with little to do. Brandt felt woefully under-prepared for the task he was now called for. "What is it I'm expected to do in there?" he asked Ren.

"Obey your warleader. Tell the truth. Do not think of this as some battle that must be won, Brandt. That will happen only among the elders. But they see with wisdom. Simply be present as you are and leave the rest to them."

"You hold your elders in high regard."

"The highest. The individuals each possess strengths and weaknesses, as do we all, but there is a higher wisdom that emerges from this chamber. They have guided us well for hundreds of years, and they have earned our trust."

Brandt looked around the antechamber, clearly worked with a skill beyond the ability of the current Falari masons. Beyond the ability of all living masons. He thought out loud. "I do not understand, Ren. Your elders meet in this space, made by those that came before, yet you do not permit the study of those same people. Why not?"

"You have no such prohibition?"

"Quite the opposite. Our first emperor destroyed as much history as he could, so little is known of the times before the rise of our empire. Our current emperor desperately searches for clues from the past."

This information seemed to trouble Ren. "Our legends tell us that those that came before possessed an incredible power. A strength that brought them untold wealth and ease, but also attracted powerful enemies. It is said their power almost broke the world. Our elders meet in these chambers to remember what is possible, and to avoid that same outcome."

"They are frightened of the power of those that came before?"

"Very. Are you not?"

Brandt shook his head. "Think of the good that could be done with abilities like these." He gestured to the room.

"Good easily matched by the possible harm." Ren stepped closer to Brandt. "Tell me, if that power was offered to you, would you accept it?"

"I would."

Ren gave him a sad smile. "Then I am sorry to say that I hope such power is never offered to you."

Ren turned away, ending the conversation. Brandt watched him make his retreat, feeling more like a foreigner than ever before.

In his confusion, he barely noticed as the door opened and Regar stepped out. Brandt couldn't tell a thing from the look on his face. "Your turn," the prince said.

Brandt stepped through the door to the chamber, then froze as he looked upon the expansive space. Though he'd had no particular reason, he'd expected the chamber of the elders to be small. Instead, it was far larger than any underground space they'd passed on the way here. Like the antechamber, it was a perfect circle, except the ceiling was three times his height.

But the size wasn't all that caught his attention. Both the floor and ceiling were covered in the symbols Brandt now recognized as the language of those that came before. The ones above glowed with an otherworldly blue light that reminded Brandt a little of the glow of the gates. An involuntary shudder ran through him. The impossible light was all that lit the space—no warm or familiar torchlight flickered here.

Standing around the edge of the circle were dozens of men and women, all well older than Brandt. The elders of the Falari. He'd only expected a handful, but to see so many gave him pause. Each stood on a smaller circle carved with a single symbol. At times, light flickered underneath their feet, the symbols sputtering light in patterns of timing and color Brandt couldn't comprehend.

Though he couldn't say why, this room *felt* different, too. The air lacked the chilly, damp feeling from the tunnels. It felt like a spring day, warm and full of the promise of new life.

How he'd drawn that comparison so far under the stone, Brandt couldn't say.

The door closed behind him, leaving him alone with the elders.

Brandt searched for the leader, but found no one that stood out. He guessed there were over sixty people in the room, but nothing he could see identified anyone as special among them.

A woman wearing dark robes gestured for Brandt to step toward the center of the room. "Please stand within the center of one of the circles you see." Her voice was soft, but still it sounded like she stood right next to him.

He followed instructions, finding seven circles near the center of the room. Each possessed the same symbol as the circles the elders stood on. What power was at play in this room?

Unfortunately, he'd come too far to have much choice in the matter. He stepped into the circle, relaxing when nothing happened.

"Thank you for speaking," a voice said. Again, it was soft,

as though spoken directly in front of him. But no one stood within fifteen paces of him. He couldn't tell who had greeted him.

"I am honored to be here." Brandt didn't know much of Falari customs, but politeness was never wasted.

"What is your purpose here?"

Brandt wasn't sure if they meant him, specifically, or their larger task. He chose to take the question literally. "I'm here to protect Prince Regar on his journey."

"And what is Prince Regar's purpose?"

Brandt considered his response carefully. He didn't dare say their purpose was to acquire the gate for the emperor. Now he understood just how volatile a subject that would be. But he also had no wish to lie. "He seeks your aid in fighting an enemy who threatens all our lands."

His words carried to every ear in the room. Though he spoke as to someone in front of him, there were no calls for him to raise his voice. The forces in this room unsettled him. He glanced down, seeing the symbols he stood upon flickering in unreadable patterns, just like those underneath the elders.

"What, specifically, does Prince Regar seek?"

He supposed it would always come to this. He hoped for the best. "Prince Regar seeks the gate on behalf of Anders VI."

"And what would Anders VI do with our gate?"

"Fight the invaders."

"There have been no Lolani at our borders, and what do we care about the fall of the empire?"

This was the first voice that spoke with emotion. The others had been curious, perhaps, but this one had an agenda.

Ren's advice had been to speak truthfully. So Brandt

spoke as the soldier he'd once been. "If the empire falls, it will only be a matter of time until you do as well."

"A bold claim. We've resisted the empire for this long. Why not a foreign invader?"

"With respect, elders, this is a force unlike any you've encountered before. Their warriors are skilled, relentless, and their affinities defy comprehension. I've fought both your warriors and the Lolani, and the Lolani frighten me more."

He feared he'd spoken too freely, but no elder argued his point.

"You know that we do not control our gate, the way Anders VI controls his, and that we consider such control unwise?"

"I do."

"You know why?"

"You fear such power does not belong to us."

"What do you reply to that?"

"It is a wise precaution. Great strength requires great control. But the power exists, and our need is great. Who among you would refuse to use a bow if Faldun was invaded? The gates are a tool. A tool of incredible ability. If they can save lives, I believe they must be used."

There was a pause, long enough for Brandt to worry he'd said too much.

"You speak well. Regar's Senki displays quality, and some of our own have voiced similar arguments. Answer this, then: why should we not just seize control ourselves and aid your emperor in that way?"

Brandt wished for an enemy with a sword, now more than ever before. "I confess that my answer is but a guess. My own knowledge of the gates is imperfect. But I do not believe such aid will prevail. Anders VI already controls two gates and could not stand directly against the queen. If any Falari attempted to give aid with only one gate, they would fall. One does not send two novice swords against a master. One sends another master."

Brandt wiped a bead of sweat from his brow. This was not his battlefield.

"You put a great deal of trust in your ruler. Such is commendable for a soldier, but is such trust wise? Should we trust a foreign emperor with such power?"

"I do not know him well," Brandt admitted, "but in my interactions I have always found him to be a man of honor. I trust him."

"And yet he oppresses your people with ruthless efficiency."

Brandt frowned. "I don't understand."

"Do you not have many slaves?"

"No." Brandt was confused. The earlier line of questioning had been difficult enough, but this caught him unaware.

"Do you not have wage-earners?"

"We have those, but they are paid for their work."

"And if they do not work?"

"The punishment is death."

"Do these wage-earners have the time and freedom to pursue their own skills and interests?"

Brandt's own parents had been wage-earners. He remembered nights when they came home exhausted from the menial work of the day. Watching them suffer in silence had been one of his primary reasons for joining the army. His parents had earned enough to keep a roof over their heads and food on the table, but nothing else.

"No."

"Is dissent permitted within your empire?"

Brandt shook his head. Private dissent was fine, and Brandt knew from his personal time with Hanns that the emperor didn't mind criticism personally, but it couldn't be tolerated in public. That was how rebellion spread.

"So the consequence of disobedience is death, and they do not have the freedom to explore other paths, and they aren't even allowed to speak out about their condition?"

"No." The confession felt like a blow to the stomach.

"So how is that not slavery?"

Brandt admitted he had no answer to the question. He knew the Falari perspective was wrong, but he couldn't explain why.

"So again we ask: You would have us trust a man who enslaves his own people?"

Brandt had never been called on to defend the empire in this way. "Our people are fed and sheltered. Crime is punished, and most everyone lives in safety. Is that not desirable?"

The elders didn't answer Brandt's question. Instead, the conversation shifted once again. "If we do offer this power to your emperor, will he return it?"

Brandt almost answered "Yes" without thinking. But then he considered the question. Would Hanns return that much power? He could be the emperor who finally unified the continent. And what if the power wasn't enough? Perhaps he needed the fourth in Etar.

Brandt didn't know the answer. The Falari had been a thorn in the empire's side for almost as long as the empire had existed. Hanns was honorable, but his life was dedicated to the empire as a whole. Would he give up such a dangerous weapon once he possessed it?

Still, Brandt couldn't say as much here. If the elders

didn't think Hanns would return the gate, why would they part with it? "I believe he will, yes."

Silence greeted his answer.

Brandt almost said more, then held his tongue. He waited expectantly for the next question.

Instead, the door opened and Ren stepped in. Without being asked, he stepped to the center and stood in a circle next to Brandt.

"Brandt, if we offered the gate to you, would you accept it?"

He had thought no further questions could surprise him, but he'd been wrong. He imagined what he could accomplish with the gate at his command. Perhaps that was the breakthrough he needed to finally understand how to surpass the cost, even without the gate.

But he thought of the words he'd just spoken to the Falari elders. The world didn't need another novice. They needed Hanns in control of all the gates. Perhaps that future frightened Alena, but it was necessary. "No."

The next question came quickly. "Ren, do vouch for this Senki? Would you fight by his side and trust your life to his skill and loyalty?"

Ren studied Brandt for a moment, his expression unreadable. Then he looked away. "I do, and I would."

Brandt thrust out his chest at that, a smile on his face.

Silence settled once again within the chamber. Then, "Very well. You both are dismissed."

The two warriors left the room together, Brandt confused by the sudden conclusion of the interview. The cold tunnels welcomed them, and Ana looked worried enough to explode. Regar was nowhere to be seen.

"What happened?" she asked. "Did they decide?"

"No," Ren answered. "But Brandt lied to them."

Brandt almost argued, then stopped. He'd only been uncertain about his answer regarding Hanns returning the gate. And that had been before Ren arrived. "How did you know that?"

"The symbols on the floor. Their pattern indicates a person's mental state, as well as a truth or a lie. It is why the elders meet there."

Brandt's stomach sank, but he was still confused. "But how do you know?"

"I was there," Ren said, as though he was explaining what should be obvious. Brandt didn't hear any accusation in Ren's tone, just a sadness he couldn't explain. At his confusion, though, his friend continued, punching a verbal hole in Brandt.

"You want control of the gate for yourself."

32

Jace lost something the day they fought off the ambush. He still laughed and joked like he had before, but where his attitude had once been full of heart and personality, it now felt empty to Alena.

In the moments after the battle, Jace had practically glowed. Pride radiated from him.

Then he had hidden behind a boulder as he emptied the contents of his stomach.

Jace was no stranger to fighting, but he had never killed.

He didn't speak much the rest of that day, only returning to something resembling normal the next morning. But it was an act. One they all agreed to pretend was real.

Alena almost spoke to him about it. She knew something of the feelings that stormed inside of him. But when their eyes met she saw the warning there. For now, he wanted to carry this burden alone.

So they walked and pretended all was fine.

Alena gave Jace space, not meeting his eyes often, but sneaking glances at him whenever she thought he wasn't looking. He endured this because of her.

They encountered one other group as they walked, but it had been a small one, and they'd been as surprised as Toren, Jace, and Alena. Toren made quick work of the four archers, killing them while Jace and Alena hid behind trees as cover.

Alena couldn't bring herself to soulwalk again in the fight. She had tried, but her mind resisted, unable to find the familiar focus required. Jace was too wrapped up in his own problems to notice, but Toren seemed to guess at her problem.

Otherwise, they walked. Broken but together, they walked.

When they reached the high point of a pass, Alena found a rock to sit on and made it her new home.

After years of wandering the plains with the Etari, she'd thought she could walk for days without problem, but the altitude of the mountains and the shattered paths of Falar made that belief an obvious lie. Every ascent winded her, and every descent served only as a reminder she would soon have to regain the same elevation again. Someday, she swore she would introduce the Falari to the concept of flat ground. Perhaps they'd enjoy it.

Jace approached her rock, having been about thirty paces behind her. He passed her a waterskin, which she gratefully accepted. The sun seemed brighter here, burning unprotected skin. She drank deeply, enjoying the cold mountain water.

"You probably don't want to sit on the highest point like this," Jace observed.

Alena sighed. She knew that, of course. She was silhouetted from almost all directions, and spotters from leagues away might see her. But she wanted to enjoy the view, and they hadn't seen anyone for days. They walked through a part of Toren's maps that was strangely devoid of markings.

The Etari hadn't had any answer to their questions about the lack of information. The Etari didn't travel frequently to Falar, and much of the information in their maps was long out of date. But the maps indicated this was the quickest way to Faldun.

Alena believed this part of Falar was abandoned. It explained the absence of information on the maps, and it explained why they seemed alone in the wild. Jace accepted that Alena's theory might be true, but without stronger evidence, he still urged caution.

Which sometimes made her laugh. Her brother had never known caution a day in his life.

And she just wanted a moment to revel in another summit, an accomplishment in these high places.

"Just give me a moment," she said. "We haven't even seen footprints on the trail for leagues. There's no one here."

Jace shrugged, apparently deciding it was one battle he didn't care enough about to fight. Alena saw it as another way her brother had changed since the ambush. She was used to him fighting *every* fight. They hadn't seen footprints for some time, and even the path was difficult to follow, nearly overwhelmed with vegetation at lower elevations.

The question she would have given anything to know was why. Food was plentiful and the game easy to hunt. Fresh water abounded, and the scenery, she had to admit, was spectacular. There was no reason she could see for the area to be empty.

Toren came up shortly after Jace. "You shouldn't sit on the high point."

Jace laughed and Alena threw up her hands. She stoppered the waterskin and tossed it back to Jace.

"Fine. I'll rest somewhere lower." She stood up, but as she did, she saw something off in the distance, a glint of something that caught her eye. "Hold on."

She peered down the mountains, squinting in hopes of finding the reflection again. Toren, anticipating her need, handed her his looking glass. She brought it to her eye, then frowned.

She wasn't going to live this down.

Far below them she could make out the exterior of a small building, then another.

A town. The first of their journey.

And the peak she stood on was in full view of several of the roofs.

Alena almost scampered down the path, but she figured any damage was probably already done. Another few moments wouldn't hurt, and something about the town seemed off. She could only make out a small part of it, but as she watched she realized she didn't see any movement. No one worked outside. No one went from place to place. The houses themselves seemed like shells.

Additional details only reinforced her initial impressions. Holes looked like they had been punched in the buildings, and the curtains fluttering in the windows could more accurately be described as rags. "I think it's been abandoned."

She handed the looking glass to Toren, who made his own study. Toren offered it to Jace, who declined. "Abandoned or not," her brother said, "it's a risk we have no need of taking. We should go around."

Alena felt a pull toward the structures, but couldn't decide if it was her own curiosity threatening to get the better of her or something more. Jace had the right of it, though. Approaching was a risk, and one better left avoided if they could. Begrudgingly, she agreed.

Their short break complete, they shouldered their packs and once again continued their journey. Alena frequently glanced in the direction of the town, but as soon as they dropped from the peak it was hidden by the mountains that surrounded it.

They dropped back into a coniferous forest, tall pine trees towering overhead, their earthy scent filling Alena's breaths. Often her footsteps felt spongey underneath her feet, cushioned by layers upon layers of fallen pine needles.

Jace led them through this section, and Alena saw the moment he tensed. Less than a heartbeat later, his sword leaped into his hands, but after taking two steps, he hesitated and froze.

Alena's momentum carried the rest of the scene into view. A lone Falari woman stood on the path before them. She stood almost as tall as Jace, her defining feature being her long dark hair, draped loosely over her shoulders.

As near as Alena could tell, the woman wasn't prepared to fight. For one, her hair would get in her way. Two, she carried no sword and her bow was slung over her shoulder. Jace could kill her half a dozen times before she sent an arrow his way.

Something else prevented her concern from rising: a sense of peace emanated from the woman. Around her, they were safe.

Alena recognized the sensations, embarrassed it took her as long as it did. "Stop," she commanded.

The woman's eyes traveled from Jace to her. She didn't seem surprised Alena had noticed her mental affinity. With a small nod, the feeling of peace faded. She spoke, her imperial precise. “I’m sorry. But I didn’t want him to attack before we spoke.”

“Who are you, and how did you find us?”

“My name is Sheren. I saw you when you crested the peak a league back.”

Toren grunted, as close as he would come to saying “I told you so.” Alena glanced behind her to glare at him, seeing he had a rock spinning and ready to launch.

“But I’ve been waiting for you,” the woman admitted, her comment directed at Alena.

“Me? But why, and how?”

Sheren looked to both sides of the path, as though concerned there might be others listening in the trees. “I felt you coming. Your ability was easy to find.”

Jace stopped her. “The Falari don’t have affinities.”

Alena rolled her eyes. Apparently he’d already forgotten the sense of peace that had stilled his blade. Sheren possessed a well-developed mental affinity, at the very least.

Sheren didn’t take offense. “There are very few of us that practice the old ways. The abilities are considered curses by most. Which is why we find ourselves here.”

She gestured in the direction of the town they’d seen from the road. “I’ve come to invite you into my home.”

“Not a chance,” Jace said. “We should kill her and be on our way.”

Behind Alena, Toren had come closer, and he kept his voice low. “The town’s not abandoned, either. Not your best day.”

She fixed him with a glare that she hoped withered his soul, but the smile on his face didn’t dim in the slightest.

Sheren’s answer to Jace brought her head back around. “Our people have long been in conflict. I understand. But borders mean little to those I live with. We would welcome you with open arms. This, I promise."

Sheren's gaze once again focused on Alena. Alena felt the invitation within those eyes. She nodded her head, just slightly, and dropped into a soulwalk.

Sheren's presence was brighter than the others and she welcomed Alena's connection. Together, the two of them traveled in Sheren's mind back over the paths that led to the town. Alena admired the vivid nature of Sheren's memory, the plentiful details that indicated the attention the woman paid to her surroundings. Alena didn't even re-create her mother's kitchen in such detail.

In a moment they were in the ruins of the town. Thanks to Sheren's re-creation, Alena saw both the extent of the ruin and the affection with which Sheren looked upon the broken city. Decay wore at every building, but the woman felt safe here. This was home.

Alena saw glimpses of faces, ghostly images that came and went as Sheren mentally introduced her friends.

The Falari soulwalker wasn't showing her everything. Alena felt the absence, the deliberate withholding of information. If she desired, she could force the woman to reveal what she hid. Now that they were in contact, Alena could feel how much her own power surpassed that of the Falari.

But she held that action in reserve. If the need arose, a mental assault was possible, but Alena didn't believe the woman withheld the information out of malice. The wall around the information seemed more the result of nervousness or fear.

A moment later, they returned. Alena came out of the soulwalk, now certain of her actions. "We should follow her."

Jace wasn't so easily convinced. "Are you sure?"

"Mostly. I am convinced that she doesn't mean us harm."

"Good enough for me," Toren said.

Jace still hesitated. Alena didn't push him. It was difficult to choose between his desire to protect her and his trust of his sister's wisdom. She also knew how much he wanted to avoid conflict right now. Finally, he sheathed his sword. Alena knew he wouldn't relax, but she was grateful she didn't have to argue with him.

She stepped in front of Jace and approached Sheren. "What is it that you're hiding?"

Alena imagined Jace behind her, tensing up again. But he wouldn't go back on his decision now, which was why she had waited to ask Sheren the question.

Sheren grimaced, hesitated, then stared at the ground. "You should know one thing about the town before you arrive."

She kicked at the ground, seeming much younger than her age.

Then she took a deep breath and looked up at them.

"It's haunted by ghosts."

33

Brandt expected to wait in the antechamber until a decision was reached, but Ren laughed when he heard the idea. "The elders have the knowledge they seek. Now their debate will begin in earnest. You are welcome to wait, if you wish, but it is not expected, and starvation is a very real possibility."

"Just how long will it take?" Brandt asked.

"As long as is needed. For a decision of this importance, I expect we will not hear from the elders until tomorrow at the earliest."

Brandt grimaced. That was a long time to sit with the knowledge of his mistake, a long time to worry that his lies had doomed their endeavor.

They followed Ren up the passages that led them back to their rooms. Brandt felt Ana's stare burrowing into the back of his head the entire way. A fight was brewing, and Ana only waited until they had four walls surrounding them to contain her fury.

Ren must have sensed something of Ana's mood,

because he left them at the door to their quarters and retreated as though before a wave of advancing enemies. The swordsman was wise.

Less than a heartbeat passed between Brandt shutting the door and Ana turning on him. Her command came out low, as though worried that if she let any more emotion out she would explode. "Explain."

Brandt had known the question was coming, and he'd spent much of the walk back to their room working out his own confused feelings. "I believed I was telling the truth."

The explanation didn't satisfy her. She kept pacing, her stare locked on his face.

"The elders asked if I would accept the gate if they offered it to me. I said no. And I thought that was the truth. I don't want to interfere with Hanns and his plans."

"And yet Ren says that you lied."

Brandt collapsed into one of the chairs in the room, unwilling to meet Ana's stare. "I know."

Silence greeted his answer.

"I didn't think that I wanted the gate. I know how important it is to Hanns, and to the empire. If Hanns needs the gate to stop the queen, it has to go to him."

Ana caught the tone in his voice. After their years together, what could he hide from her? "But?"

"But I do think about what having that power would be like. Did you know that Kyla said that if we met on equal footing, I might be stronger than the emperor?"

Ana's pacing stopped. "And you think that if you were offered control of a gate, you might be able to do more than him, don't you?"

The idea sounded harsh when she said it. But the words were true. "It's occurred to me."

"Brandt!"

The confession halfway made, he stood back up. If he couldn't convince Ana, who would believe him? "It's something to consider, Ana! I like Hanns, and I believe he has the best intentions for the empire, but what if trusting him with these gates is a mistake? What if I could do more? We need to at least ask, right?"

"The emperor is in control of two gates, and he's spent his lifetime training in their use. Do you truly believe you could do more with one against the queen?"

"I don't know! But I can't say 'no' for sure, either."

Ana continued pacing, but she no longer stared at him. Brandt felt the need to keep explaining. "I'm not going to attempt to control the gate. Yes, I do wonder if we're taking the right action, but I also believe that Hanns does have the greatest opportunity to defeat the queen."

Ana groaned. "It's not about the gate, Brandt. Honestly, I don't much care who controls it right now."

"What—?" Brandt was too confused to even figure out how to finish the question.

"It's about you."

She stopped pacing and stood across from him. "First you wanted Alena to teach you how to soulwalk so you could use the deaths of others to advance your own power. Now you're thinking about what you could do with the abilities of a gate behind you. Don't you see?" When she saw the confusion on his face, she spelled it out for him. "Your desire to grow stronger is turning into a dangerous obsession."

"I'm only obsessed with beating the queen and protecting the empire."

"Truly? Because you never consider alternatives. You

only volunteered to train soldiers around Highkeep because you felt guilty you weren't doing your part. Every effort you've taken has focused only on your own strength. Perhaps it started with pure intent, but I'm not so sure anymore."

Brandt wasn't sure how to answer, but Ana didn't provide him the space to do so. "I accepted it earlier. I've not met the queen, but I hear the fear in your voice when you speak of her. I hoped perhaps you would find a way to defeat her. I believed in you."

"You don't anymore?"

"I want to."

The loss of her faith made him feel as though he stood on shifting sands. He'd come to take her presence and her support for granted. Even when they'd argued, he'd trusted that she would aid him. He sat down, shaken.

He heard her words and grasped their meaning, yet they weren't true. She didn't understand the threat the Lolani queen posed. He didn't like considering some of these options, but they were absolutely necessary if he was going to beat the queen.

She needed to believe in him.

Like Ren did.

He thought back to the short time they had spent together in the chamber of the elders. Ren had watched him lie, yet he still stood behind Brandt and proclaimed his loyalty to the other warrior. Ren told the elders he would be honored to fight by his side.

Two strong reactions clashed within Brandt. The first was the familiar glow of pride and satisfaction. He'd earned the trust of a warrior of quality. Even with his lies on display, Ren stood by him.

Which made Ana's betrayal cut all the deeper. If anyone was supposed to understand him, was supposed to support him through his failures, it was Ana.

Some small part of him wanted to yell at her, to accuse her of betraying him, but he recognized the impulse as immature. She was his wife. They had fought together and lived together for years. Her doubt wasn't something to criticize, but to prove incorrect. "How do I gain your trust again?"

She shook her head. "I suppose leaving this all behind is out of the question?"

He kept his tone light to match hers. "We're a ways from putting this behind us, I'm afraid."

"Then I don't know. I'll fight for you, Brandt, but consider everything. We need to defeat the queen, and even if I don't understand her power the same way you do, I have an idea what it must take for you to fear her as you do. I just don't want to lose you, not to her, and not to a quest for the strength to defeat her."

He nodded, and they left their argument at that. Shortly thereafter, Ana left, claiming the need for a long walk. Brandt let her go alone.

REN'S PREDICTION turned out to be accurate. He came to them the next afternoon, and when Ana opened the door for him, he studied them inquisitively.

"I didn't hurt him," Ana said.

"I'm relieved," Ren said.

"And I appreciate what you did for me in that chamber, Ren. I'm sorry I didn't understand earlier," Brandt added.

"I only spoke the truth. Though we may not agree, I

think I understand what drives you, and I would fight by your side."

Brandt resisted the urge to glare at Ana, strong as it was. "Have the elders decided?"

"I believe they have. Both you and Regar have been summoned."

"May I accompany you?" Ana asked.

"Of course," Ren answered.

Brandt wasn't sure if Ana wanted to join because she didn't trust him, or if it was because she wanted to show her support. He supposed that no matter the reason, he was grateful for her company. Their relationship had been tense for the past day, but not unkind.

Once again they made their journey deep into the heart of the mountain. Brandt was proud that he was able to keep track of the twists and turns, and was now confident he could find his way to the chamber again if he needed to.

As before, they met Regar in the antechamber. The prince looked to be in good spirits. Brandt wished he felt even a fraction as confident.

Once Brandt and Ana arrived, the doors opened, preventing any discussion. Brandt and Regar were invited in. Again, Ana remained outside. The two men entered, taking positions upon the circles carved within the center of the room.

The voices returned, again sounding closer than they should. The elders wasted no time. "We have listened to your request and discussed it, Prince Regar. We find it wanting."

Brandt opened his mouth to reply, to argue that his own lies shouldn't reflect poorly on Regar's request. But the prince spoke faster, and he sounded as though he'd expected nothing different. “Is there nothing I may do to strengthen my argument?”

Another voice answered. “It is possible that we grant your father use of our gate. That, at least, hasn’t been decided. But to make such a decision, we must speak directly to him, here in this room. His youngest son isn’t sufficient.”

“You ask much, given the hostilities between our people.” Regar said.

“As you ask much from us. The terms of the treaty have held. The emperor would be welcome in these lands.”

Brandt clamped his jaw shut. The elder didn’t lie. The treaty, written and signed by Anders I and the leaders of the Etari and Falari, had held. The Falari never raided with numbers greater than those stipulated by the treaty. But the lack of outright war wasn’t the same as peace. Every soldiering instinct he possessed shouted at the foolishness of bringing the emperor here. The danger of the journey alone was too much to risk, especially with so much riding on the emperor’s life. But it wasn’t his place to speak.

“If it is my father’s presence you wish, I can have him here by nightfall.”

Brandt’s eyes went wide and he stared at Regar. That couldn’t be true.

The elders seemed to think so, as well. The room lit up as the circles underneath each elder flickered intensely. A chorus of voices greeted the announcement.

Regar stood tall and silent, an immovable pillar of confidence. Brandt suspected he and Hanns, if they hadn’t predicted this exactly, had at least considered it as a possibility. As Regar had confessed earlier, his father was exceedingly clever.

One voice silenced the others. "How would this be done?"

"Through the gate." Regar held up his hand to quell another outburst of defiant exclamations. "The technique doesn't require me to control the gate. I just need to be in contact with it. Anders VI has learned how to travel from one gate to the next. He can be here not long after I reach the gate."

Another commotion. Brandt forced down a smile. Regar had kicked a hornet's nest and now stood confidently in a maelstrom of angry voices. A moment later they were ushered into the antechamber to await a decision.

Brandt turned to Regar as the doors closed. "You expected that, didn't you?"

Regar's smiled echoed Brandt's feelings. "We considered it a distinct possibility."

Brandt explained to Ana.

"It's true?" Ana asked Regar.

"Yes. Thanks to the gate outside Landow, we were able to understand how it is done. Olen, my father, and I have all stepped through. It's not a pleasant experience, but the technique works."

Deep under the mountain, Brandt had no good idea of how much time had passed, but it didn't seem long before the doors opened and Brandt and Regar were invited in again.

They were barely standing in their circles before an elder spoke. "It is decided. You will bring the emperor here." The statement was issued with a sense of finality.

"If I may?" Regar asked.

"Speak."

"I can bring the emperor here tonight, but the effects of travel are disorienting. I will ask that you not summon him here, to this room, until tomorrow morning, or even the day after, if that is acceptable."

There was no discussion. The same elder spoke. "It is agreed. Now go. You will be escorted to the gate. Try nothing more than you have said."

Regar nodded. "I will bring Anders VI here. You have my word."

34

Sheren led the small party through dense pine forest, their path snaking around densly packed trees. The woods were quiet, with even their footsteps muffled. Alena knew it was just her imagination, but the space certainly felt haunted to her.

Ghosts were a subject she'd never thought much about. She'd heard countless stories over the years, but none convinced her. If soulwalking had taught her anything, it was that some part of them existed past death. She knew the gates were real and she knew they led someplace else. But what lay beyond them she didn't know. She supposed if the gate to eternity was real, it stood to follow ghosts probably were as well.

Still, the rational part of her mind rebelled at the thought. Ghost stories, in her opinion, either served as nothing more than cheap entertainment or an explanation for an unpleasant or unlucky event. No one with any wisdom believed in them.

Yet Sheren was a talented soulwalker, and she believed.

Their guide's lack of further information encouraged

Alena's own curiosity. In her experience, those who believed in ghosts would speak endlessly about ghosts if given half the chance. Sheren didn't say more, answering the few questions they asked with a simple "wait and see" answer.

The woods became less dense as they came into the valley where Sheren's village was located. In time, the trees abruptly ended, the advance of the forest stymied by axes and the need for firewood.

Alena's third viewing of the village left her just as disappointed as the first two. Holes of varying sizes had been punched in the walls of homes, but from this closer distance she saw some of the holes had been boarded up. There were people still trying to make a living here, though they hid from sight.

They came to a wide stream, the water rushing quickly. Once, a stone bridge had spanned the stream, but the center had collapsed, leaving only the abutments. A narrow wooden plank had been laid across the remains and Sheren crossed it with the confidence of frequent practice. Jace followed, his own well-trained balance serving him admirably.

Toren indicated that she should go next.

Shaking her head, she stepped out onto the crossing. The board bent under her weight and she swore she felt the vibration caused by the river's current through the board. Two more steps and the board bowed more under her weight, flexing with her steps.

She did fine until she looked down. The drop itself didn't scare her, but the rushing water directly beneath her disoriented her sense of balance.

"Alena," Jace said.

She looked up. Jace stood on the other end of the bridge, his hand extended. Focusing on him helped her find her balance. She stepped quickly, grabbing his outstretched hand and allowing him to help her cross the last few paces.

Toren followed, having none of the trouble she had. A flush of shame rose in her cheeks, and she silently promised that she would practice her martial forms with renewed vigor.

The edge of the village was less than fifty paces from the bridge. Up close, Alena realized just how vertically the village had been built. Homes appeared to spread up rather than out. She supposed with limited space and plentiful stone, the decision made perfect sense.

Closer now, the village didn't just suffer from damage, but from decay. It was more difficult to tell with stone, but the buildings appeared old. Alena wouldn't have any trouble believing they were older than the empire.

Storm clouds darkened the sky. Alena watched them for several heartbeats, feeling the change of the air on her exposed arms. Sheren's offer of shelter appeared well-timed.

Sheren led them deeper into town. The holes weren't just in the buildings, but in the streets as well. Alena knelt down to examine one, surprised by its depth.

Jace broke Alena's growing worries. "It's a nice location, but I'm not sure this village would be high on my list of places to visit. And I still haven't seen many ghosts."

Behind Alena, Toren laughed.

If Sheren took offense, she didn't show it. She stopped in front of one of the buildings, one that had been boarded up. She gestured for them to enter. "Welcome to my home."

The three stepped in, Jace going first, his hand hovering near his sword.

The room they entered surprised Alena. After soul-walking with Sheren and feeling the depth of her affection for this village, Alena expected to see Sheren's home more decorated.

Instead, bare walls greeted her. Nothing inside the room provided any clue to Sheren's past or personality, unless an absolute lack of mementos counted. A well-used fireplace appeared along one wall, and a mat had been laid against another. Otherwise, a shelf filled partway with food and pots rounded out the extent of Sheren's possessions.

"You live here?" Jace asked.

"This is home," Sheren said. "It's not much, but it's all I need, and I'm often gone for long stretches of time, so it's easier to live with less."

"Why here?" Jace asked. "Aren't there better places to live in Falar?"

"Certainly," Sheren answered. "But not if one actively develops an affinity."

"Ahh," Jace said. Alena kicked herself for not thinking of it earlier. In her academy classes she'd learned the Falari didn't have affinities. Sheren, and her presence here, made the truth obvious enough that even Jace could figure it out. Of course affinities would manifest among the Falari. It wasn't like the ability respected borders.

But those with the gift would either hide it, causing it to wither, or they would find someplace to live where they wouldn't be bothered.

Someplace like here.

Sheren stoked the fire and put some water to boiling as the party settled in. Outside, the wind picked up, causing the boards over the holes to rattle. The air began to smell like rain.

In time the rain came, but Sheren prepared them tea. They sat together as the storm pelted the walls of Sheren's house.

"How many people live here?" Alena asked.

"Less than a dozen, but it depends on the day. Most of us come and go frequently."

"And you're all gifted?"

"Or cursed."

Jace jumped in. "You must not feel that way, though, if you've decided to come out here to live."

Alena sipped at her tea to cover her reaction. That was a surprisingly astute observation from Jace. She continually forgot that he was older and wiser than she tended to think of him.

Sheren gave her brother a half smile. "My thoughts change from day to day," she admitted. "Most days, you are right. I'm grateful for my ability. But there are others where I wish for a life more in line with customs."

Through the open door, Alena thought she saw movement in the rain. She turned to see better, but when she did, the movement vanished.

She shook her head. Must have been a trick of her eyes.

Sheren began her story. When she was young, she hadn't thought anything of her abilities. Elders in her village remarked on her understanding, specifically on her ability to pick up on what people were feeling. But nothing seemed abnormal until a day about ten years ago.

"That was the day I saw my first ghost," she said.

"I was thirteen, and I came across a man wandering near our campsite. At first I thought he might be an enemy, but he carried no weapons. I was scouting with two others, and I pointed him out. The others saw nothing, but I saw him as clearly as I see the three of you. My friends were worried, but I was able to convince them I'd made a mistake, even as the man walked within a dozen paces of us."

Sheren sipped at her own tea. "That was when I knew

something was wrong. I saw the man again, in our camp, but I noticed that no one else reacted to him, so I kept my mouth shut."

Again, Alena thought she saw something moving outside in the corner of her vision, but when she snapped her head around, there was nothing there.

"You see them, too, in the rain, don't you?" Sheren asked.

"It's nothing," Alena responded.

Sheren just smiled in response. "I tried to hide it for years, but we all make mistakes. I made little ones, like paying too close attention to spaces that appeared empty to everyone else. In time, they added up and people learned my secret. I ran from my family before they could decide what to do. I wandered for a few years before I found this place. It's quiet here."

Toren spoke up for the first time since entering the village. "What happened here?"

"I'm not sure," Sheren admitted. "No warleader is permitted within two leagues of this village, thanks to an order far older than any elder alive. But I've never been able to learn what happened."

"The damage is unlike anything I've ever seen," Toren noted.

"The forces that fought here were powerful," Sheren agreed. "But I've learned little beyond that."

She turned her attention to Alena. "When I felt you coming, I hoped to enlist your aid."

"How did you notice me? You said you were aware of me before cresting the ridge."

"It's one of the benefits of living here. I said it was quiet, and I meant it. Attempt a soulwalk here and find out for yourself."

Alena did. She closed her eyes and sought out the world

of souls. And found nothing. The web of interconnectedness that bound all living things didn't exist here. A chill, deeper than any frost, ran through her veins. This village wasn't just destroyed, it had been ripped from the threads of the rest of the world. It reminded her, in some small way, of the void she had almost been trapped in the last time she faced the Lolani queen.

Unlike that void, though, there were some differences.

For one, she saw ghosts.

As Sheren had described them, they looked much the same as anyone else. They roamed the streets of the village and some seemed to live within the homes' walls.

She knew they were ghosts because they didn't possess the same threads as the living. Thanks to the complete lack of life, the bonds she, Jace, Toren, and Sheren possessed glowed like gold. The ghosts had none.

She understood now how Sheren had noticed her. Without the dim hum of a web of life, Alena could reach farther than before. It still only amounted to a league or so, if she was to guess, but it was much farther than her typical limits.

Alena came out of the soulwalk and returned to the group. "I understand." She couldn't quite bring herself to say that she had seen the ghosts. Jace would give her grief for the rest of her days. "What aid do you seek?"

"There's a new creature in these woods, one not of flesh, that is consuming the ghosts. I want you to help me find it."

"And then?"

"Then we need to kill it."

35

Say one thing for the Falari elders: once they made a decision, the whole mountain moved to make that decision a reality.

A smaller group of elders broke from the circle and indicated that Regar should follow them. Numerous guards joined the party.

Curious, and without instructions to the contrary, Brandt followed the group to the gate. Ana joined him, and before they made it past the antechamber Ren fell in beside them. "It's been years since the gate has even been visited. Change follows in your footsteps."

"Does that concern you?" Ana asked.

"Of course. But if the elders believe this is the way, I shall follow."

The elders led them deeper into the mountain. Brandt briefly considered the massive amount of stone above them, then pushed the thought from his mind. Such thoughts were the equivalent of looking down when climbing high peaks. They caused the heart to race and the mind to lose focus.

"I wonder," Ana said, "if you are continually exposed to the impossible, do you lose your sense of wonder?"

Despite the urgency of their steps and the import of their task, Ana's question thrust him into more peaceful times, reminding him of long walks and quiet overlooks. He smiled. "You're thinking of these tunnels?"

"And the gates, and the idea of bringing a person from a place hundreds of leagues away here in a moment. When we were wolfblades, all of this was impossible."

"And it still feels as though we are swimming on the surface of a very deep lake."

Ana nodded.

"Wonder is in our own eyes," Ren said, "not in the mysteries of the world."

In response to their surprised glances, Ren continued. "There is wonder in a cup of tea, in the birth of a child, the death of a foe, and in the rising of the sun. It is how we look at the world, not the world itself."

"You should have been a poet," Ana said.

"Who says that I'm not?" Ren answered with a smile.

They entered a maze.

Not as a metaphor, either. Brandt saw hallways that ended in a blank wall. They turned, turned, and turned again. Despite Brandt's best efforts, he was soon lost.

Then they came to a massive wooden door. The elders advanced as a group, each inserting a key that dangled on chains previously hidden under their shirts. Five keys, all turned at once. Brandt heard the sounds of massive weights being moved on the other side of the door. His stone affinity sang notes unlike any he had heard before.

The doors opened smoothly, revealing a now-familiar blue glow. Another gate, just like the ones outside Landow and underneath the emperor's palace.

He felt its power coursing through him and stood amazed at its construction. What had happened to those who came before? Their skills were so far beyond imagination. Had they left? Had disaster befallen them? Ren believed they'd been attacked, but what could stand against people who could create such wonders?

His questions fled when the elders gave Regar permission to touch the gate. He nodded solemnly. "It will take some time. I first must contact him and wait for him to approach his own gate."

The air in the room felt thick. Guards took position around the chamber, arrows nocked and hands on bowstrings. The elders made no effort to disguise the truth of their invitation to Regar. His welcome could be revoked, and violently, at any moment.

Regar, for his part, appeared unconcerned. Either he put on a good show or he possessed an unshakeable confidence.

With that, Regar reached out and touched the gate. It blazed brighter, causing several of the elders to flinch away. Brandt watched, listening to the songs of the elements as they crescendoed. He didn't possess the skill to unravel Regar's techniques, but he could understand the powers at play. He focused on Regar, hoping for some hint that he might use to further his own learning.

Brandt also admitted to a pang of jealousy as he watched Regar with the gate. Though he trusted the prince to do no more than he said, he couldn't help but imagine himself in control of the enormous powers of the gate. His mind might understand he stood no chance against the queen, but his heart didn't believe.

As if at the thought of her, the gate flickered, temporarily casting them into darkness. All around them, bows creaked as they were quickly drawn. His hand went to his sword, only to find himself restrained by Ren's firm grip.

When the light of the gate returned, Regar had sunk to his knees, one hand still on the gate.

For a moment, Brandt feared the worst.

But no arrows jutted from his prince. Regar held up a hand. "It is the queen. She attacks this gate as well."

Regar stood, his knees shaking at the effort. He was breathing hard, as though he'd just finished a race.

An elder gestured and the drawn bows returned to the ready position. Ren released his grip on Brandt's arm, and Brandt allowed himself to relax a measure.

Had the song of the gate changed? Brandt listened for a moment, at times thinking that it had. But he couldn't be sure, and even if it had, he didn't know what it meant.

"I've contacted my father," Regar said. "I believe we have some time to wait."

Time stretched within the chamber. Brandt's sense of time, already distorted by being so long underground, was now hopelessly confused. If forced to guess, he would have said it was early evening, but it could have been anytime from mid-afternoon to late at night. The elders waited in silence, and the guards never relaxed their vigilance. Regar remained with his hand to the gate, his eyes closed. Brandt imagined he waited for Hanns to signal that he was ready.

Brandt wanted to talk to Ana, but in the silence of the smaller space, every word would be overheard. He didn't mind, but it seemed out of place with the singular focus of most people in the room.

When Regar spoke again, Brandt jumped. He'd become used to everyone's silence. "He's connected with his own gate. It won't be long now."

Brandt focused his own attention. Regar concentrated on the gate, a grimace on his face.

Just then the gate flickered again.

Regar growled, an almost animal-like roar escaping from the back of his throat. The unnatural blue light faded, then exploded in brightness, then faded again. The guards pulled lightly on their bowstrings, but they seemed uncertain where to aim them.

Brandt stepped toward the gate, but this time it was Ana who stopped him. She shook her head.

Looking around the room, Brandt realized the wisdom of her restraint. The guards were looking for an excuse to release their arrows, eyes wide with fear. From the normally unshakeable Falari, the reaction surprised him.

Like it or not, Regar needed to fight the Lolani queen on his own.

The light from the gate disappeared, plunging them once again into darkness. A few heartbeats later, a wave of power blasted past Brandt, knocking him flat onto his back. As he attempted to return to his feet another wave rolled over him, pinning him to the ground.

Brandt struggled and reached for his affinity, but his efforts gained him nothing. He fought just to pull air into his lungs.

Then it was over, the crushing weight lifted from his body.

Brandt found his feet just as the light returned to the room. Some elders and guards appeared disoriented, their eyes dazed and wandering.

Others looked angry.

And that anger was directed at Regar.

The prince was on his knees, his hand still against the

gate. Brandt got the impression that the hand was stuck, that Regar couldn't remove it even if he wanted.

The light from the gate grew stronger, and for the first time in Brandt's experience, the center began to glow with the same cool blue light.

It was working.

One of the guards found his feet and pulled his bow back in one smooth motion. He aimed directly at Regar's back.

Brandt could do nothing but shout, "Wait! It's working!"

The archer hesitated, looking around the room for an elder to provide him guidance.

Then the issue was rendered moot as another wave of pure energy filled the room. This time Brandt saw the air shimmer and braced himself against the force.

The guard had no such luck. The wave threw him back several paces, and he released his arrow at the ceiling. It bounced off, then clattered to the floor.

The wave passed and Brandt saw an arm emerge from the light in the center of the gate. A head followed, then a torso.

Another impossible sight, but he didn't doubt what he saw right in front of him.

The emperor stepped through, but something wasn't right. His eyes were unfocused and his step uncertain. He looked old and worn, stripped of his usual bearing. Hanns took one faltering step, then fell forward.

Brandt was there to catch him. The emperor fell into Brandt's arms, and Brandt was surprised by how light the emperor felt.

Beside them, Regar groaned and fell over, his hand finally free of the gate. In the corners of his vision he saw the elders tentatively returning to their feet, studying the new arrival. If the elders planned on betraying the imperials, they would never have a better time.

But one of the elders stepped forward and kneeled next to Brandt. "Come, let us find a place for your emperor to rest. It appears the travel has taken much from both him and his son."

Brandt nodded and was about to stand when he saw the emperor's eyes suddenly focus. "Brandt?"

His voice was weak, sounding like it came from a place very far away.

"Yes?"

The emperor's lips moved, but nothing came from them. Brandt leaned closer, his ear almost to Hanns' lips. "... wrong."

Then the emperor's eyes glazed over and his lips stopped moving.

36

Sheren's description of the strange beast was frustratingly vague. It took on different shapes, often those related to a person's fears. And it devoured ghosts, but she wasn't quite sure how. All in all, Sheren could tell her little that was useful.

Which meant if Alena wanted to learn more, she needed to find the monster and study it herself.

Jace argued vehemently against the idea. As night fell and the four huddled around a fire for their meal, he made his points. "We're trying to get to Faldun as quickly as possible to stop Hanns from controlling the third gate. That will hopefully help the Etari gate in some way and allow them to keep using their gatestones. Right?"

Alena nodded, knowing well enough where Jace's argument led.

"So why do you want to stop to fight a creature which sounds plenty dangerous and has nothing to do with the gate or saving the Etari?"

Put in such stark terms, Alena wasn't sure she knew a good answer. Put honestly, it simply felt right to her. But she couldn't say why. It was most likely curiosity. She'd just learned that ghosts were real. Of course she wanted to know more. But Jace's point was valid. Staying here had little to do with their objective, and failure carried a high price.

Sheren interrupted before Alena could answer. "You're traveling to Faldun?"

"We are," Alena said.

"If you help me, I will show you a faster route. It will cut days off your travel."

Alena gave Jace a satisfied look. He shook his head. "It's still dangerous."

"So is an unescorted trip to Faldun," Sheren argued. "The war parties are more active than they have been in some time. You're safe here, but as you get closer to Faldun, the more Falari you'll run into. I can help you avoid most of them, and can help you negotiate with other war parties."

Sheren didn't completely convince Jace, but she made their reasons for remaining compelling enough to justify Alena's decision.

After the meal, Sheren, Alena, and Toren soulwalked together. Alena tried to dissuade Toren, but he eagerly sought any opportunity to learn more. In that, he reminded her of herself. She was loath to admit it, but she appreciated his presence. He, at least, was familiar, and she trusted him.

They appeared in the village, richly detailed thanks to Sheren's memories.

It didn't take them long to spot their first ghost. The village, nearly abandoned in the physical world, teemed with life in this one. Alena watched, enraptured. Here, the ghosts appeared as real and as solid as Toren. But at the same time, something was missing. Some worked endlessly at tasks, digging in gardens or nursing children. Others wandered, their eyes fixed on distant horizons.

"Why so many?" Toren asked.

"They used to live here, and many of them died in an attack. Ghosts are nothing more than souls that don't find the gate. Why they didn't, I'm not sure." Sheren's frustration expressed itself in every one of her words.

"Why do you want to help them?" Alena asked.

"They deserve better than this," Sheren said. "Death is natural. But they haven't completed the journey."

Out of curiosity, Alena reached out and touched a ghost, her hand resting on his shoulder. She fell deeper into the soulwalk, finding herself in a familiar and terrifying place.

An endless void.

Alena forced herself to breathe evenly. She searched for the threads tying her to the worlds she knew. It took time, but she felt the faint thread of her bond with Jace. She pulled on it and returned to the village, surrounded by ghosts.

Another ghost stepped by her and she flinched, not wanting to return to that void. Sheren was right. The ghosts needed to find the gate.

"What of the creature?" she asked.

"I don't sense it. You'll know when it nears. It warps the world around it."

"Then let's get these ghosts to the gate."

"How?" Sheren asked.

"I'm not sure. But I'm going to try something. When you see it, don't get too close," Alena warned. "It pulls at you."

She closed her eyes, imagining the gate, from the details of its construction to the way it made her feel. And then she imagined it standing in the main square of the village.

Sheren's sharp intake of breath was evidence enough she had succeeded.

She opened her eyes to see the gate standing there.

Already, ghosts had turned toward it, some of them breaking patterns of action they had been trapped in for lifetimes. Alena saw the desire in their eyes.

Toren, too, succumbed to its pull. Of the three of them, he was closest. Alena jogged to him and pulled him away. As she did, his eyes cleared and he shook his head, nodding a silent thanks.

From somewhere far away, something roared, shaking the trees.

"That's the creature," Sheren said.

"You two make sure the ghosts pass through," Alena said. "I'll hold the creature off."

"Alena, don't!" Sheren warned. "The creature is too powerful. Help us usher the ghosts, and when the creature gets close, we'll come out of the soulwalk. It's the only way to be safe. Trust me, I've tried."

Toren chuckled. "She's not going to listen."

Alena didn't. She turned toward the sound of the monster, then dashed forward. In this world she could become as light as her imagination would allow, and she skipped across the ground faster than any martial arts master.

The sounds of cracking trees made the beast easy to find.

But beast wasn't the right word.

It was a creature of smoky shadow, its shape amorphous. As Alena watched, the shadow gained substance, becoming a translucent giant spider with spiked legs. Alena raised an eyebrow. She didn't care much for spiders, and she certainly didn't care for spiders that were twice her size.

A leg kicked out at her. Alena imagined an unbreakable bubble around her. When the leg struck, Alena's head swam with visions of darkness. But her shield held.

The creature roared and jabbed at her with its fangs, but again her shield repelled the attack.

The shadows reared back and became amorphous once again, flowing between the trees that surrounded the village. For lack of a better description, it seemed to be thinking. Then it shifted again, shrinking down to the size of a man.

The shadow dissipated like morning fog, revealing Azaleth, eyes black as night.

Alena's stomach clenched.

Show her a spider, but don't reflect Azaleth's memory back at her.

Azaleth sprinted at her, Etari blade flashing in the moonlight. It sparked off her bubble. He deformed for a moment, turning again into shadow before he reformed, standing above her on the bubble. He glared down at her between his feet, then took off toward the village.

Alena sprinted after him, her own pace impossibly quick, pine trees flashing around her. She passed Azaleth and drew her knife, forged by her father. She dropped her shield and drove the blade into his heart.

It felt like she was killing him all over again.

It wasn't Azaleth. She had to remember that. The shadow opened its mouth in a wordless scream, and Alena drove a second knife, a duplicate of the first, from her left hand into his jaw, forcing it open. She gave herself limitless strength and pulled the blades in opposite directions.

The shadow ripped apart, causing it to bleed away from her. It remained a dark cloud, lacking form. But she wasn't sure she'd hurt it.

The two opponents studied each other. No doubt the shadow sought a way past her, and she searched her knowledge for a way to kill it. Stabbing it apparently wasn't enough.

It moved again, splitting in two and attempting to pass her on both sides.

Alena channeled her affinity through the gatestone at her navel, wanting the extra power. Through will alone, she forced the two halves to stop. She imagined them locked in place, condensing into perfect spheres of darkness. They fought against her, the sphere bulging and rippling, as though dozens of trapped creatures pushed against the skin of the sphere, trying to break free.

Strength of will decided the contest.

Alena won, and the spheres quieted. She didn't dare release her hold on them, though.

She used the quiet moments to study them. Unlike the ghosts, this shadow had threads tying it to the real world.

Alena examined those threads, a sense of deja vu coming over her. They were familiar, their handiwork too similar to be coincidence.

The queen.

Impulsively, Alena took her knife and severed the threads, cutting through them with ease.

The shadow's struggle against her containment redoubled, but Alena gritted her teeth and held it in place.

Cut off from its source, the shadows faded, roaring in anger. Alena watched them fade, only releasing her grip when she was sure the shadow was gone.

Why was the Lolani queen interested in devouring ghosts?

Her mind was too tired to even begin to guess. That was a mystery for another day.

She stumbled back into the village, glad to see Toren and Sheren were almost done escorting the ghosts. Both kept a safe distance from the gate itself.

Just as she reached them, the world shook, an earthquake stronger than any reality could offer. Had the world been physical, the mountains themselves would have crumbled. Here, Alena and the others fell, but no other harm was done.

"What was that?" Toren asked.

Alena shook her head. She had no idea. It felt enormous, like the whole domain of the soul had shifted.

Toren ran to Alena. "Was it our gate?"

She hadn't even thought of the gate. "Hold on."

Zolene had implied that distance didn't matter, so Alena fought her disbelief to connect with the Etari gate. The search took what felt like ages, but she found it. The Etari gate still worked. Her curiosity sparked, though, she turned her attention to the other gates. After finding the Etari gate, the others were easier to find. She studied the two imperial gates, finding them also in order. Then she followed the threads to the gate in Falar, wanting to check that one before venturing anywhere near the queen's gate.

She found the problem, and she backed away before she could be noticed.

"It's not the Etari gate," Alena reassured Toren. She looked to Sheren. "It's the Falari gate."

"What happened?" she asked.

"Someone took control of it."

"Who?"

Alena shook her head. She noticed the presence connected to the gate but didn't recognize it. "I don't know."

37

Hanns lived, but his breath was weak and uneven. Regar kneeled next to the emperor, concern written in every line of his face. "When I came through, I was also disoriented and felt ill, but not like this."

"Did the queen attack the gate?" Brandt asked.

Regar looked confused for a moment, then nodded. "Yes. Perhaps that was it. He passed through as the gate was under attack. When I came through, I felt better after some rest." The prince looked up at the elders. "Is there someplace we can take him where he can sleep?"

A runner was dispatched to seek aid and prepare quarters near those of the other imperials, and Brandt and Regar picked up the emperor between them and carried him out of the maze. Not long after, another runner returned with a thick sheet attached to two stout poles. He unfurled the stretcher and they laid Hanns out on it. Regar and Brandt each picked up one end and the march continued.

While the journey into the cave had been long, the journey out felt endless. The paths all sloped up, making Brandt's legs burn with effort. A few times the Falari guards offered to share the burden, but each time Brandt refused. Hanns was his emperor. In time, they stopped asking.

The stars twinkled overhead when they left the tunnels. Eventually they settled the emperor on a bed and Ana covered him up. The process unsettled Brandt. He knew Hanns better than many, but even though no formality existed between them, Hanns was still his emperor. Seeing him this vulnerable, an old man resting in a bed, made Brandt's chest tighten.

Regar addressed both Brandt and Ana. "Do you two feel safe protecting him with the assistance of my guards? I must speak with the elders."

Brandt nodded. He could only imagine the questions that would be circulating among the elders tonight. Hopefully Regar could quell any unease. Otherwise Hanns might have suffered through this journey for no good reason.

Regar left, leaving Brandt and Ana alone with Hanns. Brandt checked on the emperor one more time before taking a seat in the corner of the room. Ana sat down next to him.

He fought the exhaustion that suddenly overwhelmed him. His body ached in a dozen places, reminding him once again that even being close to the gates could be dangerous.

"Do they make you feel small?" Ana asked, her voice soft.

"Hmm?"

"The gates."

Brandt rubbed his upper arm, where he'd landed when the power from the gate had tossed him about like a child's toy. "They do."

"Do you really believe you can harness that power?" She paused, focused on her intertwined hands. "Do you think you should?"

She didn't sound like she was trying to win the argument. She was genuinely curious. "I don't know," he said slowly. "I only think of what is necessary. 'Should' doesn't come in much."

"That scares me," Ana said.

Brandt worried she would resume their fight, but she left their discussion at that.

He didn't deserve Ana. She possessed a nearly supernatural sense to know exactly how hard to push him. Tonight, her words had their desired effect.

Was he in the wrong?

He didn't know. He knew he would fight for Ana, but beyond that, all he had was questions.

Now that he was still, he felt a tug, the feeling he'd come to learn was Alena reaching out to him. How long had she been waiting?

Brandt's eyes traveled over the room. Ana looked as exhausted as he felt. They were probably safe, but leaving wasn't a risk he wanted to take at that moment. He let Alena's summons go unanswered.

In time, the sensation faded. Brandt allowed himself to close his eyes then. He wouldn't sleep, but even resting his eyes felt wonderful. "You should sleep," Ana said. "Then we'll switch."

"Deal." Brandt relaxed his body. If his years as a soldier and wolfblade had taught him anything, it was the ability to sleep anywhere. Within moments of releasing the tension, he was asleep.

HE WOKE to the sun shining through the window. Brandt blinked rapidly, surprised Ana let him sleep so long. A glance her way revealed the reason, though.

She was asleep, too.

Worried, Brandt looked to the emperor. He was fine, his breathing stronger and more even than the night before. Brandt released a deep sigh of relief. He was still disappointed in Ana for falling asleep on watch, but no harm had been done.

Brandt sat in the sun of the new day, letting his thoughts wander as the others slept. The rooms they'd been given were almost halfway up the side of the mountain, and it was quiet this high.

Hanns was the first to wake. He came to awareness in an instant, sitting up and taking in the room with a glance. He focused on Brandt, who made a calming gesture. "You're safe. You're in Faldun."

Hanns grimaced, bringing his hands to his head. "What happened?"

Brandt stood up, then walked over to the emperor's bed. "We're not sure. Before you came through the gate, the gate was acting strangely. The energy almost crushed us."

Hanns' eyes narrowed at that. "Describe it."

Brandt tried, retelling the experience as he remembered it. "It felt like waves of energy coming from the gate, incredibly powerful."

"And it stopped when I came through?"

"As far as I'm aware, yes. We left the area soon after, though, so if the gate is still acting that way, I wouldn't know."

Hanns closed his eyes. "Give me a moment."

Brandt did, then heard the sound of soft footsteps behind him. Ana was awake. "Sorry," she mouthed. She kept her eyes down and her cheeks were flushed with shame.

He nodded. She understood the severity of her failure. A

wolfblade never falls asleep on watch. There was nothing to be gained by him saying anything further.

Hanns grunted, focusing the attention in the room on him. He shook his head. "Something is wrong. I don't feel my connection with the gates the same way that I usually do."

He closed his eyes again, wandering through another world. Then he shook his head and opened his eyes. "I can feel the connection, but everything is fuzzy. Something happened when I came through the gate."

"Did the queen attack you?" Brandt asked.

Hanns shook his head again, the confusion plain on his face. "I don't know. All I remember is stepping through the gate, a tremendous pain, and then seeing you." The emperor looked up. "Where's Regar? He might have more answers."

"He left last night after ensuring you were safe," Brandt said. "He sought to ease tensions with the Falari elders after your entrance."

"Summon him, please," Hanns said. "Perhaps my connections will return in time, but I fear the consequences if I don't have full control over the gates. He might be able to help."

Behind them, Ana left to pass the order on to the guards. Brandt helped Hanns to his feet.

Alena chose that moment to tug on their bond again. Brandt must have made some expression, because Hanns took note. "What's wrong?"

"Alena is summoning me."

"She might be useful now."

Brandt waited until Ana returned, then explained he needed to meet with Alena. She nodded, taking guard while

Brandt settled into a seated position in the corner of the room. He closed his eyes and waited for Alena.

It didn't take long. No more than a few moments passed before Brandt felt his surroundings shift. Though his eyes were closed, he saw that he was in Alena's mother's kitchen. It felt peaceful here, far removed from the struggles that consumed so much of his attention. Alena sat across from him. Even here, she looked much the worse for wear. "What happened to you?" he asked.

"I fought a shadow creature of the queen's that was eating ghosts in an abandoned Falari town."

Brandt opened his mouth to reply, but found he had no idea how to respond to that. He settled for, "Huh."

"Yeah."

She didn't seem inclined to discuss it further.

"How about you?"

"I lied to all the Falari elders, argued with Ana, and was nearly killed by the Falari gate."

"Huh."

"Yeah."

"We're not doing so well, are we?" Alena asked.

"No, we are not."

They sat in silence, letting the scents and atmosphere of the kitchen relax their frayed nerves. Time passed differently here, so Brandt didn't feel the rush as he might have if they'd met in the physical world.

Alena spoke first. "When I was fighting the monster last night, something shook the world of souls. I've never felt anything like it, and I think it has to do with the Falari gate. I wondered if you knew anything about it."

"Last night the gate was trying to kill me, except in the physical world."

"Someone took control of the gate."

The sentence stopped Brandt's thoughts in an instant. He understood the words, but it made no sense. "The queen?"

"No. Someone I don't know."

"That's not—" Brandt trailed off, reviewing the events of the past night in his mind.

He knew.

He didn't understand, but he knew. Only one person had come into contact with the gate last night, and it couldn't be a coincidence that the first time the Falari elders granted access to the gate someone had taken control.

If Alena was right, control of the gate had been stolen.

Stolen by Regar.

38

The storm passed through the next morning, leaving behind a brilliant blue sky devoid of clouds. The blue appeared so rich and vibrant that Alena wondered for a moment if it was real.

Because everything in her life seemed a dream.

Or perhaps a nightmare.

She settled on unreal. Ghosts and shadow monsters existed, and she felt the boundary between her physical sensations and the world of souls slowly dissolving.

Their end of the bargain fulfilled, Sheren insisted that they waste no further time in the abandoned village. Alena wasn't sure if the rush was due to a genuine desire to help Alena or if the Falari soulwalker knew the village possessed other secrets better left undiscovered by the foreign visitors. Either way, she seemed eager to leave.

Alena wouldn't quibble with Sheren's desire for haste. Her realization, made with Brandt's help, that Regar had taken control of the gate, made her insides twist. The gates weren't toys to be played with by any passing child. She knew only a fraction of what the gates were capable of and had come to believe that the first Anders had made a wise choice in hiding their existence from his people. The fewer people who knew about the gates, the better. Their very presence invited temptation.

She couldn't believe Regar had stolen control of the gate from under the noses of everybody watching.

She knew very little about Prince Regar. His reputation, as far as she understood, was that he was brave, selfless, and completely focused on the needs of the empire.

In short, she knew only the stories that had been spread about him, and she didn't trust a single one.

If Brandt's reaction had been any indication, he felt very much the same.

Her need to reach Faldun was greater than ever. The emperor suffered from some invisible wound. Alena couldn't put the pieces together yet, but she had adopted one of Brandt's fundamental beliefs: there were no coincidences. This had the outline of a larger scheme beyond her comprehension.

So she didn't argue with Sheren when the Falari soulwalker ushered them out the door well before noon. Their guide had packed her necessary belongings in less time than it took them to gather theirs. In answer to their surprised looks, she shrugged. "As I said, I've lived most of my life on the road."

They left the village by the same route they entered. Perhaps it was just the benefit of experience, but crossing the single board over the river gave Alena no problems the second time.

She nursed a small sense of satisfaction as they left the village. Though their visit hadn't altered the physical landscape, she felt the difference in the air. Most, if not all, the ghosts had passed on. They had done some good here, however small. No soul deserved to so much as touch that dark void of emptiness.

Additionally, she had denied the Lolani queen the ghosts. She couldn't say what good her rescue did, but she was proud of herself on principle. Any action that interfered with the queen pleased her.

Thoughts of their success warmed her as they climbed out of the valley. Sheren followed a trail that Alena never would have noticed on her own. Given how overgrown the path was, it was rarely used. As they climbed higher, the nature of the trail changed, and she noticed a familiar pattern beneath her feet. The stone underfoot was flat, but not worn smooth. Much like a path high in the mountains outside Landow. A path which had led to a gate.

The old path made the switchbacks considerably easier, but Alena's legs still burned with the effort of the relentless climb. Their stop in the village hadn't exactly been restful, and she dreamed of resting for a full night in a warm bed.

Jace came to life as the day wore on. He smiled more, and she didn't catch him staring off into the distance nearly as often. Perhaps it was just time healing wounds, or perhaps something about the village had helped him. Regardless, he once again reminded her of the child he'd once been. He wasn't healed, but it was a step in the right direction.

Sheren and Jace spoke often as they walked. The two were ahead of her and Toren, and Jace's hands moved so wildly Alena sometimes worried he would accidentally hit Sheren.

She tried to embrace his enthusiasm. She followed his gaze as he turned and pointed out distant waterfalls and unique peaks. She forced herself to smile as he explained some obscure detail he'd just learned.

And it worked. Between their success in the village and Jace's infectious attitude, she began to enjoy the climb.

The whole party stopped to peer across the valley below from an overlook, the four of them precariously balanced near the lip of a boulder. Alena, distracted by something glittering in the woods far below, leaned out just as a gust of wind rushed up the mountain slope, crashing into her with surprising force.

Already near the edge of her balance, Alena stumbled forward, trying to catch herself with a foot that slipped off the edge.

Her stomach sank, but a firm grip on her wrist pulled her back before she had a chance to understand her error.

Toren.

Their eyes met, and Alena thought she saw something there she hadn't noticed before. Their gaze lingered for several heartbeats before Alena came to her senses.

"Thank you," she said.

He made a quick hand sign, then returned to the path. Alena watched him walk away, her thoughts jumbled.

Jace nudged her with his elbow. "About time you noticed."

Then he skipped back to the trail, joining the others.

No matter how hard Alena glared at her brother's back, she couldn't quite summon enough fire affinity for his shirt to catch on fire.

SHEREN LED them up the mountain until they came to what at first appeared to be a square cave. As they approached, though, Alena realized there was nothing natural about the dark hole. The cave turned out to be a tunnel, sinking deeper into the mountain than light would penetrate.

"What is this place?" Alena asked.

Sheren shrugged. "It was built by those who came before. Our legends claim that these were places of refuge." She frowned. "But I do not think that is all they were. Tunnels like these run through many of the mountains in this area. I believe that long ago those who came before may have used them for transport."

Even after experiencing the impossible underground constructions outside Landow, Alena's mind wrestled with the magnitude of the work she saw before her. Working by hand, such a tunnel would have taken lifetimes of effort. But even a cursory glance at the walls was enough for her to realize that they had not been shaped by human hands. They were nearly as smooth as glass.

Sheren lit a torch and led them deeper. "My people rarely use these tunnels anymore. Many consider them cursed. Using these will cut days off your trip and help you avoid most of the patrols. Besides," she added, "most of them lead straight to Faldun."

Jace echoed Alena's thoughts. "Well, I'm glad we stuck around to help you."

Alena agreed. This was exactly the sort of help they needed. The tunnel was as straight as an arrow, with no elevation change she could see. Passing through a mountain was far faster than walking around or over one. And not having to worry about other war parties would save them time, too. She lit a torch off of Sheren's and the party continued on.

Several hundred paces into the tunnel, when the light of day had faded to a point in the distance, Sheren's torch revealed a stone cart. As they neared, Alena felt uneasy. Something about this cart pushed at her senses.

Her reaction must've been noticeable, because Sheren commented on it. "You can feel it too, can't you?"

Alena nodded. She had no idea what it meant, but this cart had a purpose greater than she could understand.

Toren spoke. "It seems to possess a stone affinity."

Everyone turned to stare at the quiet man. "You're saying the stone possesses a stone affinity?"

Toren gestured his agreement. "At least, that is what it feels like. I don't actually know what I'm feeling."

Sheren became animated. "Come on. There's something more that I want you to see." Alena did, driven as much by her own curiosity as by Sheren's enthusiasm. Those who came before fascinated her, a mystery she wasn't sure she would ever solve.

She lost track of how far they traveled, but eventually Sheren stopped. She held her torch up to the wall, where the surface was marred with drawings that Alena did not understand.

The walls portrayed a series of sketches, drawn with a confident and talented hand. The works depicted a group of people fleeing in terror from some monster in the sky. It almost looked like a giant bird, yet different. "What is that?" Alena asked as she pointed to the creature.

"I'm not sure," Sheren replied, "but I believe it is the creature that destroyed those that came before."

39

News of Regar's betrayal froze Brandt in place. Though he knew it to be true, he scrambled to find some other explanation to fit the facts. Unfortunately, every proposal he imagined was far more outlandish than the simple truth.

Regar had betrayed the Falari. He'd betrayed his father, and he'd betrayed the empire.

Brandt couldn't get any of that to match with the man he'd come to know on the journey here. He'd sensed the bitterness toward his father, but nothing that justified an action like this.

He didn't want to believe it.

As a younger officer, Brandt had always been instructed to keep his battle plans simple. Complex strategies broke like weak pottery. What applied to battle plans applied to life, too. If two explanations for an event existed, and were roughly equal in merit, the simpler one was almost always correct.

Ana didn't suffer the same disorientation at the revelation, but she'd never gotten along particularly well with

Regar, either. What finally silenced Brandt's disbelief was Hanns' quiet acceptance. The betrayal cut the emperor deeply, but he didn't seem surprised.

"Why would he do it?" Brandt asked, more to himself than to anyone else in the room. "He loves the empire. He wants to protect it. I'm sure of it."

Ana laid a hand on Brandt's shoulder. "Why doesn't matter. Hopefully we can learn that later. But we know what he's done. We only need to figure out how to react."

Reluctantly, Brandt broke away. Ana was right. Action came first. Understanding could come later, if it came at all. Though it would be helpful if he understood Regar's goals and intentions. How could they stop him if they weren't sure what he was trying to achieve? It couldn't just be the death of his father. He'd had the perfect opportunity the night before and hadn't taken it.

Brandt's training kicked in. They were in a foreign land, far from the support they were used to enjoying. Ana looked ready to fight, and Brandt already felt sorry for the first enemy who crossed her. He was sore, but also ready. Regar's guards were a contingent of the palace guard, so Brandt didn't expect they held any particular loyalty to the prince. But he trusted them less than Ana.

The far more important, and far more uncertain, question, was Hanns.

Brandt kneeled down next to the emperor's bed. "What are you currently capable of?"

The emperor looked up at him with wavering eyes. "I can feel my connection with the gates once again," he replied. "I think I could draw on them, but I must admit," his eyes glazed over for a moment, "I do not think it would be wise to make me the cornerstone of your strategy." He paused again. "Or any piece you truly depend on."

Brandt had expected as much, but without the emperor, their task was far more difficult. If it came to a fight, Regar had a gate, and without the emperor, they had none. Those weren't odds Brandt was comfortable with.

"We need to escape," he decided.

"We're nearly in the middle of Faldun," Ana reminded him, her voice calm. "Even if we escape the capital there are still hundreds of leagues between us and safety, and for all we know every Falari alive will be hunting for us."

"It's not the best plan," Brandt acknowledged, "but I would still rather take those odds over those of fighting Regar."

Ana glanced at Hanns and considered for moment. "I agree."

Before Brandt could step outside to give the guards orders, the sharp sound of alarm bells pealed through the air.

Ana and Brandt shared a look. They had both been wolfblades. If anyone alive understood Brandt's insistence that there were no coincidences, it was Ana. The bells could only mean one thing.

Regar was making his move.

Ana realized the full implications of the bells before Brandt did. He was running to the door when she said, "It's not all the Falari. At least some are fighting against Regar. There wouldn't be an alarm otherwise."

Brandt froze in mid-stride. She was right.

If the Falari were fighting one another it opened up new possibilities, and new challenges.

He considered their options for a few moments, then shook his head. "Escape is still wisest. We don't even know who our allies would be."

Ana nodded, then turned to help the emperor prepare

for the journey. She helped him dress in traveling clothes and comfortable boots. Brandt informed the guards of their new orders, unleashing a flood of activity. The guards came into the room and began packing. Others went to nearby storerooms where they could find food.

Brandt wished they'd better prepared for this. Even with all the guards hurrying, their departure was delayed. Every moment meant the chaos would spread through the city further. They needed to leave. If he had been wise, he would have foreseen this possibility long ago. He always should have had a plan to leave the city in a hurry.

Brandt pushed the thoughts aside. What was done was done. He threw himself into his tasks while waiting for the others to complete theirs. For a while, at least, he lost himself in the bliss of focused physical exertion. He packed bags and prepared his own gear for the journey ahead.

Lost in his preparations, he barely noticed the knock on the door. Ana called for the door to be opened, revealing a concerned guard on the other side. "There is a Falari here to see you," the guard said. Before either of them could ask any questions, he added, "It's Ren."

Again, Ana understood more quickly than Brandt. The lethargy affecting his mind was fortunately not affecting her. "Send him in."

A few moments later Ren appeared, his hands well away from his swords. Brandt still tensed and took a step so that he was between Hanns and Ren.

"Regar and many of the mountain tribes are seizing control of the city. Were you aware of this?" Ren asked.

Ren had fought them both before. He knew his skill relative to theirs, but in that moment, Brandt was convinced he would draw his sword anyway if he found out the warriors had betrayed him.

"We were not."

Ren nodded. "Good, then we need your help to fight them."

Brandt shook his head. "Regar has control of your gate. Hanns is disoriented. We need to run."

"We won't run," Ren proclaimed. "If we cede control of that gate it means we lose everything."

"There is no honor in fighting a hopeless battle," Brandt argued. "Not when your sacrifice is meaningless. Come with us. Regroup. Once Hanns has recovered from whatever Regar did to him we can counter this coup from a position of greater strength."

"All the strength in the world won't matter if they take the city," Ren pointed out.

Brandt supposed he had a point there. He didn't want to be the commander tasked with capturing Faldun. Easier to tie a rope around a cloud. But that didn't change his mind.

The two warriors stared at each other, neither budging.

Ren capitulated first. "What if you come with me," he gestured at Brandt, "and I'll send several of my scouts to help you get him away from the battle." He gestured toward Hanns. "He'll be a target of those trying to take the city."

"Agreed," Brandt said. He'd be a fool to turn down such an offer. Ren's guides would be an invaluable resource for getting Hanns out of the city. On their own, Brandt wasn't sure how long escape would have taken. As much as Brandt hated sacrificing the city, Hanns was more important. Not just as the emperor, but as the man who controlled two gates.

Ana must have agreed, because she didn't argue. Instead, she stepped forward. "I'll fight with you."

Ana shook her head before Brandt could even tell her that he wanted her with the emperor. He wanted her safe.

"The guards here are among the best in the empire," she said. "My presence won't make a difference in either case. I want to fight by your side."

There were times when it was worth arguing with Ana. But from a single look Brandt knew that this was not one of them.

"Let's get going, then," he said. "We've got a coup to stop."

40

They needed to move. The longer she waited to reach Faldun, the more difficult she imagined her task would become. But Alena couldn't tear her eyes from the paintings before her. It wasn't the artwork itself. Despite the work being the product of those who came before, she had seen more superior work from artists of her own time. The painting didn't catch her eye so much as it caught her imagination.

How long had it been here?

And did it mean what it seemed to mean?

Ever since she first learned about those that came before, a single question with no answer plagued her: What had happened? Their affinities and skills were clearly so much more advanced than those of her people. She couldn't comprehend their disappearance.

She had come up with countless possibilities on her long journeys. A few seemed more reasonable than the others. Perhaps they had decided to leave this world behind. She couldn't guess how they left, or to what destination they traveled, but some part of her found the idea of a whole people moving to more fertile grounds appealing. It reminded her of the Etari, always traveling from one location to the next, just on a different scale.

That explanation still didn't answer the question of why.

Ultimately, the answer had to be one of two possibilities. Either the ones who came before had been driven away, or they had been destroyed.

Both implied that some force stronger than those that came before existed. Perhaps it had been a natural force, but Alena doubted it. The ones who came before had at least some control over the natural world. They would not have left everything due to forces of nature.

Which left the final possibility. They had been destroyed or run off by a foe far stronger than them. Just like the scene depicted in this artwork. Though it hardly served as solid evidence, it was all that Alena needed. The ones who'd come before had been destroyed by this creature. The Etari had told of a threat from the skies, but she hadn't paid it much mind. It had been a story. But perhaps it was much more.

Jace brought her back to the present. "Studying that painting isn't going to stop Regar," he pointed out.

Alena understood, but still she tarried, memorizing every curve and detail of the drawing. Perhaps this wouldn't matter today, but someday it would.

Finally, and with a reluctant sigh, she allowed herself to be pulled away from the painting. They continued deeper into the mountain, walking an endless smooth tunnel that traveled straight through the heart of a mountain. Every footstep reminded her of the powers of those who came before.

Darkness squeezed in on them from every side, held at bay only by Sheren's torches.

Eventually the light at the other end of the tunnel began to grow. Alena practically ran the last hundred paces. She wasn't afraid of tight spaces, but all the same, the fresh breeze blowing in from the mouth of the tunnel drew her like a moth toward a candle.

She passed by another cart identical in construction to the one she had seen at the other end of the tunnel, then came out into the fading sunlight of the end of the day. She basked in the last light of the sun, enjoying the feel of the breeze on her skin.

The rest of the party followed shortly thereafter. Alena glanced over and saw that Toren was smiling at her. "I guess I'm just built for open spaces," she admitted.

Toren nodded, the imperial gesture catching Alena by surprise. "Me too."

She felt guilty then. She'd been so absorbed in her own thoughts, especially after seeing the painting, that she hadn't even thought about the others.

They stood together on the ledge and admired the scenery below.

Toren's sharp eyes caught the movement below first. "There's a war party moving down there."

Jace pointed in another direction. "And there's one there, too."

The two parties were in different valleys, and Alena smiled at the thought of the two groups not even knowing that they were next to one another. It was unlikely, though. Sheren had told them all war parties on the move sent scouts ranging out far and wide. If the parties could be spotted from this distance, they were making no effort to hide. In all likelihood, the parties were well aware of one another.

"They're going the same direction we are," Jace realized out loud.

"I agree," Sheren said. "Their destination appears to be Faldun."

"That's less than ideal," Jace observed.

Sheren turned to Alena for guidance. "Your brother is right. It doesn't bode well that war parties are converging upon the capital. Only a conflict of great import would draw so many."

"Like a foreign prince stealing control of the gate?" Alena asked.

"That would suffice," Sheren conceded.

Alena closed her eyes. The temptation to throw up her hands in surrender and return home was greater than ever.

But it wouldn't solve anything. The problem would only be worse, somehow, later. "Then our task is all the more important. Will you continue to guide us?"

Sheren looked offended at the question. "I said that I would."

Alena watched the war parties for a few moments. If they knew more of the war parties and their intentions, it would influence their choices. She asked Sheren, "How far until we find a suitable campsite for the night?"

"Not far. We shall arrive well before sundown."

Not far at all, then, given as the sun was almost down. She had time to try and still reach their campsite before night fell.

"I'm going to soulwalk," Alena said.

Sheren looked dubious, but nodded.

Alena shared their guide's doubt. Despite Zolene saying that distance didn't matter in a soulwalk, Alena's own experiences indicated otherwise. The web of life was intricate beyond imagining, and while she could travel it at will now, finding a single soul was nearly impossible unless they were close. When Alena tied herself to another in the soulwalk, she could follow the thread, brighter than others. But without such a guide, she found herself lost after a few dozen paces.

It was still worth a try, though. Alena stepped back from the ledge and sat down in a cross-legged position. Then she closed her eyes and dropped into a soulwalk.

Her first impressions were those of her friends. Sheren, Jace, and Toren were all easily distinguishable and Alena felt the threads that ran between them all.

She pushed those aside, questing for the war parties.

The web of life expanded before her and she followed it in the direction of the closer of the two parties. She followed and followed, seeking a cluster of humans.

Sweat beaded on her forehead as she sought the party. For all their achievements, humans were not as unique in the web of life as they often thought they were. Her mind grew tired as she ran along the threads, seeking that small difference that indicated a human life.

She was just about to admit defeat when she thought she felt something. She latched onto the connection with all the focus she could muster. Grimacing against the effort, she attempted to bring the other mind into focus. She channeled her efforts through her gatestone, though it seemed to have little effect.

For as close as she got to the other soul, she couldn't quite connect with it. She felt as though she was running as fast as she could, but the one in front of her still pulled slightly ahead.

Refusing to surrender after coming so close, Alena pushed even harder. For a single heartbeat, the warrior's mind came into focus and she saw an image of a city built into a mountain. She saw the war that would soon take place there, at least how the warrior imagined it.

Then it was gone. Her mind, stretched to its limit, finally broke. Alena gasped as she snapped back into her own body, the transition as jarring as stepping in an unseen hole.

When she opened her eyes and glanced at the position of the sun it looked like almost no time had passed. The others gazed at her expectantly, but she shook her head. "I was close. I found one of them. It is as you suspected," she said to Sheren. "They march on Faldun. But I could tell no more."

It wasn't enough. They would need to know more. If Alena was going to be of service to this group, she needed to get stronger. She needed more power.

If war was coming, she meant to be prepared.

41

They had only advanced three levels up Faldun when Brandt made himself a promise. He swore that he would never again fight the Falari in this city.

Never again.

Even flat cities were a nightmare to fight within. That was a fact well known by military strategists. In Brandt's career the closest he'd ever come was fighting a skirmish in an outpost town near the Falari border, and *that* had been an experience he never wished to repeat.

Cities had too many corners, too many dark shadows that easily hid enemies.

It was bad enough when the attacks were made by warriors attacking with swords, but there were ways of protecting oneself then. Staying away from corners and shadows, as well as clearing spaces completely, guaranteed a warrior would at least have a warning when an attack came. A footstep or a yell, at least.

It was worse against archers like the Falari, who hid in buildings and on rooftops. Fighting against such enemies allowed for no warning. One moment, you'd be walking along the street, the next you'd have an arrow through the chest. That fate had already felled more than a few of Ren's allies.

To make the situation worse again, put the archers in a place like Faldun, which was more vertical than horizontal. Archers loosed arrows from dozens of paces above them, or even from below. Brandt and his sword were nearly useless. But he'd be even more useless with a bow in his hands.

Brandt quickly realized that this wasn't just a test of physical skill, but a test of awareness. Those Falari who best understood their environment were most likely to survive. It was in this battle Ren's true skills became apparent. Weylen's Senki was a very strong sword and excellent bow, but his awareness was preternatural.

Brandt considered himself hard to surprise, but he couldn't keep track of this fight. If not for Ren, he'd be dead a dozen times over.

Never again, Brandt swore.

Their objectives didn't make their task any easier, either. This was a battle that favored the ambush, the stationary archer with a wide field of view and protection at their back. But Ren and the others couldn't afford to lie in wait. They needed to move. They needed to join with Weylen and the others, then fight their way to Regar.

They followed intelligence Weylen had received earlier, that Regar was sheltered near the mouth of the entrance to the gate, about twenty levels above where they currently fought. Weylen and a handful of other warleaders hoped to assemble and send Regar straight to an early grave.

As they fought, though, Brandt worried they were already too late. They weren't fighting through an isolated pocket of resistance. They were fighting through a well-armed and organized defense. Somehow, this had been planned for some time.

Ana tugged at Brandt's arm and pulled him to cover just a moment before another arrow sliced through the spot he had just been standing. She glared at him. "Focus."

Brandt nodded. He and Ana both ran for the door of the building that housed their hopeful assassin. Brandt dodged another arrow just as he saw the archer release, then kicked open the flimsy wood door.

Ana led the way, running up the steps with her nearly impossible lightness. Brandt didn't bother to follow, instead ensuring the ground floor was clear. By the time he reached the top of the stairs the work would already be done.

The sound of the body thumping to the floor above him confirmed his prediction. A heartbeat later Ana reappeared, wiping the blood from her sword.

He had already lost track of the number of times they had repeated this process. And they still had a long way to go.

He would never again fight in Faldun.

They advanced through another bloody level, and then the resistance suddenly evaporated. Although they remained cautious, they were able to advance the next ten levels without a single attack. Brandt became cautiously optimistic. Perhaps they had a chance.

Ren didn't share his confidence. "They're gathering at choke points in the city." He gestured to the multitude of paths and stairs currently surrounding them. "There are too many ways up here, but the city is designed so that at some levels there are only one or two ways up. That is where we'll find more resistance."

Ren's gloomy prediction proved uncannily accurate.

They found the next pocket of resistance five levels

below the entrance to the tunnels. A wall of junk had been erected across their path, and archers behind the barricade stood shoulder to shoulder three ranks deep.

They found Weylen and the other warleaders, too. It wasn't the planned rendezvous point, but the barricade had stymied them all.

Ren and his party were among the last to arrive. They all took cover while the warleaders discussed their options. Curious, Brandt risked crawling forward, and he poked his head around an exposed corner. The barricade of tables and chairs appeared thick and sturdy, more than sufficient to halt any advance for a crucial few moments. And it was far enough away from any cover than any advance would be sure to meet a wall of arrows before it even reached the barricade.

Brandt couldn't see any easy way through the defenders. This fight was going to be bloody.

Brandt returned to cover, unwilling to risk his head any longer.

Ana stuck her head around next, then laughed. "Well, that will be easy."

"What do you mean?"

She looked at him as though he was one of the densest humans that had ever lived. "They're behind a wooden barricade."

He stared at her blankly.

"You have one of the strongest fire affinities I've ever seen," she said.

Apparently he was one of the densest human beings that had ever lived. He blamed the Falari. He'd gotten so used to people not using affinities he'd forgotten his own. He approached the warleaders. "If you wish, I can destroy that barricade."

Weylen looked uncertain. "With your affinity?"

Brandt nodded.

The warleaders shared nervous glances. In the past, they would have been honor bound to refuse such assistance, but the world had changed and Regar had stolen their gate. It was actually Merek, the once-uncertain warleader, who nodded. "Do it."

"You might get a little chilly," Brandt warned.

He returned to the corner and began to gather heat. He took it from the air and from the bodies around him. Then he reached out and took even more from those on the other side of the barricade. Confused shouts rose in response to his efforts.

He condensed the heat to two points within the barricade, causing both to catch fire. He continued stealing heat from the surroundings and funneled the power into the flames, spreading them faster than any natural fire.

The warriors on the other side of the barricade barely had time to realize what was happening. By the time they saw the smoke, the fire was already unquenchable. Flames consumed wood with the anger of a starved beast.

When the flames burned well on their own, Brandt shifted his focus. He pushed the fire from the barricade into the soldiers beyond. The rows of archers were engulfed in flame. Those who could ran, but the fire caught most of the enemy archers. Their screams filled Brandt's ears.

Behind him, Weylen and the other warleaders needed no further encouragement. They came around the corner with bows drawn, putting a merciful end to the screams of their opponents.

Brandt breathed in deeply. As a physical effort, the flames had cost him little. He had served mostly as a conduit.

The emotional toll, though, was a weightier burden to bear. Fire was a horrible way to die, and certainly not befitting of a warrior. Brandt much preferred the blade, expertly wielded to bring about a quick end. But war didn't always allow for honorable deaths.

Brandt swallowed deeply and pushed the thoughts out of his mind. He would pay for these moments later, but for now he needed to keep pushing ahead.

When the last of the screams faded away, Brandt collected the heat from the burning wood and directed it harmlessly away.

Weylen and the others stepped through the smoldering ruins of the barricade, and Brandt followed them. He forced himself to look upon what he had done. He refused to hide from the suffering he caused. The Falari pulled arrows from the corpses, unwilling to waste the precious resource.

Then the barricade and the bodies were behind them and Brandt moved on to the next challenge.

THE NEXT CHALLENGE came in the shape of the youngest prince of the empire.

Regar himself stood in front of a line of troops, but this time there was no barricade. Brandt wasn't fooled, though. Regar would serve as the barricade and more.

Weylen and their allies took cover, but no arrows came for them.

Instead, Regar spoke loudly. "Brandt. Ana. Will you join me?"

Brandt knew he risked his own death, but some part of him still trusted Regar, as unlikely as that seemed. He broke from cover and faced the prince. "Why?"

"This is needed, Brandt. The queen is not our enemy.

She has shown me the future, and although you might not see it yet, this is what needs to happen. The only reason it is a betrayal is because my father has refused to see the truth."

Brandt didn't see it. Regar's words hinted at madness, and he'd as much admitted to being under the queen's influence.

He couldn't be allowed the gate.

Brandt felt the power radiating off Regar. He didn't know what chance he had, and yet he felt as though he had no choice but to at least try. Brandt pulled heat, not from the surrounding area, but from the prince himself.

Against most people, the technique was fatal. Without heat, the body froze. But Regar was connected to the gate, to an endless source of power. No matter how much Brandt pulled, he wouldn't harm the prince.

It wasn't as good as being connected to a gate, but it was an excellent second option.

Brandt attacked, and a thin line of flame no thicker than a rope erupted from his palm.

That flame would have burned through stone and barely slowed.

Regar slapped it away as though batting away a child's plaything.

"Come now, Brandt. Be reasonable."

The buildup of power happened so quickly Brandt almost didn't have time to react. A wall of flame appeared between the two of them, the heat from it searing his skin even from dozens of paces away.

Brandt swore.

His attack had been the most powerful he knew. And it had done nothing.

In response, the prince would destroy them all.

In the face of such a strength, there was only one option.

Run.

The wall of flame pushed forward faster than Brandt could retreat. Behind him, his Falari allies scattered. Despite their determination, every warrior had a breaking point, and Regar's power far surpassed it. Brandt leaped, but the flame caught Brandt before he could land.

Brandt tried to channel the heat.

But even though he served as nothing more than a conduit, it was too much. The power filled him, the same way it had the first time he'd touched a gate. His muscles swelled and sweat poured from every gland.

Some of that power gave him strength. He landed awkwardly, rolled, and came to his feet, running faster than before. But it was still far too much energy.

He formed a ball of flame, knowing it to be useless, but he launched it in Regar's direction anyway. The prince laughed as he again slapped it away. The ball hit a stone wall and cracked it open with its strength.

But then Brandt was behind cover and he ran as fast and as far as his legs would carry him.

Behind him, the prince's laughter echoed between the stone buildings of Faldun.

42

When Alena met Brandt in the soulwalk she found herself in a small courtyard surrounded by stout stone buildings and a tall stone wall. She had never seen this place before, yet she could guess the location well enough from the descriptions she'd heard. "Highkeep?"

Standing beside her, Brandt nodded. He looked haggard, even in this realm of the souls.

Alena's curiosity pulled at her, but knowing that time passed differently here allowed her to approach the subject carefully. "Why did you choose Highkeep?"

"I'm not sure that I chose it," Brandt admitted. "But it is a place that I've been missing these last few weeks."

"Is this home for you?"

His eyes ran over the buildings and the walls, almost as if seeing them for the first time. "Maybe. But what I really miss is the routine and simplicity of monastic life."

Brandt led her through the monastery. Alena let him wander, following a step behind as he gathered his thoughts. When he spoke, it sounded as though his comments were half for him and half for her. "I didn't realize it then, but there was a joy to our days here. From the time the sun rose to when it set all I concerned myself with was training, a small set of monastic chores, and spending time with Ana. The world beyond these walls barely mattered."

They entered a hallway lined with doors that opened into small rooms that Alena guessed served as the monks' living quarters. Brandt lingered for some time on a single room. While it possessed nothing unique that would identify it, Alena noticed that more details were visible here than in other spaces.

This had been Brandt and Ana's room.

Brandt eventually broke away from the sight and led Alena back to the courtyard where he finally explained why he had called for her. "You're still on your way to Faldun?"

He barely let her nod before he continued. "Regar controls Faldun, and it's suicide to approach. We escaped with the emperor and are returning to a town where we can regroup and determine our next steps. You should meet us there."

Alena felt Brandt's emotions more acutely in this space. Between her connection with him and her own intuition, he couldn't hide behind his calm facade. A storm raged inside him, consuming him. She almost took pity on those he considered enemies.

Almost.

"What happened?"

"I fought Regar. With all my training, some part of me wondered if there might be a chance, some way to turn the power of the gate against him. But his strength made all my efforts and years of training seem like nothing." Brandt clenched his fist. "But I will get stronger. I will challenge him."

For a moment, the conviction in Brandt's voice made Alena a believer.

She felt some of the same emotion that drove Brandt. What had begun as a journey driven by curiosity had become something more, a need that demanded fulfillment. After her failed soulwalk a few days ago, she had made a promise that she would get stronger. Her weakness would no longer endanger her friends. She'd already lost Azaleth. She would lose no one else.

They spoke for a while longer. Alena asked after the others, and Brandt paused when he spoke of Ana. "She's upset," Brandt admitted. "This is the first time she's seen the power of the gates firsthand. She knows how much we have to overcome, but she still believes the queen's methods should not be ours."

Brandt gave her a pointed glance at that. Alena shook her head. "Perhaps when we are together I can figure out a way to teach you," she said, "but I don't know how to do it here."

Brandt looked disappointed, but he didn't look surprised.

Her answer wasn't wholly true. Perhaps here, teaching the technique would be even easier. She hadn't tried. But she was still uncomfortable with the idea of teaching Brandt. This, at least, allowed her time to mull the problem over.

They said their farewells, and she severed their connection.

Around a campfire, the others awaited her news.

She caught them up while she ate the food that had been prepared. Toren had assumed the responsibility of cooking, and even Jace admitted that the Etari's cooking was some of the best he had tasted. Alena almost hadn't responded to Brandt's summons because she feared she would miss the first, and possibly last, portions of the evening's food.

When she was finished, she looked around the group. She kept asking more of them. But only Jace struggled with their new destination. Her brother put his bowl down gently, but the storm clouds in his expression told the true story. "We need to return to the empire," he said.

"Why?"

"Because this is so much bigger than us," Jace said. ""We're closer to the imperial border than anyone else. We need to return and warn them."

"No." Alena took a deep breath. She didn't want to argue with her brother. "I'm certain the emperor has some way of communicating with others at home. He wouldn't have come otherwise. And I'm needed here. If anyone can stop Regar, it's me."

Jace almost stood but managed to remain seated. "Alena, do you even hear yourself? I'm amazed by you, but you're the daughter of a blacksmith. If you challenge the prince, I'm going to lose you for good, and I won't let that happen."

His admission dampened the fire burning in her stomach. The anger bled out of her. "I can't match his affinity," Alena admitted. "But I've studied the gates, and there might be something I can do. Would you turn away, if there was even a chance you could save lives?"

Jace's stare softened. "I couldn't."

"And neither can I."

Jace ran his hand through his hair, longer now than she'd ever seen it. He hadn't cut it since they left. "You know, sometimes I wish I just had a sister who had a passion for baking."

SHEREN GUIDED the change in their direction without problem. When Alena told her they were heading to Weylen's village, she'd nodded. "I know it well. It's more welcoming than most, and not far from here."

They made quick progress through the mountains. At times they used the passages that cut through the mountain, but more often they stuck to traditional valleys and passes. As Sheren explained it, they all radiated out from Faldun. While she had planned on using several in their original journey, they rarely saved time in this new direction.

The group grew more at ease with one another. Even Jace had come to trust both Toren and Sheren, making their journey substantially less stressful. Only once did they come across another war party, also heading to Faldun. Fortunately, they spotted the party from a long ways off, and were able to avoid it without problem.

The war party confirmed one of Sheren's suspicions. She explained as they resumed their journey, telling them of the divide among the Falari. She added that the party that had just passed them was one of those that held tightly to the old ways.

"So Regar is allied with those who would bring war to the empire?" Jace asked.

"It seems that way," Sheren said.

Jace's confusion mirrored Alena's own. "I don't understand."

Alena didn't either. Hopefully, once they had all reunited, someone could explain it to her.

As they journeyed, Alena offered what training she

could to Toren, but their progress remained slow. Regardless, he never complained.

One evening, his calm bothered her enough to make a point of it. "Doesn't your lack of progress frustrate you?" she asked.

"Of course," the Etari said, "but I am doing all that I can, and likewise, I believe that you are doing all that you can. Complaint is pointless. As is letting frustration get the better of me."

Alena agreed, but agreeing and living according to the belief were two very different challenges.

Toren looked uncertain, an expression Alena had come to learn meant that he had something to say but was nervous about how she might take it. "What?"

"It seems to me that you worry too much about timelines you cannot control. The presence of your brother anchors you in the past, where events have already taken place. The thought of the battles before us pull you relentlessly toward the future. But as you are lost in the past and the future, you miss out on what is happening right before your eyes." He paused. "And the present moment is a good one."

The soft conviction in his voice caught her off guard. She looked at Toren as though seeing him for the first time.

"I'll try," she promised. She meant it, too.

Three days passed. Three days of quiet hiking up and down the endless mountains of Falar. And it ended in despair.

For when they reached the valley that held Weylen's village, they saw that their destination was already under attack.

43

Their escape from Faldun and the days that followed became little more than one continuous nightmare. At first, Brandt had thought that the escape from the mountain city would be the worst of it. And it had been horrible.

Regar's planning was apparent with every step they took. The number of Falari loyal to him surprised them all, from Brandt to Weylen. By the time they made their retreat, the battle for Faldun was almost over. Regar's forces controlled the majority of the city, and Brandt and his allies escaped with the emperor through one of the last two contested exits. Had they been delayed much longer, Brandt often wondered if all hope would have been lost.

But their escape from Faldun was only the beginning of their trouble.

They first learned that harsh truth two days after putting the city walls behind them, random arrows falling among them as they ran. The patrols protecting their retreat announced that two war parties pursued them.

After a day of running, Weylen made the difficult choice

to turn and fight. Exhausted from the pursuit, his warriors still outnumbered the pursuers. They chose their battleground and settled in.

But the pursuit never closed. They waited, and although Brandt didn't understand their tactics, Weylen did. "They're waiting for others. We're being penned in."

A quick conference among the warleaders led to another hard choice. They would separate, all of them agreeing to converge on Weylen's village a fortnight hence.

The parties separated without fanfare, and Weylen's own party continued on.

Brandt didn't like the idea of separating, but he understood the logic. The time to fight hadn't come yet. They were exhausted and on the run. They were reactive. If large forces met, the odds were against them.

Separating gave them the best chance of surviving and regrouping.

As he watched Weylen, Brandt also realized that their initial expedition had stumbled upon a war party that held a position of considerable authority in the Falari hierarchy. That realization led to another: Regar had always planned to meet Weylen.

The more he thought about it, the more he understood the devious brilliance of the idea. He convinced his enemies to escort him into the trap he'd built. Had Weylen died in Faldun, Brandt didn't know who would lead the resistance.

It explained the lack of fighting on the road, as well, and why Regar hadn't tried to escape when Weylen's village was under attack.

If Brandt hadn't also been a victim of Regar's deception he would've been far more impressed.

Weylen's decision to separate the gathered war parties eased the pressure of pursuit for a full day as their pursuers decided on a new tactic, and for a while Brandt could almost relax. Perhaps they would make it without too much trouble after all.

An ambush by a Falari war party heading toward Faldun killed that hopeful belief.

Weylen and the others fought the ambush off, but they lost two more warriors.

The next four days were filled with painfully slow movement. Ren's scouts ran leagues every day, alert for the movement of other war parties. The land seemed to be suddenly swarming with them. But it only proved Weylen's belief. Regar and his allies had hoped to pen them in.

Now war parties played an enormous and deadly game of hide-and-seek in the mountains. Day after day Weylen had to make the difficult choice of hiding or fighting.

Most often they chose to hide. They were tired, and Weylen hadn't left his village with his full war party in the first place. Many remained behind to heal and to repair the damage the village had suffered. Of those that had come, too many had already fallen in Faldun and the days that followed. Against a fully armed and well-rested war party, Weylen's warriors had little chance.

Brandt couldn't remember a time when he'd been more exhausted. Silence had become customary long ago, not just because of the threat of discovery, but because the energy required to hold a conversation no longer existed. Every bit of focus and attention was given instead to the never-ending task of avoiding ambush and moving like ghosts through the mountains.

Brandt knew no way to express his gratitude for their Falari escort. Had he been responsible for this journey alone he was certain he wouldn't have survived. The constant vigilance required was too much for any single person. Only by sharing the burden could they survive.

Then, nearly a week after leaving the walls, Alena informed him that Weylen's village was under attack.

The news lit a fire under Weylen's warriors. For days now they been beaten down and pursued, with no clear objective other than to survive.

But no longer. Not only was their home under attack, but it was the place they had all agreed to meet. If it fell, they lost not only their heart, but the whole war.

Their pace had already been demanding, but Weylen increased it anyway. They rose long before the sun, taking the first steps before the first light of the day. They marched relentlessly, not even stopping for meals. They continued well into the evening, then crashed to the ground where they stood whenever the march was called.

Brandt also worried about Hanns. The emperor regained his strength day by day, but the going was slow, and the old man couldn't keep up the pace demanded by Weylen. Hanns walked when he could, but he still spent a fair amount of the day in his litter, carried by teams of guards who never uttered a complaint.

Brandt felt like something was going to crack. But when it did, it came from an unexpected direction.

One night, as they were lying down next to each other, Ana asked him a question. "Do you think we're doing the right thing?"

Brandt was too tired for the question, and he answered it by instinct. "I don't know. Does right or wrong even matter? There's only what must be done."

He'd been looking up at the stars, but Ana turned his face toward hers. "You keep saying that. And it scares me."

"Why?"

"Because I'm worried that I'm losing you."

He held her other hand between his own. Sleep pulled at him, but he sensed her unease. "I can't promise you that I'll survive, but I can promise you I will do everything in my power to always come back to you. And if I fail, I will wait for you on the other side of the gates."

"That's not what I mean," Ana said.

His tired mind didn't understand.

"I know you're focused on learning how to defeat Regar and the queen," she said, "but I fear some of the actions you'll take will destroy you."

Exhausted both mentally and physically from their days of running and hiding, Brandt finally snapped. "Do you think I like the idea of what I might have to do? I detest it! I know that to deny a clean death to an enemy might make me into a monster. But what am I supposed to do? How else am I supposed to protect you? How else am I supposed to defend the empire that I swore I would give my life for?"

Ana, apparently, had also reached the end of her patience. She didn't shrink away from his whispered outburst. "Stop hiding behind us!" she demanded. "You say you're only doing these things out of your love for us, but those of us that love you don't want you to go down this path."

She paused, then stabbed him deeper. "You're not doing this for us, you're doing this for you. That's why you lied about the gate, even if you knew it would do you no good against the queen."

Her words hit with all the force of Regar's attacks. Brandt opened his mouth to respond, but had no idea what to say. Ana saved him the trouble. She rolled away so that her back was to him, cutting off the conversation.

He saw her shoulders, softly rising and falling with her

silent sobs in light of the stars. He reached out to comfort her, but his hand stopped just short of her shoulder.

How could she believe that of him?

Brandt snarled and turned over as well. And for the first time in years, they fell asleep apart from one another.

44

Alena looked down the mountainside at the small group of warriors that patrolled the valley. The sun was setting, lighting the underside of nearby clouds with gorgeous pinks and dark shadows. The patrol below them consisted of six warriors, and each focused their attention on the village even farther below.

Beside her, Jace whispered softly, "Tell me more."

Over the past two days, that command had become shorthand for using a soulwalk to gain more information.

Alena did.

She'd practiced enough in the past few days that she no longer needed to close her eyes. She felt the shift in her mind as she reached out to explore the thoughts of the party below. She explored each for a moment, then answered her brother. "The same as the others. They're confident and eager for reinforcements."

Jace didn't respond, but she could see him assessing the situation yet again.

"Do they know how soon?"

"Nothing definite. Soon enough that their confidence is high."

Once the war party was out of sight, Jace nodded. "Let's head back, then."

They climbed higher up the mountain to a small cave that provided some protection and sheltered them from the worst of the elements. It had been home for the past few days, high enough above any commonly traveled paths to keep them relatively safe from discovery.

Once the enemy had been spotted, Jace took command of their little group, not intentionally perhaps, but completely all the same. Sheren called him her warleader, which seemed to irritate and inspire her brother in equal measures.

Jokes aside, he was best suited for the role. Toren was a skilled warrior, but his knowledge of strategy was limited. Sheren had laughed when they asked her if she possessed any military experience. "I would be beaten by a child with a stick," she confessed.

Jace had been the one who ordered the party higher up the mountain. He argued that the vantage point allowed them a better view of the situation and gave them the advantage of elevation if they were discovered.

The suggestion turned out to be even wiser than they'd expected. None of the patrols seemed interested in anything besides the village. In their days of watching, Alena had barely seen anyone do much more than glance up the mountains.

Their observations revealed the lay of the land. Weylen's village wasn't just under attack, it was completely surrounded. But the siege, if that was the best word for it, defied Alena's expectations. Occasionally an enemy warrior might wander close enough to the village to lob a few arrows at exposed targets, but for the most part they played a waiting game, content to rest until their numbers were sufficiently overwhelming the village had no hope of victory. Until then, they wore the village down by preventing the gathering of food or supplies.

The patience of the invaders, along with the certainty of reinforcements, forced Alena and the others to act.

Jace estimated the invading Falari had about seventy warriors surrounding the village. They rarely congregated, instead choosing to remain scattered around the village. That scattering prevented Alena from sneaking into the village, but it also provided ample opportunity for ambush.

Jace came up with the plan and drilled the vital aspects of it into the others. They needed to hit fast, then retreat, leaving little to no evidence of their passage. They would divide the enemy's attention, opening up further opportunities.

This was a side of Jace she hadn't seen before. He assessed and planned, and was surprisingly meticulous in his considerations.

Though he wouldn't have chosen the circumstances, she believed he commanded well.

She ended up being their greatest uncertainty. As their planning concluded, Jace looked to her. "What is the extent of your powers?"

"What do you mean?"

"Can you blind someone? Or make them flee in terror? Could you make them kill themselves?"

"Jace—"

"I'm not proud of these ideas, but I'd be a poor commander if I didn't ask. If you want to save the Etari gate, this is the way forward."

They sat in silence around the fire as Alena decided. "I

don't know," she finally answered. "It's possible, but I've never tried."

Jace nodded. "Then tomorrow we find out."

TOMORROW CAME TOO SOON, and Alena didn't sleep well. Their situation put her in a reflective mood. Part of her had always understood why the Etari feared soulwalkers as they did. What Jace proposed was a rational request in warfare. But to strip the will of a person in such a way, it did seem like a power that shouldn't exist.

They rose before the sun, scouting the patterns of those who patrolled the village. By the time evening fell again, Jace had chosen the perfect place to strike.

That location was a small widening of a path that passed underneath several sturdy trees. Patrols passed regularly underneath, and while they had a clear view of the village from the path, that section of trail was hidden from other parts of the path. They could attack without being discovered. Jace buried himself in some bushes near the trail while Toren and Alena hid in one of the trees above. Toren would attack first, hopefully disorienting the party and killing one or two before they realized they were under attack.

Jace would finish what Toren began.

Alena worried about her brother. Tonight he would be called upon to kill, which he hadn't done since that first ambush when they first entered Falar. He refused to speak on the subject when Alena brought it up in private. He insisted he was fine, and Alena had little choice but to trust her brother.

They timed their ambush well. They hadn't been settled in their position long when a group of six Falari warriors came down the path. They appeared alert, but like all the invaders, focused on the village below. They walked right underneath Alena without once looking up.

As planned, Toren launched the initial attack. He set two stones spinning the moment he saw the Falari in the distance. The Etari warrior could spin and launch two stones confidently and sometimes managed a third, a feat almost as impressive as any Alena had ever seen. Tonight she assisted him by spinning two more stones, ready for him to launch. Just spinning the stones took all her focus.

Toren's first stone struck the last member of the Falari party right between the eyes, instantly killing the unsuspecting warrior.

The man directly in front of the first victim didn't even have time to turn around before another stone caught him in the forehead.

Alena watched, amazed by Toren's precision. He made it look easy, though it was anything but.

As soon as Alena felt Toren take the stones from her, Alena dropped into a soulwalk. Time shifted, now moving at the speed of thought. Alena found the four remaining warriors with ease. She studied them. She felt their confidence, colored by their slowly growing surprise.

Alena saw Jace through the thoughts of the Falari leader as her brother stepped out in front of them. But something was wrong.

The leader was surprised to see Jace. But after that heartbeat of shock wore off, she saw Jace's stance through the eyes of a practiced swordsman, a man who had seen countless battles. The Falari leader saw the hesitation in Jace's stance, the slight widening of the eyes that gave away Jace's sudden fear.

Alena felt the warrior's confidence return, stronger than before.

She cursed, but there was nothing she could do now. The warrior and her brother were only moments away from clashing, and Jace didn't even have his sword up yet.

Then she remembered she was far from helpless.

She was a soulwalker.

And she would not lose her brother.

Alena searched the Falari leader and found his fear, the same fear they all carried. Only those with the true death wish felt nothing in the face of drawn steel. She knew she could take that fear, now suppressed by the Falari's battle instincts, and grow it into a crippling terror.

But even the thought of doing that reminded her of what she had done to Jace outside of Landow. She had stripped him of his will.

And she froze.

Toren's stones found both their targets, but it would take him a precious heartbeat or two to get the next stone spinning fast enough to launch. The lead warrior in the patrol stepped forward, drawing his bow in one smooth motion. The warrior walking just behind the leader, the only other one still standing, turned his attention to the trees above where he spotted Alena. Her attention fractured through the numerous connections in their small space. She saw the second warrior looking at her just as she saw the leader looking at Jace.

Her heart went out to Jace, driven by instinct. She desired to be with him at the end. She shared in her brother's paralyzing fear.

Move! she shouted.

Connected to him like she was, it snapped the fear that

froze his limbs. Jace sidestepped just as the archer released, the arrow flying safely to Jace's side.

His trance broken, Jace's training took over. He moved with liquid smoothness, stepping in and cutting down the lead archer with one move as the archer hurried to bring another bolt to bear.

In the confusion and excitement of the events surrounding Jace, Alena lost track of her own dilemma.

Fortunately, Toren did not. He launched himself from his branch to hers, tackling her as the second archer released his arrow. Alena's world tumbled end over end as they struck tree branches and crashed into the bushes below. She couldn't breathe, the weight of Toren limp on top of her. She felt something warm and wet trickle down her cheek and then Jace was there, a concerned expression on his face.

Together, they helped Toren to his feet and made their way away from the site of the ambush.

They recovered that night back in their cave, each of them nursing new wounds. Alena worried that she had cracked some ribs, but she was otherwise unharmed. Toren had taken the arrow meant for her, but the arrowhead had punched clean through his upper left shoulder and was relatively easily removed. Jace bandaged the wound and cleaned it, and although Toren's left arm wouldn't be much use in the coming days, he was otherwise unharmed.

They had gotten lucky, and they all knew it. After the failed ambush, Jace was the only one who kept a clear head. He had been the one to make sure they didn't leave a trail, including the blood that Toren lost.

They didn't speak, and Alena felt the anger radiating off of Jace. Her brother was upset at himself, but he didn't realize that. Instead, he glared at Alena. Though he said nothing, she understood the direction of his thoughts. He blamed her for not using her abilities to stop them. He wouldn't understand how doing so affected her. Frustrated, she stood up and walked away from the camp, finding comfort away from her brother's angry glares.

Toren came to her. He didn't say anything, but let his presence be enough. Alena appreciated him more than ever at that moment.

"He's mad at me, and maybe he should be," Alena admitted. "I could've done it. I felt their fears and I could have done it. But then I thought of Jace and I couldn't. But if I had, maybe you wouldn't be hurt and maybe he wouldn't be upset." She knew she was rambling, but she couldn't seem to stop the words from tumbling from her.

Toren reached out and grabbed her hand, the first time he had done so.

He didn't say anything, but he didn't have to.

Alena stepped closer to him and leaned her head against his chest, feeling the strong beat of his heart.

She closed her eyes and relaxed. They were alive and they were together.

The rest they could figure out.

45

When Brandt finally met up with Alena he wasn't sure which of them was in worse condition. Weylen's war party's escape had been contested up until two days ago, when the last of their pursuit had mysteriously faded away. Ren believed it had something to do with the nature of the war party's alliances, but from the tone in his voice he sounded anything but certain.

Regardless, their war party had held to a demanding pace even without pursuit. With their home under threat, they wouldn't rest until their families were safe. So when they met with Alena, he was exhausted beyond reason. And she looked about the same.

Alena's face felt like the first friendly one he had seen in some time. He and Ana hadn't spoken much since their fight several nights ago, and neither of them had apologized yet. Their ongoing fight irritated him, and he meant to end it once they'd both had a good night's rest.

Alena embraced him, but not too tightly. He saw her

wince as they broke apart. “We set an ambush several days back,” she explained. “It didn’t go so well.”

“You’re all okay?”

“Except for our pride.”

A brief period of introductions followed as the assembled parties got to know one another. They swapped tales back and forth, catching everyone up on the most recent developments.

Brandt liked Alena’s little war party. Jace he already knew and respected, and Toren had a silent strength about him that Brandt appreciated. Sheren was perhaps the outlier, but when Brandt heard what she had done for the group he elected to withhold his judgment. After the introductions were complete, talk turned to the situation in the village. The work that Alena and Jace had done proved invaluable as they considered their next steps. Ren sent a few scouts to confirm the information, but Jace’s detailed report would save both time and lives.

Hanns joined the circle as the warleaders discussed the options for attack. The unfortunate news was that no matter what, the fight was going to be bloody. The invaders had brought a substantial force and if Alena’s belief that reinforcements were coming was accurate, Weylen and his war party would be in for a rough fight.

Hans interrupted the discussion. “I’ll do it.”

His statement caused all the warleaders to look at him as one, disbelief in every stare.

Brandt reminded himself that the Falari didn’t truly comprehend the powers the emperor could summon. A few of them had seen Regar’s display back in Faldun, but without developed affinities of their own, they didn’t understand. Perhaps, in the intervening time, they had come to believe it had been a deception of some sort. The mind would always search for a comfortable explanation when confronted by the unknown.

Brandt knew Hanns could take the town if his connection to the gates was strong, but one question needed to be asked. "Are you in a condition to do so?"

Hanns' answer was brief, reminding Brandt that as much as the emperor welcomed criticism in private, he didn't accept it in front of others.

"Yes. And I need to test myself. Doing so here can save valuable lives."

Hanns had been walking most of the day the last few days. Considering their pace, the terrain, and the emperor's age, that alone encouraged Brandt.

Brandt and Hanns argued with the warleaders together. It was only when they proposed a compromise that their strategy was accepted. Hanns would attack first, coming up the main road to the village. Weylen and the others would position themselves carefully around the valley. If Hanns' attack failed, they would launch their own strike from several directions at once.

They decided to attack early the next morning. They each tried to grab what rest they could. Brandt considered speaking with Ana, but the timing didn't feel right. He elected to wait until after the battle.

In the morning, Hanns led the attack, followed by Brandt, Ana, and his guards. Alena and her war party had chosen to remain behind, content to watch and nurse their wounds. They were among the reserve Weylen could call on. Hanns' fellow imperials all stood behind the emperor, though. When he unleashed the gates, they didn't want to be between him and his enemies.

The imperials made no effort to find cover. Brandt itched to at least hide behind a tree, but Hanns gave them no chance to advance safely. He'd even waved away their idea of creating some impromptu shields.

The first arrows came without warning, shot from invaders hiding in the trees. Brandt never even saw where they came from. One moment they were walking, the next a half dozen arrows hung frozen in the air before them.

Hanns waved his hand, and the arrows spun and returned on the lines they'd come from. Brandt heard at least two archers fall from their perches.

The Falari tried again, but again the arrows stopped in midair, and again Hanns returned them to the archers who'd launched them.

Two attempts seemed to be enough to teach the Falari their lesson. The war party responded in typical Falari fashion. In Brandt's own experience, the Falari rarely retreated. When they faced an overwhelming force, they simply redoubled their effort.

It typically made them fearsome foes, but today that instinct worked against them.

The war party gathered on the road before the imperials, lining up in rows with bows drawn. On command, two dozen arrows cut through the space between the combatants.

And froze a dozen paces in front of Hanns. They fell to the ground.

If Brandt had been commanding the Falari, he would have ordered the retreat.

He heard the emperor's skill ringing in his head, his own affinity responding to the use of the gates. Brandt heard the songs of the elements, all playing at different strengths, all coursing through Hanns. The emperor's feats were a combination of awareness, control, and unbelievable power. The battle was over before it started.

But the Falari didn't think that way.

The Falari dropped their bows, drawing knives and swords. With a shouted command, they charged.

Hans came to a stop, standing calmly in the center of the road. Brandt heard the low hum of stone once again building, and the power of it squeezed his head like a melon. Ahead of them, stone of all shapes and sizes lifted from the road and the surrounding area, cracking with a rolling thunder that echoed in the valley. When the echoes faded, hundreds of small pieces of granite hung in the air like a cloud.

The Falari charge faltered, expressions ranging from anger to confusion to fear. This wasn't battle as the Falari understood it. They'd eliminated affinities from their people, and even in their fight against imperials, affinities rarely made a difference.

And they didn't understand the power of the gate.

Hanns released the cloud. It burst forward, none of the stones aimed at any particular target. Instead, they were all flung at their enemies like an angry swarm of insects.

The result devastated the invading Falari. The force of the impacts drove those in the front from their feet, the equivalent force of being shot by a dozen blunt and powerful bolts at once. The only people who survived were those near the back of the charge, and many of those looked grievously wounded.

Brandt looked to the emperor. Any worries he'd had about Hanns' readiness vanished. His ruler hadn't even broken a sweat, and he looked upon the remaining Falari with a cold disdain.

They continued walking the road to Weylen's village, but the outcome had already been decided. Those who survived the charge ran in terror, but the battle had been visible to everyone in the valley. Before long, more warriors came down to the road, but they were Weylen's fighters, come to report that every invader in the valley was running.

Weylen's village had been freed, and it hadn't cost them a single allied life.

46

Fear had many different faces. Some Alena recognized, but in the aftermath of Hanns' display of power, she discovered an unfamiliar one.

In her travels, she sometimes forgot that she was a child of the empire, exposed to certain beliefs. Within those familiar borders, affinities were largely accepted as a part of life. Limited by the cost as they were, they didn't often mean much. But they existed. While the depth of Hanns' gate-assisted abilities surprised her, her surprise was little more than an issue of scale.

But the Falari didn't have her daily experiences. To them, Hanns' attacks were a power straight from the cautionary tales of their ancestors.

Today, Alena saw the fear of a people whose legends had come to life. Legends that ended in disaster.

She wondered if Hanns and the other imperials saw as she did. Hanns grinned, no doubt pleased he had freed the town without the loss of friendly life. From a military perspective, she supposed, it was a great victory.

But Hanns had lost something, perhaps more valuable than a few lives, in his attack.

The others might not see, but she did. The Falari warriors avoided the clump of imperials, several of them making small gestures she took to be warding signs. Hanns might have won the battle, but he very well might have lost his allies.

Alena watched Weylen navigate the tricky waters of this fragile alliance. Of course he was grateful that his town was free. Horrified by the means or not, no leader wished for the deaths of his people. So Weylen welcomed the imperials and their Falari allies into the village, filling every open room with a warm and exhausted body.

Greetings were exchanged, but it was agreed that the traditional welcome feast be postponed for a day. Those who had escaped Faldun all appeared to be sleepwalking, and those besieged within the village still jumped every time a cloud passed overhead, worried it might be a flight of arrows. Alena suspected another motive as well: another day would allow Weylen to speak with his people, to calm them and discuss Hanns' presence.

Alena and the others made no complaint about the extra rest. Toren received better healing in the village, and Alena collapsed into the bed given to her. For the first time in more days than she cared to count, she felt safe, and until this moment, she hadn't realized how much she needed that feeling. Despite the sun still being in the sky, she fell asleep the moment she lay down and didn't wake until the next morning.

She woke early, the growling in her stomach reminding her it had been over a day since she'd eaten a full meal. Unable to ask the Falari for directions, she followed the scent of cooking food until she found a long hall where an assorted collection of Falari and imperial guards broke their fast. Seeing the different people together made her think her initial thoughts about the fall of their alliance were overly pessimistic.

Alena saw Ana sitting alone and joined her. The former wolfblade gave her a wan smile and gestured to the open chairs.

The whole village felt as though it was waking up from a long and luxurious sleep, but Ana looked as though sleep was a distant memory.

"It's good to see you," Alena said.

"And you," Ana replied.

"You also look like you fought the battle for the village yourself."

Ana didn't respond for a heartbeat, and Alena worried she'd offended the other woman. She liked Ana and had all the respect in the world for her, but they rarely spoke alone.

"I haven't been sleeping well lately," she confessed.

Over the course of the meal, the truth spilled from Ana, and Alena saw, for the first time, the other half of Brandt's life. Ana spoke of their disagreement, leading to the fight that drove a wedge between them.

"I'm sorry," Alena said, feeling guilty for her role. "I—"

Ana shook her head, interrupting Alena. "I've blamed you, Alena, but this isn't your fault. He would have discovered the knowledge eventually. He's pursued it too long not to find the answer." She sipped at some tea. "Once, I admired his dedication."

Ana focused on her. "Will you teach him?"

The other woman's lack of condemnation pained Alena more than an outburst would have. Had Ana raged at her, Alena could have fought back. This, she had no defense against.

She didn't know the answer to Ana's question. No doubt, Brandt would come to her, probably today, to ask for instruction. Before Ana's tale, she had decided to teach him what she could, trusting Brandt to use it wisely.

Alena thought of the Falari reaction to Hanns' abilities, their deep-seated fear of what the gates and affinities could do. Didn't she believe the gates were too powerful a tool for humans? How was her knowledge any different? Like the gates, it allowed for humans to possess powers not meant for them. And who knew how it twisted people?

Had the queen once been an honorable warrior like Brandt?

Alena shied away from that thought. Better to think of the queen only as an enemy, devoid of history or personality.

She decided she wouldn't teach Brandt. And that was what she told Ana.

The relief on her friend's face helped Alena believe she had made the right decision.

Their conversation turned to lighter topics. Eventually others joined them. Brandt and Jace came in together, sweaty and dusty, no doubt the result of an early morning training session. Alena thought Jace looked a bit like a dog following his new master. Ever since he was young, Jace had adored the wolfblades, and now he had the chance to train with one of their best. Jace might sometimes hate her for pulling him on this journey, but he'd thank her now. Toren and Sheren joined the table not long after.

Alena, already finished with her breakfast and feeling pleasantly lethargic, leaned back and enjoyed the conversation. It was awkward, with speakers coming from three different languages, and many people strangers to one another. And yet, Alena felt something here. On instinct, she dropped into a soulwalk. Her bonds with Jace and Brandt appeared first, but she saw the web already growing between others.

Not long after, Ren came to them. He looked annoyed. "The emperor has summoned the imperials."

The mood around the table soured. With a single sentence, Ren separated what had been coming together. Alena and the others said their apologies, then followed Ren out of the hall and into town, stopping at the house that held the emperor and many of his guards.

Alena had expected the emperor to receive better treatment. Despite the mixed feelings surrounding his actions, he was still the emperor of the most populous lands in the world. But his chambers were no larger than Alena's.

Hanns gestured them in. If his actions the day before had exhausted him in any way, he didn't show it. He gathered them around a table. "We need to discuss our next steps. This morning I've spoken with Olen. He's mobilized many of the empire's forces. Their orders are to approach the Falari border. He and I are in agreement; our best option is to march the army down to Faldun and besiege it."

Alena took note. Hanns had been in conversation with Olen, so he knew at least that much about soulwalking.

Brandt spoke quietly. "Faldun's never been taken."

"It's never been attacked by a man with the power of two gates before."

Alena thought of what she had learned of the Falari from Sheren. "You'll face resistance every step you take through these mountains. Your forces will be decimated by the time you arrive, even if you accompany them. You can't protect everyone constantly."

"Which is why we need the blessing of Weylen. He's considered one of the wisest warleaders in Falar. We offer him an alliance. In exchange, we'll help him crush his enemies."

In a flash of insight, Alena saw the plan behind the plan. Hanns' alliance would be designed to win him Falar. Alena didn't know exactly how it would happen. Perhaps after the siege of Faldun, Hanns would leave units of his military scattered about the land. Perhaps his methods would be more subtle. But if Weylen agreed, Falar would be the newest addition to the empire within Alena's lifetime.

She trusted Weylen to see the same, but he might not have any choice but to agree. Refusal of Hanns' offer was essentially surrender to Regar and his allies. And Weylen, as far as Alena knew, *was* interested in closer ties to the empire. Perhaps he wouldn't be opposed to Hanns' unspoken plans.

The simple brilliance of Hanns' plan angered her. Even now, every move he made seemed only to benefit him in the end. It almost seemed too perfect to be coincidence. She didn't care if Hanns was the emperor or not. She glared at him, her voice nearly a growl. "Did you plan this from the start?"

Hanns' glare made her want to cower. Though he didn't display it openly, she could feel the power radiating off him. Even without the gates, he maintained a commanding presence. While he'd always been friendly to her in the past, she couldn't allow herself to forget this man had a policy that killed those who disagreed with him in public. And one didn't become an Anders through kindness alone.

"I did not," he said, his voice colder than the mountain glaciers. "And if you imply as much again, I won't care what aid you've given in the past. Am I understood?"

She pushed out the moment as far as she dared. "Clearly."

Alena's question, and the reaction that followed, quelled

all other discussion around the table. Hanns nodded. "We'll meet with Weylen and the other warleaders tonight. It has already been arranged. Is there anything else?"

Alena's heart sank through her stomach when Brandt spoke. "Alena knows a way to ignore the cost."

The emperor looked at her, undisguised eagerness in his eyes. "You do?"

Brandt answered for her. "A soulwalking technique that bonds with a soul as it dies. The soul's strength then becomes the soulwalker's."

"Is this true?" Hanns asked.

"It is." If lying might have worked, she would have.

"Then teach it to us. It will be needed in the fight to come."

Alena took a deep breath.

"Anders I said I should not."

Hanns paused, apparently not expecting more resistance from Alena after her first reprimand. "Despite what Anders sometimes thinks, he is no longer the emperor. You *will* teach the technique to our affinity-gifted warriors."

Alena cursed Brandt for putting her in this position. He must have sensed her reluctance and hoped to persuade her through the emperor. In private, they might have spoken and reasoned together. But he had taken that opportunity away.

But what Brandt didn't understand was that she hated orders. Mother and Father would have told him that in a heartbeat, had the subject ever come up. If one asked as a friend, Alena would travel to the ends of the continent. But if the same request was framed as an order, well, they could go to the gates.

In the corner of her vision, she saw the panicked look on

Jace's face. Of those in the room, he knew her best, and he knew exactly what she was thinking.

She knew her action was foolish.

But it was also right.

"I will not."

Alena felt the warping of Hanns' power, the preparation for its unleashing. She braced herself, knowing any gesture on her part was useless. Hanns had the power to kill her with a thought.

Jace's hand was on the hilt of his sword. If Hanns acted against her, she wasn't sure how Jace would react. She and the empire tore his loyalties cleanly in two.

Alena sat calmly against Hanns' glare. For the first time in some days she felt at peace. Her knowledge would die with her.

"Get out," Hanns said. The words were spoken softly, as though if he spoke any louder he might loose the rage building within him. "Out of respect for your service to the empire, I will let you live. But you are forever exiled. Should you be found within my borders, you will be sentenced to death."

There was no use saying anything more. Exile, she imagined, was better than she could have expected. People didn't stand up to the emperor. Those who tried were swiftly cut down.

She left the room without a word, no longer an imperial.

47

Brandt focused on his breath, but his mind refused to rest on the sensation. At most, he could follow a couple of breaths before his attention wandered elsewhere. Ana's hurt glare stabbing into his back didn't help.

If Ana would just yell at him, Brandt thought it might be easier. But for all her anger and all her disappointment, she refused to speak unkindly to him.

That didn't mean she hadn't expressed herself, though.

Competing desires tore him not in two, but into shreds. He loved Ana, respected Alena, obeyed Hanns, and would die for his empire. What did he do, though, when those desires all pulled him in different directions?

Once, when he'd been training as a wolfblade, the instructors had made him complete an unusual exercise. A circle of other candidates stood around him, shoulder to shoulder, about a pace away. His instructions were to stand stiff as a board, arms crossed over his chest. He was pushed, and so fell toward the circle, where another candidate would catch him and push him again.

Forced to remain stiff, Brandt had no choice but to trust the other candidates to catch him. He failed if he lost his posture. The others failed if they let him fall.

Being young and aggressive, the pushes hadn't been gentle, and it had taken all his control not to break form and catch himself. But he'd been tossed about in that small circle for what seemed like an eternity.

He felt like that now, too. Tossed about violently, his direction changing moment by moment. But now there was no one to catch him.

If he had more time, he might be able to think his way out of this mess, but there was none. Hanns expected him shortly for their meeting with Weylen.

Brandt opened his eyes and stood up, stretching after his prolonged and failed attempt at meditation. Ana glared at him with red-rimmed eyes. He almost went to her, but stopped. What had broken between them would take more than an apology. It would take time and effort. Both of which he was willing to give.

But not now.

"I'm sorry," he said. He watched, hoping his apology would melt some small part of the ice from her stare. When it didn't, he turned his back and left.

He would make it right. He would.

As soon as he had the chance.

Hanns paced the small quarters he'd been given. Brandt had mixed feelings when he saw the emperor. He still felt respect, both for the man and the position he held. He agreed with the emperor's decisions on what the empire must do next. But he wished the emperor had worked with Alena somehow, instead of exiling her. Given what Hanns might have done, Brandt supposed the decision had been merciful, but it still upset him, if for no other reason than he disliked being torn between friends.

Hanns barely acknowledged Brandt, too wrapped up in his own thoughts. Eventually, a guard informed him they had been summoned, and a focus returned to the emperor's gaze.

Their audience wasn't just with Weylen. More warleaders had arrived, the next wave of the many that would come. Weylen was still the key, but the emperor needed to persuade more than one person.

They were ushered into a small hall where there were no chairs. Weylen and Ren stood together in a circle of men and women. Brandt assumed he was seeing a group of warleaders and their Senkis.

Weylen, never one to mince words, began. "I expect you seek an alliance between our people, Emperor Anders VI?"

Some hint of menace in Weylen's tone brought Brandt up short. Hanns noticed the same tone, and a slight frown darkened his face. "That had been my hope, yes." His reply was cautious, as tentative as a man knowing he took steps onto thin ice.

"What are your terms?" Weylen inquired, his question as sharp as a blade.

"For us to determine," Hanns replied. "But Regar has committed treason, and he cannot be allowed to control your gate."

"Will you kill your son?" This from another warleader.

Brandt saw Hanns take the question like a physical blow, flinching away from it. He realized in all this time he hadn't thought much on what Hanns must be suffering. His own blood had betrayed him, stolen from him what the empire needed most. Now his duty demanded he march against the child he had raised.

Hanns answered the question slowly. "I would prefer not to, but if no other option is left to me, then yes."

Silence greeted the answer, broken a dozen long heartbeats later by Weylen. "And if we succeed, you wish the gate for yourself."

Hanns looked uncomfortable under the questioning. No doubt, he'd never tasted this flavor of diplomacy. Even by Falari standards, Weylen's inquiries were direct. "Yes. At least until the queen is defeated."

"It is said you already control more gates than her, yet cannot defeat her. What difference will a third make?"

The question finally broke Hanns' composure. "I'll only know if I have the gate to try!"

Surprisingly, the emperor's outburst appeared to impress the warleaders more than his composure. They nodded as he spoke.

"Tell us more about your proposed alliance," one of the other warleaders asked. There was no edge in her voice.

"I've already ordered my troops toward the border," Hanns answered. "They will not cross unless ordered, but they are accompanied by monks and warriors with strong affinities. With your permission, we will march side-by-side to Faldun. We will take back your capital and deliver it to your hands. And Prince Regar will be defeated."

"And after?"

"After, I use the power of the gate to defeat the Lolani queen."

"What about your troops?"

"They will leave."

The warleaders glanced from one to another. They spoke quickly, in Falari. Brandt looked to Hanns, but if he could understand their language, his face betrayed nothing.

The warleaders spoke for some time. They didn't shout

or wave their arms about, but the passion with which they argued was evident. Watching them, Brandt couldn't tell if Hanns' argument swayed them or not.

Eventually, Weylen nodded, ending the final conversations around the circle. He locked eyes with Hanns. "We reject your offer."

Brandt saw Hanns' fist clench, fingernails digging into the palm. "You will die without our help."

"Better that, we think, than allowing the empire a foothold in Falar. Your ways will never be ours, and should your army cross, the treaty shall be broken."

Weylen's threat landed heavily. Perhaps Hanns would risk war with the Falari. But the treaty wasn't just between the two nations. It included the Etari, as well. If Hanns brought his troops across the border, he risked fighting both independent countries on the continent as well as the queen. That conflict, should it come to pass, would be impossible to win.

"I'm offering to help," Hanns said through gritted teeth.

Brandt wasn't sure if it was imagination or not, but he swore he felt Hanns' power growing. Weylen took a mighty risk angering Hanns further.

"And for that, we thank you. But we do not want those with affinities coming through our land."

"Even if they are your best hope for survival?"

"Even then."

It was only then that Brandt understood Hanns' mistake. He should not have fought to free Weylen's village. The emperor saw it as a chance to save lives. The Falari saw it as a confirmation of their worst fears.

To Brandt's imagination, the silence that stretched between the Falari warleaders and Hanns was full of threat. The Falari understood the gate's importance, but they didn't understand how much it meant to Hanns personally. Brandt had seen Hanns fight for his life, but he'd not seen the emperor this angry before.

Which made Hanns' next words all the more surprising.

"Very well. Then escort me to Faldun alone."

From the expression on Weylen's face, the statement surprised him as much as it did Brandt.

"Take me back to Faldun," Hanns said. "You can't fight against a man with a gate, especially if half your people support him. And you won't let my warriors over the border to assist. So take me. Escort me, make me your prisoner, do whatever you need to satisfy your sense of honor." The last words were laced with disdain. "Just get me close enough to fight my son."

Hanns' offer set off another round of debate among the Falari, but this time, Brandt thought he had a better idea of their disposition. This offer of help was too generous for the Falari to refuse. The warleaders had to know they had no chance without Hanns. Their discussion was louder than their first.

Brandt leaned over. "Are you certain about this?"

The plan left Hanns completely at the mercy of the Falari. Brandt trusted the mountain warriors, but the opportunity to betray Hanns was a temptation he'd rather not offer anyone.

"There's no choice," Hanns whispered. "I'd rather they trust me, but this does have the advantage of keeping more imperial soldiers out of harm's way. Regar can't be allowed to maintain control of that gate."

The discussion ended suddenly. Weylen spoke to Hanns. "Your offer is accepted. You may join us on our march to Faldun."

Hanns bowed. "Thank you."

They said their farewells, and then the two imperials left the room.

They marched to battle.

48

That anyone would knock on her door surprised Alena. That the person who did so was Ana surprised her even more.

Alena let her friend in. A cold evening breeze gusted from the peaks as the town bustled to prepare for the march ahead.

Runners had gone throughout town not long ago, informing the village's inhabitants of the decision of the warleaders. Their choice didn't surprise Alena, because she didn't think Regar had left them one. The warleaders could fight and die quickly, or they could hide in the mountains and die slowly.

Ana paused when she saw the preparations among Alena's small group of warriors. It only took her a heartbeat to guess Alena's purpose. She met Alena's gaze, and for the first time, Alena noticed Ana had been crying. "You're joining them, aren't you?"

Alena nodded. "I can't return to the empire, but regardless, my task has always been in Faldun. We plan on following the rest of the war parties."

"The emperor is traveling with them."

"Really?" The runners hadn't shared that piece of news.

"The warleaders refused to permit the army to cross the border. Hanns offered his strength, not as an emperor, but as the man who controls two gates."

Alena wanted to hate Hanns. He'd exiled her, a decision whose full weight Alena still hadn't felt. With a word, he'd torn apart her family again. She knew he was wrong, but it was hard to rage against a man who would fight against his own son, alone, to save the empire.

Hanns' choice also complicated her life. Between her and Sheren, they'd already decided it would be wiser to follow behind the war parties than to join them, but if the emperor was present, she'd need to stay well behind. She didn't dare risk his anger.

She turned to her guest. Ana hadn't taken more than a couple of steps into their place, as though she wasn't certain this was where she belonged. Alena, recognizing a need Ana wouldn't voice, stepped toward her friend and embraced her.

Ana returned the gesture, wrapping Alena up tight in her strong arms. Alena felt the woman's determination, even in her distress.

When they separated, Ana wiped a tear from her eye. "I'm sorry for coming here, but I wasn't sure where else to go."

"You're always welcome, wherever I am," Alena replied. She studied the former wolfblade. "Brandt?"

Ana nodded. "This path he walks, I'm not sure I can follow him on it much longer. He hides it well, and I think even he believes he only does it out of love, but I don't believe him anymore. If he continues, I fear his desire to grow stronger will consume him."

Ana paused. "Perhaps it is already too late. The Brandt I know never would have let the emperor exile you. He would have fought on your side, even if he disagreed with you. When he remained silent against the emperor, I realized just how much he's already lost."

Alena put her hand on the woman's back, strangely relieved Brandt's actions had cut Ana as deeply as they had her. When she made contact, though, she dropped halfway into a soulwalk. Lately, it had been happening more often. Some instinct within her connected with others without conscious direction. It was the same ability that had first made her realize her gift. It didn't happen every time she touched others, but it was more common now than in the past.

When she dropped into a soulwalk, Alena understood the other part of Ana's distress. She took a step back, as though Ana had burned her. "Oh."

Ana guessed Alena's reaction well enough. "You felt it?"

"Yes." Alena paused, digesting the information. "Congratulations. Does he know?"

"Not yet," Ana said. "I only learned myself a few days ago, just before the attack on the village. It didn't seem an appropriate time."

No, Alena agreed, it wasn't. "Do you know what you'll do?"

Ana's laugh was bitter. "I haven't the slightest idea."

Alena didn't have any ideas, either. Her heart ached for the other woman, but she couldn't think of a single way to help, outside of offering her support. "Whatever happens," she said, "you're always welcome here."

Ana took several deep breaths. "Thank you." She glanced over their preparations. "And what, exactly, do you hope to accomplish at Faldun?"

"I intend to separate Regar from the gate."

"You can do that?" She didn't believe her.

"I hope so."

"And if you are successful, then what?"

Alena chuckled. "I haven't the slightest idea."

Ana smiled at the echo. "You intend to prevent Hanns from controlling the third gate, don't you?"

Alena grimaced. She supposed it would have been too much to slip that past Ana, and there was no point attempting to lie. "I do."

Ana smiled at her own private joke.

"What?"

Ana shook her head. "It's just that everyone else is fighting to control the gates, and you're here, trying to prevent them. You've taken on the most challenging task of all, and you aren't even hesitating to confront a traitorous prince, an emperor, and an invading queen."

"You make it sound hopeless."

Ana laughed out loud at that. "The fact that you don't speaks volumes about you, Alena. And I appreciate that."

Jace joined the women. "Well, if you're looking to join our hopeless cause, we'd be delighted to have you. Although I'll warn you, we don't accept just anyone. Our application and training are very rigorous."

Ana and Alena both rolled their eyes, but Alena appreciated her brother all the same. As a child, he'd regaled them all with his academy adventures, but somewhere along the line Jace had learned how to say exactly what a group needed to hear. Tonight, he'd stepped in just before the conversation became awkward.

Ana spoke of Alena as though she were a hero, which Alena knew she wasn't. She just refused to do nothing while those with the power of the gates destroyed their world.

Alena didn't think Ana had found her answers, but she bid farewell to the group. Alena walked her out, standing in the street with the former wolfblade. "I'm not sure what I can do to help," she said, "but if you ever need anything, I'm here."

Ana gave Alena a deep bow. But before she could say anything in response, Brandt came around the corner. "Ana! I've been looking—" His voice trailed off when he saw who Ana stood next to. Concern transformed into disgust. "What are *you* doing here?"

Alena was no stranger to those who didn't accept her. Her years among the Etari taught her how to deal with those barbs. But coming from Brandt, a man she had so much respect for, the words broke her heart.

Her response was colder than she meant. "I was exiled from the empire. In case you haven't noticed, we aren't there."

A part of her flinched from the sound of her own voice. She wanted to repair the wounds in their relationship, but Brandt's words crawled under her skin, making her feel unwelcome among her own friends.

Brandt turned to Ana. "What are you doing here?"

Alena felt the storm brewing. Ana's fists were clenched, and Brandt looked ready to draw his sword if given the excuse.

Ana unleashed her anger. "I'm here with our friend! The woman who risked her life for us, the woman who helped you with your memories after Landow! She's not a traitor."

Ana's fire met Brandt's cold reply. "She's been exiled for defying the emperor. She's no friend of ours."

Alena stumbled back a step, her knees unsteady beneath her.

"You don't mean that," Ana said.

"I do," Brandt said. He turned and walked away, back to the rooms he and Ana shared.

Ana looked at Alena. "I'm sorry," she said. Then she chased after Brandt.

Alena stood alone in the street. Brandt and Ana were friends, and people she admired. To see them come to this made her want to weep.

But no tears would come.

She heard the sound of footsteps behind her. Jace stood a few paces away, his face a mask of anger.

"You know I'm loyal to the empire, right?"

Alena nodded. Of course she did. Jace had always wanted to serve. He was, perhaps, one of the most loyal subjects the emperor had. She expected, at least until her exile, that he would rise far in the government.

"Then you know what this means when I say it," he said. He paused, closing his eyes as though the next words required tremendous focus. "I think you're doing the right thing."

He gave her a smile and returned back to their chambers.

Alena looked up at the stars above. What had she ever done to deserve such a brother?

Though she was the only soul on the street, she no longer felt alone.

49

Brandt sat on the edge of a rooftop, watching the sun rise over Weylen's village. Ana had barely spoken a word to him last night, and they had again spent the night apart. Brandt didn't want to fight, but he didn't know how to fix what was broken between them.

He'd spoken rashly last night. Yes, he was angry at Alena. She possessed a secret of limitless potential, and she still didn't understand how many people might die because of her moral certitude. But he'd still been too quick to react, and once started, hadn't been able to stop.

He looked down at his hands. Control was part of the creed of the wolfblades, and outside of a few occasions in his life, he'd always maintained it. But now his emotions always seemed to get the better of him.

He felt unbalanced. And that had driven him to the rooftop this morning.

As Brandt watched the sunrise, he studied Weylen's village. He felt an absence here, and it seemed more acute on this quiet morning. After a long study, he found what he missed.

Nothing decorated the buildings of Weylen's village. The stone walls were sturdy but simple, lacking the craftsmanship of an imperial building. There were no statues here, no paintings. No thought was given to the aesthetics of the place.

Once he saw, he couldn't unsee.

A society so focused on the art of war lost its art.

Brandt heard soft footsteps behind him, and Ana held a cup of steaming tea in front of his face. He felt his heartbeat calm just by virtue of the small act.

"Thank you."

She sat down next to him, a cup in her own hands.

He recognized the tea as an offering, a truce, if only for a few precious moments in the morning.

"I would die for you, you know," Ana said.

A lump formed in his throat. "I know."

They each sipped at their tea.

"I don't know how to make this better," Brandt confessed.

"Neither do I. I want you to put this all behind you, to return to the empire with me. But you can't do that, can you?"

Brandt wouldn't admit he found the idea tempting. Ana wouldn't believe him, but he didn't want to return to Faldun. He didn't want to be anywhere near a fight between Regar and his father. His imagination couldn't begin to envision the power of three gates clashing.

He wanted to be with Ana, isolated from the world in a place almost like this. Some of his most cherished memories of the past decade were of the two of them resting in the mountains above Highkeep. If he could live in those moments forever, he would.

But the stakes were too high, and he couldn't live with

himself if he abandoned Hanns now. The battle at Faldun would be the key to the future of the empire. He imagined it as a fulcrum.

And, although Brandt also couldn't admit this out loud to Ana, the answers to the questions that had plagued him for over a decade called to him. He shook his head.

"I'm pregnant."

Brandt almost spilled tea down his shirt. "Really?"

Ana smiled. "I've suspected for a few days, but Alena confirmed it last night."

The mention of Alena almost sucked the joy out of the moment, but even she couldn't spoil this. "I'm going to be a father?"

"You are."

Brandt heard the question in the statement. Knowing that, would he still march to Faldun?

He considered, examining his own emotions.

The decision came easier than he expected. Far from making him reconsider, the knowledge that he had a child to protect only buttressed his determination to defend the empire.

"Then I need to finish this at Faldun," he said. "It could be the chance to make everything right."

Ana's mouth was set in a tight line. "Then I'll need to go with you."

Brandt started to argue, but when he saw Ana's expression, he relented. She'd no doubt expected this and had come here with her decision already made. He couldn't convince her to flee to safety any more than she could convince him. The thought made him smile.

"What?" she asked.

"We really were made for each other."

"I already feel sorry for our child."

They sipped at their tea as the sun finally broke free of the mountains. Below, the town stirred to life. The war parties would set out today, leaving messages for those still to arrive. They couldn't waste time. The warleaders had decided any delay only served to allow the usurpers longer to prepare. Those still on their way would have to catch up.

"You should apologize to Alena," Ana said.

Brandt let out a slow exhale. He wished he could take back his words to her the night before, but he still felt some of that anger.

"She's doing what she believes is right," Ana continued. "She knows what it means, and she's willing to sacrifice ever seeing her family again. Do you think she would do that without a compelling reason?"

"Her decision could cost countless lives." She denied the empire a strength they could use to overwhelm their enemies. In so doing, any life lost was partly her responsibility.

"Or perhaps she's saving them. Maybe some powers aren't meant for this world."

"That's not her choice to make!"

"And why not? She knows more about soulwalking than anyone on this continent, as far as I know. Why shouldn't we trust her? We did in Landow, and she saved our lives."

Brandt gripped the tea cup tightly in his hand, squeezing against it. Then, with a sigh, his anger broke and he felt his body relax. He wasn't sure which argument, exactly, had won him over, but Ana was right. He put down the cup before he broke it. "Fine."

The smile on Ana's face immediately made his decision worth it.

. . .

THEY LEFT that morning after breaking their fast. Brandt and Ana began the journey near the head of the column, but after they cleared the first pass they took a long rest and waited for Alena's group to approach.

The small group trailed a few hundred paces behind the last war party. They remained close enough to enjoy the party's protection, but far enough behind that they were mostly out of mind. When they appeared, Brandt felt his spirits lift. Despite their differences, he liked Jace and Alena. The group stopped short of Brandt and Ana, and Brandt saw the way they refused to meet his gaze.

Fortunately, Ana navigated the waters of relationships better than he did. "Brandt decided to apologize."

Brandt stood up. "Alena, I'm still not sure that I agree with you. I fear your decision will cost lives. But I understand your reluctance, and I'm sorry."

He found the apology easier to give than he'd expected.

Alena offered him a short bow. "You don't know how much that means to me." She ran forward and embraced him. Brandt, caught by surprise, returned it awkwardly.

It felt good, though.

Under Ana's careful supervision, they continued the process of reconciliation throughout the day, as they hiked up and down mountain passes.

By the time the sun set on their first day, Brandt almost felt as though the rift had been healed. The scar of the argument remained, but the only cure for that was time.

Ana remained with the group, who now called themselves Alena's war party, as Brandt returned up front as the day's journey ended.

Ren, Weylen, and the emperor sat together with the other warleaders as the camp sprang to life around them. One warleader gave a report. Brandt caught the end of it.

"We know they have scouts out, tracking our progress from a distance, but we haven't seen any indication of an opposing force."

Hanns pulled at his beard as he thought. "Why wouldn't they attack?"

The other warleaders looked as though that question would keep them awake all night. But to Brandt, the answer seemed plain as day. He spoke up, drawing attention for the first time. "It's because of you," he explained, pointing to Hanns. "Both Prince Regar and the enemy warleaders know the power you have at your command. An ambush might pick off a handful of our warriors, but they risk your retaliation. Unless Prince Regar accompanies an ambush, it's suicide."

"And he won't accompany one because he needs to defend the gate," Hanns completed the thought. "That makes sense."

"Does he intend to allow us to approach Faldun uncontested?" The warleader who spoke sounded as if such a thought was the height of madness.

And until Hanns and Regar arrived in Falar, the warleader would have been right. The mountainous land almost demanded the wise commander lead one ambush after another. The war party on the move had every disadvantage.

But the tactics only worked when both sides brought approximately the same weapons. Hanns could bury an entire ambush in flame or stone with little more than a thought.

The Falari, for all their martial skill, weren't ready for this new warfare. Regar was. He knew the better use of his troops was defending their most vital asset.

Weylen suggested they increase the number of scouts

surrounding the war parties. Brandt suspected the measure was unnecessary, but the other warleaders agreed with it. It made them feel safer to do something, useless as it might be.

The days continued to pass without incident. Brandt found himself spending more time with Alena's war party than up front. Though he unofficially served as Hanns' Senki, there was little for him to do. The Falari scouts were better suited to their protection than him, and as Brandt had predicted, their march was uncontested.

It made their journey pleasant, but Brandt feared the conclusion even more. Their enemies would be packed into Faldun and the area surrounding it. After the trouble they'd had last time in the city, he already had nightmares about what awaited them.

At night, he could almost convince himself that life had returned to normal. Alena usually retired early to soulwalk, accompanied by Toren. Brandt knew she was seeking a way to unravel the connection Regar had formed with the gate, but she spoke little about it. Despite the apology and the intervening days, a tension still ran between them when Alena spoke of soulwalking. Though Brandt refused to ask, he still wanted her secret. Astute as she was, she no doubt guessed his thoughts.

His evenings were spent with Ana. The scars remained between them as well, but the healing had begun. They didn't talk about the gate or the battle that awaited at the end of this journey. Instead they spoke of their future.

The idea of fatherhood excited and terrified him. He looked forward to meeting their child, but he kept his fears unspoken. He was a warrior, with blood on his hands. Did he even have the right to raise an innocent child?

He didn't have answers, but Ana's presence reassured

him. Together, they would figure parenthood out. Together, they could raise a child better than either of them could alone.

All they had to do was win at Faldun.

Their party grew as they marched. Those who had come to join Weylen in his village caught up to them, swelling their ranks. Numbers were hard to guess, spread out in the mountains as they were, but Brandt suspected thousands of Falari now journeyed toward Faldun.

From early reports, nearly that many waited in Faldun to oppose them.

It didn't take long for a grim attitude to settle over the warriors. Skirmishes between Falari war parties weren't uncommon, but a conflict of this scale was unheard of, at least in recent memory.

And then their journey ended late one afternoon. They entered the valley where Faldun waited for them. The valley itself was empty, save for a number of scouts returning to the safety of Faldun's walls.

Brandt watched the scene with the other warleaders. Beside him, Weylen studied the capital of his people. He nodded, as though convincing himself that an assault on the city was even possible.

Then he turned to the others.

"Prepare your people," he said. "Soon, we will attack."

50

Faldun was as impressive a sight as Alena had ever seen. Sheren, Brandt, and Ana had prepared her in some sense, telling her what they could of the city, but seeing it in person still almost knocked her over.

As night fell and torches were lit, Alena thought it looked like the entire mountain was on fire. The homes were stacked higher than she ever believed possible. She kept thinking they would collapse at any moment, but they continued to defy her expectations.

Faldun frightened her in more ways than one. The thought first in her mind was that attacking such a city was no different than falling on your own sword. The valley before it had been cleared for hundreds of paces, and the archers within the city had the advantage of much higher ground.

Arrows would blacken the sky as they approached, and if they made it into the city, the fighting would be even worse. Brandt and Ana had told of their escape, and Alena didn't wish to live through a single moment of such an event. Sheren informed them the city had never fallen, and now that she'd seen it for herself, Alena wasn't sure it ever would.

But another fear, more subtle and yet deeper, concerned her even more. Faldun was impossible. Not even the best masons, gifted with the strongest affinities in the empire, could come close to making a marvel even a quarter as impressive. Those who came before had made this, and they had vanished.

Alena feared the battle of Faldun, but she feared what came after even more.

Toren, standing by her side, no doubt understood her thoughts. They had spent so much time soulwalking together Alena had tied a permanent bond between them. She could feel her awe at the sight before them echoed in his own emotions.

Their soulwalking attempts had been well spent. Together they had studied the gates, even going so far as to examine the connections between Hanns and Regar and the gates. Alena believed she could separate either of the rulers from their power, with one caveat. She needed to touch the gate. She'd tried separating Regar while at their campfires at night, but some force prevented her.

She considered practicing their soulwalking again tonight, but she found she wasn't in the mood. She wasn't close to any new breakthroughs. Her skills wouldn't improve in any way between tonight and tomorrow. Better instead to rest.

When Toren grabbed her hand, Alena barely reacted. Though they rarely touched, it didn't take a soulwalking connection to understand his feelings. She squeezed his hand. Then she pulled him toward her tent.

. . .

When she awoke the next morning, Toren had already left. She felt the warmth where he'd been, so it hadn't been long.

Her emotions were too complex to sort through, so she pushed them away. More important tasks demanded her full attention.

Alena dressed and stepped out of the tent, surprised to see she was the last one awake. Jace sharpened his sword while Toren examined every stone in the pouch that rode at his hip. No words passed between the men, but Alena didn't notice any tension, either. She focused on the bond between her and Jace, curious what she might find.

She felt his concern, as she often did. But the bond between them radiated a warmth that made her smile.

She joined them, reassured by the presence of both men.

For a moment, all felt right in the world.

That moment ended too soon. Suddenly, Alena felt as though she was going to throw up. Beside her, Toren turned pale, and Sheren collapsed from where she'd been standing off to the side. Alena's mind, acting more on instinct than conscious choice, dropped into a soulwalk.

Alena appeared in a flat space, empty as far as the eye could see.

She spun around, swearing.

She knew this place.

The last time she had been here, Lolani troops had been lined up, prepared to walk through the gate and invade the empire.

Alena kept turning, and both Toren and Sheren appeared next to her.

She hadn't thought this possible.

Then *she* was there, terrible in her beauty, a spear in her hand. Her arm snapped forward, a smooth motion Alena barely caught. Alena's mind, still in shock, couldn't defend.

The spear stabbed into her stomach and pinned her to the ground below.

Her vision flashed red as the agony of the wound overwhelmed any conscious thought. Somewhere, far away, she heard Toren shout.

The queen's cackle, though, rattled her bones. "This will be the least of your pain."

Alena felt something about the environment shift, and a hand yanked her head up by her hair. Her eyes opened through no effort of her own and she saw Toren pinned to a wall by several spears, his face a mask of unrelenting agony.

The queen let Alena's head drop, then she spun, rose her heel up high, and drove it down onto Alena's chest. Her body slid down the spear until it smashed against the ground.

Alena gasped and coughed up blood.

This isn't real.

Knowing that, though, and believing it, were two different things.

The queen walked over to Toren, hips swaying with each step, every movement exaggerated for effect. A knife appeared in her hand, one whose lines were as familiar to Alena as those on her palm.

The knife her father had made for her.

The queen stabbed it into Toren's leg, then pulled it free and repeated it with the other leg.

An arrow struck the queen in the back, but the point of it bounced off her as though she was stone. Both the queen and Alena turned to see Sheren holding a bow.

The queen shook her head. "Witness now the weakness of your people."

A dozen arrows fell from the sky. Sheren brought her arms up to protect herself, but the arrows stuck into her like a pincushion. She fell, joining the other soulwalkers in their distress.

The Falari's attack might not have damaged the queen, but it distracted the woman's attention long enough for Alena to find some focus. Fighting against the agony, she imagined herself whole and healthy, holding her father's knife at the queen's back.

The image wavered, both due to her struggles to focus and the resistance of the queen's own will. But Alena opened up the connection to her gatestone, flooding her with a burst of power she desperately needed. She fought for a moment longer, then found herself standing behind the queen, knife in hand.

Before the queen could react, Alena thrust the knife between her ribs, right where the heart should be. If she could counter this ambush and kill the queen here, their troubles would be over.

The knife stabbed into the queen, but slowed to a crawl well before the tip reached the heart. The queen's skin was as hard as steel.

Alena recognized the sensations for what they were. Her will and strength battled against those of the queen.

The queen screamed, spinning around with inhuman speed. Alena held onto the knife as the queen wrenched her body away, throwing Alena off balance.

The queen attacked again, but Alena's wits had returned. She vanished and reappeared behind the queen, stabbing at the same place.

Unfortunately, Alena's technique was easily duplicated by the queen, who vanished as Alena stabbed through empty air. For a handful of heartbeats both combatants disappeared and reappeared, attacks missing by the narrowest of margins. Sometimes they moved only a pace.

Sometimes they vanished only to reappear hundreds of paces away. Distance didn't matter, not here.

The queen ended the chase, deflecting Alena's stab with a parry instead of a dodge. The two fought at the speed of imagination, but here the queen's fighting skill and greater strength overpowered Alena.

Alena vanished before the queen's sword cut her, then reappeared before Toren and Sheren. With a focused effort she freed them from their torment. They fell to their knees, not in pain but in shock, their minds fighting to remain balanced.

The queen approached the trio at a leisurely pace, her confidence absolute. Alena attempted a few attacks, manifesting spears and arrows and launching them at the queen. None came close to harming her.

Her friends were more a liability than a help. Their surprise was absolute, and by the time they found their balance this would be over. Until then, the queen could attack them at a whim.

The queen stopped short of the group. "No one has cut me in lifetimes," she said. She almost sounded respectful.

Alena couldn't have heard her right, but something in the queen's attitude seemed different. The few times they'd fought, Alena had felt only malice and anger. This growing regard from her enemy unsettled her almost more than the initial attack.

A wave of power forced Alena to her knees.

But for all the power, there was no hate. Instead, the queen watched her closely, as though Alena was some creature caught in a trap, its behavior a fascinating study.

Alena felt her own strength coursing through her limbs, collecting at her navel next to her gatestone. She couldn't challenge the queen, not in this place. But she wouldn't die on her knees, either.

With a snarl she focused her energy. Gravity pulled at her, stronger than she'd ever felt. Toren and Sheren were pressed flat against the ground next to her, although Toren was slowly pushing himself to his knees.

Grunting, Alena stood, her balance precarious. She manifested a knife in each hand, daring the queen to attack with her gaze.

But the queen didn't attack.

"Remarkable," she said.

Perhaps it was her brother shouting to her, or perhaps the queen simply lost her focus briefly, but Alena felt her connection to Jace, just for a moment.

She didn't waste it.

Letting gravity take her, she fell down, touching both Sheren and Toren. Then she followed Jace's connection, fighting against the queen's will with the last of her remaining strength.

When she opened her eyes again she was on her back, concerned faces all around her.

"How long?" she asked.

"Not very," Jace replied. "A count of sixty, maybe ninety."

It had felt like so much longer. If she ever was trapped in that place, eternity would last even longer.

She tried to sit up, but Jace held her down. "You should rest."

She shook her head. Mentally, she'd taken a beating, but her body was fine. "You need to find Brandt," she said.

Because in those final moments, when she had followed

Jace's thread back to the physical world, she had gained a sense of perspective.

And she understood why the queen had been able to attack them in such a fashion.

"You need to find Brandt," she repeated. "And you need to tell him the Lolani queen is in Faldun."

51

Anger broke them apart, but necessity reunited them sooner than anyone could have guessed. News of the Lolani queen ran through the Falari camps like wildfire, sapping determination wherever it was spoken.

Brandt's own stomach felt hollow as he considered the implications. Regar hadn't just been planning this, he'd been planning this alongside the queen. No other story explained her sudden appearance on the continent.

Ren and Weylen joined Hanns, Brandt, and Alena's war party. The animosity between Alena and Hanns hadn't been forgotten. Hanns hadn't revoked her exile, and she hadn't agreed to teach the technique. Both sides stood by their decisions.

But they still gathered in the same circle. Brandt hoped the two would resolve their argument, but they had more pressing problems.

Weylen spoke the truth everyone else thought. "Our chances were already slim against Prince Regar. Against him and the queen, there is no point in attacking."

"We don't need to take the city," Hanns replied. "Our goal has always been to separate Prince Regar from the gate." He looked to Alena. "You say you think you can do so, without killing him?"

The hope in Hanns' voice pulled at Brandt's heart.

"I think so," Alena said. "But I need to be close to the gate. I need to touch it."

"There is an opportunity here," Hanns said, almost muttering to himself. "The queen is impossible to defeat within the soulwalk, but if she is physically here, I don't think she can withstand the power of two gates. If I can find her, perhaps we can end the Lolani threat for good."

Brandt shook his head. "That's all well and good, but unless we have a way into Faldun, it's a moot point."

The Falari soulwalker with Alena, whose name Brandt forgot, spoke with a trembling voice. She'd been clearly uncomfortable with this gathering from the moment she joined. "There's a passage on the other side of the mountain."

Weylen shook his head. "Those passages are not for our use, and its exit in Faldun is sealed."

Brandt looked between the two Falari, not understanding.

"Besides," Weylen continued, "even if we could convince our war parties to approach that way, it's still suicide. Our movement will be easily spotted, and the guard on the other side will be reinforced before we reach them. Even if we do pass the guard, with the queen and Prince Regar I have no doubt they could simply seal us in."

Brandt's memory traveled far back, to when Ana had almost been caught in a collapsing cave. He had no desire to relive that moment, nor the fear he'd experienced afterward as he sought a way out.

Still, he was curious about this route. Hanns beat him to it, though. He said, "Tell me of this passage."

Weylen refused to answer the question, leaving the Falari soulwalker in the uncomfortable position of answering to a foreign emperor. "Those who came before left a series of tunnels through the mountains. Most, if not all, lead in the direction of Faldun. There is one that travels through the mountain Faldun is built into."

"Where does it go, and why is it not to be used?"

"It enters Faldun near the top of the city, and the tunnels are not used by my people. Like most remnants of those who came before, we avoid them."

"But there is no particular danger?"

"None that I've ever experienced."

Hanns played with his beard. "And the defenses?"

"Most tunnels are unguarded. This one is not. A fort is built around the entrance, with warriors there at all times."

"How many?"

The soulwalker grimaced. "I don't know. Fifty?"

Weylen finally interrupted, looking almost as uncomfortable as the soulwalker. "It's no better an option than a direct attack. If anything, it poses more risks. It would funnel all our warriors into a single tunnel."

Brandt found the solution first. "We don't need to move the war parties. This has always come down to Prince Regar and the gate. The only people who will make a difference are sitting around this circle."

Hanns nodded, his thoughts following Brandt's. "The war parties' attack on Faldun will be a diversion."

"Better if they don't even attack," Brandt thought out loud. "Unless it becomes necessary to hold the defenders' attention. How long to reach the tunnel?"

The soulwalker considered. "The better part of a day, a little longer if we hope to remain unobserved."

Brandt sketched out his plan. Weylen, Ren, and Hanns all challenged different parts, pushing and pulling until they came up with an approach that, if it didn't excite any of them, at least they didn't object too strongly to. A silence fell over them. Ultimately, the decision rested on Weylen's shoulders. Hanns and the others would bear the greatest risk, but they couldn't succeed without the warleader.

Weylen nodded.

Ren turned to his warleader. "I would like to join them."

Weylen agreed, and their course was set.

THEIR DEPARTURE, as a matter of necessity, was accomplished without fanfare. All morning the scouts attached to both sides of the Falari conflict had been fighting small battles. By late morning Weylen received word a path away from the camps had been cleared. They couldn't hold the path open long, mostly because they didn't want it to seem like they were clearing a path.

Their party was small. Hanns commanded them, followed by Brandt, Ana, and Alena's whole war party. Hanns had questioned the need for the war party, but none of them were willing to abandon Alena, nor she them. In the end, Hanns had shrugged, the emperor deferring to the young woman.

Brandt suspected Alena didn't even understand what she had accomplished. Imperial, Etari, and Falari, all joined together in common purpose.

All following her into mortal danger.

Brandt had argued with Ana, too, though he'd expected failure from the start. She'd ended the argument by stating she didn't plan on leaving the father of their child behind. Brandt hated the risk, but knew a losing argument when he saw one. Besides, Ana was no fool. She'd keep herself as safe as it was possible to be on a mission like this.

Hanns even left his guards behind. They were all gifted with affinities, and their role in the deception was to make it seem as though Hanns was with the main party. One of the guards, who looked eerily like Hanns, would act as emperor in Hanns' absence. The ruse was far from perfect, but it didn't need to be. It only needed to distract the defenders' attention for long enough.

The soulwalker, named Sheren, guided them. From the way she moved and the paths she found, Brandt guessed she was no stranger to walking through these lands unobserved. In truth, they couldn't have found a better guide had they searched all the assembled war parties.

Their journey was made in silence. Ears strained for the sound of enemy scouts, while eyes restlessly wandered near and far. They made it to the base of the path by early evening, making camp for one last night of rest. They slept under the stars.

Brandt slept easily. Despite his worries about tomorrow, he was tired, and he knew tomorrow would come no matter his choices. Better to face the day well rested.

He woke well before the sun, as did several others. Some, like Sheren, appeared as though they hadn't slept at all. They planned to attack the fort just before dawn.

Under other circumstances, Brandt didn't think their assault of the fort would have a chance. At times he could see it between the trees, and was impressed by its location and construction. The fort possessed a commanding view of the path below, and there would be no stealthy approach.

Like Faldun itself, those walls could hold back countless attackers with only a handful of defenders.

Unless one of the attackers possessed the power of two gates.

Hanns changed everything.

Thanks to the cover of darkness, they weren't spotted until they were within three hundred paces of the wall. Brandt kept his eyes on the guards pacing the lit battlements. When one stopped and drew his bow, he gave the signal Hanns had been waiting for.

Once again, Hanns chose stone as his weapon. Small sharpened rocks split the air with a crack, decimating the warriors on the walls.

Brandt watched in awe. He knew Hanns' power. He'd seen it before. But it still impressed him every time. With that strength, Brandt couldn't help but imagine what he might accomplish.

He could protect Ana and the empire from all harm.

He pushed aside those thoughts for the moment. Hanns' attack served as the signal for Brandt, Ana, Ren, and Jace. The warriors became light and sprinted forward. They hit the wall at full speed and climbed it hand over fist, the rough stonework easy to grasp. Even Brandt launched himself over the top of the wall in less than three heartbeats.

As they fell, swords were drawn, and Jace and Brandt fought side by side. Alena's brother had demonstrated his skill several times before, and he fought without hesitation. He'd been hardened by battle.

Ren fought behind them, his sword making quick work of the few enemies Brandt and Jace left standing.

Ana turned her attention to the gate of the fort. The mechanism to open the gate was easily operated by a single person, and before long Hanns and the others came through the front.

Their assault ended almost before it began. Sheren's estimate of fifty warriors turned out to be a gross exaggeration. Less than twenty had been stationed here, and after Hanns' initial assault, the odds had nearly been even.

Brandt sought Ren out. "Was that too easy?"

Ren looked around the fort. "I don't think so. Neither Prince Regar nor the queen likely know the area around Faldun well, and this isn't an approach that would occur to the Falari." He paused. "Also, twenty would be more than enough to hold off most assaults, at least until the bell was sounded." He pointed his sword at a large bell above them, untouched by the guards.

Brandt supposed Ren was right, but the ease of it still made him nervous.

His worries didn't alter their course, though. It didn't take them long to find their destination. They gathered together at the mouth of a tunnel, a long stretch of perfect darkness.

Hanns lit a torch and took the first steps in.

Brandt took a deep breath and followed his emperor into the darkness.

52

In the darkness of the tunnel, Alena found it too easy to relive her memories. This was the second time she'd seen Hanns unveil his power, and she hoped she wouldn't have to see it again. He must have killed a dozen men in less than a heartbeat. She saw their bodies, most of them dead before they realized they were even under attack.

Hanns turned everything she believed about war on its head. This wasn't a conflict of skill against skill, where the better sword or bow won the day.

Hanns didn't fight.

He murdered.

Some part of her wanted to strip him of his power. She wanted to make him nothing more than a man again, to make him understand how unnatural his power was. But it wasn't possible, and even if she could, she couldn't even begin to guess the consequences. So she followed, a mute witness to the horrors he committed.

The party only carried a handful of torches. Hanns walked in front of them all, so as not to ruin what little night vision he had.

She wasn't sure how long they had been in the tunnel when he called for her. Although her first instinct was to disobey, it would do little good. She walked ahead, until they were side by side, well ahead of the others.

He spoke softly, his words barely reaching her ears. "Do you hate me, Alena?"

She lost a step, then caught up to him again. She'd been ready for many questions, but not that one. "No. I disagree with you. And I hate what the gates allow you to do."

The emperor smiled, and Alena suddenly suspected that his smile hid a sorrow that had no end. "Would you believe I once thought as you do?"

Alena's first response was to say such thinking was many, many years behind him, but she bit her tongue. But he must have caught some hint of her thoughts from her expression. "It's hard to believe, but when I was named as Anders V's successor, I also hated the secrets. I feared the power of the gates."

"What changed?"

"Nothing. I still hate the secrets, and I still fear the power. Although I have, perhaps, gotten too used to them."

"Then why don't you change everything?"

"Because I've not found a better path. I saw your face, back in the fort. You hated me then, for a moment."

"You murdered them." Alena didn't believe she would confront the emperor like this, but she suspected he wanted her to challenge him. He invited it.

"I did," he admitted. "But could it have been done better? Their deaths were quick and relatively painless. How would you have done it?"

She struggled for an answer, but had none.

"I've spent years searching for a better path than the one Anders I set for us. Every time I receive word that a public dissenting opinion has been crushed, some part of me weeps. But in my decades of rule, I've never invented anything better."

"Why are you telling me this?"

The emperor laughed, soft and bitter. "Because I fear my death, and I want at least one person to understand me before I travel to the gates."

"You exiled me."

"And you defied me in front of others. Most Anders would have taken your head." He paused, sighing. "And you make me angry. You remind me of the man I used to be. A man who never would have considered your soulwalking technique."

"But you want it now."

The emperor shook his head. "I don't *want* it. But I fear the empire needs it. I don't want to control the gates, but if I don't, the empire will fall before the queen. I respect your idealism, Alena. But idealism crumbles like dust against the forces of this world. All that remains is what is useful."

Alena walked in silence for a few paces before deciding how she wanted to respond. "I hope I never believe that."

Hanns smiled at her. "For what it's worth, I hope the same."

They walked for a bit, then Hanns said, "I revoked your exile, Alena, before I left. I spoke with my guards, and I don't think anyone here would turn you in. I spoke rashly, and I apologize."

A lump formed briefly in Alena's throat. "Thank you."

Alena believed the conversation to be over, so she slowed. But Hanns reached out and pulled her to his side again. "If you can, don't harm Regar. He's a good man, twisted by the gates and the queen." He paused. "The trappings of power are far too easy to fall into."

She wasn't sure if he spoke about his son or himself. "I will do what I can."

"As do we all."

With that, Hanns let her join the rest of the party, leading the way down the tunnel alone.

As had been the case in the tunnels before, Alena lost track of time. But their journey came to an end too soon.

Hanns came to a stop about a dozen paces in front of a wall. Unlike the walls that made up the tunnel, this wall was formed of rougher stone. Hanns stepped up to the rock and put his hand against it. He looked to Sheren. "Do you know what's on the other side?"

She shook her head.

Hanns shrugged. "Get ready."

With a gesture, the rocks crumbled and turned to sand. She blinked, both to clear the dust from her eyes, and to ensure she'd seen correctly.

They were greeted by an empty balcony and an endless vista. Brandt stepped over the sand first, sword ready. A moment later he sheathed it. The others followed after him.

As Alena approached the balcony edge she fought a wave of vertigo. After the long journey in the tunnels her eyes had become used to the dark. Now the bright cloudless morning sky burned her sight, which now extended for leagues.

She'd never stood over such a drop. She was no stranger to mountains, but this was outside her experience. The world wavered underneath her and she steadied herself against the short stone wall in front of her.

Beside her, Sheren pointed out several mechanisms. "I

think these were used to move supplies. They came in through the tunnel, then were dropped to the city below."

Sheren might have found the proof for her theory about the tunnels, but Alena couldn't find it in her to be pleased for her friend. Her attention was focused elsewhere. Far below, the Falari were arranged in loose formations, preparing for their diversion.

The others joined her.

Alena had seen Faldun from a distance, and she had some sense of its scale, but she didn't truly understand until she stood near the top of it. To build something so high defied everything she believed possible. From up here, the war below seemed puny and insignificant. She wondered if this was how Hanns felt, so high above everything.

As spectacular as the view was, it wasn't complete. From on high she couldn't feel the nervous tension running through the ranks, the visceral fear of death clawing for purchase in the hearts of the soldiers. From so high, one gained perspective but lost the meaning of it all.

Faldun was built so that lower levels extended out beyond higher ones, matching the slope of the mountain. This high, the drop felt vertical, but it wasn't quite. Alena could look down and see dozens of levels below, and she could see the enormous square where the defenders of Faldun gathered. They were packed tightly together, except for a small space near the center.

Though she couldn't make out individuals, she suspected that was where they would find the queen and Prince Regar.

Despite the threat of violence, the scenes below looked peaceful. Weylen's war parties didn't advance, nor would they, if the plan held. All that was needed was for them to attract attention, which it appeared they'd done. Alena didn't see a single Falari within several levels.

A glowing ball of fire interrupted her consideration of the scene. The ball hovered over the hole in the center of the defenders. Either the prince or the queen had just surrendered their location. It grew rapidly, almost too bright to look at. Then it arced into the sky, toward Weylen and their allies.

The Falari might have remained well out of bow range, but the fireball knew no such limits. Alena watched, unable to respond, as it dropped out of the sky toward a discolored patch of warriors.

Hanns' palace guards.

Someone wanted the emperor dead.

The ball of flame paused briefly in the sky, no doubt resisted by Hanns' guards. But it was a one-sided battle. The fire crashed among the guards, sending people running in all directions.

"Well," said the emperor grimly, "there goes our ruse. Brandt, you're with me. The rest of you, go with Alena."

Hanns tore up some of the rock around them with his affinity, fashioning two platforms.

"Alena, go to the gate. Ren can guide you. Break my son's connection."

Alena nodded, her attention distracted by whatever Hanns planned.

Hanns, satisfied with his project, pulled her aside. "Do you want the power of the gate for yourself? If you know how to break a bond, then you certainly know how to form one."

Alena shook her head. She might be filled with questions and doubts, but that answer she knew for sure. Never did she want the responsibility of such power.

"Good. If you do separate Regar, don't let anyone else have control. Not even Brandt." The emperor reached out and grabbed her arm. His grip was firm, but his hand felt warm. Too late, she realized he performed a soulwork on her. She dropped into the waking trance, seeing the threads he tied between them.

At first glance, she thought they were little different than the connections she'd woven between her and her loved ones. But as she focused, she saw the weave was more complex than hers. This almost appeared to be an intricate chain. Some of the power of the gates flowed through it. She felt stronger.

"What did you do?" she asked.

"You'll be able to draw on some of my strength if you need it," Hanns said. "And you can let me know the moment you free Regar from the gate."

They rejoined the rest of the group. Ana and Brandt stood apart, wishing each other well.

"Hurry now," the emperor said. "You won't have much time."

"Aren't you going to descend with us?" Alena asked.

Hanns looked at the stone platforms he'd made, a smile on his face.

"No. We have a quicker way down."

53

The others disappeared down the stairs, leaving Brandt and Hanns alone. Hanns looked over the edge one more time. Now that the others had gone, he didn't seem to be in such a rush.

"She's a remarkable woman," the emperor said.

Brandt joined the emperor at the edge of the balcony. The scene below had been quiet after the fireball. To their credit, Weylen and the others didn't break, and no more devastation was launched from Faldun's walls.

"Alena?"

"Yes, but I was referring to your wife. She follows you into battle, but leaves when ordered to without complaint. Loyalty and discipline are a rare combination."

"We were wolfblades together, before," Brandt explained.

"Ahh, you've told me that before. I'm sorry I forgot. But a companion worth a great deal of suffering, I think."

Brandt thought of their last few weeks together. "I agree."

"Would you give up your strength for her?"

Brandt paused. "I want to think so. But how does one choose between duty to the empire and their love?"

The emperor chuckled softly. He seemed somehow... lighter, than before. Brandt worried the stress of the upcoming battle was affecting him, but that wasn't it. Hanns' gaze was sharp, missing nothing down below. He seemed more aware than before. More alive. "If you figure out the answer to that, Brandt, please let me know."

Brandt nodded. "What are we waiting for?"

"The others to get closer to the gate. I imagine they've got the harder journey in front of them. No doubt, Regar and the queen suspect something by now, but I think we have a little time yet before they make a decision and act on it."

"I can't protect you against that many," Brandt pointed out.

"You can draw from me," Hanns replied.

Brandt's pulse quickened at the thought. He'd drawn power from a man with a gatestone before, but the full power of two gates? His imagination ran wild. "Then I will protect you."

They watched the scene below together, and for a while Brandt didn't feel as though they were emperor and subject.

They felt like friends.

"Brandt?"

"Yes?"

"Protect her, and cherish what time together you have."

"I will." It wasn't lost on Brandt that Hanns had lost his wife early in his reign and never remarried, or that they were about to attack Hanns' son.

"It's time." Hanns stepped away from the balcony and placed himself firmly on one of the stone platforms he'd created. He gestured for Brandt to do the same.

"What are these?"

"Just become light, and stay balanced." A narrowing of the emperor's eyes was the only warning Brandt had before the platform moved under his feet, picking him up.

Hanns appeared delighted, and perhaps even a little surprised. "I wasn't sure these would work, but it's an idea I had years and years ago, when I was a much younger man." His own platform lifted and they hovered together.

Brandt's platform hung in the air. Intellectually, Brandt knew Hanns was using the power of his stone affinity and the gate, but his body thought he was flying. "Hanns, what are these?"

"A quicker way down!"

The platforms flew out into open space. Brandt felt his bowels tighten. A moment ago, a fall would have been a minor inconvenience. Now he would fall hundreds of paces to a certain death. But they were over the Falari defenders, so he supposed he would take out at least one or two with his falling body.

"Let's go meet my son."

It felt as though the platform had dropped out from underneath him, but it was just that it had dropped quickly. His feet remained firmly planted. They passed level after level in less than a heartbeat, and it seemed little better than a freefall as far as Brandt was concerned. He fought the urge to scream. He thought he saw a flash of color that looked like his friends, but he fell too fast for his eyes to focus on any single object.

The square where the Falari gathered approached with frightening rapidity. For something that had seemed so far away moments ago, he could now make out individual faces. A few were looking up, curious about the shadows passing overhead.

Of course they needed speed. This fall was the only way to approach Regar without giving him time to react.

Just when Brandt thought they had gone too far to recover, the platform slowed quickly. The deceleration forced Brandt into a squat, even light as he was. When he was close enough, he jumped off the platform toward the empty circle around Regar.

He looked left and right, but the queen was nowhere to be found. The prince stood alone. His eyes met Brandt's, but there was no understanding there.

Hanns landed beside him, and together they faced Regar. For a long moment, no one moved.

In the confusion of their landing, Brandt seized the advantage. He pulled heat from Hanns, worried for a moment that he endangered his emperor's life. Against most warriors, it was a fatal technique.

His fear was misplaced.

When he pulled from Hanns, he pulled whole lakes of energy from a limitless ocean.

This, then, was the power of the gates. He'd approached this power before, but without the ability to control the energy it had nearly torn him in pieces. But pulled and controlled through Hanns' connection, Brandt was invincible.

Brandt turned first to fire. Even after all his years of study it remained the element he felt most comfortable with. Flame erupted in the air, blooming like a wildflower, and Brandt drew a circle around him, the prince, and Hanns.

The Falari warriors, already shocked by the arrival of fighters who had literally fallen from the sky, panicked and broke against the wave of fire. Brandt pushed the fire further, encouraging their retreat. He wouldn't be satisfied until the square didn't hold a single breathing Falari.

Many unfortunate souls were caught in the fire, and their cries were enough to shatter the courage of the few warriors who still considered taking part in the fight, those who hovered near the edges of Brandt's flame. Before long, Brandt was satisfied. The square was completely emptied, at least for the moment.

He split his attention between watching for any approaching threats and the situation developing between Hanns and his son.

"Must we fight?" asked the emperor.

"We need her, father. We need the change she brings. You know what's coming! She showed you the same as she did me. I know she did."

It took Brandt several heartbeats to realize Regar was speaking of the queen. Somehow, she had gotten to him. She had corrupted him. Perhaps even now he was compelled.

"She has shown me the same visions," Hanns admitted, "but they are lies! She creates a threat in our minds so we can justify treachery against the oaths of Anders. But she has been a soulwalker for hundreds of years. There is no truth in anything she says. They are all illusions, designed only to grant her more power. That is all she has ever cared about."

"You're wrong." Regar's voice gained confidence with every sentence. "The evidence surrounds us even now. Faldun was built by people who disappeared, a people destroyed by the threat that approaches even now. It is you who lies to yourself." Regar paused and Brandt saw the set of his shoulders change. Whatever uncertainty the prince had felt no longer existed. "And unless you recognize that, I have no choice. This is the only way to save the empire."

A new sphere of flame appeared in front of Regar. Even fifteen paces away Brandt felt the heat burning off it. How Regar could be so close and not be burned defied Brandt's understanding.

"Don't make me do this," Regar said.

Brandt heard the son's pain, but determination as well. If Hanns didn't back down, Regar most certainly wouldn't.

Hanns' shoulders slumped. For a moment, Brandt thought Regar had convinced his father.

Then Hanns stood up straight. "I'm sorry, too, Regar. I should have taught you better. I should have prepared you better for her attacks. Your failure is mine."

The ball of fire hovering in front of Regar transformed, flattening and expanding into a wall of orange flame, licking at the air like a hungry animal. With every pace it advanced it grew in size, speed, and intensity. Brandt considered absorbing it, but there was nowhere for the heat to go. The air was already blistering hot.

Hanns remained, waiting for the wall of destruction to reach him.

When it did, the battle began in earnest.

54

Stairs. Alena decided that if she never saw another staircase again she would die a contented woman. Why would anyone choose to live in a place like this? Sure, it had never fallen to a siege, but she wasn't sure safety was worth the never ending burn in her legs. Making matters worse, Ren wasn't as familiar with Faldun's winding ways as she would have liked. Several times they were forced to climb up the stairs they had just descended.

Alena was also surprised to find that going down stairs could be just as torturous as going up them, but in wholly different ways. Her knees and legs ached, and her most vivid wish was only for flat ground.

Fortunately, they ran into no resistance as they descended and searched for the entrance to the lower tunnels underneath the mountain. It seemed that the entire might of Faldun was focused below, preparing to defend against an attack that would never come.

When Alena saw Hanns and Brandt fall from the sky she swore her imagination had finally gone too far. She thought perhaps she'd taken one stair too many and her mind had shattered. But she leaned over the wall and saw the conclusion to their wild descent. Jace joined her, grunting as the two landed safely in the square below. Alena might have been without words, but that was a problem that rarely afflicted her brother. "Didn't know that was possible."

Alena shook her head, still not sure she should believe what her eyes were telling her.

"I want to try that someday," Jace announced.

Alena just shook her head again. She had no other response.

Ren urged them on and Alena resumed their descent. When Ren finally announced they were on the correct level, she almost hugged him. They took a moment to shake out their legs before continuing.

The party ran through the empty streets of Faldun, Ren becoming more confident in his directions the closer they came to the entrance. The emptiness of Faldun unsettled her. Unlike Sheren's village, Faldun was clean and tidy. It looked like it should be occupied, and the fact that it wasn't jarred her senses.

Then Alena saw it, a square entrance that led deep into the mountain behind Faldun. They ran closer, but when they were about ten paces away Alena came to a stop, along with everyone else in the party.

Why had she ever wanted to enter a tunnel like that? She hated caves, tight spaces, and the darkness that knew no sunlight.

There would be another way to the gate, she was certain of it. Those who had come before wouldn't have limited themselves to one entrance. They could find another route, one that would no doubt be safer.

Beside her, Jace spoke. "Alena, I know this might sound

odd, but I'm certain that if we go in there, you're going to die. Let's find another way."

The others all bobbed their heads, except for Toren, who signed his agreement.

She had already turned around to begin their search when she realized what had happened. The thoughts were her own, but they had been shaped and exaggerated. Her dislike of tight spaces had grown into a crippling fear. She dropped into a soulwalk and saw the weaving they had walked through. It wasn't terribly strong or complex, which meant it hadn't been left by the queen, but by someone else.

Alena could guess. The queen rarely, if ever, was alone. She had brought some of her priests with her through the gate.

With a thought, she brushed away the weavings wrapped around her and the others. She detested compulsions of all kinds, but hated it most when her own emotions were used against her. The others blinked. Most of them quickly realized what they'd experienced, but Ren looked properly horrified.

Now wary of traps and weavings, Alena scouted ahead. Her soulwalk revealed another barrier, stronger, stretched tight across the entrance of the tunnel. It looked vicious. But now that she was aware of it, she was confident she could overcome it.

She addressed the group. "She brought priests. Jace, Ren, and Toren, take the lead, but don't enter the tunnel until I give the signal. Once I do, charge in and kill anyone in front of us. Even if they stand still. The real battle won't be physical."

Jace looked uncomfortable with the order, but they both silently agreed. Alena had Sheren stay behind her. She didn't want her in the soulwalk, not in battle against the Lolani.

Then Alena focused on her soulwalk. She followed the threads the priests had left. They weren't far from the entrance, no doubt ready to finish whoever managed to pass through the first two levels of compulsion.

Alena stepped up to the weaving and her father's knife appeared in her hand. She sliced through the barrier, cutting the compulsion into pieces. In the physical world, she gestured the warriors forward. Hopefully they wouldn't have to go far to find the soulwalkers.

Until then, she could distract them.

Alena followed the withering threads of compulsion to their owners, two women who reeled backward in surprise. They hadn't expected an attack from a fellow soulwalker.

Alena connected with them and pulled them into a reality of her shaping.

They appeared on the roofs of Landow, the place where Alena had spent far too much of her childhood.

Before the Lolani could gather their wits, Alena was on them, slashing and stabbing with the knife. She wasn't a natural born warrior like her brother or Ren, but she made up for her lack of skill with intensity. She reminded herself that she didn't need to win. All she needed to do was distract them long enough for the others to complete their task in the physical world.

The soulwalkers reacted quickly. Despite their disorientation and Alena's attacks, she never managed to do more than scratch them. In very few heartbeats, they had their own weapons in hand and began to fight back.

Before the fight could escalate further, they suddenly vanished from the soulwalk. Alena couldn't find them at all.

Jace and the others had done well.

She dropped out of the soulwalk and joined them. Just as she had felt, two soulwalkers lay at the feet of Jace and Ren. Her brother looked shaken, and she supposed for good reason. Distracted as they were by Alena's attack in the soulwalk, they wouldn't have put up any defense.

It had been years since she had seen a Lolani soulwalker up close, but there were several things different about these two. The ones in Landow hadn't carried swords, but these did. And their soulwalking skill, while not weak, wasn't as strong as those who had visited Landow. Their clothes were different, too. Alena wondered if there were different categories of soulwalkers serving the queen.

There was no time to consider the question, though. The sounds of battle echoed faintly from outside and they had one task above all others. They ran, led by Ren.

Every so often, Alena stopped to soulwalk ahead of them. She remained alert for traps and weavings, but it seemed like the priests had focused their attention only on the entrance.

She wished they had more time. This tunnel was even more fascinating than the others they'd passed through. It was lined with scripts begging to be translated, crying out their secrets to any who would open their eyes. They passed more knowledge and history with every step than she had even realized existed through most of her childhood.

They made it to a maze without encountering another soul, and Alena soon forgave Ren for every false staircase they had climbed. As Weylen's Senki, he knew the path through the maze and led them through with unfailing precision, never once taking a wrong turn. Given its size and complexity, without him she wasn't sure she ever would have found her way.

After a while, the now familiar blue light of a glowing

gate appeared and guided them the last steps of their journey. There had been a heavy door here once, but it had been broken wide open.

Alena checked once more for weavings, but there were none. She frowned. This was too easy. Either they were walking into a trap, or their plan had been so unexpected no one had prepared for it.

Her greatest fear had been that she would run into either Regar or the queen at the gate, but the room was empty. She assumed that both must be down in the square fighting Hanns. That thought alone compelled her closer to the gate. Hanns would need everything just to fight the queen. He couldn't deal with his son at the same time. She took a deep breath, reached out, and touched the gate.

It was time to take Regar's prize away from him.

55

Brandt wondered if this was how the world ended. The power of a single gate defied comprehension. The power of three gates left him senseless.

The wave of fire, hot enough to crack the stone it passed over, vanished before it reached Hanns. Brandt took a step back. One moment, an impossible inferno had sped toward him. Then he blinked and it was gone.

How?

A vicious wind rose as the air shifted in response to the rapid changes in heat, howling against Brandt. Brandt lowered his center of mass, genuinely worried the wind might carry him away.

Hanns, still as a statue, lifted a dozen stones into the air and launched them at his son. The speed of the projectiles was almost too fast for Brandt's eyes to track. But none came close to Regar. He stood like a boulder in a stream, the rocks passing to either side of him. The stones, now forgotten, crashed into the walls and buildings far behind the prince, cratering the fine masonry of those who had come before.

Incredible feats of strength and control passed back and forth between the two men as quickly as thought. Fire, stone, and air were all utilized, often in combinations Brandt had never dreamed possible, limited by the cost as he was. At one time, vortexes of fire formed between the combatants, the pull of the wind threatening to suck in both the fighters and anyone foolish enough to be nearby.

At first, Brandt had worried about the Falari taking advantage of the battle, launching arrows down on the emperor. But no attacks came. He caught glimpses of faces in windows, but most Falari had vanished.

He figured they were the wise ones.

Brandt couldn't leave. He had a duty to Hanns. Beyond that, he wanted to understand. As far as he knew, a battle like this had never been fought before. He wanted to learn from it.

But Brandt could make little sense of what he saw and felt. Everything happened too fast. His affinities screamed at various pitches, the sounds a disorganized cacophony ringing in his head. Every time he sensed a pattern, it shifted away from him.

Slowly, one fact did become clear.

Hanns was winning.

Brandt wasn't sure it was a matter of power, either. This close, and at the levels these two were fighting at, it was hard to be certain, but Hanns didn't feel twice as strong as Regar. His advantage instead seemed to come from experience. He dealt with Regar's attacks more easily and responded with more creative counters that forced his son back with every exchange. It wasn't much. In many ways, the two were closely matched. But Regar gave up a step, and then another one.

Perhaps Regar felt the same, because after another failed attack he drew his sword and dashed at his father.

The charge didn't last long. Stone assaulted Regar from all sides, and the focus required to keep himself safe prevented him from advancing more than a single slow step at a time.

But he did advance. Hanns increased his efforts, but through sheer determination, Regar continued to close. The advance cost him. Stones cut through his arms, and one appeared to embed itself in his stomach. But Regar didn't falter.

When Regar closed to within four paces, Hanns unleashed a fire attack that put all the previous ones to shame. Regar, no doubt acting on instinct, raised his sword to block the blast and was then enveloped in fire.

Brandt thought it was over.

But Hanns didn't stop. He took one step forward and then another, fire pouring from him. Stone cracked and shattered with every step.

The song of the fire brought Brandt to his knees. He'd been able to endure the previous attacks, but the sheer focus of this one was too much. His head felt as though it might explode, and he clutched his hands to the side of his head, holding it together.

Then Hanns stopped, leaving nothing but echoes pounding in Brandt's skull.

Regar still stood, a feat of impossible strength. His clothes smoldered, wisps of smoke drifting into the sky. The fine sword he held in front of him had been slagged, little more now than a melted and misshapen piece of steel.

The prince looked at the sword in his hand in disbelief. Then he tossed it aside. Even that small motion looked as though it might throw him off balance. Somehow, he found his center once again, made two fists, and stumbled forward.

In one smooth motion Hanns was there. His hand chopped at Regar's throat, and his son's defense was too slow to block it. The prince collapsed to the ground, choking and gasping for air.

Brandt frowned. The strike had been debilitating, but with more force, it could have been fatal. A martial artist of Hanns' quality knew that. The emperor could have finished the fight.

Hanns leaned over his son, who still gasped for air, his face red. "Don't push this any further. Please. Don't make me go any further."

Regar just lay there, spasming as his body slowly recovered.

Brandt wasn't sure what to do. For the moment they were safe, but he didn't trust the moment to last forever. The vast energies had driven the Falari away, but how long would it take before they returned?

Perhaps he should finish what Hanns clearly did not want to.

He couldn't bring himself to move, though. This was a battle for the empire, but it was also a fight for his son's life. Brandt thought of his own child, yet unborn. Could he go as far as Hanns already had? He felt as though he had no place in what happened between those two.

Once Regar caught his breath, his first words made Brandt glad he had withheld his sword. The words were faint, the prince's voice still weak. "I'm sorry, Father."

The remorse in Regar's voice signaled the end of the fight. Brandt heard the same remorse in the emperor's voice as he responded, tears falling from his cheeks. "It's all right. All will be forgiven."

With surprising quickness, Regar drew a knife and stabbed it deep into his father's stomach.

Brandt could do nothing but watch as a thin beam of fire erupted from his emperor's back.

56

When Alena touched the gate, she entered another world.

As always, the initial rush of power threatened to pick her up and carry her away. This was the power of the gate, and she couldn't imagine controlling it. She was certain that if she let so much as a trickle in, it would fill her past bursting in moments. Why Hanns thought controlling such power was wise was beyond her.

Alena relaxed and focused. She couldn't control this power, but she could ride it. After a long heartbeat she broke free of the current and skipped across its surface.

She didn't allow herself more than a few heartbeats to recover. Even if time passed differently here, every moment mattered. Brandt and the emperor would need every advantage she could give them.

When her mind was calm she dove deeper into the gate, deeper into the web that connected all life.

How long it took her to find the manifestation of the gate she was in contact with, she had no idea. This space left her bereft of time and distance, a sensation that disoriented her if she allowed herself to think about it for too long.

But eventually she found herself before the gate. It appeared as diamond, but if she focused, that latticework she'd discovered in Etar was present here, too. The gate was a weaving, albeit one of dizzying complexity.

She had worried that Regar's control would be difficult to undo. Back in Etar, Zolene's bond with the gate had taken her considerable time to remove, and that was without the added pressure of a battle to affect her concentration. From a distance, she hadn't been able to sense more than the basics of Regar's bond.

Up close, she was surprised to see how clumsy Regar's control of the gate actually was. Where Zolene had woven her own soul closely to that of the gate, Regar's bond looked more like a hasty lashing. His technique appeared like something she would have tried back before she had learned anything useful about soulwalking.

It always came back to Anders.

As Alena looked at the crude working, she thought she could feel history squeezing at her. She'd suspected Anders had learned soulwalking, but he'd had no instruction. Of course the techniques he'd passed on had been crude. And with the restrictions he insisted on placing on his successors, it was little wonder they had never developed their technique.

Alena's knife appeared in her hand.

Regar had tied several bonds between him and the gate. Alena put her knife to one and focused her will. Her blade slid through the lashing with ease. The lashing fell from the gate and withered as she focused on it.

Could it really be this easy?

Only three strands remained, and Alena set herself to a

second strand, cutting through it with just as much ease as the first. These bonds were weaker than those Alena had tied between her and Brandt, and she'd thought that weaving weak.

For all the power they controlled, she thought of the Anders like children now, playing a game for which they didn't even know the rules.

She turned her attention to the third strand.

Before she could make the cut, though, she felt a presence. Not in the soulwalk. She spun around, the motion slow, but she remained alone.

The feeling, she decided, was an echo passed down from her physical body. Her time had run out.

Hoping that Zolene's comments about the self-healing properties of the gate were true, Alena reached up with her knife and made one cut running down the length of the gate. Where the tip of the knife met the gate, it slowed and burned a bright white light. Though she focused all her will, she barely made a scratch in the gate.

But she did make a scratch, and she now had some idea of what would be required to destroy a gate like Etar's. Her blade sliced all the way down, cutting through the final cords wrapped around the gate. When she finished her cut, all Regar's connections had been completely severed. She stepped back and studied the gate one more time. It was free, just as she believed the gates should be.

In that moment it occurred to her just how easy it would be for her to take control of the gate. It was right before her, with no one to contest her claim. If her physical body was in danger, that power might mean the difference between life and death. She didn't feel the same debt of honor to the Falari that she felt to her Etari family. She could join Hanns in fighting the queen.

The temptation grew. It would be easy, and she even suspected she could learn to do more with the gates than those who feared soulwalking. She thought of the good she could do, of the changes she could make. Together, she and Hanns could find a new way forward for the empire.

She could protect others, the same way Brandt wanted to protect them all.

The thought stopped her in her tracks. She knew where these thoughts led. If she continued walking that path, how long would it be before she considered the stealing of souls from the gate justified? How long before she couldn't tell the difference between herself and the queen?

She looked longingly at the gate for another long heartbeat, then turned away.

She came out of the soulwalk quickly. She passed through the levels separating her from reality with ease.

When she opened her eyes, back underneath the mountains, she came face to face with the Lolani queen.

57

Prince Regar stood over his father, aloof and detached. Fifteen paces behind him, Brandt stood frozen, unable to will his body or mind into motion.

The knife wound was fatal. Unless Hanns possessed some healing skill beyond Brandt's awareness, his time remaining in the world was limited.

Brandt could still pull on the power of the two gates through Hanns. The emperor drew breath, so he was still connected to his gates. Brandt could finish what the emperor hadn't been able to. He heard a primal scream echo in the square.

A moment later, he realized the scream was his.

Whatever fear held him in place vanished. He charged the prince. He didn't care that Regar controlled a gate. He didn't care that Regar had trained his entire life for this moment. All that mattered was that Regar had killed his father.

And betrayal demanded blood.

Brandt's charge ended the moment Regar turned his attention to the former wolfblade.

Regar's gesture was dismissive, but it was no less dangerous for that. A gust of focused wind struck Brandt like a wall, picking him up off his feet and throwing him straight back. He hit the stone of the square hard. His training kicked in and his body relaxed. He rolled twice before coming back to his feet, sword still in hand.

Undeterred, he charged again. Another gust of wind, even stronger than the first, knocked him back off his feet. This time he landed hard, the wind expelled from his lungs. He coughed and struggled first to hands and knees, then to his feet. He wouldn't stop, not until Regar was dead. Even if it meant drawing from the gates through Hanns' dying body.

Regar's voice sounded heavy, as though even speaking challenged him. "Don't, Brandt. There's no point."

Brandt stumbled forward anyway.

Regar raised his hand, no doubt preparing his final attack.

Brandt was out of ideas. But he wasn't going to stop, either. Before Regar could unleash his attack, his face went pale. He frowned, then he crumpled to the ground.

Less than ten paces separated Brandt from Regar, and he didn't plan on wasting the opportunity. He closed the distance in less than two heartbeats, risking lightness to skip across the square.

Disoriented as he was, Regar still possessed the presence of mind to roll away from Brandt's sword. But while he dodged the deadly edge, he left himself open to Brandt's knee. The two collided with a crack of bone on bone. Brandt overextended and lost his balance, tumbling over the prince. Worried about cutting himself, Brandt let go of his sword, which clattered behind him as he rolled to a stop.

Brandt recovered before Regar. In a moment, he was on

his feet, pummeling the prince with fists, elbows, and kicks. Not every blow connected, but when one did, a surge of satisfaction filled Brandt.

In the midst of the beating, Regar collapsed again, his muscles losing all their strength. He folded like a rag doll, and Brandt wasn't sure the prince would ever get up. Brandt didn't think he was the cause. As vicious as his attack had been, it hadn't been fatal.

He needed to end this. As satisfying as beating Regar to death with his bare hands would be, the sword was quicker, a more certain solution.

Brandt turned and walked to his sword. His body was sore and tired. More than anything, he wanted this to be done.

Brandt picked up his sword, turning around to see Regar back on his feet.

He swore and rushed toward Regar before the prince could summon his affinity again. He hadn't expected Regar to recover so quickly.

It was already too late. Regar hit Brandt with another gust of wind. Brandt braced himself, then realized the gust of wind was little more than a stiff breeze. Regar frowned, looking down at his hands like they had somehow betrayed him.

But Brandt understood. Alena had done it. She had severed his connection to the gate. She'd actually succeeded.

A surge of hope filled Brandt as he charged forward.

And then he was met with fire.

Instinctively, Brandt turned the fire away, allowing his body to absorb that which he couldn't deflect.

Sweat broke out on his forehead, and he felt the tremendous power coursing through his body. Regar might not have his gate anymore, but he still had a gatestone, and that was more than enough to kill Brandt. Brandt was still limited by the cost.

More fire washed over Brandt, and he couldn't control the power anymore. He released the energy, letting it go in any direction it pleased. All that mattered was ridding himself of it.

When the power finally faded, he was on his knees, surrounded by blackened stone.

Regar stood several paces away, well out of reach of Brandt's sword. Even if the prince had been closer, Brandt wasn't sure it would make a difference. He wasn't sure he possessed the strength to even lift the weapon.

Regar laughed, a hint of madness at the edges of his voice. "It doesn't matter. The gate will be mine again, just as soon as I'm done here."

Brandt sighed. Even the idea of arguing sounded exhausting.

After everything, he was still useless in this fight. He still wasn't strong enough. And Alena had denied him his best chance to get stronger.

He wasn't sure if Regar moved with incredible speed or if he was just that weak. But one moment Regar was standing in front of him, and the next the prince was driving his knee into Brandt, mirroring the attack he'd just endured.

Brandt tumbled, managing to hold onto his sword but little else. Regar came again, apparently not concerned that he was an unarmed man fighting against a former wolfblade with a sword. His fists found Brandt's kidneys, stomach, and face. They landed like bricks.

Brandt could barely summon the energy to see the blows coming, much less avoid them.

One kick sent Brandt skidding across the stone.

"Get up," Regar said. "Get up and die like a real warrior."

Brandt wasn't sure where he found strength. Perhaps it was fueled by anger or perhaps his body was slowly starting to recover from the elemental attack. Either way, he found his feet. His balance wobbled for a moment and then steadied.

A ball of flame appeared in Regar's hand, not as impressive as his earlier displays, but still several orders of magnitude greater than anything Brandt could summon.

It seemed fitting he would meet his end through the power of the same affinity he had used against so many others.

Regar raised his hand and aimed the ball of fire at Brandt. "Goodbye, Brandt."

58

The queen looked at Alena with her icy gaze. Despite this being their first meeting in the physical world, that gaze seemed all too familiar. But it was not filled with hate, the way Alena expected. Instead, it seemed contemplative. The queen studied her.

"You are the soulwalker. Alena."

Hearing her name voiced by the queen sent a shiver down her spine. There was strength even in the queen's voice, power that reverberated in every syllable. It promised wisdom, the experience of lifetimes, condensed into one soul. It was intoxicating, though Alena didn't feel even a hint of compulsion.

The queen's eyes traveled from Alena to the gate, and something in her gaze seemed off, like it was focused both here and somewhere else. With a start, Alena realized the queen walked in both worlds at once. After examining the gate for less than a heartbeat, the queen's eyes returned to Alena. "You didn't take it for yourself."

"The gates were never meant to be controlled," Alena said.

"Foolishness," the queen said. "The gates are but a stepping stone to true power."

There wasn't a hint of madness in the queen's voice, but Alena didn't believe her. How could the gates be a stepping stone? No power surpassed them.

Except the gates hadn't saved those who came before, and they had created the weapons.

Some power had overwhelmed even the gates.

It didn't make sense, but at the same time, it had to be true. It was the only story that fit what she knew. What did the queen know? What was she after?

Despite the fact they had fought several times, Alena couldn't answer those questions. The queen was a mystery.

But a dangerous one at that. Alena broke away from the queen's blue eyes to examine the room. She had been so distracted by the queen's presence she had forgotten that very presence spelled doom for her friends. Every member of her war party lay scattered around the floor. None moved that she could see.

"I haven't killed any of them, yet."

The threat of Alena's noncompliance was clear.

"Why didn't you take the gate?"

Alena was reminded of a young child, asking why the sky was blue or why apples fell. For all her lifetimes, the queen seemed unable to comprehend her decision. "The gates are not meant for us to control," she repeated.

"Nonsense! You could've fought against me, perhaps better than anyone else, and yet you refuse. Why?"

Had she been a fool? The queen seemed to think that Alena was more dangerous than the others, but was she? Did her soulwalking abilities somehow make her use of the gate more of a threat to the queen?

So many questions, and no answers. The Anders weren't

the only ones playing a game they didn't understand the rules to.

Even though the queen didn't move a muscle, her next words almost knocked Alena over. "Take control of the gate."

Alena stared, incredulous.

The queen looked to the gate. "Nothing taken without struggle has value. Take control of the gate and let us see whose will is greater. It has been far too long since a worthy challenge has appeared before me. I will not waste it."

Alena licked her lips. The gate was still close enough to touch. She hadn't moved since coming out of the soulwalk. All she needed to do was reach out. Then she could fight the queen on more even terms. She even knew how to make a stronger connection than the Anders. If not her, then who else? She didn't like the gates, but perhaps commanding one was her duty.

She looked again around the room. Her friends needed her. And right now, there was nothing she could do to save them. She reached toward the gate.

Then she stopped.

"What are you waiting for?" the queen demanded. "It's right there."

Alena didn't have an answer. Something inside her held her back.

"Do it!"

Knowing that touching the gate and controlling it was what the queen wanted solidified Alena's determination. What good were her beliefs if she didn't live them?

She let her hand drop. Then she stared directly into the queen's cold eyes. "No."

The queen's rage was immediate. With a gesture, a gust of wind unlike anything Alena had ever felt picked her up off her feet and threw her across the room. She hit the opposite wall at speed, and the back of her head cracked against the stone. She collapsed to the cold stone floor of the cave, smooth the way that only those that came before could create. Then the queen stepped forward and touched the gate.

Alena's whole world went white.

59

Brandt and Regar felt the heat at the same time. They both turned their heads, mirroring each other exactly. Considering that Regar held a burning ball of fire in his own hand, the fact that he even noticed the additional heat was indicative of how hot the new source of heat was.

"I'm sorry, son," said Hanns.

And with that, the dying emperor unleashed an attack of flame, a white-hot tunnel of light and heat that cut into Regar.

Brandt was convinced that the beam was strong enough to cut through a mountain's worth of stone. It could melt a mountain glacier in a heartbeat, sending a deadly wave of water to some unsuspecting valley. Yet somehow, Regar's body absorbed it. The beam winked out of existence almost as quickly as it had appeared, and Brandt stood in shock.

There came a point where a mind couldn't take any more. When wonder followed wonder, awe eventually faded. Brandt wasn't sure he'd ever be amazed by anything ever again. Regar should be nothing but dust and memories, yet he still stood.

Regar gritted his teeth, and Brandt saw the prince struggled with the same inability to handle the heat Brandt had fought just moments before. Except this time, the scale of the attack was far beyond a mere gatestone.

Off to the side, Hanns collapsed, the last of his energy spent on the attack.

Brandt came to his senses. It wouldn't take long for Regar to either die from the emperor's blast or to overcome it, but there was no reason to take a chance.

Brandt reached out with his sword and stabbed it into Regar's chest. He pushed it through the heart and out the prince's back.

A father should never be the one to kill his son.

For a long moment, nothing happened. Regar looked down at the sword sticking through his chest with a look of disbelief, then he collapsed, giving up control of the incredible energies coursing through his body.

They found their exit through Brandt's sword. A wave of pure energy that warped the air blasted from the tip of Brandt's blade, channeled out through Regar with his dying breath.

The blast tore apart stone, shattering it as though it was nothing more than a brittle pot.

Regar's mouth moved, but no sound came out. One moment his eyes were full of life and dreams of the future, and the next they were blank orbs, their animating force gone.

As Regar fell he slid back, off Brandt's blade.

He had killed a prince.

Brandt stared at Regar for a moment and then turned to the emperor. Remarkably, the man was still alive. Brandt rushed over to him and knelt beside him. For a moment, Brandt dared to hope. If the emperor had enough strength for that attack, perhaps he had enough to surprise Brandt one more time. But it was a fool's hope.

Seeing the emperor's wounds up close, Brandt didn't understand how the emperor had attacked at all. The man's face was pale, his eyes were unfocused, and his hands trembled. The hole in his back bled freely. Tears ran down the emperor's cheeks, and perhaps for the first time, Brandt saw the emperor not as a ruler but as a man. An old man who had felt honor bound to kill his own son. Brandt didn't know what comfort it would be, but it was all he had to offer. "You didn't kill Regar. I killed him. I'm sorry."

Brandt didn't know if the emperor heard him or not. His eyes stared at something beyond Brandt's shoulder, possibly already looking to the gates beyond.

So Brandt repeated himself, over and over, until Hanns breathed his last.

Brandt braced himself. Hanns had been connected to two gates and he couldn't guess at what the death of such a man might mean.

But the emperor passed to the gate without incident. A slight mountain wind whispered its sorrow, but that was all. He had been one of the most powerful men in all of history, but when he died, the world took no notice.

Brandt allowed himself a moment to grieve. Then he stood and walked over to Regar's body. He used the tip of his sword to cut away the prince's shirt around his navel. There, just as the prince had once claimed, was a gatestone embedded in his skin. Brandt cut it out and held the bloody stone in his hand. He felt the power of it the moment he channeled even the slightest amount of his affinity into the stone. He looked up.

His body demanded rest. Just being near the prince and his father as they battled had been exhausting. He was certain that if he lay down and closed his eyes, he'd sleep on the burnt stone of the square for a full day.

But Ana was up there, and the queen was still in Faldun.

As much as he wanted to rest, this didn't end with the death of the emperor.

It was a long hike to the gate, but that was where this ended.

60

Alena pushed herself to hands and knees, fighting the nausea that made her stomach clench. Her body ached from the impact against the wall, but her true concern was her head. She struggled to focus her thoughts.

The bright light faded. The queen stood next to the gate, eyes closed, hand against the diamond of the weapon.

Alena didn't know how long it took to control a gate. She couldn't count on having much time. Soulwalking moved at the speed of thought, faster than the physical world. Anger wrestled with despair. The queen couldn't have the gate, but Alena didn't know how to stop her.

Alena channeled her will through her gatestone, desperate for any scrap of power she could acquire. She studied the room through a soulwalk, disappointed but not surprised to see a shield of pure force surrounding the queen, similar to the one her priest had created under Landow. Alena didn't possess the strength to even crack that protection.

But she had to try.

She pushed against the bubble, then imagined herself attacking it with her father's knife.

No matter how she struck at it, though, the bubble resisted every attempt she made. The queen mocked her through indifference.

Still soulwalking, Alena raged against the bubble. She stabbed and swung, over and over, screaming as she did.

Nothing.

She fell to her knees in the soulwalk, mirroring her posture in the physical world, her anger burned out.

All she could do was watch as the queen's plans came to fruition.

Out of nowhere, a wave of power crashed over her, throwing her out of the soulwalk with physical force. Suddenly she was in her body again. Her head rushed toward the floor, but she got her hands in front of her in time to prevent a broken nose.

Bile rose in her throat, and stopping it was hopeless. She vomited on the floor, losing what little she'd eaten today. The stomach acid burned her throat and tongue.

Her heart pounded. What was happening?

The power didn't stop. It filled every bone and muscle of her body. Her focus returned, sharpening details in the room. She felt every current of air in the room, heard the heartbeats of each of her friends.

To find answers, she dropped into a soulwalk. New connections had been anchored to her, strong threads that glowed with power. She followed those threads and found the gates at the other end.

For a long heartbeat, her mind was blank.

The emperor. When he had tied that weaving to her before they separated. Hanns had bequeathed his gates to her. *She* had control of both of the imperial gates. Why?

No answers came, but that didn't change the facts.

She found her feet and clenched her fists.

Then she paused.

If she controlled the gates, Hanns was dead.

She grieved for his loss. They hadn't agreed on much in his last days, but with the gift of these gates, Alena realized her arguments had hit closer to his heart than she expected. She wasn't sure she could forgive him, but she understood him better than before.

Now that her choice had been taken away, a lightness settled over her heart. She would fight the queen, and they would see whose will was greater.

If the queen believed the only worthwhile rewards were gained through struggle, Alena would give her that struggle.

Alena looked down at her hands. She saw in two worlds. Both the physical and the soulwalk. She felt light and strong.

Alena studied the queen. The weaving she worked on the gate was more similar to Zolene's careful threads than the rough lashings of the Anders. Even with the additional complexity, she looked to be nearly done.

Alena stepped up to the sphere of energy protecting the queen and laid her hand upon it.

It burned, but she did not flinch away. With a thought, the sphere shattered. With another thought, she blasted the unprepared queen across the room, using the same wind technique she'd just been the victim of a few moments ago.

The queen recovered before she hit the cave wall, using wind to slow herself. Her eyes were unfocused, uncertain.

Alena didn't waste the moment of confusion. She didn't believe she could win a fight in the physical world. Even with the power of the gates, she hadn't trained the elemental affinities enough to challenge the likes of the queen.

But she could soulwalk better than anyone in the empire.

Alena dropped into the other world, connecting with the queen and dragging her along.

They appeared on the rooftops of Landow.

The queen had taught Alena one lesson she'd never forgotten in their first fight. In a soulwalk, it wasn't physical skill that mattered. One was limited only by their imagination and will.

Here, it didn't matter if she couldn't throw a solid punch in the real world. If she could envision it here, she could do it.

Alena attacked, vanishing and reappearing behind the queen. She drove her fist into the queen's kidneys, gloating at the feel of her blow striking true. The punch folded the queen in half and sent her skipping across the roof.

Before the queen came to a stop, Alena vanished and reappeared again, this time directly in the path of the queen. She kicked, the blow launching the queen high into the air.

Alena imagined a sword in her hand and it was there.

It was time to end this.

She vanished and reappeared again, this time in the sky, again in the path of the queen. She raised her sword and cut.

But her sword didn't cut through the queen's body. It struck steel, the sound deafening. The queen now held her own sword, and had blocked Alena's cut with ease.

Alena swore as she saw the queen grinning viciously.

She swore again as the queen's image blurred and she found herself impaled on the queen's sword.

The queen flung her down. Alena crashed against the

roof, sending shingles flying in all directions. She clutched at her side as her lifeblood drained from her.

Landow flickered, and she remembered this was a soulwalk. She took a deep breath and imagined herself whole and healthy.

And she was.

Alena stood up.

She'd lost the element of surprise. Now it was just her against the queen.

She gripped her sword so tightly her knuckles turned white. The queen controlled an entire continent and had lived more lives than Alena could imagine.

Despite that, she was bouncing on her toes. She leaned forward, ready for the queen's next move.

She wanted this.

The queen vanished, and Alena formed a sphere of protection. The queen's sword cut into the sphere. The protection didn't stop the cut, but it did slow the attack enough for Alena to respond.

She didn't bother with the sword. Instead, she stole another idea from the queen. She imagined a sky full of spears, all pointing at the queen. Then she threw them all.

Alena turned to see her enemy impaled by nearly a dozen spears.

Unfortunately, the queen had protected her head and torso. None of the spears were immediately fatal, and soon they fell away from her body, which healed a moment later.

The queen studied her, and Alena's own mind raced.

Killing most people in the soulwalk would be a simple matter. But Alena realized that killing an experienced soulwalker of equal power might be a challenge she wasn't prepared for. Damage could happen almost instantly, but both Alena and the queen now shielded their most vital organs, and wounds could be healed as quickly as they were made here, so long as one kept their focus.

Alena settled in for a long fight.

But the queen didn't attack.

"Join me."

Alena took a step back. "What?"

"I need warriors like you."

Alena prepared another attack, this one a single spear floating in the air over her shoulder. Perhaps she could throw it hard enough to pierce the queen's shield.

The queen didn't defend herself. Instead, a creature appeared between them, one fashioned from the queen's knowledge. It appeared far less serpentine than Alena had seen before, but still recognizable.

The creature from the tunnels.

The creature that killed those that came before.

It radiated a cold menace, its regard gelid, making the queen seem a roaring campfire in comparison.

"You've seen this before, haven't you?" the queen asked.

Alena nodded. "They killed those that came before."

"I didn't think anyone in your empire knew that."

Alena realized she and her brother were probably the only two. "Not many do," she admitted.

"They return, even now, as we speak."

Alena took another two steps back, as though distancing herself from the representation between them would keep her safe. "You're certain?"

"I am. Will you soulwalk with me?"

Alena suspected a trap. How could she not? And yet, curiosity pulled her forward, relentless. She protected herself, strengthening her shield even more. "Very well."

The queen used their existing connection. She took Alena, not pulling her, but guiding her.

For the first time, Alena understood how little distance could mean to a soulwalker. And she understood how hopeless beating the queen in this space was. They traveled from Falar to the land of the queen in less than a heartbeat, then connected to a gate on a different continent. The queen made each act seem as easy as breathing, though Alena would have struggled to complete such tasks.

For a brief moment, Alena felt the presence of others. She expanded her sense, finding a dozen priests, all interconnected in a complex web with the queen and the gate. But the threads binding them weren't just of connection.

They were also of compulsion.

Before Alena could even consider the implications, her attention was focused by the queen's interaction with her gate. She learned more in a moment of studying the queen's soulwalking than she did in a week of learning on her own.

The gate now served as a passage. The queen dove into and through the gate, launching herself untold distances.

Alena could do little but observe, events happening too fast for her to understand.

As usual, distance meant little in the soulwalk, but when they encountered the creatures, all Alena knew was that they were very, very far away. Farther even than some of the stars that lit the night sky. But the strength of the creatures was beyond reckoning. The only comparison Alena could make was that of the source of the gates' power. And it was possessed by each.

But they were cold.

How did an insect understand the power of a human? The thought was the closest she could come to explaining what she felt, but even that didn't accurately describe the separation. The queen was nothing but a child compared to these beasts.

They were ancient. Alena's own life would be nothing but a blink compared to what they'd already lived. They might be mortal, but were so close to eternity the distinction barely mattered.

Her blood froze just contemplating them.

They sensed the queen's presence.

They sensed Alena.

But they didn't care.

They approached at speeds faster than Alena believed possible, and yet the distances were so vast they still had a long time to travel. Alena couldn't judge how long it would be until they arrived, but it was sooner than she wished.

They returned to the rooftops of Landow, to the soulwalk Alena began. This fight suddenly seemed insignificant.

Everything Alena had accomplished seemed insignificant.

She controlled two gates, and those beings would still swat her like a fly.

"I need warriors," the queen repeated.

Alena nodded. The queen didn't exactly speak true. She didn't just need warriors. The whole imperial army wouldn't do a thing against those beings. She needed individuals with the potential to do more.

In a way, the queen's request honored her.

"But you need the gates, don't you?"

The queen nodded. "I do. I need all five."

Alena gave herself time to think. After encountering those beings, the queen's desires now had context. What frightened Alena was that the desire to control all five gates didn't seem unreasonable.

She had so many questions. But one, seemingly inconsequential, wouldn't let her go. "Why do you compel your own priests?"

"It's the only way to ensure none rebel. Otherwise, to be that close to such power corrupts the soul. I don't have time to deal with petty rebellions. You've now seen my true purpose."

Alena shook her head. She thought of Brandt, of the loss he'd suffered due to compulsion. Yes, she now understood the purpose the queen worked toward. But that didn't make her methods any more palatable.

"There has to be a better way," Alena said.

The queen growled. "There isn't. You know what's at stake. Tell me this better way, knowing what's coming."

Alena didn't have an answer, but she searched for one.

As she failed to find a better way, she began to empathize with the queen. Yes, some of her methods might seem horrible, but they were talking about the fate of all people. What choice did they have?

She nodded.

The queen was right. If Alena gave her the gates, it would give the world the best chance of survival.

Alena frowned.

Something wasn't right.

She focused, drawing on the power of her gates.

A thin thread, nothing more than a wisp of smoke, connected the two of them.

Alena cut the subtle compulsion with her knife.

The fire in her heart roared to life.

She summoned the single spear once again, throwing it with all her will.

The spear stopped a hair away from the queen's chest. Alena willed it forward, but it wouldn't budge.

The queen couldn't be trusted. An incredible threat approached, but slavery wasn't the answer. Taking the power of the souls of the dead wasn't either. Alena believed that with her whole heart.

The spear crawled forward.

Her will against the queen's. No battle could be more simple.

Alena focused everything on the point of that spear. The queen grimaced, her own will crumbling before Alena's.

But the queen hadn't become the ruler of her people through a lack of focus. The spear finally froze. No matter what Alena did, it wouldn't move.

The queen raised her hand, slowly, and pushed the spear out of the way. She pushed hard, as though wrestling a boulder three times her size.

Bit by bit, she moved the spear. When she was safe, she let go, and the spear blasted past her, cracking the air as it disappeared off into the distance.

A sword appeared in the queen's hand. She advanced on Alena, fire in her eyes.

61

Brandt's ascent to the tunnel that led to the gate turned out to be easier than he expected. The battle between Regar and Hanns had driven the Falari away from the square, but most of them had massed in the alleys and streets just beyond.

Brandt led with fire. He didn't have time to wage honorable combat. If the Falari were close, they were enemies. He sent fire ahead of him down streets and into houses through doors and windows. The screams that echoed in reply barely registered against his consciousness.

After a few levels, his path cleared. The Falari avoided him, thanks to the power he now possessed. Next to that of a full gate, it was nothing, but the gatestone still allowed him to pull more than he ever had before.

He hiked up two more levels before realizing his foolishness. With a gesture, he tore stone away and shaped it to his will, a platform not unlike the one Hanns had made not long ago. He stepped upon it, then lifted it into the air, ascending the levels between him and the tunnel entrance with ease. His memory of his last trip to Faldun guided him.

When he came to the tunnel he found two bodies. They were pale.

Lolani.

It looked like they'd been killed without a fight. Of course, he already knew Alena had reached the gate. Regar's death was proof enough of that. It didn't surprise him her war party had to fight to reach it.

Brandt traveled deeper, following the passages he remembered from his trips below. He reached the maze outside the gate without making a wrong turn. But the route through the maze he didn't remember. And he didn't have time. So he channeled stone once again, tearing the maze asunder and creating a straight path for himself. He stopped when he saw the blue light of the gate ahead.

Brandt ran, sliding to a stop when he entered the room. His attention was first drawn to Alena and the Lolani queen. They stood on opposite sides of the room, their eyes closed. Despite their lack of movement, he could tell they were twin poles of enormous power.

He didn't understand. Alena was a gifted soulwalker, but not nearly strong enough to stand against the queen. But the evidence was there, right in front of his eyes.

Then he saw the others. Ren, Toren, Jace, Sheren, and Ana were all in various states of pain. Ren appeared unconscious, blood flowing freely from a wound on the back of his head. Likewise, Sheren didn't look like she'd be moving for a while. Her eyes were closed and one of her legs appeared broken. Toren's right arm rested at an unnatural angle, but he was sitting up, eyes watering with pain. Jace was on his feet, tending to Ana.

Brandt ran to Ana. She looked dazed but otherwise unharmed. He and Jace lifted her to her feet. "Are you all right?" Brandt asked.

Ana nodded. "I think so. I feel like I got hit by a brick, though."

They looked at the two women occupying the room with their power. "What happened?" Brandt asked.

Their blank looks were answer enough.

He supposed it didn't matter. The two women in the center of the room fought on nearly equal terms. That was all he needed to know. For a moment, he felt the now familiar pangs of jealousy. It should have been him fighting.

He also knew the queen was distracted. So he stepped forward, drawing his sword, ready to end it all.

He swung, his cut clean.

But the queen moved. Though her eyes were closed, she sidestepped as he cut. His blade sliced through nothing but empty air.

The queen's eyes opened, but Brandt had the distinct feeling she wasn't truly there. She attacked him with a gust of wind, but he heard it building, and using his own gatestone was able to negate the attack. Her eyes focused on him for a single moment. "Brandt."

Her attack wasn't as strong as he'd expected. Below, Hanns and Regar had fought with far superior strength. Was it possible she was weaker than they expected in the physical world?

The queen didn't give him time to answer his question. She carried a sword at her hip, and in a moment it was in her hand and she was attacking him.

Her movements were smooth and precise, and Brandt found himself on the defensive. Her attacks left no openings to exploit. They passed each other twice, neither gaining an advantage. Brandt felt like he had the edge, but she was better than he'd guessed her to be. After so many years relying on her affinity, he'd expected the sword would be little more than decoration.

A small stone suddenly appeared in the air between them. Brandt stared at it, not sure where it had come from. Only the queen's glance toward Toren helped him understand. She'd stopped an Etari attack while fighting him.

She *was* as strong as he'd first thought.

The stone dropped, but Brandt saw Toren already had another one spinning.

Then Ana and Jace were at his side, their swords cutting toward the queen.

The queen focused on Jace, somehow finding the focus to blast him off his feet with air. It left just Brandt and Ana.

Brandt almost yelled at Ana to leave. If nothing else, their child needed to survive this. But the queen left them no chance to retreat.

Together, though, he and Ana were too much. They'd fought and trained side by side for over a decade. They knew each other's moves intimately, stepping into the gaps the other left, always relentless in their assault. Behind them, Toren supported them with well-placed stones that never quite found their mark but distracted the queen anyway.

Brandt drew first blood, a cut across the queen's thigh that elicited a low hiss.

It was only a matter of time. The queen gave up another step and then another. Soon she'd run out of space to give.

"Enough!" Her shout echoed in the small chamber, repeating again and again.

A wave of force bent the air around them. Though Brandt saw it coming, and heard the power through his affinity, there was nothing he could do. Even with the gatestone, he was helpless before the force. It threw him off his feet and sent him slamming against the wall of the cave. Beside him, Ana fared better, skidding across the floor until she slid to a stop against the wall.

Only Alena stood against the force. Brandt didn't understand how, but she remained unmoved. As he watched, she opened her eyes and he realized that she, too, had that same distant look the queen had. She was both here and not here.

And then Brandt felt true despair.

The queen had been fighting both he and Ana, blocking Toren's attacks, and fending off Alena in the soulwalk the entire time.

They had no chance against her. No chance at all.

But he was the first to his feet. Chance or no, he'd never understood surrender. He'd fight until he couldn't. He flexed his grip on his sword and stepped forward to attack again.

"Stop," the queen said.

She didn't shout, but the power in her voice caused him to pause. The queen sheathed her sword. "There is no need for you all to die. I came here for the gate, and it is now mine." The queen glanced to Alena, as if in challenge. Brandt wondered what had passed between the two women. But Alena said nothing.

The queen looked down at her cut leg, blood trickling down to her calf. Then she looked to Brandt. "I offer you a truce."

Brandt's eyes narrowed in suspicion.

"Come with me," the queen told Brandt. "Study under me, and I will teach you all that I know. You have my word. Any question you have, I will answer to the best of my knowledge and ability."

"Never!" said Ana behind him.

"Why?" Brandt asked.

"There is a threat coming, more dangerous than you could understand. Ask your friend, Alena."

Brandt glanced at Alena. "She speaks true," the soulwalker said.

The queen gestured to her injured leg. "I need warriors strong enough for the fight that is coming. I've already won the gate. I plan to return to my own land soon. I gain nothing by killing a man who may someday have the strength to save not just his empire, but his world."

Brandt stared into the queen's crystal-clear blue eyes. He saw no lie within them. He was tempted. Just like that, all his questions could be answered. The strength he needed to protect his family could be his.

But if something was too good to be true, it often was. "And if I gain enough strength to kill you?"

The queen smiled at that. "Then you are better able to defend this world than I. The Lolani don't shy away from strength," she cast a pointed glance at Alena, "no matter the risk."

Brandt knew then the queen understood him in a way his imperial friends and family did not. This was a woman who knew the sacrifices sometimes required for the protection of others.

"Stop compelling him!" Ana shouted.

Brandt didn't feel compelled, though. These thoughts were completely his own. It didn't feel at all like it did before, when Kye had used the technique.

Alena confirmed his guess. "She's not."

The queen finished her offer. "All I ask is for one year. I shall protect you from all harm and teach you all you desire. In exchange, so long as Alena doesn't interfere with my control of the Falari gate, I promise not to attack the continent."

"And then?" Brandt asked.

"Then we all have choices to make. I will need the gates to defend this world. If you so choose, I will send you back here after one year, even if that means you'll oppose me. Alena, too, will need to decide what course to take. I can spare one year, but no more."

Ana came up behind Brandt, her hands around his upper arm. "She's scared, Brandt. I can hear it in her voice. All of us together, we can defeat her. She knows it."

The queen said nothing in response.

Perhaps there was some truth to Ana's suggestion. They'd already cut the queen, and behind them, Ren had finally woken up, and Jace was on his feet and looking ready to attack again. If they fought again, she'd have to avoid four swords.

But he wasn't sure. Whatever her motivations, he believed the queen spoke the truth. And if they fought, he was far from sure that they would win. The queen now had two gates. That type of power couldn't be underestimated.

He turned to look into Ana's eyes. If he left for a year he would miss the birth of his child. He would miss a year of being with Ana.

Brandt didn't know how to answer the demands of both duty and love.

He thought of the empire, filled with over a million lives, all helpless before this unnamed threat that even the queen feared.

He remembered quiet nights with Ana in the mountains above Highkeep. The perfect contentment he'd felt in those moments.

Perhaps he didn't need to save the world.

Perhaps he only needed to save his family.

Brandt pulled gently away from Ana. He turned to her. "I love you," he said.

Her eyes were filled with doubt. But she nodded. "I love you, too."

Brandt stepped forward, his sword held in front of him. He sensed, rather than saw, Ana prepare for a fight. He could imagine her settling into her favorite stance. But he didn't dare risk a backward glance.

He took another step.

It was time to end this war inside of him.

Brandt kneeled before the queen.

"I accept."

The queen smiled. There was a flash of light and a force that lifted him through the gate.

And he was gone.

EPILOGUE

Alena and Jace sat together on an overlook across the valley from Faldun. In the valley below, several camps had appeared as if grown from the fertile ground.

The queen might be gone, but she had left their world a mess.

Between the camps and Faldun, a large tent had been pitched. Within that tent, the future of the Falari was being determined. After their assault on Faldun, and particularly in the moments after Hanns and Brandt had dropped into the square, hundreds of mountain warriors had died or been injured. As a result, those who wished for endless war against the empire now numbered significantly fewer than those who wished for peace.

But those who wished for war still controlled Faldun, a city that would be nearly impossible to besiege. Any attempt would be long and bloody.

So the two divisions searched for some agreement. Their gate was no longer theirs, and the queen had made them aware of a threat greater than the empire.

The warleaders and elders had plenty to discuss.

Weylen was optimistic. When he'd last spoken to Alena, he'd asked if he could use the threat of her strength if necessary. Alena had agreed, but wasn't sure if she would even be able to follow through if needed.

Hopefully, it wouldn't come to that.

Jace passed over the flask he'd been sipping from. She nodded her appreciation and took a pull. The Falari liquor burned stronger than anything she'd ever tasted, but she admitted it had grown on her. Probably more than was healthy.

"Has Ana spoken to you today?" Jace asked.

Alena shook her head.

"She will, in time. She doesn't blame you, not really."

"I know," Alena said. The knowledge didn't stop Ana's silence from hurting, though. "I might have been able to do something, though."

"Brandt made his choice." Jace spit out the words.

Alena wanted to defend Brandt. Some part of her understood. But she still couldn't believe he'd left them. His desertion was an enormous open wound over her heart, and she didn't carry Brandt's child.

She understood Ana's anger, too.

Alena took another drink, welcoming the relaxation it brought to her tight shoulder muscles.

"Sometimes I think I should have taken her offer," Alena said. "Then Brandt never would have had a chance to make that choice."

"Why didn't you?" Jace gestured for the flask and Alena handed it back to him. "It wasn't because you wanted to see more of my charming good looks."

Her brother took another long sip. Jace had considered Brandt a hero.

Alena wondered if Brandt knew how many people his decision had hurt.

She suspected he did. He was no fool.

But she still felt like punching him in the kidneys.

Repeatedly.

"I'm still not sure," Alena admitted, "but the queen is wrong. The threat is coming—that much is true. But it's not just about surviving." She paused. "How we fight matters."

Alena snatched the flask from Jace and took the last pull.

"What next?" Jace asked.

Alena sighed. That was the question, wasn't it? The one she'd been thinking about for days, ever since the queen had so suddenly disappeared from their lives. The Falari weren't the only people in disarray. The Etari gate remained the only one unclaimed, and no doubt it suffered even more now that the queen pulled from two gates.

They'd stopped Regar's coup, but they'd lost to the queen.

And though almost no one knew, the emperor was dead.

"Are you going to become the empress, Anders VII?" Jace's question was only half-joking.

Alena shook her head. Did control of the gates come with control of the empire? She had no idea. "I don't want to be the empress. I'll have to speak to Prince Olen."

"Who is where, exactly?"

Alena didn't know the answer to that, either. He'd been on a mission, but to where, she couldn't imagine.

Their conversation lapsed into silence. They'd covered the same ground many times in the past few days, but still didn't have good answers. They already planned on returning to the empire. Weylen had promised a substantial escort once negotiations were complete. Toren and Sheren had both asked to join, and Ana would accompany them, despite her current hatred for Alena. Alena's war party remained intact, even if their hearts were broken.

Alena had a year to find the answers. Answers she hoped would be in the gates.

Jace stood up. He extended his hand to help her up. "I'm glad you decided to stay with us," he said.

"I am, too."

Alena reached up and accepted his proffered hand.

Then they walked down toward their uncertain future together.

WANT MORE FANTASY?

As always, thank you so much for reading this story. There's an amazing number of great fantasy stories today, and it means so much to me that you picked this book up.

If you enjoyed this story, I also have two other fantasy series, filled with memorable characters. My first fantasy series is called *Nightblade.*

Links to all of my books can be found at www.waterstonemedia.net

THANK YOU

Before you take off, I really wanted to say thank you for taking the time to read my work. Being able to write stories for a living is one of the greatest gifts I've been given, and it wouldn't be possible without readers.

So thank you.

Also, it's almost impossible to overstate how important reviews are for authors in this age of internet bookstores. If you enjoyed this book, it would mean the world to me if you could take the time to leave a review wherever you purchased this book.

And finally, if you really enjoyed this book and want to hear more from me, I'd encourage you to sign up for my emails. I don't send them too often - usually only once or twice a month at most, but they are the best place to learn about free giveaways, contests, sales, and more.

I sometimes also send out surprise short stories, absolutely free, that expand the fantasy worlds I've built. If you're interested, please go to https://www.waterstonemedia.net/newsletter/.

With gratitude,

Ryan

ALSO BY RYAN KIRK

The Nightblade Series

Nightblade

World's Edge

The Wind and the Void

Blades of the Fallen

Nightblade's Vengeance

Nightblade's Honor

Nightblade's End

Relentless

Relentless Souls

Heart of Defiance

Their Spirit Unbroken

Oblivion's Gate

The Gate Beyond Oblivion

The Gates of Memory

The Primal Series

Primal Dawn

Primal Darkness

Primal Destiny

Primal Trilogy

The Code Series

Code of Vengeance

Code of Pride

Code of Justice

ABOUT THE AUTHOR

Ryan Kirk is the bestselling author of the *Nightblade* series of books. When he isn't writing, you can probably find him playing disc golf or hiking through the woods.

www.waterstonemedia.net
contact@waterstonemedia.net

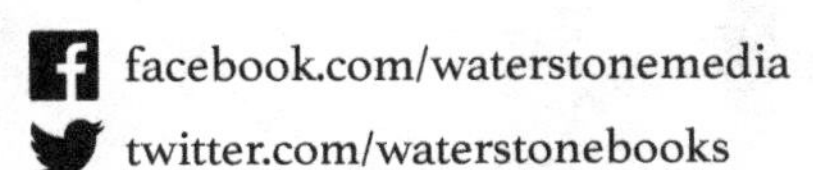

facebook.com/waterstonemedia
twitter.com/waterstonebooks
instagram.com/waterstonebooks

CPSIA information can be obtained
at www.ICGtesting.com
Printed in the USA
LVHW011950081220
673650LV00004B/631